WILLIAM WILDE AND THE NECROSED

THE CHRONICLES OF WILLIAM WILDE

DAVIS ASHURA

William Wilde and the Necrosed

Cover art and design by Deranged Doctor Design

Interior design and art by Mikey Brooks (mikeybrooks.com)

Printed in the United States of America

First Printing: 2018

DuSum Publishing, LLC

Paperback Edition

ISBN: 0-9911276-8-4
ISBN-13: 978-0-9911276-8-9

DEDICATION

To my fantastic sister.
She's a big part of why so much of what I've written
turned out so much better than I expected.

OTHER BOOKS BY DAVIS ASHURA:

The Castes and the OutCastes

A Warrior's Path

A Warrior's Knowledge

A Warrior's Penance

Omnibus edition (available as eBook only)

Stories of Arisa — Volume One

The Chronicles of William Wilde

William Wilde and the Necrosed

William Wilde and the Stolen Life

William Wilde and the Unusual Suspects

William Wilde and the Sons of Deceit (available Spring 2019)

William Wilde and the Lord of Mourning (available Summer 2019)

ACKNOWLEDGMENT

No book is written in a vacuum, and this one is no exception. Thank you to Scott and Julie and all the kind folks at Tasteful Beans in Hickory, NC, who let me drink their delicious coffee (there's something addictive about their snickerdoodle) and use their free Wifi while I write. Also thank you to the kind people at Barnes and Noble who do the same. In addition, I've had some fantastic editors that helped make this book immeasurably better, and I'd be remiss without mentioning them, especially Tom Burkhalter, the Master of World War II Aviation Fiction. Then, of course, I can't forget my lovely wife and her gentle forbearance. She somehow easily manages the hat-trick of being funny, sweet, and wicked smart.

CHAPTER 1: A CHANGED LIFE

January 1986

Kohl Obsidian lifted his cleft nose to the cold, winter wind and tasted the air for blood. His wet nostrils made sucking sounds as they flared in and out like filters. He inhaled deeply one last time before snarling silently. The iron-rich scent of blood suffused the air, but none of it held the delicious flavor of *asra*, the aroma of magic.

Nearby, an overturned car rested upon its roof. Oil, gas, and other liquids leaked onto the road, and a large dent, one shaped like Kohl's bulky form, marred a door panel. Within the car slumped two dead humans, a man and a woman. A third, a youthful male, still clung to life.

Kohl hissed in annoyance.

Had the adults still lived, they could have served as a flesh depot for the necrosed's decaying form; he could have used a new heart. Of course, even the boy could function in such a role, but it had been his potential for *lorethasra*—the magic within him—that had drawn Kohl's attention. That potential yet coursed through the youth's veins, but without priming it would remain forever dormant. Forever untapped. Forever useless to Kohl's needs.

Once again, the necrosed hissed in annoyance as he surveyed the wreckage.

Movement along the road, though, brought a grim smile to the creature's leathery lips and stone-like face. There had been one other survivor of Kohl's recent attack. Another boy, likely a brother to the one trapped in the car. This one also had the potential for *lorethasra*, but it was weak and worthless, essentially an insult. And for such a sin, Kohl had marked the boy with blood, shriven him with the corruption that flowed through a necrosed.

That older boy, even now stumbling off with no clear direction of where he was going, would take years to die. Kohl had emptied all his weaknesses into the boy, made him a vessel for all his pain. The boy might suffer decades of anguish and loneliness, with no memories of his prior life to bring relief to his wretched state.

A fitting punishment for his worthlessness. A mental nudge from Kohl's degenerated *lorethasra* sent the useless youth into the woods where no one would find him.

Kohl watched the older boy stagger off into the dark, and a moment later he returned his attention to the car. What to do? No necrosed, except their leader, Sapient Dormant, had ever possessed an easy ability to scheme, and Kohl pondered long before coming to realize that the boy trapped in the car might eventually be of use. Perhaps he was worth saving.

The necrosed ripped off one of the vehicle's doors and tore away the seatbelt holding the boy in place. Kohl paused, studying the youth's features. No, he realized. Not a boy. Almost a man.

Kohl's weak eyes hadn't registered the truth until just now, but young man or boy, it didn't matter.

The necrosed pulled the youth from the wreckage and carried him effortlessly to a nearby embankment. Kohl's joints grated like grinding gears. There, the necrosed unceremoniously dropped the boy before turning back to the car. The dead within the vehicle were useless to him. Their corpses would burn.

With a gesture, black lightning poured from Kohl's hands, and the car exploded into flames. The fire raised a smile on Kohl's broken visage as the bodies within burned to ashes. Destruction, death, and murder. Those were the hollow sentiments that drove a necrosed, the actions that brought the forever-dying a kind of pleasure.

Kohl again studied the boy he had spared. So young and weak, helpless as a worm. But perhaps the boy would one day come in contact with a *saha'asra*. Then his power would flare to life, and the worm would grow powerful in his *lorethasra*. Then he would prove useful to Kohl, ready for harvest.

But to be kept safe, the boy would need strength, something he clearly lacked based upon his thin limbs and brittle build. He would need a sturdier frame. With a touch of his corrupted *lorethasra*, purified as best he could make it, Kohl changed the boy. A small change. Undetectable, but profound. One day the worm might even thank Kohl for what he'd done. Right before Kohl killed him.

August 1986

The first day of school marked summer's end, and for most students it represented the transition from lackadaisical days of cruising, movies, games, and golden sunshine to schoolroom tedium. With a single sunrise, drowsy hours of boredom and moments of transcendent clarity became months of dedicated dullness. The fact that the final days of August—sweltering and unbearable as they were—would also be banished, carried only the most meager of comforts.

But none of these issues brought discomfort or relief to William Wilde. For him, the first day of school inspired a Cheshire-cat grin. For him, a charge filled the school, electric with potential and vibrantly glowing. Today meant happy reunions with friends not seen all summer long. Today meant new teachers and new classes for William to either love or hate. And most of all, today meant the joy of returning to his beloved St. Francis High School, this time as a newly minted senior. As such, there was no sadness for William on this, his last first day of school. There was only room for happiness.

"Wrong way," his friend, Jason Jacobs, said.

William furrowed his brow in confusion at Jason, but an instant later the meaning of his friend's warning became clear. An involuntary, high-pitched yip escaped William's mouth, and he pulled up short. He'd almost wandered into the girls' bathroom.

Jason grinned.

"Jerk," William growled. "You could have said something sooner."

"I could have," Jason agreed, "but it was funnier this way."

"We'll see how funny you think it is when—" William drew up short, and an embarrassed flush chased away his annoyance when Sonya Bowyer, the most beautiful, most popular girl at St. Francis High School, edged past him in order to exit the girls' bathroom.

Her face scrunched into an expression of disgust. "Freak," she muttered as she slid past him. She had clearly assumed the worst regarding his intentions.

William shook his head in disbelief. Sonya Bowyer just *had* to be the one to witness his near mishap. "Guess everyone's going to think I'm an even bigger dork than before, huh?"

Jason shrugged in his inimitable, laid-back fashion. "Probably not. They're more likely to just think you're a pervert."

"Screw you," William replied to Jason.

William's coarse response elicited an openhearted, generous laugh, every bit as carefree as Jason himself. It bubbled from within with a kind of joy that often left William feeling wistful or envious. Even before his family had died last winter, he didn't think he'd ever laughed the way Jason could, a realization that once more made him aware of what a mismatched pair they were.

Jason had only moved to the area a few years back—just him and his grandfather and right before the start of sophomore year of high school—but he'd quickly found his place at St. Francis. Everyone liked Jason. Probably something to do with his easy smile and his exotic appearance: blond, California-surfer good looks mixed with Polynesian dark skin.

William, on the other hand, had moved to Cincinnati when he was nine, but sometimes he still felt like an outsider. Maybe it was because of his North Carolina-mountain accent and his unique dark-skinned, dark-haired appearance. His dad had been Scotch-Irish and his mother from India, by way of Trinidad. But then again, there had been his older brother, Landon, who had shared the same features, skin tone, and accent as William, but who'd been every bit as well-liked and popular as Jason.

"Who do you have for homeroom?" Jason asked as they continued down the hall.

"Mrs. Wilkerson," William answered.

"Doesn't she have some kind of sweater contest every Christmas?" Jason asked.

"The uglier the better. Who do you have?"

"Coach Rasskins."

"Didn't he try to pressure you into trying out for the football team again this past summer?"

"Yeah," Jason said with a self-deprecatory shrug. "He obviously knows greatness when he sees it."

William rolled his eyes. "I'm sure that's the reason."

"Either that or he heard how I dusted Lance Owens in a race last spring."

"If you didn't want Coach's attention, then maybe you shouldn't have done that," William noted. "Lance is supposed to be his fastest wide receiver." He shook his head in mock disappointment. "Not too bright, are you?"

Their conversation paused when a group of harried-appearing students rushed past.

"Freshmen," they muttered at the same time.

It was the same all down the hall. The freshmen, generally small, whippet-thin, and with worry creased on their harried faces, slammed shut their lockers as they raced along in their mad dash not to be late. Their eyes scrunched as their gazes flitted about in mild panic.

But seniors like William and Jason ambled along with a much slower, more confident pace. It was an unspoken rule that seniors were expected to maintain a certain decorum, a certain calm demeanor, and never reveal anything that might suggest they were intimidated by high school life. One guy even had a radio in his locker, playing "Jack and Diane" as he sorted through his books.

William paused when he noticed a girl—a tall, thin blonde—standing frozen in the middle of the hallway. Rather than looking fearful or worried, she wore the bewildered expression of someone who was lost as her gaze flitted between a paper in her hands—probably her class schedule—and nowhere in particular.

William felt an upwelling of sympathy for her. He still remembered what it had been like to be a freshman, new to the bustling hustle of St. Francis's first day, to the harrying nature of it, and how relieved he'd been when an upperclassman had been kind enough to show him around.

"I can help you, if you like," he offered.

The tall girl mutely handed over her class schedule.

William glanced at it. "It's this way," he told her. "I'm heading in the same direction."

The warning bell for homeroom went off, and a surge of urgency filled the air.

"See you at lunch?" Jason called over his shoulder as he hurried off toward a nearby set of stairs.

"Same bat time, same bat table," William answered.

"Dork," Jason shouted.

William grinned before turning back to the girl. “You have a name?”

“Jessira.” Her voice had an odd, impossible-to-place accent.

“Nice to meet you, Jessira.” He held out his hand. “I’m William. Are you a freshman?”

She nodded.

“Well, Jessira. We gotta run.”

They sprinted down the rapidly thinning hall, dashing around other students hustling to their homerooms and off into the old wing of the school, down some stairs, up some stairs, down another hall, and up one more flight of steps.

“Here you go,” William said, delivering Jessira to her homeroom. “Your first class is back in the new wing, not far from my own, so if you want I can show you where it is after homeroom.”

Jessira’s face broke into a relieved grin. “I’d very much appreciate that.”

Again, William noted her odd accent. “I’ll see you then.” He doffed an imaginary hat before racing to his own homeroom, barely making it before the bell rang.

As a result his seating choices were limited. Only one desk remained unoccupied, and William sighed when he realized that it would place him next to Jake Ridley, the bane of his existence. The two of them had clashed ever since they’d first met in fifth grade. In William’s opinion, Jake put the ‘jack’ in jackass, and his girlfriend just happened to be the lovely Sonya Bowyer.

She sat next to Jake and whispered in his ear. The two of them briefly flicked their attention to William before breaking out in laughter.

William's face burned as he remembered the incident at the girls' bathroom, and their mocking laughter triggered a fiery knot of anger in William's chest. It flared like heartburn.

Before the car accident that had killed his parents and his brother—all of them burned to ashes in the flames—William had been low-key, almost laconic. Now it didn't take much to get him heated up. Sometimes a cross word or challenging glare was all it took. The anger always lay there, bubbling right below the surface, waiting to be let loose.

He stared at Jake for a hard instant before forcing his unconsciously clenched fists to relax and taking a deep, cleansing breath. He shoved down his anger and took the empty seat.

Seconds later, Mrs. Wilkerson strode into the room. Their homeroom teacher was a small woman with tidy white hair pulled back in a bun, and wire-rimmed glasses that perched on the tip of her nose. She peered over the edge of them and glanced around the room with a sardonic smile on her seamed face. "I know you're seniors, and you think you should get to do things on your own terms, but in here we'll still have assigned seating." Her voice had a trace of a German accent. "That's to say, don't get too comfortable in your seats."

A rumble of groans met her words, but a few minutes later she had the room reorganized, and the muttered complaints and conversations slowly faded.

"Good," Mrs. Wilkerson said. "Now that we have that out of the way, we can go over my expectations for homeroom."

Just then a middle-aged woman—a secretary from the principal's office—minced into the room. Her wooden-soled stilettoes clacked like a typewriter as she walked. She whispered something to Mrs. Wilkerson, who listened intently before looking over in William's direction.

"You're wanted in the principal's office," Mrs. Wilkerson said.

William arose from his seat. "Is something wrong, ma'am?" he asked as he approached. A stab of unreasonable worry rose. His stomach hollowed, and his heart raced. Unexpected panic—fear for no reason—had also become a common part of his life since the death of his family. "Is Mr. Zeus hurt? Am I in trouble?"

"Who's Mr. Zeus?" Mrs. Wilkerson asked with a frown of confusion.

"Jason Jacob's grandfather. I live with him now."

Mrs. Wilkerson's face cleared. "Ah, yes. Pardon me. I forgot your home situation. But not to worry, Mr. Wilde. Nothing's wrong. No one's injured. There's merely a new student in school. We only found out about her today, and Principal Walter wants you to show her around. It turns out the two of you have the same class schedule."

"Come along," the secretary commanded with an imperious snap of her fingers.

"Yes, ma'am," William said, and they set off for the administrative offices.

Once there, the secretary gestured for him to have a seat. "The new student is meeting with the principal. They should be finished up in a little bit."

William tried not to groan. In adult speak, a little bit really meant twenty or thirty minutes. "Yes, ma'am," William said with a sigh before sinking into a hard, plastic chair and settling in for a long wait.

Muzak played in the background. *Ugh! Soul rot.* William wished he'd brought something to read. Anything to distract from the horrific strains of faux violins trying—and failing—to capture the badassery of Billy Idol's "White Wedding".

He glanced around. An old edition of *Sports Illustrated* from a few years back caught his attention. Michael Jordan graced the cover. William mentally snorted. Jordan was just a scorer. He'd never be as good as Magic or Bird. As William flipped through the *SI*, he tried to ignore the Muzak and prayed that Principal Walter would finish up soon with the new student.

He knew it would be unlikely, but . . .

The door to Principal Walter's office opened, and William perked up.

"If you have any other concerns, please let us know," Principal Walter said in his hearty baritone to someone in his office.

"I'll be sure to," a young woman replied in a confident contralto. It also held a hint of . . . was that mockery?

William sat up further, his curiosity piqued.

The new student, whatever her name was, stepped out of Principal Walter's office, but her back remained toward William. He couldn't see her face, but he could see enough. Tall and slim, she had dark hair that cascaded to her shoulders, and if her face was anything like the rest of her . . .

"I know changing schools in the middle of high school can be difficult," Principal Walter said in sympathy, "but we'll do anything you need to make the transition easier."

"It's more difficult than you know," the girl said with that same barely heard hint of amused irony.

"Of course," Principal Walter said with a brief smile.

The girl glanced toward William, and his heart picked up the pace. Sonya Bowyer suddenly had stiff competition for being the prettiest girl in school.

"Mr. Wilde. Come meet our new student," Principal Walter said. "You'll be showing her around."

William stood, and sent a silent prayer of gratitude that his hands weren't sweaty.

"William Wilde," he said, offering his hand to the girl.

"Serena Paradiso," she replied, taking his hand in a firm grip and shaking it. Her full lips were turned up in a smile, and her dark eyes sparkled with amusement.

"Well, Ms. Paradiso, I'll leave you in the capable hands of Mr. Wilde," Principal Walter said, "and with him to show you around, I'm sure you'll have no problems settling in."

"I'm sure Mr. Wilde will make sure I have no problems at all," Serena replied in her cool, composed voice.

She held William's gaze all the while, and he began to fidget. Her regard held an intensity that he found unnerving.

The principal eyed her uncertainly before clearing his throat. "Yes. Well, the two of you had better head on back to your homeroom. First period starts in a few minutes."

"Please lead the way, Mr. Wilde," Serena said with a sweeping gesture.

"William. My name is William," he corrected her, leading her out of the administrative offices.

"And your preference is that I call you William?"

She spoke in a formal manner, and William studied her in momentary puzzlement before answering. "Yes. No one calls me 'Mr. Wilde.'"

"Then perhaps I shall be the first," Serena replied with a half-smile.

"I'd prefer if you wouldn't," William said.

Serena held him with her disconcerting gaze for a beat before facing forward. "As you wish," she said.

William eyed her sidelong. Pretty girls tended to put him off-balance, and Serena was definitely pretty. He tried not to trip over his feet as they continued down the empty hallway.

Serena chuckled, low and throaty. "Or perhaps I'll call you Will."

William grimaced. "Please don't." *Only his parents and his brother had ever called him Will.*

CHAPTER 2:
THE NEW GIRL

By the time William and Serena made it back to homeroom, it was nearly over. Mrs. Wilkerson only had a few minutes to meet Serena and introduce her to the rest of the class.

William wondered how Serena would react to twenty pairs of assessing, curious eyes focused on her. He would have melted into a puddle of nervous sweat had their circumstances been reversed.

However, Serena evidently had greater self-assurance. She gazed over the other students like a queen surveying her rapt subjects before eventually offering them a composed smile. "It's good to meet all of you, and I look forward to getting to know you in the coming year," she said.

Warm smiles greeted her words, which William thought unsurprising. Serena had a presence, something unassociated with her beauty, something indefinable, but perhaps related to the surety in her eyes and the confidence of her carriage and voice. William figured that Serena could have been plain as a manila folder, and many would have still found her intriguing.

In fact, she had already been noticed. Many of the more popular boys in the class gave her admiring appraisals, while some of the girls viewed her with indecipherable, speculative gazes.

William mentally smirked and placed a wager with himself. Serena would get bored with him before second period and move on to join one of the popular cliques.

After homeroom ended, William led her out into the packed hallway. Conga lines moved in both directions, but some students stood like rocks in a stream as they talked, laughed, and postured, with the boys speaking a little too loudly and gesturing too flagrantly. William wrinkled his nose in disdain. *Peacocks wearing too much cologne.*

"Where to?" Serena asked.

"American History, but we've got to make a pit-stop first," William replied. "I promised to show a freshman how to get to her first class."

Serena lifted her brows in an unspoken question.

"She was lost and needed help," William answered.

"How very generous," Serena said with a faint smile.

William couldn't tell if she was mocking him or not, and he simply shrugged before searching around for Jessira. He quickly found her, surrounded by a gaggle of giggling girls. She stood out like a giraffe, easily a head taller than the others.

"You know where you're going?" he called to her.

Jessira flashed a smile. "I think so," she said, gesturing to the other girls. "But if I don't, apparently these others will help me figure it out."

William nodded, glad to see her fitting in. "Let me know if you need anything else."

"I will."

"That was kindly done," Serena said after Jessira and her new group of friends had moved on.

"It wasn't much," William replied. "So where are you from?"

"San Diego," Serena replied.

William did a double-take. "San Diego? Why'd you move here from there? I mean, Cincinnati is great and all, but San Diego? Isn't it always warm and sunny?"

"My father's job," Serena answered. Her lips curled in scorn, the first sign William had seen from her of something other than amusement. "It wasn't my choice."

"Moving right before your senior year? That sucks," William empathized.

"Yes, it does."

"Well, there's only one thing I can say to that, and we both know what it is." William waited a beat. "Dress warmly, because you're going to hate the winter."

Serena blinked in surprise before offering a slow, warm chuckle. "I'm sure that'll be true," she replied. "And I'm also sure that I'll miss the ocean."

"My mom used to say the same thing." William smiled in remembrance. "She was from the Caribbean."

"Was?"

Once again, William found himself the focus of Serena's disconcerting scrutiny.

"She died last year. Car accident," William answered, his answer curt even though saying the words no longer caused a lump in his throat. At least not on most days.

"I'm sorry to hear that," Serena said. "I know what it's like to lose someone you love." She wore a tight-lipped expression of sympathy and squeezed his forearm.

"It's fine," William said, as they skirted a couple of slow-moving students. He forced a smile even while he shoved down a flash of anger. He had long since grown tired of everyone's sympathy. "We're here." William gestured to the room they were about to enter. "First period, American History."

As soon as they entered the room, William noticed the stares. From the boys came slack-jawed expressions of awe, and from the girls, cool-eyed gazes of assessment.

"I think they're staring at me," Serena said, amusement back in her voice.

"No. It's me," William said, sighing in feigned weariness. "I get this kind of attention everywhere I go."

Serena chuckled. "I'm sure you do." She looked out at the class. "They're still staring."

"Ignore it," William suggested. "It's tedious, but you get used to it."

"I'll have to trust your expertise." Serena smiled and nudged him with her elbow. "Where do we sit?"

"Over there." William led her to a pair of unoccupied desks.

They settled into their chairs, and he tried not to squirm about in his seat, but he could feel the interest from the rest of the class upon Serena. By reflection, it fell on him, too. Jennifer Miller, one of the prettier girls in their class, sat to Serena's right and began speaking to her. William tried not to eavesdrop.

"Switch seats with me," a voice hissed from behind him. It was William's friend, Daniel Karllson. He'd moved into William's neighborhood a few years back, right after Jason.

"Why?" William whispered. "So you can sit next to Serena?"

"I'm just trying to be a good friend," Daniel said. "You know she's out of your league. You'll just embarrass yourself when she dusts you off."

"You think this is a favor you're doing me?" William asked with a laugh.

"On my honor," Daniel replied. His face split in a grin. "That's what friends are for."

"Right. I'm sure they are, Dionne Warwick."

"What?" Daniel's face creased in confusion.

"The song," William reminded him.

"What song?" Daniel asked. His face cleared. "Oh. That song." He grimaced. "Dude, that was a sucky song. Why would you even remember it?"

"And just for that, you can't have my seat."

"Fine," Daniel pretended to huff. "But don't come whining to me when she drops you."

"Whatever."

Mr. Callahan strode into the room on William's final word. He shut off the various murmured conversations with a gruff, "Quiet down, wise guys," in his thick Brooklyn accent with an idiom perpetually stuck in the forties.

"See you at lunch?" Daniel whispered while Mr. Callahan rifled through his briefcase.

"Sure thing," William agreed.

"Will your new girlfriend be there?" Daniel asked. He nodded toward Serena.

Judging by the swift upturn of Serena's lips, William was sure she had heard, and he wanted to strangle Daniel. "I don't know. Now shut up."

As if on cue, Mr. Callahan barked, "I said quiet down, fat-heads." He spoke directly to William and Daniel. "Or do you want a jug on your first day of school?"

William shot Daniel a glare of annoyance.

As soon as Mr. Callahan's attention shifted elsewhere, Serena arched her brow at William. "Jug?" she mouthed.

"Justice under God," William whispered as quietly as he could. "Detention."

"Keep talking and you'll have it," Mr. Callahan said without glancing his way.

William shut his mouth.

Thankfully, the rest of the class passed quickly, and after History came English, and then Biology.

The teacher for the latter was Mrs. Nelson, a mousy appearing woman with a heart of ice. She had a boa constrictor for a pet and fed live rats to the beast. The one time William had seen a feeding like that, he'd almost lost his lunch.

Right after being dropped into the cage with the boa, the poor rodent had scurried about, obviously terrified, and William had felt an unexpected surge of sympathy for the rat, especially when the dead-eyed snake had slowly uncoiled, menacing, quiet, and deadly. The sight had sent shivers down William's spine. He hated snakes. He always had and always would. Plus, as the preacher at his church had once said, any animal that walked without legs had to be the devil.

"This semester we'll be dissecting a number of animals," Mrs.

Nelson said. "Now, first things first. Find yourself a lab partner. I don't particularly care who you choose."

William immediately thought of Serena. Why not? She was standing right next to him, fingering a small, silver cross that hung from her necklace. "Do you want to be lab partners?" he asked.

Serena spun his way, appearing relieved. "Absolutely," she quickly answered. "I was afraid I'd be left out in the cold."

William smiled. "Has that ever happened?" he asked, genuinely curious. "I mean, have you ever been the odd man out?"

"Well, first of all, in case you haven't noticed, I'm a woman, not a man," she said. "And secondly, no, it hasn't. But there's always a first time."

"Not for something like that," William said. "At least not in high school."

"You never know."

Steve Aldo approached them with a confident gait and a cocky grin. Steve was handsome, athletic, and one of the popular boys. "We haven't been introduced yet," he said.

"What are you talking about, Steve?" William asked, purposefully misreading Steve's statement. "We've known each other for years."

Serena covered her lips, hiding a smile while Steve frowned.

Good.

Of course, Steve wasn't always a bad guy. Sometimes he could actually be genuine and friendly. But he was insufferable in Jake Ridley's presence. Then, like all of Jake's friends, Steve became a sycophant, trading his confidence to be an orbiting planet to Jake's sun.

"I was talking to *her*," Steve replied.

"Oh, right," William said. "In that case, Serena, this is Steve. Steve, Serena."

"It's nice to meet you," Steve said, grinning widely again and flashing his perfect white teeth. "I'm still looking for a lab partner. So how about it? You and me and all that." He lifted his brows suggestively.

William rolled his eyes. *What a tool.*

"Thank you, but I already have a partner." Serena put her hand on William's forearm.

Steve's grin slowly faded into disbelief. "William? Seriously?" At Serena's nod, he made a Herculean effort to cover his shock and appear nonchalant. "Well, when you get tired of him, I'm sure Mrs. Nelson will let us switch." He gave a final cheesy grin and a wink.

"What a himbo," Serena said, staring after Steve.

"What?"

"A himbo. A him-bo. Like a bimbo. Steve. Your friend. That's what he reminds me of."

William chuckled and glanced at Steve, who once more offered Serena a cheesy grin.

"Does that smile actually work for him?" Serena asked.

"Yeah," William answered. "At least it seems to, maybe even on some of the guys now that I think about it."

Serena covered her mouth as she stifled laughter.

William grinned in bemusement. It hadn't been *that* funny of a joke, but hey, whatever made Serena smile was fine by him.

Serena got her laughter under control and glanced at him, but her eyes were still shiny. "I'll have to remember that about you."

"What?"

"How funny you are."

"Funny-looking?"

Serena chuckled again and William puffed up, strangely proud that he'd made her laugh. After that, Biology and the rest of the morning quickly passed, and the lunch bell rang.

On the way to the cafeteria, Serena hummed a song. William couldn't place it at first, but eventually he figured it out. "Gloria" by U2. *Good song.*

In the cafeteria, just like in the hallways, the students formed another conga line while they waited to file through for their food. Serena's humming ceased. No doubt the unappetizing aromas of over-cooked institutional food put her off. Eventually, they entered the kitchen and reached for the bland, flavorless cardboard rectangles that masqueraded as pizza, and something in the shape of macaroni and cheese. Dessert was a pudding pretending to be chocolate.

Serena eyed her food with antipathy. "Is any of this actually edible?"

"Sure," William said. "If you're a billy goat. But whether it's digestible or not is another question."

Serena grimaced. "That would be funnier if it wasn't true. I think I'll be packing my lunch from now on."

"Beautiful *and* wise," William said without thinking. The words simply slipped out of the sieve that was his mouth before he could think to hold them in.

"You think I'm beautiful?"

William eyed Serena askance. She wore either a teasing smile or a mocking one. He couldn't tell, and his annoyance riled at the sight. "Sure, I do," he said, managing a nonchalant shrug. "But don't let it go to your head."

"I wasn't—"

"Let's go sit down," William interrupted.

He spotted Jason and Daniel. Seated with them was Lien Sun, the pretty Chinese foreign exchange student who'd been with Daniel's family since last year. William led Serena to their table, where they sat down after brief introductions.

As usual, Jason had already slurped down his lunch and was in the midst of taking a tentative taste of the chocolate-colored pudding. His lips curled, and William grinned.

"Why do you even bother?" Daniel asked with a bemused shake of his head. "You know the pudding sucks. It's always tasted like stool, and it always will."

"How would you know what stool tastes like?" Jason asked.

"I . . ." Daniel gaped stupidly. "I don't," he finished lamely. He reddened when Serena and Lien pealed with laughter.

William smiled but didn't join in the hilarity. Daniel hated looking bad in front of girls—all guys did—and William sympathized with him.

"Anyway, the reason I keep trying it is because I keep hoping that *just once* it'll actually taste like chocolate pudding," Jason said. "It's stupid, I know, but . . ." he gave an eloquent shrug.

"It is stupid," Lien said, all blunt truth. She didn't sugar-coat anything, and while at times it could be annoying, at least a person always knew where they stood with her. "If something has never changed in the past, it is not likely to change in the future."

"It's not dumb," Serena disagreed. "Seeing if something that was once bad might have improved seems worth doing."

"*The definition of insanity is doing the same thing over and over again and expecting a different result*. Albert Einstein," Lien countered.

"Quoting Albert Einstein isn't a proof of anything," Serena said. "Jason isn't conducting an experiment on universal laws. He's tasting food. Food changes."

A brief tension rose between the two girls, but Lien ended it with a smile. "I like her," she announced. "Welcome to the coolest, smoothest lunch table at St. Francis."

"I don't know if we're cool or smooth," William said.

"Speak for yourself," Lien replied tartly.

"Exactly what brings you to our fair city anyway?" Jason asked Serena.

"My father," she answered. "He works in an import business. A job opportunity came up, so here we are."

"What does he import?" Daniel asked.

"I have no idea."

"None?" Daniel asked in surprise.

"None."

"What about your mother? What does she do?" Lien asked.

"She doesn't." Serena's face clouded. "She died a long time ago."

"I'm sorry to hear that," William said.

"Sorry I said it, or sorry about what happened?" Serena asked.

Her intense focus caused William to fidget, but he forced himself to meet her gaze. "Both."

"How did you get such wonderful hair?" Lien asked. She directed her question to Serena. "It's so dark and pretty, like Terri Garber's."

"Who's Terri Garber?" William asked.

"The pretty brunette from *North and South*."

"The one who was also in *Star Trek: Wrath of Khan*?" William asked.

"No. The other one."

"Oh. That one." William grinned widely. "Yeah. I wouldn't kick her out of . . ." He coughed into his hand. "Never mind."

Lien rolled her eyes. "I knew you would eventually remember her."

After lunch Serena continued to accompany William from one class to the next, and while she remained friendly whenever members of the popular cliques struck up conversations with her, that appeared to be the extent of it. William got the sense that she didn't want to prolong the conversations with them. Even when some of those same popular girls offered to show Serena around to the rest of her classes, she chose to stay with William.

He tried to appear indifferent whenever it happened, but inside, his heart and self-confidence soared. In fact, when the day ended he realized that this had been the best first day of school in his life, and his shoulders slumped in disappointment when the final bell rang.

"See you in the morning?" William asked on their way to their lockers. Serena's locker, which she had to herself, stood next to the one he shared with Jason.

"Definitely. And thank you for showing me around school, Mr. Wilde," Serena replied, her tone teasing once more. "You were an excellent tour guide."

William doffed an imaginary hat. "It was my pleasure to squire you about, Ms. Paradiso."

Jason arrived just then. “Ready to go?” he asked. “Daniel and Lien should be waiting by the car.”

Serena’s head swiveled as she glanced around, appearing lost or like she was looking for something. For the first time that day, William thought she appeared unsure of herself. It took him a moment to figure out why.

“Do you have a way to get home?” he asked.

“I’m not sure,” Serena said. “I don’t have a car, and I don’t know which bus to take.”

“I can take you,” William offered.

“You’d do that?” Serena asked with a hopeful expression.

“Of course,” William replied, surprised at her surprise.

Jason turned to Serena. “You’re sure you’re fine hanging around us?”

“Why wouldn’t I be?”

“Because we’re what the French call ‘le nerds,’” William answered.

“Speak for yourself,” Jason said.

“A nerd, huh?” Serena smiled. “I think I figured that part out by myself.”

“What gave me away?” William asked.

Serena tapped her chin, pretending to ponder the matter. “Maybe it had something to do with that doodle you made in English, the one of the man with claws. Bearman. Is he supposed to be friends with Superman?”

“That was Wolverine,” William corrected. “He’s from Marvel. Superman is DC.”

“Same difference,” Serena pronounced with a dismissive wave of her hand. “And you just made my point.”

William's mouth dropped open. *Marvel. DC. The same? Sacrilege.* "It's not the . . . " He quieted when Serena arched her eyebrows in challenge. "Never mind," he muttered. "Where do you live?"

The address she supplied was the home in which William had grown up, a couple houses down from where he now lived with Jason and his grandfather, Mr. Zeus.

"That's my old house," William said.

"Seriously?"

"Seriously."

Serena's face fell. "I'm sorry if—"

"I didn't see you move in," William interrupted, knowing what she intended on saying—probably something sympathetic—but he didn't want to hear her pity.

"We got in late last night," Serena answered. "The moving company is supposed to deliver our furniture later in the week."

"Moving into my old house. Same class schedule. Locker near mine. Those sure are a lot of coincidences," William said with a teasing smile. "You sure you aren't stalking me?"

Serena held her hands up in surrender. "You figured me out," she said. "I'm actually a member of a super secret spy organization. I'm here to test your skill set and recruit you to our cause. And by recruit, I mean by any means necessary."

William knew her words were most likely spoken in jest, but he couldn't help himself. "Really?" he asked, his voice quavering with suppressed hope.

"No. Not really." Serena shook her head in disgust.

Jason brayed laughter.

"Let's go," William muttered.

CHAPTER 3: DRIVING AND SECRETS

The parking lot rang with sounds of celebration as everyone grinned and laughed that the first day of school was over and they'd all survived. Freshmen and sophomores chattered away in excitement before boarding their school buses, while upperclassmen stood next to their cars, many of them intentionally speaking and laughing loudly enough for others to notice.

William rolled his eyes. *More peacocks signaling their coolness.*

Based on Serena's dismissive smirk, she wasn't impressed by their poses, either.

"Are we dropping Serena off?" Daniel asked. He and Lien waited by William's car, a lemon-yellow T-Bird.

"I bet it isn't out of our way either," Lien said, wearing a smile like butter wouldn't melt in her mouth.

"It's my old house," William answered.

Lien's knowing grin faded.

"William told me after lunch about what happened to his family," Serena said. "I'm sorry if it bothers—"

"Don't worry about it," William cut her off. "Someone was bound to move into it eventually. And it's not my home anymore. I've barely set foot in the place since . . . you know."

Daniel rapped the T-bird's roof. "Let's get going," he said, and William privately blessed him for changing the subject.

"Who gets the front seat?" Lien asked.

"Shotgun," Serena said.

"Wait!" Jason protested. "I always sit up front."

Serena gave him a condescending smile. "Then you have to speak up faster next time."

"But—"

"No," Serena said.

"I'm his—"

"Still no."

With a deflated sigh, Jason acquiesced. "Fine," he huffed.

Everyone clambered into the T-Bird with William and Serena up front and the others in the back.

"Nice car," Serena noted.

"Thanks. It was my father's," William said. "Dad bought the car junked, and Landon and I helped him fix it up. We put in a new dash and leather seats. Same with the headliner, stereo, engine, and chassis."

"I like it," Serena said, as she stroked the upholstery. "Corinthian leather?"

William laughed. "No. That's a Chrysler. This is a Ford. And I'm guessing you don't have a car of your own."

"Good guess."

"None of these losers do, either." William gestured to the back. "They don't like to drive."

Daniel slapped the side of William's seat. "Let's go," he urged. "Look at that line forming up."

The single exit from the school grounds was backing up and getting longer by the second.

William keyed the ignition, and the T-Bird's V-8 engine rumbled to life. The radio came on, and everyone rolled down their windows as William eased forward, waiting for his turn to pull into the exit lane. Patience and cooperation were needed to get out of the packed parking lot.

As if he wanted to put a lie to William's silent assessment, Jake Ridley rolled up in his Corvette, and even though William had the right of way, he stuck the nose of his car in front of the T-Bird. Sonya Bowyer rode with Jake, and the two of them gazed imperiously upon William and his friends.

William's anger fired, and he strangled an urge to flip Jake the bird. He wasn't worth the aggravation. He decided on a pissed-off scowl.

The notes of a familiar song playing over the radio soothed the last of his anger.

Lien shouted in his ear. "Turn it up!"

William did so, and grinned in anticipation.

Lien belted out the first line of the song in her Chinese accent. Daniel's tenor soon joined her high-pitched wail. Jason added his voice next.

Their loud singing drew Sonya's and Jake's attention. The two of them stared in bemused disbelief at Jason, Daniel, and Lien before they started laughing.

"Losers!" Jake yelled.

Jason must not have had William's reticence. He flipped Jake the bird and sang louder.

William turned up the radio and added his voice to those of his friends.

Jake flipped them off in return while Sonya wore a sour grimace, as if she'd just smelled something bad.

There had been a time, just this morning, in fact, when earning the good opinion of Sonya Bowyer had been of great importance to William. *Now? Not so much.* He gave Sonya a mocking salute. The entire situation became perfect when a few other students tuned their radios to the same station and sang along.

Jake shook his head in disgust at William and mouthed something coarse.

William's answer was an easy grin. He knew it would piss Jake off even more, and best of all, with Jake distracted, William cut in front of him and pulled out into traffic.

Jason crowed in triumph. "Stupid Corvette's worth nothing if the driver's a moron."

"Is leaving the school grounds always like a musical?" Serena asked, wearing a dazed expression.

"Only on the good days," Lien replied with a grin.

"Anyone want to go to Graeter's?" Jason asked.

"Hell, yeah!" Daniel said.

"What's Graeter's?" Serena asked.

"The best ice cream in the world," William replied.

Five minutes later, they sat ensconced in a booth with their luscious riches arrayed before them. Before they ate, though, of one accord they all leaned in toward Serena, waiting for her verdict.

She slipped a lock of hair behind an ear and took a delicate bite of her chocolate chip ice cream. Her eyes rolled up in an unmistakable expression of bliss.

"I think she likes it," Lien chuckled.

"It's divine."

William took that as a sign to tuck into his Cookies n' Cream. He tried to eat slowly, wanting to take small bites and savor it, but despite his best intentions, it was gone all too quickly.

He glanced at the others.

As usual, Jason had gobbled his down as though it might run away from him, while Lien and Serena were just about finished with theirs as well. Daniel, though, being the slow-motion eater that he was, hadn't yet reached the halfway point of his own dish.

William surreptitiously surveyed the others again. No one was paying him any attention, and he wondered if could get away with licking his cup clean.

Serena noticed his speculation. She raised a questioning eyebrow an instant before a knowing smile lit her face. "You're thinking of licking your bowl clean, aren't you?"

William sniffed. "I have no idea what you're talking about."

Her throaty laugh told him that she didn't believe him.

William pretended to ignore her amusement as he looked around the ice cream parlor. A few other students from St. Francis had come in, a trio of skinny juniors whom William recognized. He'd played D&D with them.

"What is that disgusting, desiccated creature on their shirts?" Serena asked, nodding at the other students.

Jason looked where Serena had indicated. "Eddie the Head," he answered. "Iron Maiden's mascot."

Serena's eyes widened. "You know who this thing is, this celebration of the horrific?" she asked, sounding appalled.

William shifted in his chair, not wanting to admit that he had a poster of Eddie on his bedroom wall.

"He's famous," Jason said, sounding as defensive as William felt.

"He's repulsive," Serena countered, sounding like a schoolmarm.

"They couldn't have left the Ring with Tom Bombadil!" one of the skinny juniors shouted. "He'd lose it in the barrows and not even remember he did it."

"They're barrow-downs, dumbass," one of the other boys corrected.

"Whatever. The point is that the Ring would have ended up back in Mordor in two snaps of a Balrog's whip."

"If the Balrog got ahold of the Ring . . ."

"What are they talking about?" Serena asked with a perplexed expression.

"*Lord of the Rings*," Jason answered. "William could tell you all about it."

Lien also appeared to be eavesdropping on the other group's conversation. "I know we're kind of nerdy, but those three take it to an entirely new level," she noted. "And what is a Mordor anyway?" She sounded both contemptuous and baffled.

William did a double-take. "You don't know about Mordor, the land of shadows?"

"Of course not," Lien replied. "I try to have a real life instead of living it through some book."

"Your loss," William replied. "Some books contain the truest magic."

Lien rolled her eyes. "Yes, Master Yoda."

"Hi, Kettle. I'm Pot. You're black," William said, calling Lien out on her knowledge of geek culture.

"Shut it," she replied.

"I think it's sweet that they long for magic," Serena interrupted, "but the land of shadows sounds as awful as the creature on their shirts."

"Mordor is much worse." William briefly explained to Serena about the One Ring of Power.

"One Ring to give its wielder unfathomable power," Serena mused.

"And corruption," William reminded her.

"I think I should read this book they're talking about."

"You can borrow my copy," William offered.

"Yeah. He's only read it like twenty times," Jason said with an insufferable grin.

"Do you read it so often in order to study the nature of evil?" Serena asked.

"Pretty much," William lied. The truth was that he read *Lord of the Rings* because he loved losing himself in Middle-Earth, a better, brighter world than the real one. While reading Tolkien's epic, William often imagined himself as a member of the Fellowship, journeying into danger and performing great deeds while singing songs of love and valor. But he didn't want to admit that to Serena.

"That's too much philosophy for me," Daniel said, finally surfacing from his still-unfinished bowl of ice cream. He waved his spoon for emphasis. "Life's complicated enough. I like my entertainment to be light-hearted and simple."

"Like your brain?" Lien asked.

"Ha, ha," Daniel replied.

"Or like *Hardcastle and McCormick*?" William asked. "How does that theme song go again? Something about slow-motion men."

Daniel gave him a sour scowl. "Again, ha, ha. I don't eat in slow motion."

Serena wore an air of bemusement. "Is this how your group always interacts?"

"Interacts?" Lien asked. "A big word when all we're doing is joking around with one another."

"Done," Daniel announced as he pushed away his empty dish.

"Finally," Lien said.

They piled back into William's car and drove the short distance to their neighborhood. It was a newer subdivision that ended in a cul-de-sac with homes that were all less than fifteen years old.

William pulled into the driveway of a tan-brick tri-level with an attached two-car garage, and everyone got out of the T-Bird. Daniel and Lien called out their goodbyes and crossed the street to go to their home, a two-story with a gray vinyl siding.

Serena stood by William's car and appeared to be waiting for something. Jason caught the hint and excused himself to head inside.

"We leave for school around seven if you need a ride in the morning," William said.

"You have no idea how much I was hoping you'd say that,"

Serena said with a grin of relief. She hesitated a moment later, appearing as if she wanted to add something more but then changing her mind. "See you tomorrow." She headed off to her home—William's old simple ranch. As she departed, she gave William a final glance over her shoulder.

Within three strides of leaving William and facing her new house, Serena schooled her face to stillness. No one could be allowed to read her true thoughts. Where she had been brought up and taught, doing so could lead to unfortunate consequences.

And she wanted to avoid 'unfortunate consequences' given who her "father" truly was. He was related to her, but his importance stretched further than familial ties. He was her Isha, the person charged with her education, her final training. And displeasing him, not accomplishing what he had taught, was unforgivable. Not only would his punishment be more severe than anything her true father would have ever administered, it would set her back, maybe too far to recover, in what she hoped to accomplish with her life.

Even as Serena thought about her future, she sensed William's regard. She glanced at him over her shoulder and feigned a shy half-smile before facing forward once more. Lastly, she tucked a stray lock of hair behind an ear—William seemed to like when she did that—before opening the door.

One last glimpse, and she caught him smiling in return.

Good. William could never see her as anything but a happy, well-adjusted new student. She had plans for him.

Serena still wore the half-smile as she crossed the threshold, but as soon as she stepped inside, her expression became inscrutable.

The house she entered, a modest, single-story ranch, opened into a large space that held the kitchen, dining room, and the family room. Down a darkened hallway to the right lay three bedrooms. Compared to some of the houses in which Serena had resided, this one was small, but its humble nature wasn't what ended her smile.

It was the presence of her Isha, Adam Paradiso, a big man whose size and aura shrank the room. He sat at a card table, which currently served as a dining table, with his well-muscled arms folded across his broad chest and his bearded face displaying a frown of impatience.

"You're late," he snapped.

"I was delayed, sir," Serena replied.

"The reason?"

"I was asked to accompany the *Mayna* for ice cream." Serena kept her voice level and composed. Isha disliked reports given with any sense of emotionality. He felt it biased the listener.

Her instructor's impatience receded and he raised a sardonic brow. "And I'm sure that brought you great suffering."

Serena allowed a smile of true humor to cross her face. "It was necessary, but yes, I did enjoy the ice cream. I'll not lie."

"Why not? I've taught you to lie at need."

"You have," Serena agreed. For her, lying had become as natural as breathing, and she no longer bothered with who might be hurt by it. Ambition had become her sole motivation. "But in this case, the truth suffices for my purpose."

"And what purpose is that?"

"To give you an accounting of my movements."

"So be it," Isha said. The last of his annoyance fell away. "Tell me about the *Mayna*." His visage had tightened into one of raptor-intense interest, the same expression that Serena sometimes unwittingly mimicked. He steepled his fingers beneath his chin. "Who is William Wilde?"

Here was Isha's true self: the meticulous, controlled taskmaster. In fact, he had never truly been upset with her. All along, his annoyance had been a ruse, a means to see how Serena would react. Constant testing and training had always been Isha's way.

"He is young and—"

"Meaningless."

Serena tilted her head in acknowledgment of the rebuke. "He is naive. Weak." She fingered the cross hanging from her necklace. "He also thinks I'm a Christian. He likes that."

"Why?" Isha asked, appearing truly puzzled. "God doesn't love the meek."

No, He didn't, but Serena sometimes wondered what the world would be like if He did. She knew better than to voice her treasonous thoughts.

"What about his *lorethasra*?" Isha asked.

"Quiescent. He has no need for a *nomasra*."

"What of his friends? Who are they?"

Serena pursed her lips, uncertain. "Of them I am less sure," she admitted. "I can't tell if they're magi of Arylyn or friends who are as simple and harmless as the *Mayna*."

"You think him harmless?"

"In comparison to what we are? Yes," Serena replied with no hint of her prior uncertainty.

"And therefore, you believe that if circumstances require force to accomplish our task, he will be unable to deny us?"

Serena carefully considered Isha's question before answering. "No matter what you believe about his potential, right now he is untrained. He knows nothing. He could not stop us."

A true smile broke across Isha's face. "Excellent. Finally some good news. I'm already tired of this place." His air of intensity returned. "Pay close attention to William. Stay close to him. Ingratiate yourself to him. If he is a *raha'asra*, we need him. Our people need him, and those who bring him in will rise high in our ranks. You will do this." There was no hint of a question in Isha's voice. It was a command.

"Yes, Isha," Serena said. "Already he likes me as a young man likes a young woman. Our task won't be as difficult as I was initially led to believe." Serena let a smile, lupine and cunning, slip across her face. It hid her true feelings, which were uncomfortably close to affection for William. She had genuinely enjoyed talking to him, enjoyed his sense of humor, and listening as he and his friends had sung that song and eaten ice cream. It was so different from anything she had experienced thus far in her life.

It changed nothing, though. Friends were a liability.

"Do not let confidence blind you to the dangers we face," Isha warned.

"Yes, sir," Serena said. "But there is one other thing." She hesitated. "The *Mayna*—"

"William. If you wish to earn his confidence, start thinking of him by his true name. Consider him the *Mayna* and you deny his humanity. You begin to think of him as an object. It will come across in your interactions with him."

"I already know this, sir," Serena said, allowing none of her annoyance at his simplistic advice to taint her voice. "After so many years, do you not trust that I know how to do as I have been instructed?"

"A reminder is not always—or even often—meant as an insult," Isha said. "But this other thing you wished to tell me? What is it?"

"I hadn't realized that William's family was killed last year. Burned to death in a car accident. It's tragic."

"Tragic?" Isha rubbed his chin. "Failure is tragic. What he experienced was the sorrow of a puppy who lost his master."

CHAPTER 4: MR. ZEUS

William watched Serena walk home, noting how she smiled at him one last time before tucking away a strand of hair and opening her front door. Such a small gesture—a smile—but it could convey much: amusement, sarcasm, satisfaction, acceptance, joy . . . In Serena's case, it had been pleasure.

At least that's how William read it.

"What are you doing?" Jason asked from the front stoop of their house. "Are you coming in or what?"

William broke from his reverie and quickly climbed the steps from the driveway to the front doorway.

After his parents and brother had died in that horrible car accident last winter, William could have gone to live with some aunts and uncles, but everyone figured he'd be better off staying close to his friends in familiar surroundings.

In the end, it had been Jason and Mr. Zeus who had taken him in, and William reckoned he'd remain forever grateful for their generosity. He didn't know what kind of state he'd have been in if they hadn't. Their patience, friendship, and love had been key to William's recovery.

That didn't mean Jason couldn't be a pain in the ass, such as now. Jason was probably itching to make fun of him about Serena. William kept his head tucked as he trotted up the stairs. He didn't want Jason to see his blush of embarrassment. Still, he risked a glance.

Jason smirked. "Something have you so mesmerized you forgot where you were?"

"Shut up," William growled. He knew it had been too much to hope that Jason wouldn't tease him about Serena.

"What did I say?" Jason asked.

"Just get it out," William replied.

"I have no idea what you mean." Jason tried to keep his face innocent, but his twitching lips and twinkling eyes gave him away.

"Ri-i-ight," William said. "I'm sure you haven't been dying to say a whole bunch of things you think are funny."

"Well, of course," Jason said. "If jokes at your expense were ammo, right now I'd be loaded for bear. Some of my jokes are even as funny as your face. You know what I mean?"

"You mean when I'm doing my impression of you?"

Jason didn't go for the bait and fall into a war of insults. "Of course, we could ask Serena what she thinks of your looks," he continued, still wearing a smug smile.

William rolled his eyes. "Why don't you get right on that, himbo?"

Jason's smile curled into a frown in puzzlement. "What's a himbo?"

"You know, a guy who's a bimbo. A *him*-bo. The kind of guy

who does this." William arched his neck, closed his eyes, and used both hands to slick back his hair.

Jason erupted in laughter. "A himbo. I like it. Where'd you hear it?"

"A girl I met today. Lives down the street from us," William said, wearing a grin of his own now. "She was talking about one of my friends when she mentioned it."

"Uh-huh," Jason said. He sounded dismissive, but worry lingered in his eyes.

"All right. It wasn't about you," William admitted. "She was talking about Steve Aldo."

Jason chuckled as they climbed the short flight of stairs to the main living area. "Serves him right. I'll have to spread that word around tomorrow."

"What are you two laughing about?" Mr. Zeus asked, immediately recognizable by the aroma of his wafting pipe smoke.

As usual, Jason's grandfather sat ensconced in his throne, an ugly, pink-plaid recliner as comfortable as it was hideous. He held a pipe between his teeth and a folded newspaper in his lap. He stroked his long, lustrous, white beard, and his eyes twinkled. They always did, as if he was secretly laughing about something. He was an odd man, William thought, as odd as his true name: Odysseus Louis Crane III. All he needed was a pointy hat and he'd look like Merlin.

"Himbos," Jason replied to his grandfather's question.

An arched eyebrow and a perplexed expression prompted William to explain the nature of himbos once again.

When he finished, Mr. Zeus cackled. Puffs of smoke escaped his mouth with every guffaw. "That's clever," he said. "But now, what's this about a girl?"

William didn't want to discuss Serena. There wasn't anything *to* discuss. He liked her, but they'd only met today, and as soon as she was settled in at school, she'd probably find her own tribe—her own circle of friends. It wouldn't end well for him if he hoped for something more. And Jason teasing him about her wasn't helping matters. "Nothing, sir," William answered.

"To me, 'nothing' describes the void between the stars. Or the empty space in your brainpans," Mr. Zeus said. "A girl is *never* nothing."

"I didn't say *she* was nothing."

"Which means she's something."

"William met a new girl today," Jason supplied.

William ignored their conversation and tried to pay attention to whatever was on TV. President Reagan was talking about the Soviet Union and the Chernobyl disaster, and stating that Commies were basically Nazis with better press.

"She just started at St. Francis," Jason said, "and she's beautiful."

"And William is worried she'll forget about him as soon as she figures out her way around the school," Mr. Zeus guessed. "Which is why he doesn't want to talk about her."

William groaned. *How had the old man known?*

Mr. Zeus chuckled. "I'm old, but I'm not that old." He went back to stroking his beard, and William noticed that he seemed to be checking to see if it was symmetric.

A few months ago, Mr. Zeus had burned off a good five inches of his chin moss during an accident in his smithy out back. Forging was how he spent his days. That, and taking long hikes in nearby Winton Woods, or if he was feeling really adventurous, the Arboretum at Mt. Airy Forest. Of course, getting to the Arboretum necessitated that Mr. Zeus drive, an activity he loathed almost as much as Jason did. Otherwise, he spent most of his time in his shop. In that claustrophobic space of metal and fire, Mr. Zeus forged, creating armor, tools, and weapons straight out of the Hyborian Age.

"Who saw her first?" Mr. Zeus asked.

"Me," William replied.

The multitude of Mr. Zeus' laugh lines crinkled as he chuckled in what seemed like amused understanding at Jason. "I see."

Jason bristled. "It wasn't like that."

"Are you sure?" Mr. Zeus' eyes twinkled even more than usual, and his smile widened. "William saw her first, she likes him more, and now you're making fun of him out of jealousy."

"I said it wasn't like that," Jason protested. "Yes, he saw her first, and yes, she likes him, but I'm not jealous. I'm happy for him. But it also doesn't mean that I can't make fun of him about it."

Mr. Zeus arched his caterpillar eyebrows and peered over his wire-rim glasses at the two of them.

"Her name is Serena Paradiso," William answered in response to his unspoken question.

"Serena Paradiso." Mr. Zeus seemed to be savoring the syllables of her name. "Serena Paradiso," he repeated. "Is she truly as fetching as her name?"

Jason smirked. "William thinks so."

"And you don't?" William challenged.

"She's beautiful," Jason accepted. "But only *you* think she's lovely."

William scowled.

"Lovely, eh?" Mr. Zeus asked. A smile creased his seamed face. "Like the young woman you admire so much on that television show?"

"Stephanie Zimbalist. She's on *Remington Steele*," Jason unhelpfully supplied.

William reddened. He really didn't want to talk about Serena with Mr. Zeus. It felt wrong on some fundamental level. "Yes, I think she's lovely," William said. "Can we move on now?"

Mr. Zeus eased back into his chair, and a faraway memory appeared to stir him.

"What?" Jason asked.

Mr. Zeus shook his head, and his eyes seemed to film over. "I remember what it was like to be young, and having my heart led astray by a beautiful woman. It's so hard to keep your head straight, and the prettier they are, the worse it is." He sat silent for many seconds, apparently lost in his recollection, until he shook himself back to the here-and-now. His misty smile faded, and a serious expression took its place. "Keep your wits about you when you're around this girl and don't do anything foolish," he advised both of them.

"Yes, sir," William and Jason mumbled together.

Mr. Zeus studied them for a moment before harrumphing. "At any rate, I have something for you," he told William, standing up and passing over a small jewelry box resting on the coffee table.

"What is it?" William asked.

"Look inside and find out."

William cracked open the box and discovered a platinum chain with an oval locket made of gold. The locket had a small latch, and William snapped it open. Inside lay a picture of his family: his mother with her dark skin and bright smile, his red-headed father, grinning in the cheesy way only he could, and Landon, his big brother, with an arm thrown carelessly across William's shoulder.

William's eyes misted.

"I made it last week," Mr. Zeus said softly. "I thought you might want a way to see your family whenever you wished."

"Thank you," William said, blinking to keep away the tears.

Mr. Zeus gave a tight-lipped, sympathetic nod before relighting his pipe. All it took was a flick of his hand, and a flame somehow appeared on the tip of his finger. Mr. Zeus was something of a magician, but William had yet to figure out how he made fire appear.

"One more thing," Mr. Zeus said. He pulled a box off the fireplace mantle. "I fixed him."

William slipped the chain around his neck and took the box, grinning. He lifted the lid, and a stuffed black dragon stared back at him.

"Is that Bartholomew?" Jason asked.

William nodded, unable to stop smiling. "My dad gave him to me."

Bartholomew had been the first present William had ever received. His father had given the stuffed dragon to him on his first birthday, and for years, he and Bartholomew had been inseparable. They'd gone everywhere, on every vacation, sleepover, and summer camp.

Eventually William had outgrown the small, stuffed dragon, and several years back, he had shoved Bartholomew into a box under his bed. Bartholomew had lain there, forgotten as time slowly ravaged him, leaving him dust-covered and moth-eaten. It had broken William's heart to rediscover Bartholomew ruined like that. Now here he was, all fixed up and looking new, thanks to Mr. Zeus.

"Thank you," William said to Mr. Zeus, choked up with emotion. The little dragon had a nick on his right ear and was still missing a claw on one paw, but other than that, he was fine. He was Bartholomew.

"Thank you," William repeated, holding Bartholomew close as flashes of memories played in his mind: Bartholomew's first bath; his tears when Bartholomew's claw had torn off; Landon teasing him about having a 'baby' toy.

"Think nothing of it, my boy," Mr. Zeus said.

The basement of Mr. Zeus' house was a large, open space with a ceiling high enough to play basketball and one of William's favorite places in the world. He and Jason spent most nights there, training in kickboxing, judo, or the longsword. Mr. Zeus knew quite a lot about martial arts, and he'd readily agreed to take William on as a student.

Over the past few years, the hard practices had slowly transformed William's soft, skinny frame into one that held glimpses of strength, dexterity, and coordination. The changes in his body had accelerated over the past few months, and sometimes, when no one was looking, William would preen in front of the mirror, proud of his new muscles.

Just as important, the time spent sparring, grappling, or swinging a sword had given William a shelter, a place where, for a few precious hours each day, he could forget about the pain and anger from his family's death . . . or at least have a physical outlet for them.

He didn't need much of either anymore, though. At this point, he genuinely liked training.

Tonight was judo, and since Mr. Zeus had already gone upstairs, William and Jason had turned on the boombox while they got in some final sparring. "Fight for Your Right (To Party!)" wailed through the speakers, music Mr. Zeus would have ridiculed as rhythmic noise.

"Last one," Jason called out. "Go!"

William slipped his right hand inside the collar of Jason's gi. They pushed and pulled against one another. Jason tried for an inside trip, but William stepped over it. Again, they strained for position. William snaked a leg between Jason's and twisted at the hips. Incipient hope rose when he felt his friend's feet come off the ground. William couldn't help it. He grinned in anticipation.

His budding joy crashed down like a Jenga tower. Jason fought off William's attempted throw. A hard pull put William off-balance. The world rotated, and in those few seconds where time seemed to stretch forever, he realized his mistake and cursed aloud before slamming into the mat.

William groaned. *He'd been so close.* He lay on the ground, staring up at the ceiling and the bright, fluorescent lights as self-directed anger built. He slapped the mat. *Idiot!*

"A little more focus and commitment to your throw and you would have had me," Jason said, flopping down next to him. "Plus, you gave up too easily when I fought off your throw. You should have tried harder to get it."

William snarled as he slammed another fist into the padded mat before rising to his feet. It wasn't anything he hadn't already heard or figured out on his own. He *had* given up too easily. He'd quit. He was a quitter. That's how it had always been with him when it came to sports.

"Are you all right?" Jason asked, eyeing him in evident concern.

"I'm fine," William snapped, struggling to get his anger under control. "I'm just mad at myself."

"You sure?" Jason rose to his feet as well.

"I'm sure," William answered. The anger abated. "I'm just tired of losing. I don't care if it's lack of focus, lack of will, or lack of strength, I'm tired of it."

"It's not lack of will," Jason said. "If that was it, you would have stopped sparring against me a long time ago."

"Then what was it?"

"I already told you: loss of focus," Jason replied, tapping him on the forehead. "You smiled. That was when you lost. That's when I knew I'd win. And you're plenty strong enough, even with your noodle arms." Jason grinned, and the tension between them popped like a soap bubble as William's anger drained away.

"I may be stronger, but I'm not strong enough. Not yet, anyway."

"You'll get there," Jason said.

"Sometimes I think you're right," William said. A strange, but familiar sadness took him, and he sighed. "And sometimes it seems like I'm no better than I was when I first started."

"Stop," Jason said. "We both know that's not true. What's really got you so bothered all of a sudden?"

William frowned, unable to explain what he felt. "I don't know," he finally answered. "Ever since the car accident, it's like something's missing from my life, you know? There's something that should be there, but it isn't. I've got all this sadness and anger. They're like waves trying to pull me under. . . ." He ground to a frustrated halt. "Forget it."

"There *is* something missing," Jason said. "Your family. Anger and sorrow are understandable. I wouldn't expect you to be all sunshine and rainbows. Give it time."

"I know," William agreed. He breathed out in relief as the sorrow let up. "Let's go up and see what we have left to eat. I'm hungry, and food always makes me feel better."

"I know what you mean," Jason said with an understanding smile.

"You think Mr. Zeus left us some pizza?" William asked.

"Not likely. It's LaRosa's, remember? You know how he is with that stuff."

"Do we have any Pringles?"

"I think I saw a couple of cans."

William grinned. "Then if we can't have pizza, there's always that. Plus, it's not too late to watch a movie."

"Which one?"

"*Dragonslayer*?"

"Sounds like a plan, Galen."

CHAPTER 5:
THE FIRST WEEKEND

"Pay attention," Serena hissed, elbowing William in the ribs.

His eyes snapped open. "I'm awake," William mumbled.

"Uh-huh. Right."

William didn't bother protesting since Serena was correct. He had been dozing, but he didn't think it was entirely his fault. Mrs. Nelson, their Biology teacher, was just so boring. She presented the lessons like a robot, with no emotion or life.

William glanced at the clock and mentally groaned. *Thirty-five minutes to go? How? Was the clock not moving any faster? It felt like they'd already been here for an hour.* He sighed. *At least it was Friday. Only a few more hours and the first week of school would be over.*

William sat up straighter and tried to pay attention. But once again his eyes drooped and his head bobbed.

"William," Serena hissed.

"I was just blinking."

"If blinking means closing your eyes and keeping them closed, then sure you were."

Mrs. Nelson chose that moment to pause in her dry recitation of facts and ask a question of the class. "Does an insect have an endoskeleton or an exoskeleton?"

William prayed she wouldn't pick him to answer.

"William," Mrs. Nelson said.

He mentally groaned. "Exoskeleton," he said. It was a blind guess, but he forced confidence into his voice.

Mrs. Nelson cracked a bare smile. "Good. Now what is an exoskeleton?"

Shit. Now he was going to look stupid in front of Serena. Exoskeleton. What the hell was an exoskeleton? Wait. 'Exo' meant outside. Maybe . . . "Um. A skeleton worn on the outside," he stated.

"Very good." Mrs. Nelson's smile broadened. "Maybe you were paying attention in between all that dozing."

The class laughed, and William grinned as Mrs. Nelson went back to lecturing.

"How'd you know the answer?" Serena whispered. "You were asleep during that part."

"Logic and brilliance," William whispered back. "Now shush. I'm trying to pay attention."

Serena elbowed him again even as she smiled in amusement.

The lecture finally ended—William even managed to stay awake during the rest of it—and afterward they were expected to dissect a beetle.

William eyed the bug in disgust. "Gross."

"Aw, is the big, bad bug too scary for you?" Serena teased in a baby-voice.

William shot her an annoyed scowl. "Let's just get this over with. The quicker we do, the quicker I won't have to look at this B.E.M."

Serena wore a frown of confusion. "What's a B.E.M.?"

"Bug-eyed monster."

Serena appeared to consider his words before breaking into a grin. "I like it. Let's get this bug-eyed monster dissected."

Like a flipped switch, she became all business, telling William to hold the beetle here, cut it there, and hand her the scalpel or forceps. Under her direction, they quickly had the insect turned inside out and dissected.

"Sweet. We're all done," William said, amazed they'd finished so quickly.

"Hi, Serena. William," a voice said.

William glanced up. Steve Aldo wore a friendly smile, but William's hackles rose.

"Hi," Serena replied.

William merely grunted acknowledgment.

"These bugs are pretty gross, aren't they?" Steve asked. "I don't even want to touch mine." He did a double-take when he saw their already-dissected beetle. "You can't be serious. How'd you finish so fast?

"Teamwork," William replied.

"Well then I want to be on your team," Steve said, sounding awed.

"It was mostly Serena," William admitted.

"It was both of us."

Steve glanced from one of them to the other and shrugged. "Whoever it is, I'll trade you a Kim Morris and a Sonya Bowyer if I can work with you guys."

"Maybe next quarter," Serena said with a chuckle.

"Is that when we do the pig?" Steve asked.

"Yeah," William answered, although he didn't want to think about it. *A fetal pig. It sounded grosser than the B.E.M.* He happened to glance down, and noticed Steve's shoes. "Those new Air Jordans?"

"Yep," Steve replied, puffing up with pride.

"I thought the Air Jordan 2s were supposed to come out in a few months," William said.

"They are, but I couldn't pass these up. They were on sale."

"Can you dunk in them?" William asked.

"No. Can you?"

"Can I dunk in *your* shoes?"

"No. Can you dunk?" Steve clarified, sounding annoyed.

"I've got a vertical leap like you wouldn't believe," William answered.

"Really?" Steve said in a tone of obvious skepticism.

"Oh, yeah."

"How high?"

"I can jump right over a piece of paper."

"A piece of paper?" Steve barked laughter before casting an appraising gaze upon William. "You're a lot funnier than I remember."

"Funnier-looking is what he always says," Serena supplied.

"Yeah, that too," Steve agreed. He appeared ready to head back to his table, but he turned to William. "You know, we should hang out sometime."

William almost fell off his stool in shock.

The first week of school had ended and the weekend had just started.

On the ride home, Serena hummed along to the song playing on the radio. Humming was the most she was willing to do, though. She never sang. Singing made her feel vulnerable, exposed. Singing was too uncontrolled and emotional. It left her desiring things she could never have, things she told herself she didn't want.

Lien, on the other hand, had no such reservations. She crowed out the words to the song in full-throated splendor, her delight obvious. Maybe she did so because it was the end of the school week and she was overjoyed that they were heading home. Or maybe she was just a passionate person.

Whatever the reason, Serena secretly admired her, and she sometimes wondered what it would be like to live in Lien's world: open and carefree.

"We still doing movie night tomorrow?" Daniel asked.

Serena set aside her useless speculations and returned her attention to the conversation.

"Sure," William answered in his pleasant drawl. "As long as Mr. Zeus doesn't mind."

"He doesn't. I already checked," Jason said.

"Then we're set?" Daniel asked.

"We're set," Jason confirmed.

What's movie night?" Serena asked. "Other than the obvious."

"We hang out and watch a movie," William explained.

"And we throw popcorn at the TV if the movie sucks," Lien added.

"No, we don't," William corrected.

"We should," Lien countered.

"Then you can vacuum it up afterward."

"No, thanks. I like it better when you do that." Lien gave William an unrepentant grin.

"You want to come?" William asked Serena. "I mean, I know all your furniture and stuff just got in yesterday and you're busy unpacking, but if you want, it'll be tomorrow at eight."

"Yeah, you should definitely come," Lien agreed. "The guys always choose stupid movies about spaceships and robots. It'll be nice to have another girl pick something good for once."

"I'll be there," Serena said offering a feigned pleased smile.

Her true satisfaction derived from her work, and her work was progressing nicely. Matters between her and William were advancing much as she had hoped they would. He liked and trusted her, wanted to be around her, which meant that her father, the one to whom she and Isha answered, would give her the time she needed to bring William in to join their people. And he would join. It was just a question of when and how willingly.

"What are we watching?" Serena glanced at the others through guileless eyes. After long practice, she knew that no hint of her actual thoughts marred her features.

"*The Goonies*," Jason said.

"Thank God! Something funny," Lien said. "I was afraid it would be *The Terminator* again. You guys chose that movie like ten times in a row last year."

"I'll be back," Jason quipped in a vaguely Germanic accent.

Serena didn't know what that meant, but it must have been a bad joke since the others groaned.

"Dork," William said.

"But it got you to groan," Jason said with a pleased smirk.

"More like made me want to punch you in the nose," Lien muttered.

"How do you decide what movie to watch?" Serena asked, changing the topic since she didn't know what the others were talking about.

"We rotate," Daniel explained. "I choose one week, then William, then Lien, then Jason, and so on. And whoever chooses has to make sure there's enough snacks and everything."

"Is it always at William and Jason's house?" Serena asked.

"Pretty much," Daniel answered. "They've got a nicer TV."

"Anyway, you'll like *The Goonies*," William said.

"You think so?" Serena asked.

"Yeah. I think I've gotten to know you well enough this past week to figure what movies you might like."

Serena studied his face. He wore a generous smile, and it struck her how much William was like Lien. They were both so open-hearted and trusting.

All of them were. They shared a camaraderie Serena had never before experienced, and she didn't like admitting how much she enjoyed it. It felt good and right, even as she recognized its naivety.

A weight of years rested on her shoulders as she viewed their innocence through the prism of her far more experienced life.

"You okay?" William asked. "You look sad."

"I'm fine," Serena replied, blinking away unexpected tears. "I was just thinking of my mom. We had something like your movie nights, too." She added the lie as an excuse for the tears even while she pushed aside thoughts of friendship and camaraderie and focused on the task at hand. William was her mission, the focus of her pilgrimage. She had to deliver him to her people. Nothing else mattered.

William offered her a tight-lipped smile of sympathy. "I understand."

He would, given what had happened to his family last year. Serena offered him a brief nod of 'thanks' even as she did her best to keep his sympathy from touching her heart. She didn't need it. She didn't want it.

At least, that's what she wanted to believe. But Isha had taught her too well. He had taught her to lie at need, but also to spot a lie, even one she told herself.

"You sure you're okay?" William asked. "You still look off."

"I'm fine," Serena replied again. "Tell me about the movie."

William thankfully dropped the subject of her sadness. "It's about a group of friends who need to save their homes, and they go searching for a pirate ship full of treasure. There's also this ugly giant, a family of criminals, and a maze full of traps."

"Another fantasy, then," Serena said with a teasing smile and shake of her head.

William smiled ruefully. "Busted."

"One-Eyed Willy," Daniel announced. "He's the pirate who hid the treasure. That's a pretty cool name when you think about it."

Everyone, even Serena, burst out laughing.

"What's so funny?" Daniel demanded.

"Don't you know what a one-eyed Willy is?" Jason asked.

"It's the name of the pirate," Daniel said, still sounding confused.

"It's also a name for—"

Daniel's face went bright red. "Oh, yeah."

"Pass the popcorn," Jason said.

William obliged.

He had to reach past Serena to pass the bowl to Jason. The two of them shared the love seat while Jason and Daniel slumped on the couch. Lien huddled in a sleeping bag with a mountain of pillows propping up her head.

William laughed when, on the screen, Chunk screamed. "I don't know what it is about that chubby kid, but I swear Chunk could be reciting the *Declaration of Independence*, and I'd still think he's funny."

"Shh," Serena said to him. "Stop talking over the dialogue. I've never seen this before, remember?"

William quieted down, but everyone laughed when Mouth promised ridiculous punishments in Spanish to the new housekeeper. They missed half his words, but the closed-captioned subtitles helped them keep up.

The movie played on, and Sloth appeared for the first time.

William's eyes widened. His heart began pounding. A nightmare from right after the death of his family took him.

An icy stretch of twisting, country road, a fearful shout from his father, and a swerve that ended in the tortured sound of tearing metal. Trapped in the car. His mother's face, her eyes wide and lifeless, her head twisted in the wrong direction. His dad. The steering column punched through his father's chest. Blood everywhere. Where was Landon? He wasn't in the car. But in the distance, a figure stumbled and wandered down the road, blurred and out of focus, like a mirage.

Another figure stood nearby. He loomed large, easily the size of Sloth, but even more grotesque. His arms hung long, like a gorilla's, and his face looked like melted wax with oversized, lipless teeth held in a perpetual sneer. From him rose the stench of rotten meat and evil. He studied William, and menace and cruelty wreathed the monster like smoke.

The figure strode toward the car, reached for William and hurled him aside. The car burst into flames. The bodies of both his parents burned to ash.

William started.

For a moment, he didn't know where he was. He glanced around and realization came to him. He was in Mr. Zeus' house. His friends were with him, and they were watching *'The Goonies.'* Only a few seconds had passed. He and Serena still shared the loveseat, while the others remained scattered about the family room.

William wiped a sweaty palm across his face. The nightmare always seemed so real, but even more so this time. It had been months since he'd last had it.

"You all right?" Serena asked. Her face was filled with concern.

"Just resting my eyes," William answered.

"You sure?" Serena asked. "For a second there, it looked like you were terrified."

"I remembered the night my parents died," William admitted,

although he didn't want to discuss the nightmare any further. He reached for his can of Coke on the coffee table and took a swig. *Flat.* He grimaced. "I'm fine now."

Serena still seemed to study him with concern. A moment later, she squeezed his hand. "I think you might have missed some of the movie."

"It's all right," William said. "I've seen it before." His heart slowly settled down, and he was able to push aside the nightmare. "You like it?" he asked.

"Love it," Serena answered. "Now shush. I want to see how it ends."

"How was the movie?" Isha asked when Serena entered their house. He sat in his newly arrived recliner, reading the newspaper with no light on except for the lamp arching over his chair.

"It was fine," Serena answered even as she suppressed a smile.

The movie had been better than fine. It had been wonderful, but Isha could never know that. Nor could he know the delight that coursed through Serena's mind as she recalled it. The movie had been fun, comical, and fantastic.

"What did you see?"

"A silly movie called *The Goonies.*"

Isha grunted acknowledgment. "Did anything happen with William?" he asked, returning his attention to the newspaper.

"Nothing important," Serena said. "We sat together."

Isha glanced up and wore a pleased expression. "Good.

You've gained his confidence and affection, then. I imagine it shouldn't take much to convince him to join us, if he truly is what we hope he is."

"Yes, sir." Serena was about to tell Isha what had happened to William during the movie. The strange terror on his face. His eyes wide open but his awareness stolen away. He'd proffered an explanation that might have been true, but it hadn't been the entire truth. In fact, if Serena didn't know better she would have sworn William had had a vision. Which should have been impossible since his *lorethasra* had yet to flower.

Whatever occurred had left him shaken and terrified. It had been obvious on his face, and Serena had found herself unexpectedly worried for him. She'd even reached for William's hand and squeezed it in support. It had been an unconscious, natural motion, unplanned and instinctual.

While it had been the right move to earn William's ongoing trust and affection, the fact that it had occurred because of compassion rather than due to rational planning worried Serena. *What if her actions and thoughts meant that she actually liked William as a person?* It was a horrible thought, implying a weakness Serena couldn't afford.

"You have something more to add?" Isha asked. "You appear troubled."

Serena mentally cursed her lapse and schooled her features to stillness. "I was considering what will happen to William if he chooses wrongly."

Isha's focus sharpened on her like a raptor's. "We'll take him anyway. The importance of a potential *raha'asra* cannot be overstated."

CHAPTER 6: CONFLICTS

September 1986

Over the next few weeks, the inevitable chores of homework and study took the shine off the new school year, and summer's endlessness blurred into a memory. Life eased into a new routine.

For William and Jason, the new routine began a few hours before school. Every morning they readied Mr. Zeus' forge for the day's work by straightening up the workshop. Jason's grandfather had many wonderful attributes, but cleanliness was not one of them. Dirty dishes, soda cans, and trash always littered the workshop.

After that came school.

On one particular morning in the middle of September when fall's blessed crispness had finally washed away summer's humidity, William and his friends pulled into the parking lot at school.

"Don't turn it off yet," Lien said. She'd been belting out the song on the radio while Serena hummed along with the tune, which is what she always did: hummed and never sang.

William winced when Lien tried to hit a high note. It sounded like a cat with its tail pinched by a rocking chair.

"I think it's sweet how she likes to sing," Serena whispered, apparently noticing his wince.

"Yeah, but I could use some earplugs, you know," William whispered back.

Serena chuckled, and the song, and Lien's singing, ended.

William keyed off the engine and opened the door. He was about to step out of the car when Jake Ridley squealed into the adjacent parking spot in his new, monster-sized pickup truck. William had to slam his door shut or have it torn off.

"Jackass!" Lien shouted through the rolled-up window.

William felt the same way, and in a heartbeat his anger blazed, lava-hot and roaring through his veins like a flood. His thoughts ripped away like flotsam, and all he could feel and see was a red wave of rage.

"He's not worth it," Serena advised, putting a hand on his arm.

With her calming touch and words some of William's fury bled out, and he hesitated. Anger still roiled within him, anger at Jake Ridley's careless conceit, his years of taunts and bullying, but at least William could think clearly again. William realized that Serena was right: Jake wasn't worth it. He forced down the anger and unclenched his fists.

Sonya got out of the passenger side of Jake's truck and had the grace to appear embarrassed. Jake, though, grinned at William and revved his engine before hopping out of the driver's seat. He wore not the least hint of apology on his arrogant face. Instead, he sauntered off with a cocky strut, holding hands with Sonya.

William again saw red. He threw open his car door and jumped out. “Learn to drive, asshole!”

Jake turned around. “What did you say?” he asked, in what William imagined was supposed to be a menacing tone.

“You heard me, dickhead. Learn to drive.”

Jake’s face darkened. He took a step toward William, but pulled up short when he saw Jason and Daniel standing nearby. Jake sneered. “You’re lucky you’ve got your loser friends with you, or I’d beat your face into the pavement.”

William’s boiling anger faded into icy coldness. *Why had he ever let this thug push him around?* William stared Jake straight in the eyes, never looking away as he marched forward, pressing into the other boy’s space. “I don’t need them to deal with someone like you.”

“William,” Lien warned.

He ignored her. Something like concern passed across Jake’s face. But then his own friends arrived and he puffed up in their presence. “Sure, you don’t, William Wilted,” Jake smirked.

“Whatever,” William said, not backing off as he stood loose-limbed and ready. “I’m right here.”

“You’re nowhere, Wilted,” Jake sneered. “See you around, loser.” He made the words sound like a threat before he withdrew, heading toward the school as he laughed in the midst of his friends and their girlfriends. They sniggered with Jake, slapping him on the back as if he’d done something wonderful even as they gave William dismissive smirks.

“Who’s hiding behind his friends now?” William shouted at Jake’s retreating back. “Or maybe it’s your girlfriend you’re hiding behind.”

Jake stopped in his tracks and slowly turned around.

"You sure about this?" Jason whispered.

William didn't bother responding.

By then the confrontation with Jake had gathered the attention of other students in the parking lot. They stopped whatever they had been doing and eyed the situation with an air of expectant curiosity.

Jake's face darkened with anger. "One-thirty. Behind the old chapel. Just you and me."

"Don't tell me where and when in public, stupid!"

Jake snarled. "Fine. I'll send you a love letter. Just be there, chickenshit." He gave Serena a brief, contemptuous assessment. "Or bring your girlfriend, if you don't think you can handle me on your own."

Sonya gave Serena a withering glower. "You should have taken up my offer and become friends with me. Now my boyfriend is going to ugly up your boyfriend."

"Your boyfriend's a pretentious thug, which doesn't say much about you," Serena retorted.

Sonya's lips curled in outrage.

"What? Do you honestly think you can take me?" Serena eyed her with a smirk. "Step back before I break you in half."

"This is between me and Wilted," Jake said to Serena as he moved in front of Sonya. "Just us. No one else." He focused his attention back to William. "You better show up where and when I say, or everyone here will know you're the little wuss I've always said you are."

With that, Jake and his friends departed, but excited mutters rose from those standing about. Most shot William looks of pity.

"What are you going to do?" Jason asked.

"I'm going to beat his ass." A large part of William anticipated the coming conflict. He couldn't wait to shut that bully down.

"Tell us when and where," Daniel said.

"He said just him and me." William replied. "And that's how it's going to be."

William shifted about, filled with nervous energy as he waited for Jake's arrival.

Serena stood with him, and as she so often did, she hummed *"Gloria"* by U2. "He's late," she noted, appearing as uncertain as he felt. "Maybe he won't show."

William grunted and wondered if that might be the best outcome for him. Although he'd been sparring with Jason for two years, he had never actually put the training to use. Plus, Jake was big, fast, and strong. That would count for a lot.

"Are you sure this is the place?" Serena asked.

"It's what the note I got in homeroom said," William replied. "Ten-thirty in the garden behind the old chapel, just like he said in the parking lot."

"I still wish you'd told Daniel and Jason about this."

"It's only supposed to be me and Jake," William said. "I'm not even sure you should be here."

Serena stood with her arms crossed over her chest and an expression of derision on her face. "You really think someone like

Jake would come here by himself?"

William hesitated. While he didn't want anyone to say that he'd only won because of his friends, the same couldn't be said of Jake. Jake *would* come here with others. He wouldn't care if anyone found out that he'd beaten William with the help of his friends. Bullies never did.

"Well, do you?" Serena pressed.

Once again, William found himself the focus of her strangely intense gaze. "No," he finally admitted. *How could he have been so stupid?*

"Then it's a good thing I made you tell me when and where Jake wanted to face you."

William was forced to agree, and they fell quiet.

The small, walled garden in which they waited was a quiet space where the Jesuits who ran St. Francis often came for prayer or meditation. Stacked, gray stones, rising to a height of ten feet, walled the garden on all sides except the west. There the border was formed by the looming bulk of the old cathedral. A narrow wrought-iron gate served as the only entrance, and it opened on a white-gravel pathway that wended its way amongst flowers, shrubs, and ferns. A small bench faced a trickling stream and a koi pond.

William slapped at a mosquito. "Stupid motorized freckles," he muttered.

"What?" Serena asked.

"Mosquitoes. They're like motorized freckles."

Serena smiled at his description, but her humor dropped away when Vice-Principal Meron entered the garden. Mr. Meron was a short, squat man with beady eyes, a permanently red face, and meaty jowls that shook whenever he spoke. But despite his orc-like appearance, Mr. Meron was fair.

"What are the two of you doing here?" he demanded.

William and Serena shared a glance.

"I was showing Serena some of the older parts of the school, sir," William said with a quick-witted lie.

"Really? Didn't you and Jake Ridley get into an argument this morning?"

William's insides twisted, and he tried not to show his sudden nervousness. If Mr. Meron knew about the argument, he probably also knew about the fight that was supposed to take place here and now. And St. Francis took a dim view of fighting. "We did have an argument," William admitted. "He almost ran me over with his monster truck and I got mad, but there wasn't much more to it than that."

"You're telling me he didn't challenge you to a fight at this exact time and place?" Mr. Meron demanded with a snort.

William's anxiety rose, and he tried not to squirm. "Yes, but—"

"That's why you're really here, isn't it? Waiting for Jake Ridley so the two of you can settle your disagreement?"

"It was my idea to come here, not William's," Serena answered, stepping forward. "I wanted to see the garden. My mother gardened a lot, and she used to teach me. I . . ." Serena shrugged. "I just wanted to come here and remember her."

William held still. If he looked at her Mr. Meron would know Serena was lying, that they both were. Even now the vice-principal's face held a distrustful frown. Still, William also saw a touch of sympathy.

"That's the real reason you're here?" Mr. Meron asked.

Serena shook her head, appearing reluctant. "No. I also didn't want William to fight. I was hoping that by keeping him busy during study hall he wouldn't have time to get into another argument with Jake. He isn't worth it. As far as I'm concerned, if they fought, even if William won, he'd still lose because of whatever punishment you'd have given him."

Earlier in the morning, after the heat of his anger had cooled, William had come to the same realization. However, by the time he'd figured that out, it had been too late to back down. He'd already agreed to the fight, instigated it, really, and there was no way to get out of it. Not without the entire school thinking he was a coward.

Mr. Meron's features relaxed further, and he no longer seemed so suspicious. "I see. Well, the garden isn't really a place for students, even seniors. Head on back to the main campus."

"Yes, sir," William said.

As they stepped past, Mr. Meron called after them. "Ms. Paradiso, a moment of your time, please. Before you go, since you were taught so much about gardening, maybe you can tell me the name of that plant." He pointed to an unassuming one with green and white leaves. "I've always thought it was pretty."

"It's a variegated hosta," Serena said, "and these have been planted in too much sunlight. It's why their leaves are burned. Hostas like partial shade. I'd also thin them out. They're crowded."

Once again, William had to hold back from staring at her in shock. *She'd sounded like she actually knew what she was talking about.*

Mr. Meron smiled. "I'll make sure to mention it to the priests who tend the garden. It sounds like your mother taught you well."

Serena offered a slight smile. "She taught me some, but she knew so much more."

"Head on back," Mr. Meron ordered.

"Yes, sir," William replied again.

"That was some quick thinking." William said to Serena after they left.

"I just stretched the truth a bit. That's all." She quirked a smile at him. "That was some quick thinking on your part, too."

William shrugged. All he had done was lie, and poorly at that. "Did your mom really teach you all that stuff about plants?"

Serena's expression went flat. "It was a long time ago."

The rest of the day passed without any further incident, and the next morning, Jake thankfully wasn't around when Serena and the others got out of the T-Bird. She made a point of lifting her nose to the air. "I don't smell skunk, so Jake must not be here yet."

Lien lifted her nose as well. "Me, neither."

"But if he *were* here, and it came to a fight, William would take him," Jason said. "No doubt about it."

William gave his friend a look of appreciation, but Lien gave him a look of disgust. "Why am I not surprised," she said.

"What?" Jason protested.

"Not all problems need to be solved by fighting."

Serena partially shared Lien's sentiment, but not for the reason the other girl probably thought. Fighting was sometimes necessary, but it was far better to cut an enemy from the shadows, destroy him when he couldn't defend himself.

"Maybe in some situations, but not all," Jason countered. "Besides, I've been sparring against William for two years now. Just because Jake's a big, bad football player doesn't mean he can fight. William would have leveled him."

"There are ways to show up someone like Jake Ridley without resorting to violence," Serena said. "In the end, William beating up Jake wouldn't have proved anything."

"Maybe not to you, but it would have proven something to everyone else," William said. "At least the other guys in our school."

"What?" Lien demanded.

"It would have told them that you can't pick on William without having your teeth knocked down your throat," Daniel said.

"That's stupid," Lien replied.

Which was true, as far as Serena was concerned, but she also understood Daniel's point of view. Nevertheless, to her fighting was simply too primitive, too inelegant for what she hoped to accomplish in life.

"Why's it stupid?" William asked.

"I can't explain it," Lien said. "If men were half as civilized as women, you'd understand what I mean."

"Women aren't any better than men," Jason said. "You're just as bad as we are. You're just sneakier about it."

"We aren't like guys at all," Lien protested.

"Yes, you are. You're exactly like us," Daniel said. "You're telling me girls can't be mean? Catty and cruel?" He laughed. "That's almost a stereotype when it comes to teenage girls. You never hear about catty teenage boys."

Lien wore a stubborn expression, as if she didn't want to admit the validity of Daniel's words. "That's different. What we do doesn't leave someone bruised and beaten."

"But it can still leave someone badly hurt," Serena said.

"I thought you were on my side!" Lien exclaimed.

"I am, but I also think they have a point," Serena said.

The boys straightened, standing taller, and Serena gave them a withering stare. "It'll probably be the one and only time that they do."

Lien grinned. "Kind of like a stopped clock is right once a day."

"It's right twice a day," William reminded her.

"What?"

"A stopped clock is right twice a day. At least in the U.S. it is."

Lien's grin departed. "Shut up!"

Jason, Daniel, and William chuckled, and while Serena smiled with them, maintaining the carefree persona she'd carefully built, she felt little amusement. She was concerned, and she unconsciously chewed the inside of her lip.

Jake Ridley would likely say or do something else to antagonize William. It would happen today or tomorrow or the next day, and Serena worried how William would react.

While she figured William could handle himself in a fight, she couldn't allow him to be damaged. And just as important to his future, if he wanted to thrive among her people, he had to develop better control of his emotions. Those to whom she answered would chew him up if he couldn't.

Serena's fears about what Jake might do to William were realized in English class.

Jake strutted into the room proud as a rooster, and surrounded by his friends. They clucked about as if they were the lords and ladies of St. Francis, speaking in brash tones and preening too hard, especially the boys in their football jerseys. Today was Friday, a game day.

"I heard Mr. Meron almost suspended someone yesterday," Jake said in a tone meant to carry.

"Who?" someone asked.

Jake shrugged. "I wouldn't know, but maybe you can ask Wilted."

His sycophants laughed.

"I heard he was making out with a rosebush."

"I heard it was Serena."

They laughed again.

Meanwhile, William stiffened, and his jaw clenched.

"Don't pay attention to them," Serena whispered. "Their power is only what you give to them. Don't let their words touch you and there will be no anger."

William nodded, but he remained tense. Serena could see it in the tightness of his shoulders and neck.

Another pointed finger from Jake along with something else he uttered produced another round of braying laughter.

William reddened. "I'm fine," he said before Serena could warn him to remain calm. "Those guys just need their asses kicked."

"They do, and one day they will. Life has a way of doing that. They'll grow up and face a hard world where their immature cliques won't help them. They'll be cattle among hard men and women who will use them for their own purposes."

William turned to her with his brow furrowed in confusion.

Now it was Serena who reddened, and she mentally chided herself. She'd spoken too bluntly, expressed herself too clearly. William, with his open-heartedness and naiveté, made it too easy to forget who she really was. "Sorry. I get carried away sometimes."

"I guess," William said, still wearing a bemused expression.

Serena was saved from further explanation when Mrs. Clancy, their English teacher, arrived and stilled any further conversation.

"Quiet down, everyone," Mrs. Clancy said. "We have a lot to cover today."

The class began and there was peace, but afterward the harassment from Jake and his hangers-on picked up right where it had left off. They followed Serena and William down the hall, taunting them and whistling in ridicule.

Other students watched the unfolding drama.

"Let's go this way," William said, leading Serena on a different route than she expected.

"Where are we going?" she asked. "This isn't the way to Biology."

"Trust me," William replied.

But Jake and the others persisted in trailing after them and calling out their childish taunts. The situation had quickly passed from annoying to infuriating, and Serena started giving serious thought to doing something she might later regret.

William unexpectedly wheeled about. "Shut up. You've made your point. You think I'm weak and Serena's ugly. Just leave us alone."

"She's not ugly," one of Jake's friends muttered.

"She's hot," said another.

"Yeah, she's hot," Jake agreed, "but she's glitched. Why else would she be with that loser?"

"She probably likes slumming," Sonya said with an ugly laugh.

"Or maybe, unlike you," Serena said to Sonya, "I appreciate those who have qualities that go beyond chasing a ball around like some simple-minded dog." She gave a derisive snort. "But then again, you look pretty simple-minded yourself."

"Go fu—" Sonya began.

"You don't get to talk about my girl like that," Jake snarled.

"I'll talk to her anyway I want," Serena replied in an even tone. She kept her anger leashed and controlled even as she took a challenging step forward. *Better to have Jake's energy and attention focused on her rather than William.*

Sonya retreated behind her boyfriend, and Serena gave her a chill smile. "I thought so."

"Whatever," Jake said. "This isn't about you anyway. This about me and your loser boyfriend." He turned to William. "What? You're going to let your girlfriend do all your talking?"

"I can talk," William replied. "And I'm telling you to leave me alone."

"That'll happen when you face me one-on-one. Meet me tomorrow at noon, the football fields out back. They'll be empty. If you're any kind of a man, you'll show up."

"And if I don't show up?" William asked.

"Then your life will be hell. I'll make sure of it." Jake sneered. "You're getting lit up one way or another, boy. Either by me or by the rest of the football team. Any chance we get, you're going to get touched, and I don't mean a light tap, either. We'll beat you down every day. There won't be a place in this school where you'll be safe."

William didn't reply.

"What? You scared?" Jake snorted. He lunged at William, feigning a punch.

William never blinked or backed down. Instead, he smiled.

"That's enough!" Mr. Meron stepped up next to Serena and William, his face even redder than normal. "Jake Ridley! Explain yourself!"

Serena felt like cheering at Mr. Meron's fortuitous arrival. If she'd had to intervene, it would have sent Jake and his friends to the hospital.

It was then that she took in William's expression. He seemed *very* pleased with himself.

Jake, on the other hand, stood white-faced. "Mr. Meron. I don't know what you thought you heard, but we were just playing around. Nothing serious. Right, Wilde?" Jake turned to William with a murderous gleam in his eye. "Say we were playing around or you're dead," he mouthed.

"And you're an idiot, Mr. Ridley. You think I didn't see what you just said to Mr. Wilde?" Mr. Meron said. "Get to my office, right now. If you're lucky, you'll only be in detention for a week. No football for any of you tonight."

Mutters of outrage and disbelief met his words.

"Another word and it becomes a month," Mr. Meron added. "And if I hear of any kind of bullying of Mr. Wilde or Ms. Paradiso, you'll be suspended from school. Now move it!"

Many of the passing students heard his words, and most of them grinned.

Jake shot one last glare at William. "This isn't over," he muttered as he shuffled past.

"It's over unless you want a suspension," William said. He still appeared insufferably smug.

Serena eyed William in speculation. *He'd done something here.*

Mr. Meron leveled his gargoyle glare at Serena and William. "You two better get to your next class."

"Yes, sir," William agreed.

"What just happened?' Serena asked as soon as the vice principal moved on.

"Mr. Meron always checks the grounds for smokers at the end of second period," William said, "and he always comes back into the building at that entrance. I knew he'd show up. I just had to keep Jake and his friends talking long enough for Mr. Meron to hear them."

Serena stared at William in unfeigned admiration. Impressive. William had just defeated an enemy without lifting a finger. She'd never expected him to have such resolve or cunning, and she made a mental note to be more careful around him.

Maybe he would be able to handle some real monsters after all.

CHAPTER 7:
A DINNER. NOT A DATE

"I heard you and William had an interesting talk with Jake Ridley today," Mr. Zeus said to Serena. His eyes twinkled in amusement.

"You could say that," Serena replied in a wry tone.

"What's this?" asked Daniel's mother, Trace Karllson, a tall, willowy woman from east Africa with a brilliant smile.

She and Magnus, her husband, had invited Serena, William, Jason, and Mr. Zeus over for dinner.

Isha had also been asked but, as usual, he'd declined. Personally, Serena thought it was a mistake that he kept himself so isolated from others, a recluse. As a result, he'd become the topic of much speculation, which could be dangerous to someone in his position. A mystery invited too many questions. Jason had even joked as to whether he existed, since he'd yet to meet Serena's supposed father.

"William crushed his enemies, saw them driven before him, and heard the lamentations of their women," Jason said in response to Mrs. Karllson's question. He wore a wide grin and again spoke in that vaguely Germanic accent.

Daniel laughed. “Yes. That is best in life!”

Serena raised her eyebrows in a silent question to Lien.

“Nerd stuff,” Lien explained with a pitying eyeroll.

Oh. One of those things.

“What really happened?” asked Mr. Karllson, a Norwegian giant whose deep, resonant voice matched his build. Serena reckoned that a thousand years ago, if someone like Mr. Karllson had been witnessed disembarking a Viking longship, everyone would have run for the hills.

“Nothing much,” William said, clearly trying to sound dismissive though his pride in what he’d accomplished shone through.

“The way Jason told it, it didn’t sound like nothing,” Mr. Zeus said, eyes still twinkling. “I heard you defeated the Dark Lord and rescued the princess without having to lift a finger.”

William blushed, and Serena took his hand and stared into his eyes. “My hero,” she said breathlessly.

William’s blush deepened, and everyone laughed.

Serena laughed along with them, but inside she felt abject horror. Once again her actions had been driven by instinct rather than rational thought. They were unacceptable occurrences that were taking on the frequency of habit, and she had to put an end to it. While her natural inclinations hadn’t yet led to any mistakes, they eventually would. It was inevitable, and Serena recognized that she courted the cliff’s edge if she couldn’t find a way to rein in her thoughts and emotions.

Thank God Isha hadn’t been here to witness her lapse in judgment.

Serena counted backwards from one hundred by sevens,

seeking to settle her thoughts and regain her composure. It was a far harder task than it had been only a month ago when she'd first met William Wilde and his friends. In fact, a large part of Serena wished she had never met them. If so, there wouldn't be these traitorous feelings to cloud her judgment.

More importantly, there was her sister, Selene, to consider. If Serena proved unsuccessful in her pilgrimage, she alone wouldn't bear the price of her failure. Her sister would pay as well.

". . . then Mr. Meron showed up just like I knew he would," she heard William say.

"Well, I think you handled the situation splendidly," Mrs. Karllson said.

Mr. Karllson murmured his approval as well. "Such clarity of thought should be rewarded," he said in a rumbling basso as he passed William another piece of lasagna. "Eat. I know how much food you teenage boys need to fill your growing frames."

"Is there enough lasagna left for me?" Mr. Zeus asked, wearing a hopeful expression.

"Perhaps," Mr. Karllson rumbled. He glanced Mr. Zeus up and down, pausing at the older man's protruding belly. "But you look like you've already had an extra piece." His mouth curled upward. "Or three."

"How droll," Mr. Zeus replied.

"Besides, I was thinking of saving the last piece for myself," Mrs. Karllson said.

"Just let your tapeworm starve this one time," Mr. Zeus urged.

"Oh, hush," Mrs. Karllson said with a trill of laughter. "You're just jealous."

"Of course, I'm jealous," Mr. Zeus said. "Look at me. I have to walk endless miles, literally starve myself, and I still look like an apple. You, on the other hand, eat twice as much as the rest of us, and . . ." He gestured to Mrs. Karllson's slim form.

"If you're going to starve yourself, can I have the rest of your lasagna?" Jason asked.

"No, you may not," Mr. Zeus said, whacking at Jason's reaching hand.

"Ouch!"

"Serves you right," Mr. Zeus said. "I almost died today getting in my exercise, so I think I've earned this lasagna."

"What happened?" Daniel asked.

"I was taking a walk when some lunatic on a bicycle almost ran me over. He had on one of those new-fangled contraptions, a portable cassette player."

"A Walkman?" Lien asked.

"I don't know what it's called," Mr. Zeus said, waving aside her words, "but it was emitting sound—"

"You mean music?" William asked.

"No. I mean sound," Mr. Zeus said. "It was noise. There was no relationship between whatever was coming from his headphones and music."

"Right," Jason said. "There hasn't been any good music since . . . How old are you again?"

"I'm old, boy, but I'm not cold," Mr. Zeus said.

Serena chuckled, genuinely amused.

"At any rate, this fool on a bike, wearing his contraption, was so caught up in his noise that he almost rode me down. I had to hop lively to get out of his way." Mr. Zeus shook his head in disgust. "Wicked devices."

Mr. Karllson laughed. “Mr. Zeus is a man of a different era. He still hasn’t completely come to accept the internal combustion engine.”

“More like the *infernal* combustion engine,” Mr. Zeus said.

“Anyway, having someone almost run you down probably isn’t as bad as Magnus’s day,” Mrs. Karllson said. “You see all sorts of things in the plumbing business.”

“I didn’t think it was a competition,” Mr. Zeus said.

“I don’t think you need to tell us what happened,” Daniel said in a pleading tone.

“I thought it would be another routine call,” Mr. Karllson began, ignoring Daniel’s entreaty. “The fellow said he was a doctor, but his bathroom was utterly filthy. Imagine all the dried-up stains of things unimaginable and you begin to understand my work environment. Worst of all, his toilet was plugged, and when I took it off, I found . . .”

“Yuck! I don’t want to know anymore,” Lien cried out.

“We’re eating!” William exclaimed.

Mr. Karllson chuckled at their reactions, but at least he didn’t finish his story.

Thank goodness for that, Serena thought. Any discussion about bowel and bladder habits always left her unsettled. It reminded her of childhood as a slave in her true father’s palace where she had to clean out the latrines every morning.

Later on after dinner, Daniel and Lien cleared the table while Mr. and Mrs. Karllson brought out coffee and peanut butter brownies.

“Dig in,” Mrs. Karllson said. “There’s enough for everyone.” She gave Mr. Zeus an assessing gaze. “Although you might want to do without, my apple-shaped friend."

"Too late!" Mr. Zeus grinned around a mouthful of brownie.

"You are incorrigible!" Mrs. Karllson exclaimed.

"And quite pleasantly stuffed."

"Like a Thanksgiving turkey," Mrs. Karllson quipped.

Serena smiled at their interaction. She had never seen people speak mockingly to one another and yet with obvious love.

"We were thinking of going camping over Christmas break," Jason announced. "There's a park in West Virginia, out past the light pollution, where we can watch the stars and go hiking."

"Daniel and Lien are more than welcome to come with us," said Mr. Zeus. "It should be a lot of fun."

Warning bells went off in Serena's mind. The discussion involved more than camping and hiking. A strangeness filled the air, but she couldn't pinpoint its meaning.

Her thoughts were interrupted when William closed his eyes and quoted a poem:

Gazing at her mysteries, I wonder,
What is more lovely.
The crowning glory of her silvered moon,
Or her gifted shawl of shining bright stars.
My eyes seek the truth, but my soul ne'er learns.

"Very pretty," Mrs. Karllson said.

"Thank you," William replied.

"You wrote it?" Lien asked, sounding surprised.

William nodded.

Serena arched an eyebrow. "Strong enough to face down your

enemies, and also a romantic? There's a lot to learn about you, William."

Jason groaned in disgust. "Oh, come on . . ."

"Don't worry, Jason," Daniel advised. "I'm sure we won't hear anything that sickeningly sweet from Serena ever again after she finds out just how much of a geek William is."

"I think I already have that part figured out," Serena said.

"I'm a geek?" William asked in a disbelieving tone. "What about you two and how you keep quoting things in that terrible German accent?"

"Well, that's different," Daniel said. "That's quoting Arnie. Quoting him is nowhere near as bad as what you do, especially on Fridays."

William blinked and wore a sickly expression. "Err. Why don't we . . ."

"Daniel Karllson," Mrs. Karllson said in a warning tone.

"I'm missing something," Serena said, glancing around the table.

"It's just Daniel and Jason thinking they're funny," Lien said. "Don't listen to them."

"That's not true," Jason protested. "Daniel and I were talking about it, and we think Serena should know something about our friend, William."

"You guys suck," William muttered.

"The reason he's never able to talk to you or see you on Friday nights at ten is because he's watching *Miami Vice*," Daniel announced with a gleeful relish.

"His life revolves around that show," Jason added, appearing equally gleeful.

"I hope you dick—" William shot a glance at Mrs. Karllson. "I mean, I hope you two enjoy walking to school on Monday."

Daniel and Jason didn't seem the least bit worried about William's threat. Instead, they kept on grinning in evident triumph.

In that moment, several things became clear for Serena. Daniel and Jason truly loved William. Though they had tried to embarrass him, their words hadn't been spoken in spite. They had been spoken in the teasing fashion that could only be shared by the deepest of friends.

As for William . . . Serena gave him an appraising glance. He obviously liked to live vicariously, whether it was through the books he read or the TV shows and movies that he watched. He enjoyed seeing greatness in others, perhaps hoping to one day see it in himself. But what he didn't understand was that greatness was earned, not received like some magic ring.

Serena pitied him his lack of insight.

William held up his hands in mock surrender. "I'm sorry. Yes, I love *Miami Vice.* Yes, I love the theme song. And yes, I think Tubbs is the coolest person of all time. Guilty."

"Tubbs? He's a character on the show?" Serena asked.

"Yeah, and he's just so laid-back and cool and badass—"

"And he probably doesn't spend his Friday nights watching TV," Serena finished for him.

"I had a great time tonight," Serena said to William. "Maybe the best night I've ever had." The words slipped out without thought, and while they were the truth and worked for her purpose, she also spoke them with the same unintentional emotionality for which she had mentally castigated herself earlier in the evening.

"Really?" William asked, sounding surprised.

"Really."

"Then you haven't lived much."

The two of them stood alone on the Karllson's front porch—Jason and Mr. Zeus had already left—and she leaned into William, knocking him off-balance. "Very funny, Tubbs."

William grimaced.

"You know you aren't going to live that down, right?"

"I know." William sighed.

"See you at home?" Jason called from across the street.

"Sure," William shouted back. "I'm just going to walk Serena home." He glanced her way. "Do you mind if I walk you home?"

"I don't mind," Serena answered, offering William what she hoped was a shy smile.

He smiled in return.

Good.

"It's starting to get cold," William said as they set out for her house. His breath frosted in the night air.

"Yes, it is." Serena had worn a thin dress, and it didn't offer much protection from the chill. She drew her shawl closer about herself and pretended to shiver. Of course, she wasn't actually cold. In fact, she'd spent most of her life in an environment where this late September evening would have been considered balmy. Instead, the shiver had been meant to elicit a reaction from William.

A moment later, William did just as she had hoped he would: he draped his jacket around her shoulders.

Serena's confidence rose. There might be times when she wasn't as fully in control of her actions and emotions as she wished, but she still had enough control to execute her assignments. She could still manipulate William and finish her final pilgrimage.

"Thank you," Serena said.

"It looked like you needed it," William replied.

As she and William crossed the street and made their way to her house, Serena pulled the coat closer about herself. It smelled like William, a warm blend of something as earthy and real as his lovely drawl. Unconsciously, she shifted closer to him.

Immediately she realized what she had done and why.

Damn it. There went her control again. She mentally cursed. It was all William's fault. She liked him and his friends too much. If she was honest with herself, she liked who she was when she was around them even more. They made it so easy for her to simply lose herself in the moment and live her life freely, without considering the lies she had to tell, or determining how best to use someone to her advantage.

She counted backward by sevens again, this time from one thousand, and by the time they reached her front step, Serena had control of herself again.

She noticed that William's face had scrunched up like he had a question in mind.

"What is it?" Serena asked.

William flushed, and Serena smiled to herself. There was something refreshingly clean about William. Whenever he spoke or laughed, it was his truth. It was an expression of exactly what he felt at that time. He didn't lie, at least not to her, and she liked that.

And his dark, good looks weren't bad either.

A moment later, she mentally chided herself. *Control.*

"It's movie night tomorrow. My house. Do you want to come?"

"Sure, as long as it isn't *American Ninja II*," Serena said, needling him over a movie choice he'd made last week.

"It won't be," William promised.

"Then I'll be there." *Time to seal tonight's importance.* Serena leaned forward and kissed William on the cheek. Only a brief, butterfly brush, but his eyes widened. It would have been perfect if Serena's own heart hadn't started beating so fast. "Here's your coat," she said, hating the uneven tone in her voice. "Good night, William."

"Good night, Serena."

Serena stepped inside her home and closed the front door, not bothering to hide her smile of triumph. Even with her clumsiness, her inability to set aside her traitorous thoughts and emotions, events were proceeding quite well.

"Dinner was good?" Isha asked.

Before answering, Serena set her features into blandness, even as "Gloria" played in her mind. She only wished the lyrics to the song were true, that God loved His fallen creations. "It was fine," she said, infusing her words with carelessness. "But more importantly, it's furthered our plans very nicely. You heard William's invitation?"

"I did," Isha replied. "I also sensed that you kissed him. Was that wise?"

"I think so, sir" Serena replied. "He likes me. He thinks of me as a friend, but as you've always taught me, love and desire are more exploitable than friendship."

"Yes, they are," Isha agreed, even as he studied her with his raptor gaze. "In turn, you don't feel friendship for him?"

Her heart skipped a beat, but Serena didn't let her anxiety show. She snorted in derision. "Friendship is a weakness. Your first lesson, sir."

"Yes, and you learned it well," Isha said. "However, allow me to instruct you further. Upon your face and in your heart, I sense something unexpected."

"And what do you think you see or sense, sir?" Serena asked, maintaining a mildly curious tone.

"I sense the most dangerous emotion of all," Isha answered. "Contentment."

Serena blinked in surprise. His observation wasn't what she had expected, and yet . . . he was right. Serena forced a sarcastic smile. "Really? If that is what you sense, then perhaps your powers of observation are not as fearsome as they once were."

"Perhaps not," Isha said, sounding unperturbed by her waspish words. "So long as you don't lose perspective of the true reason we are here. The true reason why we care for this boy."

The doorbell rang. And rang and rang and rang.

William hustled down the hall. Only Daniel, that numbnut, did that. Mr. Zeus hated it. He generally hated any kind of loud noises, other than his hammer and anvil. Probably something to do with being old.

Jason came out of the kitchen. “Mr. Zeus is going to kill him.”

“I know,” William said as he raced for the door.

Daniel probably didn’t know that Mr. Zeus was home or he wouldn’t be pounding away on the doorbell as if it were a drum.

“Someone get the door!” Mr. Zeus yelled from his room.

William arrived and threw the front door open. Daniel stood on the porch wearing an unapologetic, cheese-eating grin. “What took you so long?”

“Mr. Zeus is home, stupid.”

Daniel’s grin fell away. “Oh, man.”

“Daniel Karllson, next time you think about ringing my doorbell like that, don’t!” Mr. Zeus shouted.

“Sorry, sir.” Daniel replied in a chastened voice.

“I don’t care. Don’t do it again, you little vagrant!”

“Yes, sir,” Daniel said. “He sounds really mad,” he whispered to William.

“You think?” William rolled his eyes. “Let’s go to my room. And be quiet this time. We don’t want you bugging Mr. Zeus again.”

Jason joined them, and William closed the door after he entered. Daniel flopped onto the oversized beanbag in the corner while Jason sat in the desk chair.

Pennants for the Reds and Bengals and a poster from *Back to the Future,* decorated the walls. Eddie the Head had been over the bed, but William had taken him down after Serena’s comment about Iron Maiden’s mascot. A poster from *Blade Runner* had replaced him. Other items, like Star Wars miniatures of a TIE fighter and an X-wing, hung from the ceiling, while the *Battlestar Galactica* and the United Starship *Enterprise* faced off on a bookshelf. The *Millennium Falcon* stood watch from a bookshelf.

"Why do you have Wonder Woman's bracelets on top of Superman's logo?" Daniel asked, fingering the articles.

"They just seem like they belong together," William answered as he thumbed on the boombox. "Kyrie Eleison" came on, but he quickly dialed down the sound, once again for Mr. Zeus' behalf. *Ted Nugent would say Jason's grandfather was too old.*

"What movie did you guys get for movie night?" Daniel asked.

"*The Road Warrior*," William said.

"Again?" Daniel frowned. "The girls aren't going to like that."

"It's a Saturday afternoon," Jason said. "All the good, new movies were already gone by the time we got to the video store. The place was pretty much cleared out."

Daniel shrugged. "Whatever. Do you guys want to finish that D&D campaign, *The Vault of the Drow*?"

"Is that really how you want to spend a Saturday afternoon?" Jason asked.

"Well, yeah. It's why I came over."

"You mean it wasn't because you missed the company of your friends?" William asked.

"I missed Jason. You, not so much."

"Very funny."

"Don't ask a question if you don't want the answer," Daniel said, sounding smug.

"You do remember I'm the Dungeon Master, right?" William asked.

"Crap."

"Yeah, exactly. Crap," William said. "I'm pretty sure any time you roll, Razorclaw the Ranger is going to have the runs."

"Razorclaw the Ranger." Jason snorted. "That's so lame."

"Shut up."

CHAPTER 8:
FALLOUT

"Good job, Wilde," Sonya Bowyer huffed, pushing into his personal space and glaring at him. "We lost the game on Friday because of you."

"The football game?" William asked.

"Yes, the football game, stupid!" She poked him in the chest. "We lost, and it's your fault. Half our defense was suspended because of what you did on Friday, and Lance Owens got hurt in the game, too. He was our best wide receiver."

How's that my fault?" William demanded. "I'm not the reason Jake and those guys got suspended. They did that on their own."

"We had a chance to win the city title," Sonya screeched. "Maybe even state. It would've been our first title ever. Because of you Jake might lose his scholarship to Notre Dame, and—"

"Thanks to *him*," William interjected, his blood starting to simmer. "What happened was his own fault."

William and Sonya had been among the first to arrive for Biology, and the rest of the class slowly filtered in. The other students stood by in rapt silence, watching to see what would happen.

"You knew Mr. Meron would be there." Sonya poked him again. "You knew, and you didn't care that Jake would get suspended from the team. Or that we'd lose because of you!"

"So what?" William snarled, a red film filtering over his vision. "Jake didn't try to get me in trouble with Mr. Meron first? He didn't threaten to sic the entire football team on me? You think I should have just sat back and taken it? That's not going to happen. Don't blame me for what your asshole boyfriend did."

Sonya must have seen something in William's face, and fear flitted across her face. She stepped back.

Guilt filled William at seeing Sonya afraid of him. His anger quickly drained away.

Mrs. Nelson walked into the room. "What's going on?" she asked, approaching them and obviously sensing the tension.

Serena arrived as well. She waited behind Mrs. Nelson, chewing her lip in concern.

"Sonya seems to think I should sit back and let her boyfriend beat me up whenever he feels like it," William answered.

"That's not true!" Sonya blurted.

"Didn't Mr. Meron tell you to stay away from Mr. Wilde?" Mrs. Nelson asked Sonya.

"Mrs. Nelson, I was just—"

"Get back to your table."

"But—"

"Now."

Sonya snapped her mouth shut, spun on her heel, and stalked back to her table, her back ramrod straight. Mrs. Nelson followed a pace behind, as if to make sure that Sonya did as she was told.

"What was that about?" Serena whispered.

"Nothing," William grumbled, still upset. The worst part of his entire interaction with Sonya had been the shame of making her afraid. "I just scared a girl I used to have a crush on."

"And?" Serena persisted.

William sighed before explaining his confrontation. "Have you seen the looks I've been getting from the football team?"

"Dirty looks are all they can do," Serena reminded him.

"I know."

"They can't touch you, or Jake and his friends won't be reinstated. That's what Mr. Meron said."

William grimaced. Her words brought him no solace. Between the ugly stares he'd received all morning from the football team and the argument with Sonya, his victory over Jake Ridley a few days ago seemed like ancient history or Pyrrhic at best.

"Settle down, everyone," Mrs. Nelson called. "We'll be starting class now."

"Great," William muttered. "A crappy Monday morning, and Biology to top it off."

"I don't know why you're complaining," Serena said. "I do most of the dissecting."

"It's just all the formaldehyde and all those disgusting creatures and worms," William replied. "It'd be easier if I could chop them up with my sword."

"Like a ninja from that movie you like so much?" Serena teased. "The one where the bad guy sounds like a Japanese Elmer Fudd?"

William gave her an offended expression. "It's *American Ninja*, and it's an instant classic."

"*He possess great skills*," Serena said with a chuckle.

William smiled, unable to maintain his sourness in the face of Serena's humor.

"I have some exciting news," Mrs. Nelson said. "Today we move past invertebrates and insects and get to start on frogs."

"Don't backtrack," Serena warned, taking in William's expression. "You were finally breaking out of your moodiness."

"But it's so disgusting." William hated how whiny his voice sounded. "Dissecting frogs."

"Before we start we'll watch a short video," Mrs. Nelson continued. "After that, I'll pass out the frogs."

"Try not to fall asleep this time," Serena said.

"What are you talking about?" William asked.

"You know what I'm talking about," Serena said. "As soon as the lights go out, so do you. Stay awake this time."

The room darkened.

"I'll try," William replied, "but the only thing worse than dissecting a frog is watching a video about dissecting a frog."

Serena rolled her eyes. "Shut up, and pay attention. I'm not doing all the work this time."

The film was blessedly short, but narrated by someone from the sixties or seventies. He had lank hair combed over to the side, oversized glasses, and the dull, lifeless diction common to that era of instructional videos. Despite his droning, soporific monotone, William managed to stay awake through the entire video.

When the lights came back on, Mrs. Nelson gathered everyone around her lab table at the head of the class. "You won't be expected to do everything seen on the film," she said, "but for today I want each table to have the skin dissected off one leg. Let me show you what I mean."

William and Serena stood toward the back of the group, and they had to step onto stools to see Mrs. Nelson's work. She had her mousy head bent over the demonstration frog.

William wrinkled his nose at the stench of the formaldehyde. "Does it stink so bad because it's dead?" he asked Serena in a whisper.

Serena's eyes crinkled as she bit her lower lip, shaking with silent laughter.

Steve Aldo, who stood nearby, chuckled as well. "I hate the way this stuff stinks, too."

William shot him a surprised expression. Steve's friendliness was unexpected, especially since he was on the football team and friends with Jake. "I'm sorry the team lost," William whispered to him.

"Me, too," Steve replied. "But that wasn't your fault. That was Jake's." He shrugged. "They shouldn't have done what they did."

Once again, William's eyes widened in surprise.

Before he could reply, Serena interrupted their conversation. "Will you two be quiet?" she whispered. "I'm trying to listen."

William gave Steve a shrug and returned his attention to Mrs. Nelson. With a few efficient slices, their teacher had the skin removed from a thigh of her frog. "See how easy it is?" she asked. "Simple. Now go back to your tables and I'll get the frogs." She ducked into her office and returned with a sloshing, white bucket. "Glove up and grab one," Mrs. Nelson said. When she reached William and Serena's station, she paused and waited expectantly.

William reached into the bucket and scowled in disgust. Though the frogs were dead, with their cold, slimy, squishy gross skin, they still managed to flop through his grasping fingers.

"Just grab one," Mrs. Nelson said impatiently.

"They're slippery," William said.

"For heaven's sake, just pick it up," Mrs. Nelson said in exasperation. "It's not that hard."

William gritted his teeth and grabbed a frog. It almost slipped free, and he had to grasp it more firmly so it wouldn't escape. With a firm jerk, he pulled the frog out by one of its hind legs and all but threw it onto the dissection tray. It plopped down with a wet smack.

"Ack!" Serena cried out. Some of the liquid had splattered into her hair.

William gasped. The first girl who had ever showed any interest in him, a beautiful one, too, and he'd splashed frog juice in her hair.

"William Wilde!" Serena exclaimed.

The class burst into laughter.

"Settle down, everyone," Mrs. Nelson said, trying to remain stern, but her quivering lips gave way to chuckles as she moved to the next station.

"William," Serena said, drawing his attention to her. She glared at him, something she'd never done before. "This is unacceptable!"

By the barest margins, William managed not to shrink away from the intensity of her gaze. "I'm so sorry," he said.

"I don't care," she snapped.

"If I say sorry again, will that make you even angrier?"

Her jaw briefly clenched, but then she sighed. "Never mind." Her voice and posture no longer seeped anger, but coldness laced her tone. "Let's just get this done."

William nodded. "I paid attention to the film. I can skin the leg if you like. You know, that way you don't have to get your hands covered in frog goo."

"Dissect," Serena corrected. She shoved the tray toward him. "You dissect the leg."

William carefully grasped the dead frog the way Mrs. Nelson and the monotonous man had, but it escaped from his hands. He tried again and had the same result.

Serena growled. "Just give it to me. The way you're going, we'll be here all day."

She took the tray, pulled it close to her, and used her forceps to clamp down on the frog and hold it in place. With a few deft slices, she had the skin filleted off one hind leg. The muscles were clearly visible.

Serena wasn't finished, though. She plucked William's forceps from his hands, inserted the head into the frog's open thigh and pried apart the various muscles, separating them until they stood out. She'd been as efficient as Mrs. Nelson and as skilled as the man on the film.

William's jaw dropped.

"Now that we're done, I'm going to try and wash this gunk out of my hair," Serena said as she stood up.

"You cut that thigh apart like it was nothing," William said, still gaping.

"If you haven't noticed, I'm pretty good with a scalpel," Serena replied.

"Remind me not to ever get on your bad side."

"Finally, you demonstrate wisdom," Serena said.

After the confrontation with Sonya Bowyer, the rest of the week passed uneventfully. But then came Friday, and another loss for the football team. Hell followed on the following Monday. The other students' anger at William—not just from the football team this time—was palpable. Somebody even vandalized his locker, writing 'traitor' on it. Serena told him to ignore the veiled insults and pissed off stares, but that was easier said than done.

On Tuesday, the anger from the team and everyone else continued, but that was when Jason came up with the not-so-brilliant idea for the two of them to try out for the football team. It was midseason and doing so shouldn't have been possible, except that with Lance out for the season and half his defense still suspended, Coach Rasskins needed the players.

William thought that trying out this late in the season was a dumb idea, but he went along with it anyway. Miraculously, they both made the team. Of course, Jason had been a shoo-in, but William's own athleticism had been surprising, especially to himself. He still thought of himself as being weak and slow, and to find out he was strong and fast took getting used to.

However, during that first practice, the rest of the team gave William a scornful once over and voiced their opinions about him in no uncertain terms.

"Who let that loser on the team?" someone muttered.

"Probably got Jake suspended just to take his spot," another answered.

"How did I let you talk me into this?" William asked afterward.

"It'll be fine," Jason promised.

It wasn't.

Jason thrived while playing football. He had natural instincts and an athleticism that few others possessed, and in three days he transitioned from walk-on to starting wide receiver, but William struggled mightily. He had been assigned to defense, and while he had plenty of speed and strength—two years of martial arts hadn't been for nothing—that wasn't enough for football. Positioning was critical, and William was always out of position. The offensive players enjoyed blocking him into the dust while he was busy trying to remember his assignment.

William ended up playing third or fourth string, and being way down the depth chart was fine as far as he was concerned. That way he wouldn't be expected to actually play.

Lord forbid if that happened!

Friday, game day, eventually arrived, and the morning dawned cheerfully sunny, unlike William's worried, gray mood.

"I still don't know how I let you talk me into this," William said to Jason at their lunch table that day. "Tonight's Homecoming. We *have* to win."

"Stop worrying," Jason replied. "We will. Besides, you probably won't even make it out onto the field. You're third string, remember?"

"Fourth."

"Whatever. You're overthinking it," Jason said. "That's always been your problem."

"Thinking is what I do best. It's who I am."

"Maybe you need to change that," Jason said. "Maybe you should trust yourself. Let your muscle memory and instincts take over."

"Jason's right," Serena said. "When you tricked Jake Ridley, you had a plan and you executed it. This game is the same. You play, you make a decision, and you go with it. It doesn't matter if it turns out wrong because at least you've made a commitment. Freezing up and doing nothing would be worse."

When put like that, it sounded so simple, William thought. Nevertheless, he continued to worry after the conversation around the lunch table moved on.

The rest of the day passed in a blur, and after school, Serena stood with William on his front porch.

"I have something for you," she said, handing him a small box. "I made it this week and I wanted to give it to you before I forgot. Open it."

William unwrapped the present and found himself holding a gold-colored handkerchief bearing a Chinese pictograph on a shield. William looked to Serena for an explanation.

"The shield is you," Serena explained. "Your name means 'warrior' in German, and the pictograph is the Chinese word for 'serenity.' Wear it during the game and maybe it'll help you."

William smiled, his first moment of pleasure all week. "Thank you," he said, drawing Serena into a hug.

Rather than her typical composed confidence, Serena wore a shy, uncertain expression. "Do you like it?" she asked.

"I love it."

"Good." Serena kissed him on the cheek. "Then good luck with the game."

CHAPTER 9: HOMECOMING

October 1986

An hour before kickoff, William kept twitching like a live wire. Nothing helped to settle his nerves. Not prayer, not meditation, not even listening to "Bad" by U2. He paced about in the locker room, alone, restless, and anxious.

Tonight's game wasn't just homecoming. It was also against the Blackward Crusaders, St. Francis' bitter rival. Bragging rights for a year would be determined tonight. Plus, St. Francis still had an outside chance of winning the city title and making the playoffs. But it all started with a win tonight.

As he waited for kickoff, William's nervousness gnawed at him, stealing his confidence and leaving him nauseated and angry. Jason kept telling him the emotions were only natural, but William didn't care. He just wanted the feelings gone. And he wanted this game over with, and of course, St. Francis the victor.

Shortly before the team exited the locker room, they all gathered round when Coach Rasskins entered the room. The team greeted him with a riot of sound. Feet pounded the floor, hands slammed the lockers, and a shouted call-and-response of *'We are! . . . St. Francis!'* roared out.

William's heart stirred, and some of his anxiety abated.

Coach Rasskins grinned and clapped along with the players before lifting his hands, calling for quiet. "Before we go onto that field, boys, I want to talk to you. I've got words to say." The room quieted. "Some people will tell you that this is just a game, and they aren't wrong. Some people will tell you, it's only high school football, that it's not important. They aren't wrong, either." Coach paused. "But those are just some people. They aren't you. They won't have to wake up in your shoes tomorrow. You will."

William listened in rapt attention. He'd never heard anything like Coach's words before.

"And I want you to think about that. Pretend tomorrow comes and think about what that'll be like. How will you face the day? Will you think about this night and have a clear conscience? Will you know that you gave everything you had, everything in your heart, your soul, and your body for the boys sitting next to you? That you fought to the end, never quitting, never letting go of the dream you share with every member of this team."

The room stilled utterly.

"They say you only get one chance to live the life you want, but that's not true. You get many chances, but in each of those chances, there will be obstacles that you can't handle by yourselves. You'll need friends and family. People to help you. A team. Think about that. Obstacles you can only overcome with a team." Coach Rasskins paused to glance around the room, meeting every player's eye.

William's heart soared. He wanted to leap and roar defiance, ready to reach for something he couldn't name.

"Obstacles that only a team can overcome," Coach repeated. "Tonight we play a game, but it's also an obstacle. Remember that." His voice rose, and he enunciated each sentence with a downward thrust of his hand. "And the only way to overcome that obstacle is by giving everything you got for the boys in this room. Everything."

William's heart pounded in response to Coach's words.

"The legacy you want to leave starts with that choice: *will I fight for my team, for my brothers?* Will you?"

William shouted out, one voice amongst many as the team roared response to Coach Rasskins' question. He felt part of something larger than himself, an unstoppable force.

"And that's why we're going to win! Because we're a team. Every one of us. Nobody out on the field, not Blackward, not their fans, not even *our* fans, nobody believes it, but I do. I know it. Be angry that no one believes in us. Be angry for greatness, and be angry for your team!"

Another roar, stomping feet, and pounding hands greeted his words, William as loud as any of the veteran players.

"Now huddle up with me, and let's pray."

The team closed in around Coach Rasskins, each one lifting an arm so they formed a tent of hands above him.

"*Hail Mary, full of grace. The Lord is with thee. . . .*"

William bent his head and joined the rest of the team in saying the Hail Mary, and afterward, Coach led them through the dark tunnel that opened out onto the field.

The team roared like some prehistoric beast as it emerged into the blazing lights of the stadium. The hurricane sound of "Shoot to Thrill" blared over the loudspeakers. A cry like a battering ram met the team as the student body of St. Francis cheered them on.

William stumbled at the lights and the sound, but he quickly caught his footing and gazed about in wonder. The last of his anxiety receded. Adrenaline burned through his veins, and he screamed out with an undefinable passion alongside his teammates.

With the opening kickoff, the game started with a rolling, thunder roar from the St. Francis side of the stadium. Afterward, the riotous energy calmed into a more placid but still electric excitement. The game transformed into a tight contest, hard-fought, with both sidelines a feverish beehive of activity.

Neither team could establish much of a lead, and St. Francis was bitten by the hard luck of several injuries. Coach ended up waving William onto the field to play on special teams on both kickoffs and punts.

With only a minute or so left in the game, St. Francis clung to a slim lead of 21-17.

Blackward got the ball back, though, needing a touchdown to win. They began their drive pinned deep in their own territory. On two consecutive passes, Blackward gained huge chunks of yardage, driving to St. Francis's two-yard line. Even worse, three of St. Francis' defenders were injured and forced to hobble off the field. There was time enough for one more play. The Crusaders needed only a short run to win.

"Get in there!" Coach Rasskins shouted to William. "Don't play scared. You can do this!"

William's heart pounded. Fear coiled in his stomach like a wriggling worm. Their entire season was on the brink. "Lord, help me," he prayed before strapping on his helmet and racing onto the field.

St. Francis' defenders wore sagging demeanors. Several of them muttered in forlorn disbelief when William joined their huddle.

"We haven't lost!" exhorted Jeff Setter, the defensive captain. He slapped players on the shoulder. "Get fired up! We got this. Remember your role. Remember your place. Don't give them an inch. Your teammate's right by you. He'll fight for you. Goddamn it! You better fight for him!"

William took heart from Jeff's words. Resoluteness stiffened his spine. *He would not be the reason St. Francis lost tonight.* The anger that never entirely left him flickered to life, and William used it crush any remaining doubts. He bit down on his mouth-guard and slapped the sides of his helmet.

Ready!

Blackward broke their huddle and set up in a simple I-formation with their running back, the Notre Dame-bound, all-state standout Marcus Reed. A wide receiver went into motion, setting up on William's side of the field. He paused just outside the tackle.

William recognized the play: a handoff to Reed.

William's vision tunneled to what lay directly before him. The rest of the world faded, and silence reigned along the line of scrimmage.

The quarterback took the snap. Handoff to Reed. William darted straight to where he thought the running back would make his cut. The right guard pulled, rumbling along the line of scrimmage like a dump truck clearing a path for a Porsche. The lineman outweighed William by a hundred pounds.

In that moment, instinct took over, and William went with it. No doubts. No indecision.

He rushed straight at the pulling guard, feigning a direct assault. It was foolhardy, he knew. The Blackward player lowered his shoulder, ready to hammer him into next week. William got even lower, but just before the point of impact, he spun around the lineman. Reed was one stride away, and William had no chance to prepare himself. The Blackward running back smashed into him with a thud.

Without thought, William wrapped his arms around Reed. *Hold.* That simple word became the entirety of his world. William gritted his teeth and strained to keep the Blackward running back from pushing forward. For an endless second, William and Reed were locked in stasis.

William suddenly found himself stumbling forward. His teammates had arrived. They added their strength and weight to his own and buried Reed.

The world returned with a jarring crash, and the St. Francis stands erupted. St. Francis had held.

He had held.

They'd won.

William stood in shock as his teammates bellowed their triumph. Many of the St. Francis defenders smacked him on the helmet as they streamed past.

William shouted in joy.

After the game, Mr. Zeus invited all of William's and Jason's friends to his house for a celebration with lots of pizza.

"Then during Biology, William reaches into the bucket and basically flings the frog at me," Serena said, trying to sound exasperated.

"I hurled it. I didn't fling it," William corrected through everyone's laughter. "And if any of you had handled that thing, you'd have done the same. It was disgusting."

"Well, I'm sure none of them would have splashed me with frog juice. It got all over my hair," Serena replied.

"Gross," Lien said with a chuckle.

"I did say I was sorry," William said. "At least twenty times."

"And I eventually forgave you," Serena said. "It's just that the smell lingered all day, so I think I'm allowed to tease you about it. I swear, sometimes I think I can still smell the formaldehyde." She held a lock of hair out to William. "What do you think?"

He inhaled. His eyes closed for an instant. "It smells like flowers."

William's words sent a thrill tingling up Serena's spine, and she managed a shy smile even as her heart skipped a beat. Thoughts filled her mind, treasonous thoughts of freedom, ones in which she rebelled against all her commitments and orders and lived her life on her own terms.

In the next heartbeat, Serena cursed her foolish longings and bit down on her pizza as if it were the weakness that threatened to undo her control. *Selene*, she reminded herself.

Jason, thankfully, changed the subject as only he could, by snickering.

Lien threw a piece of garlic bread at him, but he ducked out of the way, and it smacked Daniel on the side of his head.

"Hey!"

"Oops," Lien said. "I was aiming at Jason."

"What did I do?" Jason protested.

"You know what you did," Lien said before turning to Serena. "Don't mind Jason. He's an asexual ass—"

"Language," Mr. Karllson warned.

"Oops again. Sorry," Lien said, sounding unapologetic. "Anyway, Jason isn't interested in romance, or what it means when a boy likes a girl."

"Uh, Lien," Daniel warned. "I don't think you should . . ."

"Don't think I should what?" Lien shot a glance at William, who seemed inordinately interested in his food. "Oh!"

Kohl Obsidian awoke with a hiss and a start when his singular dream was interrupted.

In his fantasy, Kohl fed upon long lines of frenzied *asrasins*. One by one, he stole their succulent, pure *lorethasra*, enjoying their panicked pain and sweat-ridden fear as their life's grace grew corrupted and pustulant. It was his favorite dream.

And after his gorging, Kohl, now more fell than any necrosed in history, challenged and destroyed Sapient Dormant, the Overward of the necrosed, their leader, the one being in all the worlds whom Kohl feared.

His ability to lucidly dream was a remnant from his previous life, from the time when he'd been a holder, from when he'd been human. He didn't like to dream of those times, though. He didn't even like to remember them.

But tonight his singular dream had been interrupted by an unexpected stirring of something familiar, of *someone* familiar.

Kohl concentrated, and the answer to the disturbance came to him. The boy from months ago. The boy Kohl had spared, but whose family he had killed. The boy with the potential for *lorethasra*.

Emotions, powerful and strong, raged through the boy. Blazing triumph filled his thoughts. He had done something he considered worthy of praise. What it was, Kohl didn't know or care, but what he did know was this: the small seed he had planted within the boy those many months ago had found fertile soil. The child had grown fleet of foot and strong.

Kohl considered harvesting the boy now. It would be poetic justice. He had become who he was because of the necrosed's polluted *lorethasra*. Plus, Kohl needed new parts for his body. The boy's extremities and organs would serve nicely.

But if he waited, the boy would grow even stronger. His *lorethasra* might flower fully, becoming as delicious as a ripe mango. Kohl hesitated, and the boy's potential for *lorethasra* became the ultimate temptation. If it came to fruition, the boy would be a rich reward for Kohl's patience.

The necrosed pondered long into the night on what next to do.

CHAPTER 10: HEIGHTS REACHED

Everyone on the football team knew that the one play William had made, that one instinctive effort to hold on, had saved St. Francis' season. Coach Rasskins knew it. Every student in the stands knew it. Even Jake Ridley and his suspended friends knew it.

And by Monday, everyone in the school had suddenly become William's friend, and the football team welcomed him into their brotherhood with open arms. Even Jake Ridley, imbued by whatever magic winning created, managed civility toward William. He offered a nod of acknowledgment in homeroom although his eyes seemed to burn with resentment.

Two more games followed the one against Blackward, along with two more wins. Then came Halloween, Jake's first game back on the team, and the final one of the regular season. It would be against Archbishop Roman, the undefeated, defending city and state champion. The game would determine the league championship and whether St. Francis would go on to the state playoffs.

Since his play against Blackward, William had occasionally seen the field, but only on special teams, and never in critical situations. The truth was that while his play had improved during practice, Coach still didn't trust him on game day, but against Archbishop, another late-game injury pressed William into service. Archbishop was driving for a score that would put the game out of reach. This time William had to fill in at safety, covering the void in the center of St. Francis' defense.

"They're coming right after you, look sharp!" Jake shouted to William.

"Just like against Blackward!" Jeff Setter exhorted. "You got this!"

Both players slapped William's helmet in encouragement.

William nodded, and untapped his latent anger, leaving him amped up but focused. He clamped down on his mouthpiece, and just as it had against Blackward, the world receded. Archbishop was up by four points. If they managed a touchdown, the game would be lost.

William scouted Archbishop's formation. They had two running backs in a power-I, with their wide receivers bunched up tight. *A running play.* William eased forward to be at the point of attack.

He was about to edge closer to the line of scrimmage when he noticed one of the wide receivers drift into motion, moving from left to right onto William's side of the field. He caught the glance between the quarterback and the wide receiver.

Warning bells went off. "Watch the pass!" William shouted as he shifted back and cheated closer to the wide receiver.

The ball snapped. Joe Skipper, the cornerback who had initial coverage on the wide receiver in motion, shot toward the quarterback. He must have thought it was a run, too. The wide receiver shucked past Joe and sprinted down the sideline, uncovered. It would be a game-sealing touchdown.

William was on him. He didn't bother searching for the ball. It would be in the air. *Faster. He had to close.* Anger fueled adrenaline. *Faster!* William took an angle and ran flat out.

The Archbishop wide receiver looked back. His arms rose into position, ready to cradle the catch.

William jumped up with arms raised. He felt an impact as the ball bounced off his hands. The wide-receiver's eyes widened. He was still looking up. The ball was still in the air. Still in play. William shoved the wide receiver to the ground and spun about. A flicker at the corner of his vision. He reached out, and the ball landed in his hands.

Before him lay a wide open field.

William took off down the sideline. His heart pumped. His cleats dug in, and he ran flat out. His teammates set up blocks. They smashed aside the Archbishop players who desperately tried to bring him down.

William dodged or plowed through tackles until only two players remained. He slammed to a stop, and one Archbishop player flew past him. He spun, and the other player's hands slipped off him. The way to the end zone stood clear.

William ran the last few yards untouched and unopposed. He spiked the ball and roared triumph. His teammates mobbed him. They screamed wordlessly and thumped his helmet and shoulders.

St. Francis had the lead, and two minutes and twelve seconds later, the game was over.

William was mobbed by his team and the student body. St. Francis had won the city championship and would be advancing to the playoffs.

The next day, All Saints Day, everyone's schedule worked out so that after a long month of football practice and games, William finally had time to hang out with his friends and go to the movies.

"What are we seeing?" Lien asked when they arrived at the dollar cinema.

"*Highlander*," William said.

"There can be only one," Daniel quoted.

"Not another boy movie," Lien protested. "Why can't we see *Peggy Sue Got Married*?"

"Because *Peggy Sue* doesn't have cool swords and immortals," Jason said.

"I thought we were seeing a movie about Scottish people," Serena said, looking confused. "Isn't that why it's called *Highlander*?"

William gave her a double-take. *She'd never heard of Highlander?* "Are you serious?"

"Well . . . yeah," Serena said. "I thought it would be something about Scots."

"It is, and it isn't," Jason enthused. "You'll love it."

"Only if you're a nerd," Lien muttered.

"Hey! I like *Highlander*," Daniel said.

"And like I said, if you're a nerd."

Jason laughed. "You set yourself up for that one."

"I'm a nerd," Serena quietly announced.

"No, you're not," William scoffed. "If there's a bright center to nerdom, you're about the farthest from it."

"Then there are supernova nerds who mangle lines from *Star Wars*," Lien said.

"Or the ones who know the lines to begin with," Daniel replied to Lien. "Who's the nerd now, eh?"

Lien tried to backhand Daniel on the shoulder, but she ended up hitting Jason.

"Watch it!" Jason said.

"Sorry. I was trying to hit Daniel."

"Well, aim better next time."

"Maybe I'm not a nerd," Serena said, "but I do like nerds." She smiled at William as she spoke, and her eyes glowed with that intensity he'd grown used to seeing.

William smiled back, and he knew what he should do, what everyone expected him to do, but for whatever reason he didn't want to. Not only because he had an audience—his friends—but something else, something he couldn't understand. Serena was beautiful, smart, and funny. She'd already declared her interest in him, and he had most definitely been interested in her, but now . . .

A few days ago, a warning bell had gone off in his head, a sense that something wasn't right, either about Serena or her interest in him. He couldn't shake the feeling no matter how stupid it seemed.

Serena didn't seem to notice his troubled thoughts. She hummed "Gloria" as they entered the theater.

“So, what did you think of *Highlander*?” William asked Serena as they left the theater.

“I’m still trying to figure it out,” she replied. “It wasn’t what I expected.”

“Anyone want pizza?” Daniel asked. “I’m hungry.”

“You’re always hungry,” Lien said.

“Then you don’t want any?” William asked.

“I didn’t say that.”

“Then we’re going to LaRosa’s,” William said.

They climbed into the T-Bird, and a few turns and a couple of minutes later, they wheeled into the parking lot of a small, white building from which a delicious aroma emanated. The place was packed, but sooner than William expected they had seats and food.

“This is *really* good,” Serena said after her first bite.

“Cincinnati has crappy weather, but it does have good eats,” Daniel said.

“I know,” Lien said. “And Serena probably hasn’t even tried Montgomery Inn.” She brightened. “You should take her there someday,” she suggested to William. “She’ll love it. It could be your first date.”

William almost coughed up his mouthful of pizza and shot Lien a glare.

She smiled sweetly back. “Did I say something wrong?”

Yes, you said something wrong.

“No, you didn’t say anything wrong,” Serena replied to Lien. She turned to William. “I would love to have dinner with you . . . as long as it isn’t Cincinnati chili.”

"No Cincinnati chili," William agreed.

"What's wrong with Cincinnati chili?" Jason asked.

"It's spaghetti sauce pretending to be chili," Serena said with a wrinkle of her nose. "Real chili is Texas style."

"If you like chili-flavored tomatoes," William said.

"Really?" Serena asked in an arch tone. "That's what you think of Texas-style?"

"I try not to think about it," William said. "It's not worth wasting the brainpower."

"And you definitely need every last ounce of your brainpower," Serena said. "You're running on fumes."

"Ooh. She got you," Daniel chortled.

"Why don't we just agree to disagree," William said to Serena.

"Can't keep up with me?" she asked with an arch of her eyebrows.

"I could, but my mother always told me to never pick an argument with a pretty lady." *Which was true.*

Serena grinned. "Compliments will get you out of most any problem," she said. "But even if I don't like your chili, I do like Glier's Goetta."

"When did you try Glier's?" Jason asked.

"I get around," Serena told him. "While you were off doing football things, I went out and discovered the city."

"Have you discovered the downtown library?" Lien asked.

"No," Serena replied. "Why?"

"If you like books, it's like walking through the gates of heaven," Lien said with a faraway expression in her eyes.

Serena lifted her brows. "Really? And do you need a cigarette when you're done?"

"What?" Lien asked in confusion.

Everyone else chuckled.

"Never mind," Serena said. "Maybe we can all go there sometime."

"Sure," William said. "We can even go to the zoo, if you want. Make a day of it downtown."

Serena smiled. "I'd like that."

Jason wore a shit-eating grin.

William scowled at him. "What's so funny?"

"Nothing," Jason said. He made a whipping sound that only William could hear.

"Shut up," William said with a roll of his eyes. *Jason had no idea what was going on, but whatever.* "Did you ever figure out what you thought of *Highlander*?" he asked Serena.

"I liked it," she replied. "It was sad, though, especially when Connor held his dying wife in his arms and described the Highlands."

"That scene always gets me, too," Lien said.

"I thought you didn't like *Highlander*," Jason said.

Lien graced him with pitying glance.

"You're back later than I expected," Isha said when Serena arrived home.

"We went out for pizza after the movie, sir," Serena explained.

"I take it you aren't hungry, then?"

"No, sir. I doubt I could stomach another bite at this point."

"Are you also too tired and too full of pizza to train?"

Serena *was* tired and full. All she really wanted to do was to go to bed, but to admit to either would be admitting weakness. "I'm ready whenever you are, sir," she said. "Should I change first?"

"Would an enemy allow you to do so?"

"No, sir."

"Then, after you." Isha gestured to the stairs leading down to the basement.

Serena went first, alert in case he decided that training would begin before they reached the basement. Sometimes he was like that, attacking when least expected. However, this time Serena reached the bottom of the stairs without incident.

The basement floor was covered by a thick, black mat and lit by fluorescent lights that illuminated the mostly empty space with a stark whiteness. The brightness removed all shadows.

"Your interactions with these others continues to show in your carriage and your mannerisms," Isha noted.

Serena had an inkling of what he meant, but she couldn't afford to allow him to believe she possessed such a weakness. "I don't know to what you refer," she said, keeping her expression bland.

Isha paused. He must have noticed the tension in her posture. "You've changed."

"What do you think this supposed change indicates?" Serena asked. Rather than deny his charges she did as he had always taught her: shift the focus of the conversation toward the other person and subtly interrogate them.

Isha didn't answer at first. Instead, he warmed up, doing

stretches, lunges, pushups, and pull-ups.

Serena followed suit.

"In my time in the Far Abroad, I've seen many things," Isha said, seeming to choose his words carefully. "Some things have been amusing, others pathetic, and a few have made me wish . . . Some have made me wish for something you and I can never have."

Serena paused in mid-stretch, surprised by Isha's openness. "What do you wish for?"

Isha didn't answer. Instead, he attacked.

Serena angled away from his punches and checked a kick. He snapped a jab. Serena tried to weave aside, but the punch clipped her cheek. She kept circling before she suddenly changed directions.

She stepped in with a straight right, and missed. Isha shot forward and tried to grapple with her. Serena pushed him off, and partially connected with a right hook on the break.

Isha grinned and wiped away a trickle of blood from the corner of his mouth.

He feinted for a single-leg takedown, but Serena slid to her left. As expected, he sent a straight left tunneling through the air where her head had been. It missed by inches.

"Good," Isha said. "Whatever changes you are going through, at least you still remember how to fight."

"What are these changes you keep referring to?"

"Must I explain everything to you? Or can you not deduce it on your own?"

"I can deduce truth, but what you see may only be your imagination or misinterpretation."

Isha nodded agreement. He wiped at his mouth again, but it was a ruse. Before Serena could dodge, Isha bull-rushed her. He clasped his arms beneath hers. Serena leaned down at the waist, making him carry some of her weight. She sprawled, doing her best to hold him back, but he pulled her off balance and snuck one foot between hers. A simple trip, and she crashed to the mat.

Before he could gain control she slipped out from beneath him. She placed her feet on his hips and pushed. He twisted away from her thrust. She pushed again, but once more he moved aside. He fell back on top of her, a threat to gain control.

"Contentment," he said. "You like it here. You like your life here, and I sense your desire for what we both know can never be."

She recognized the truth in his words, and they fired an anger inside her. *How could she have been so foolish? Worse, how could she have allowed* Isha *to see it? Stupid, stupid girl. Her sister might pay the price for her idiotic dreams.*

Serena made a grab for Isha's wrists. When he worked to twist them free, she used the distraction to kick again at his hips. This time it worked. She got him off her and regained her feet.

"Break," Isha called.

"There is no contentment, sir," Serena lied. "I am as I was when we first arrived here, focused on the completion of my pilgrimage."

Isha shook his head. "You're lying, but your secret is safe with me."

"You are mistaken."

"I am your Isha. Do you really think you can lie to me on such an important matter?"

Serena blinked, unsure what to say. Isha was right, and she

tried to mask the sudden fear that filled her. *What would he do with this truth? Would he tell her father about this failing?*

"Leave it be," Isha said. "I know what's in your heart, but your father, the Servitor, never will. Not from me."

His words allayed Serena's worries; nevertheless, she shook her head again and denied Isha's words. "There is nothing in my heart that is worthy of the Servitor's attention."

Isha scowled. "You take me for a fool?" A moment later he sighed. "So be it. We will pretend that what I sense is merely my imaginings. Now, tell me. What do you know of these friends of our *Mayna*, William Wilde?"

"I'm almost certain that Mr. Zeus and Jason are *asrasins*, both are magi, masters of the craft," Serena answered. "I'm not as sure about Daniel and his family, though."

"Why Mr. Zeus and Jason?" Isha asked.

"There was a quiet tension about Jason when I raised the notion of true magic once. His reaction was telling."

"What kind of reaction?"

"A quick intake of breath, a narrowing of his eyes, and tension in his shoulders. The kind that told me he knows magic is real," Serena answered. "Also, while his interest in Eastern martial arts isn't exceptional, his training with the longsword is an oddity. He has apparently mastered a dead European fighting style, one hardly known by anyone anymore."

"Except those who remember it as it was originally taught," Isha mused.

"And if Jason is an *asrasin*, it would logically follow that his grandfather must be one as well."

"You may be right," Isha said. He stroked his chin in thought.

"If you are, then you must be extremely cautious around those two. All of them really, including Daniel, Lien, and the rest of the Karllson family."

"When have I been anything less?"

"Do you truly wish an answer to that?" Isha asked. "Or do you not recall our earlier conversation about contentment? Or what your father would do if he knew."

Kohl Obsidian gradually woke and stared at the ceiling of his cave. He blinked. Stalactites, broken like his teeth, met his gaze, but no bats. They wisely avoided his cave. All animals did.

Kohl had been dreaming again. It had been so pleasant, a true memory.

A young *asrasin*, newly birthed to his power, had knelt helplessly before Kohl, begging for mercy. Kohl had pretended to consider it, and just as hope had bloomed on the youth's face, he had killed the *asrasin* and feasted upon his pure *lorethasra*.

It had been the last time he had tasted such a lush meal. In fact, he could count such occurrences on just one of his mangled, decaying hands, the one with four fingers.

But something insisted on breaking into his repetitive litany of desires. He sensed a tremor on the wind, a stirring of *lorasra* that drifted across the world, a current only a necrosed could feel. Something to do with the boy. He remained nothing more than a potential, but . . . Kohl tasted something about him, something unfelt until now.

Kohl frowned and focused on the boy. *What was it? What was different about him?* Kohl strained his senses, trying to piece together what he had felt.

Minutes passed before the answer came to him.

Carried along with the boy's scent, for a single, easily missed moment, came the rich aroma of uncorrupted *lorethasra*, mature and vibrant. He detected *asrasins* about the boy, *asrasins* who were alive and powerful.

Excitement built, and Kohl's decayed heart beat faster, circulating the pus-like fluid that was his life's blood, even as he struggled to hold onto caution. What he had briefly sensed had been as faint as a single flick from a dragonfly's wings, and it might still be nothing more than his imaginings.

With a soft hiss, Kohl straightened his stiff limbs and rose to his substantial height. The cave in which he nestled would have been considered large by most men, but the necrosed was no man. When he stood up, the cave seemed to shrink as Kohl's head brushed the ceiling, and he crawled out of his barrow, like a massive, deformed wolverine. Outside, he held still and inhaled the cold air, trying to recapture the scent that had awakened him.

His heart slowed to its regularly irregular, bradycardic tempo, and Kohl lifted his nose to the winter wind. He stood poised like that for hours. Snow dusted his head and shoulders, collecting at his feet, but Kohl remained unmoving.

There! He sensed it again, the pure, potent *lorethasra* of a mature *asrasin*.

Kohl's heart beat faster once again, and hunger thinned the gelatinous pus of his blood. His thoughts, as sluggish as the rhythm of his heart, grew crisper and colder, more certain. As the fog cleared from his mind, his hunger, easily unheeded when he slept, grew more difficult to overlook.

He had to feed, and if the sensations carried upon the *lorasra* were true, he soon would. The scents of *asrasins,* many *asrasins*, had been wrapped up in the feeling of the boy. Enough for Kohl to feast as no necrosed had in thousands of years. Possibly even enough to challenge Sapient Dormant for leadership of their kind.

A tingle of pleasure sparked along Kohl's pustulant heart.

He would soon collect the boy, and it would be good.

A realization came to Kohl, one that took away his budding pleasure. He was weak. He wasn't prepared to defeat so many *asrasins*. They would overcome him in his present condition.

His thoughts turned inward. Kohl needed to wait. He needed to ready himself with proper rest. He needed the dreamless state, the deepest sleep a necrosed could achieve. It was always a risky proposition. The dreamless state would leave him vulnerable, but it was a risk worth taking.

The boy and those *asrasins* with him would make it so.

CHAPTER 11: THANKSGIVING TRUTHS

November 1986

The football season ended late for St. Francis because after defeating Archbishop Roman on Halloween, they advanced to the playoffs. Two more grinding wins led them to the state championship game against St. Loyola, Cleveland's powerhouse city champion. St. Francis won in a blowout, the school's first state football championship.

The Monday following the state title victory, a school-wide assembly acknowledged the football team's success and prepared for the upcoming Thanksgiving holiday.

For most folks it was a time of celebration, but for William, the holidays remained a time of melancholy. He missed his family, especially now around Thanksgiving, his favorite time of the year. There wouldn't be any gathering in the kitchen in the morning, all of them cooking together, talking, laughing, and sharing in the feast. There would be no watching football in the afternoon while Mom read a book. There would be none of the joy of simply being together.

And with football season finished and no other worries to occupy his mind, his family's absence ached like a wound. William tried to console himself that maybe the holidays wouldn't always be like this, that maybe with new memories and the passage of time it would eventually get better.

But that time had yet to come.

With those doleful thoughts in mind, William attended Thanksgiving dinner, along with Jason and Mr. Zeus, at the Karllsons' home. Their food and company proved to be exactly what William had needed.

He found a way to laugh and temporarily put aside his sorrow.

The only problem was that he ate too much. After the feast, he could barely manage a waddle, stuffed like the Thanksgiving turkey he'd helped consume.

"Do you think you can make your way home?" Mr. Zeus asked him with an amused twinkle in his eyes. "There's something I want to talk to you about."

William groaned. "Now? I thought we were going to see the new *Star Trek* today."

"Another nerdboy film?" Lien asked.

"You say it like that, but we both know you want to see it, too," William said.

"Aren't there whales or something in it?" Daniel asked.

"It won't take long," Mr. Zeus said with a flash of annoyance. "You can see the movie later."

William sighed. "Yes, sir." He levered himself to his feet.

Jason already waited by the front door. The three of them said their 'good byes' and 'thank yous' to the Karllsons and headed back to their own place.

"What did you want to talk about?" William asked after they settled into the family room of their home. Jason and Mr. Zeus both wore uncharacteristically serious expressions, and unease wormed across William's mind. "What's wrong?"

"Nothing is wrong," Mr. Zeus answered. "But it's time you learned the truth about who you really are, and who *we* are."

William flicked an uncertain glance between Mr. Zeus and Jason. "What's this about?"

"I don't mean to sound so ominous," Mr. Zeus said with a rueful smile. "But what I'm about to tell you will tax your trust in us." He cleared his throat. "Let me start at the beginning.

"Jason and I are not from Louisiana, as we originally told you. Well, Jason is, but our true home is an island called Arylyn. It's a secret place, hidden away in the South Pacific, and not recorded on any map you've ever seen. It is an island of magicians. Magi, or more generally, *asrasins,* is what we call ourselves."

William barked a laugh and waited for the punchline.

None came. Mr. Zeus and Jason didn't crack a smile. Their faces remained somber.

William's laugh trailed away. "Wait. This is just a joke, right? You guys aren't serious?"

Mr. Zeus shook his head. "This isn't a joke, and we are serious. Maybe it would be easier if you saw what we mean."

Jason fetched five butter knives from the kitchen. "Watch." He began juggling the knives, and they arched through the air. But not once did Jason touch them. The knives moved in slow and sedate arcs, supported by nothing but air. They came to a halt, shifting about until they formed a perfect circle in midair. Then they stopped moving.

William's mouth dropped open. *What the hell?* He blinked his eyes, rubbed at them, but the unmoving, unsupported knives mocked his attempts at rational thought. *Impossible. It made no sense.* William wanted time to rewind so he could figure out what Jason had done.

"It's a trick, right?" William asked, glancing between Mr. Zeus and Jason. "Some kind of illusion."

"No trick. No illusion," Mr. Zeus said. "It is true magic. *Asra*, we call it. The Beautiful Art." He held out his right hand, and a marble-sized ball of fire slowly formed on his palm, neon-purple with small streaks of crackling, white lightning. He transferred it to his left hand and rolled it along the back of his knuckles.

A flick of Mr. Zeus' wrist, and the ball flew to William. It orbited him, radiating heat like a miniature furnace. Then it dashed off, flitting through the room and lighting all the candles before popping out of existence in a puff of smoke. With its disappearance, a lavender scent filled the room.

William realized his mouth had fallen open again, and he shut it. Mr. Zeus and Jason had his undivided attention.

"We show this to you because when we came to Cincinnati it was for one reason and one reason only. You."

William's heart beat as fast as a rabbit's, cornered by a wolf. "Me?" His mouth was dry, and the word came out as a squeak.

"You," Mr. Zeus affirmed. "Those born on our island, Arylyn, are all magi, and those born in the Far Abroad, the rest of the world, are not. *Lorethasra* does not usually course through the ley lines of their lives, but sometimes it can and sometimes it does."

William recognized most of the words Mr. Zeus used, but taken together they sounded meaningless. *Lorethasra? Ley lines?*

What was Mr. Zeus talking about? William struggled to make his mind work, to bring order to a suddenly disordered world, but it was hard to think with so many random questions flooding his thoughts. Of course, Jason's floating butter knives made it that much harder.

"At its most basic," Mr. Zeus explained, "there is *lorethasra*, the inner magic, what's inside a person, and *lorasra*, the outer magic, what's inside a place, like a field or an island. The inner magic cannot survive without the outer, and in such a situation the magus dies."

William finally got his mind moving. "Cincinnati has enough of this outer magic?"

Jason chuckled. "Cincy is a great town, but no, it doesn't have enough outer magic. There's one place here that has some of it, but it isn't enough for what we need. Thousands of years ago it was different. Places with *lorasra*, the outer magic, we call them *saha'asras*, were all over the place, but not anymore. Now they're rare."

"Why?"

"An explanation for another time," Mr. Zeus said. "Let's return to why we're telling you this in the first place.

"We came to Cincinnati because you are one of those rare individuals who, should you be exposed to a *saha'asra*, your *lorethasra*—your inner magic—will kindle to life. Your priming."

Surreal didn't begin to describe how this Thanksgiving had ended up, and William shook his head in disbelief. "If I go to some place that has this outer magic, my *lorethasra*," he stumbled over the unfamiliar word, "will change or something?"

"Exactly," Mr. Zeus said with a nod. "Your *lorethasra* will come to life, and you will become a magus."

William kept thinking he'd wake up, that all this would turn out to be a very vivid, eating-too-much-Thanksgiving turkey-induced dream. But nothing changed. Mr. Zeus and Jason continued to wear solemn expressions as they stared at him.

"But it comes with a price," Mr. Zeus continued. "Once your *lorethasra* comes to life, you can only ever live in a *saha'asra*. If you go too long without the outer magic, you will die.

"As far as we know, there are only two such *saha'asras* on Earth that can support our kind," Mr. Zeus continued. "Arylyn is one. The other is a place called Sinskrill. It is the home of humanity's mortal enemies."

Mortal enemies? A fog blanketed William's thoughts. He nodded stupidly, but he knew a million questions would come as soon as the shock of all this wore off.

"Those of Sinskrill are jealous, cruel, and vindictive," Mr. Zeus said. "Think of goblins and orcs from *Lord of the Rings*, and you will understand the kind of people who call Sinskrill home."

Understand? William wanted to laugh at such an absurdity. He remained as far from understanding Mr. Zeus' story as an ant might understand the sun.

"It's a lot to take in, isn't it?" Jason asked.

"You think?" William scoffed. "You're telling me magic is real. I have it, and if I want to stay alive I have to go to some place that no one's ever seen because of something I've never heard of." His eyes narrowed, and his slumbering anger stirred. "If all that's true, then how do the two of you get by?"

"We have a way, but it isn't easy." Mr. Zeus grimaced. "Our lives here are pale shadows of what we experience on Arylyn. Here we always feel less than we should, a little slower, weaker, and duller. It is unpleasant. You would understand what we mean should you decide to trust us and choose what we offer."

"Trust you?" William's anger burned hotter. "The two of you have been lying to me for two years, and you think I should trust you? Give me one reason why!"

"We've had reasons for our secrets," Mr. Zeus answered.

"We would have told you the truth a long time ago, but then your family . . ." Jason said.

His words did little to mollify William's growing outrage.

"We truly would have spoken earlier, but we needed to get to know you," Mr. Zeus said. "We needed to learn if you were worthy of a magus's power. By the time we determined that you were, your family had tragically died and you were in no position to hear us out. I'm sorry we had to hide this from you. Believe me, we would have spoken to you sooner if we could have."

William's anger simmered down some, but his sense of betrayal lingered.

"Listen. We don't want or need anything from you," Mr. Zeus said. "But we can offer you so much, something of which many dream but only a rare few are fortunate enough to receive. We offer you magic. Can you conceive it? All you have to do is come camping with us over the Christmas holidays. It'll be to the state park in West Virginia, as we said. It's near a *saha'asra*, a place of *lorasra*. We can protect you so your *lorethasra* will not fully come to life, but you'll get to experience a taste of what it means to be a magus."

William's anger calmed enough for him to think again. "Why can't we just go to this place Jason said was here in Cincinnati?"

"We need privacy," Mr. Zeus explained. "In addition, the *saha'asra* in Cincinnati is too frail for our purposes."

"If I go to this place in West Virginia, I get to do magic?"

"No. You'll learn what it's like to be a magus," Jason answered.

"Remember the cost, though," Mr. Zeus said. "If you become one of us there is no going back. The rest of the world becomes poisonous to you. You will be trapped on an island with few opportunities to leave."

"But I get to do this whole magic thing?" William persisted.

"*Asra*," Mr. Zeus corrected.

"*Asra*. Whatever," William said. "Why can't I just live here and do what you and Jason do? You guys aren't trapped."

"It isn't as easy as that," Mr. Zeus said. "Once you experience Arylyn, life everywhere else will seem like a pale shadow. Additionally, if you're *lorethasra* doesn't allow your survival in the Far Abroad, you will never again see the rest of your family."

His words struck like a splash of ice water. To also lose his aunts, uncles, and cousins would be hard to accept.

"How did you know about me?" William finally asked.

"It's different for everyone," Mr. Zeus said, "but when someone with the potential to become a magus reaches a certain age we can feel it. It ripples through all the *saha'asras* scattered throughout the world, but the disturbance is softer than a feather falling on a lake."

"The truth is, it was blind luck that we found you," Jason said. "Most people with the potential for *lorethasra* are never discovered. In your case, Lien happened to be interested in this city and felt—"

"Lien's a magus?"

"So is Daniel and the rest of his family," Jason said. "But Lien is like me and you. She was born in the Far Abroad and came to Arylyn when it was her time."

"Then why is she here in Cincinnati?"

"She's from Liuzhou, Cincinnati's sister city in China, and she wanted to see more of the world," Jason replied. "She thought Cincinnati would be a fun place to visit."

A niggling suspicion wormed its way to the surface of William's thoughts, and his distrust flared again. "You all came here because of me," he said. "Does that also mean that you're only friends with me because of this potential I have?"

"No," Jason answered immediately. "We did come here because of you. That part's true. But we're friends because we like you. You can be mad at me for lying to you, but our friendship has always been real. It's got nothing to do with what you might one day be able to do."

William studied him, and Jason stared back wearing the guileless appearance of a true friend. But that friend had also been lying to him for two years. It wasn't something William could just blink away and forget.

"I'll go camping with you," William finally replied. "I'll listen to what else you have to say. But what about Serena? I invited her, too. I can't uninvite her."

Jason grimaced. "I still wish you hadn't done that," he said.

"I wish you hadn't lied to me."

"We'll take care of Serena," Mr. Zeus said. "We're magi. We have ways to keep her unaware of what we're doing."

CHAPTER 12: FORGIVENESS

"Where's everyone else?" Serena asked.

William shrugged.

They stood in line at the movie theater. Misty rain fell, and headlight beams glowed off oil-slick pavement. The smell of popcorn wafted through the air and mixed with exhaust fumes as parents dropped teenagers off in front of the theater.

"I thought it could be just you and me," William said.

"For *Star Trek*?" Serena asked. "I thought Jason and Daniel wanted to see it, too."

"They do, but they wanted to go some other time," William said. It was the truth, but not the entire truth.

"What happened?" Serena asked. She held his eyes with her disconcerting gaze.

"What do you mean?" William tried not to fidget.

"I mean, what's the real reason we're seeing *Star Trek* without the others? There has to be something else. You're upset. What's wrong?"

William scowled. The pain of betrayal remained a deep cut. How could Jason, Mr. Zeus, and the Karllsons have lied to him like they had? Who were they really, and how could he ever trust them again?

In that moment, had he been able, William might have told Serena all about Arylyn, magic, and magi, but the uneasy sensation that kept him from thinking of her as anything more than a friend also warned him to stay silent about this. Best to keep it secret.

Besides which, he wasn't able to tell her even if he wanted to. He couldn't. Another of Mr. Zeus' betrayals. Jason's grandfather had done something to him, used his magic and made it so William was physically incapable of communicating what he'd learned about Arylyn and magic. No writing, speaking, or even miming what he knew. A collar was what Mr. Zeus had called it.

The notion that control of his body had been stripped away caused William's anger to surge like a tide beneath a vast, black moon.

"That bad?" Serena guessed. She offered him a tight-lipped expression of sympathy.

"That bad," William admitted. "I . . ." For a moment, he couldn't think or speak clearly. A red haze of fury trapped his mind, but with a shudder, he managed to push it to the back of his thoughts. Rather than raging like lava down a mountain, it only bubbled like a pot on boil.

"William?" Serena frowned in concern.

"Jason and I got into a pretty big argument yesterday."

"What happened?"

"He lied to me, and I'm trying to figure out some stuff about us."

"Was it really that serious?"

"You have no idea," William said.

"Maybe I don't, but I know this much: you and Jason, I've never seen two people who are friends like you two are. You love each other."

William snorted.

"It's true, whether you want to admit it or not," Serena said. "The two of you have a special bond. I'm jealous. I wish I had someone in my life I could trust like that, someone who made me a better person the way Jason does for you. And if I did, not even death could tear us apart."

Yesterday William would have been in complete agreement with Serena. But now? Now he didn't know. "You don't understand."

"Maybe not, but ask yourself this: did the lie benefit Jason?"

William opened his mouth to answer but shut it when he took the time to consider her question. He knew the answer, and while the sense of betrayal remained, the last of his anger simmered down, returning to linger like it always did just beneath the surface.

"By the way, what happened to your face?" Serena pointed to William's swollen lip.

"Oh, that." William gingerly touched his lip. "Jake."

Serena's eyes widened. "You fought? I thought the two of you had made peace with one another."

"Not exactly," William said. "We're not enemies any more, but we're not exactly friends." He shrugged. "But this . . ." he pointed to his lip, "had nothing to do with fighting. It was part of the end of season rituals that Coach Rasskins put us through. It's called an Oklahoma drill."

"What's that?"

William sighed. "Something stupid in football. Two guys line up and bash each other. It's like sumo wrestling. That's how me and Jake worked out our feud." He grimaced. "We bled all over each other, but he won."

"How was the movie?" Jason asked, standing in the doorway to William's bedroom.

"It was all right," William said. He sat at his desk with his feet propped up, and he didn't look up from the book he'd been reading: *The Stainless Steel Rat.* He'd thought a lot about what Serena had said before the movie, about his friendship with Jason, and how Jason made him a better person.

It was all true.

In all their time together, Jason had been the truest friend William could have ever hoped to have. Yes, he and Mr. Zeus had lied, but they had their reasons—good reasons—and maybe it was time for William to tell them so. He could start by apologizing to Jason for the way he'd been behaving.

But William had never been good at it. His eyes scanned the same words on the page and his thoughts swirled while he tried to muster up the courage to say sorry.

Jason remained at the doorway. "You still mad?" he asked.

William looked away from his book and exhaled heavily. "No. But I said some things, and I need to tell you how sorry I am about it. You didn't deserve how I treated you."

"Don't worry about it," Jason said. "It's done."

William looked up, hope rising. “You sure?”

“I’m sure. You should be pissed off at us.”

“Yeah. I guess, but . . .” William shrugged. “You know.”

“I know. Don’t worry about it.”

William chanced a smile. “We’re good, then?”

“Always,” Jason replied.

William smiled more broadly. “In that case, the new *Star Trek* movie *is* about whales.”

Jason blinked in apparent disbelief. “Seriously? Whales?”

“Whales. And hardly any Klingons.”

“What the hell! Whales and no Klingons?” Jason sputtered. “How stupid is that?”

CHAPTER 13: SEMESTER'S END

December 1986

The last day of school before Christmas break always felt like a Friday. This year it fell on a Thursday and was a short day, with Christmas Mass in the morning and no classes afterward. Throughout the service the auditorium sparked with an anticipatory buzz, and as soon as Mass ended all the students made a beeline for the exits.

William buzzed with as much anticipation as everyone else. Maybe more so. He'd spent most of his time since Thanksgiving thinking about what his future might hold, and during Mass, he almost vibrated in his chair with excitement.

Magic. Asra. It was like having an unasked-for dream made real. What would his parents and Landon have thought?

He figured they'd have been thrilled. All of them, even his mother, had been nerds of some sort, but what would they have wanted him to do? William wished they were still around to tell him, or at least to share in the joy of knowing that magic was real.

Arylyn. A hidden island of magi.

What Mr. Zeus had described sounded so impossible, and early on there had been times when William had doubted all of it, but those doubts hadn't lasted long. Mostly because he saw Jason and Mr. Zeus use magic on a daily basis, things as simple as a pot of water freezing to ice over a hot stove, or a seed growing to a flowering plant in seconds.

And later today, they'd head out to the state park in West Virginia, for the *saha'asra*, the place of *asra*, and William would have his first glimpse of what it meant to be a magus.

He couldn't wait, and he grinned in excitement, not caring that it made him look like a slack-jawed yokel.

Mass finally ended, and the auditorium emptied. The hallways quickly crowded as an infectious joy filled St. Francis. Students stood about and talked, most of them laughing and calling out to one another. Some discussed vacation plans for the holiday. Others talked about getting together during the break. And everyone smiled in relief at the notion of no school for the next two weeks.

"What's got you so excited?" Serena asked at their lockers. "You've been smiling all morning."

"Christmas holidays," William said. "Same as everyone. No school. Camping." He managed to fake a smile past his guilt at lying to her, even if the lie was one of omission.

"Don't tell me you're actually excited about camping out in the cold," Serena said. "I don't think it sounds all that much fun."

William glanced at her in surprise. "You're not coming?"

"I'm coming, but I'm bringing a kerosene heater. My California blood's too thin to go camping out in the freezing cold in the middle of nowhere."

"Well, lucky for you, we won't be camping in the middle of

nowhere," Jason said. He came up in between them and threw an arm around their shoulders as they left the school and entered the parking lot. "We're staying in a lodge in the middle of nowhere. Big difference."

"Seriously?" Serena asked with a hopeful expression.

Jason nodded. "Seriously. It's got a kitchen, electricity, plumbing, all the modern conveniences a wimpy Californian could ask for."

Serena punched him playfully in the shoulder.

"Punch him harder," Lien advised as they approached the T-Bird. "He deserves it."

Daniel stood with her. "Took you long enough," he complained.

"You can always walk," Jason noted.

"Shut up, and let's get going. It's cold," Daniel said.

"What are your parents doing over the holidays?" Serena asked Daniel.

"Vacationing in Key West," Daniel said. "They started kissing when they said that, and the way they looked at each other . . ." He gave a shiver of revulsion. "Gross."

William shared Daniel's disgust. *Parents shouldn't do stuff like that.*

After an early lunch, everyone stacked their gear into Mr. Zeus' old International Harvester Scout. It was the only vehicle big enough to hold all of them and their luggage. Otherwise they would have needed two cars.

“How long do you think we’re going to be gone?” William complained as he piled Lien’s overstuffed suitcase onto the roof rack.

“You never know,” Lien answered.

“And you really need all of this shi . . . stuff?”

“Just put it away,” Lien ordered in a haughty tone.

William muttered under his breath but did as he was told. “All done," he said as he tied down the last strap.

He climbed into the Scout, stuffing himself into the undersized third row next to Serena. It barely had enough room for both of them. Mr. Zeus and Jason sat up front, while Daniel and Lien occupied the middle row.

Mr. Zeus cranked up the engine, and the Scout rumbled to life. He slowly backed out of the driveway, and they were off.

A glorious energy trembled in the air, different than back at school; a sensation similar to when William and his family had driven out west to visit the Grand Canyon, or when he’d seen *Star Wars* for the first time. But this time it felt so much more potent. The greatest adventure William might ever take awaited, and he almost expected fireworks and fanfare to buoy them along their travels, something majestic to mark the moment.

Of course, there were no such spectacular events, and he had to resign himself to imagining them.

“You still excited?” Serena asked with a teasing grin.

William shook off his thoughts and returned his attention to the here and now. “Is it that obvious?”

“I don’t know. Maybe it’s that empty-headed smile you’ve worn all day.”

"It's not that bad," William said.

"Sure, it is. The lights are on, but the house is empty."

"I wonder how hard it'll be for you to stack your luggage on the way back."

Serena wore an unrepentant grin. "Not hard. I'll just ask Jason or Daniel to do it."

"Just make sure to ask them nicely," William advised. "They're not nearly as kind as me."

"Probably not."

"What's your father going to do while you're gone?"

Serena shrugged. "Work, I guess. He says he has a lot to do before Christmas. Bunch of customers needing last-minute orders filled."

"Yuck. Sounds like we'll be having way more fun."

"Probably, but he'll be fine. He likes what he does."

"My parents were like that, too. Same with Landon. He was the scholar in the family." William frowned. He shouldn't have brought up his family. Most times, doing so didn't bother him so much any more, but sometimes, like now, talking about his parents and his brother triggered melancholy.

His excitement ebbed.

Serena noticed. "Still hard, isn't it? Thinking about your family. This is your first Christmas without them."

"It's not easy," William admitted.

They fell into silence, and William continued to stare out the window, not really seeing or thinking about anything, until he turned to Serena. "You never told me why you decided to come with us," he said. "I mean, you thought we'd be freezing and uncomfortable, but you still wanted to come."

"Maybe I like the company," Serena answered. "Some of you guys tend to grow on a girl."

"Like a fungus?" Daniel suggested.

Lien smacked Daniel on the head.

"Ow!"

"Stop eavesdropping," Lien said. "It's rude."

"So is smacking someone on the head."

"You deserved it."

"Let me smack you on the head next time I think you're being rude," Daniel replied.

"Sorry," Lien said, not sounding the least bit apologetic.

Serena and William shared a smile.

"You know, I don't have cooties," Serena said after a moment of quiet.

William's brow furrowed in confusion.

"You're all squished up on the other side of the seat," she explained.

She was right. He was cramped into the corner of the back bench.

William straightened, but when he did, his leg touched Serena's for most of the length of their thighs.

He shifted to pull away, but Serena reached out and held his knee in place. "I won't bite," she whispered so only he could hear. "Unless you want me to."

William tried not to gape. *Had she really said that?* That was as explicit an offer as he would likely ever hear in his entire life, and yet William felt . . . nothing. He searched his heart, trying to figure out what was wrong with him. *How could he not be crazy about Serena? It was that stupid sense of . . . whatever it was.*

As William silently berated himself, he realized the silence between them had lasted too long. He had to say something. "No biting. Kissing is a lot nicer."

Now why the hell had he said that?

Serena noticed none of his anxiety, and she grinned. "That can be arranged."

CHAPTER 14:
THE SAHA'ASRA

The drive to the state park wended through the hill country of southeastern Ohio and West Virginia. The road they followed twisted and turned through long valleys with fallow fields, and steep inclines of forested foothills, gray-brown and bare, that would eventually transition into the Appalachians.

Eventually, they left the highways behind and traveled ever-smaller country lanes. Mr. Zeus took a final turnoff from one such road, and they drove along a gravel driveway. The Scout's tires crunched as they journeyed through a dense, copse of trees. Half a mile later, the driveway reached a dead-end, and Mr. Zeus killed the engine.

Full dark reigned, and the only light came from the moon, the stars, and the lit windows from a few nearby cabins.

William stepped out of the Scout and arched into a back-cracking stretch before taking in his surroundings.

A handful of rustic lodges clustered along the northern edge of a small meadow. They pressed like a peninsula into the surrounding woods. Warm light spilled out of their windows, and the smell of wood smoke scented the air. The world lay quiet as a cold wind caused William's breath to mist.

"Move," Serena said.

William stepped out of her way, and helped Jason and Daniel unload the Scout. After everyone had their belongings, they followed Mr. Zeus to their cabin, a simple log home nestled amongst several tall pine trees, with a stream gurgling in the back, and a wide front porch overlooking the meadow.

"Where's the blasted key?" Mr. Zeus grumbled as he fumbled about in his pockets. A moment later he gave a satisfied grunt, threw open the door, and stepped inside to turn on the lights.

The others pushed in after him.

An open space took up the front room of the cabin and included a kitchen, dining table, and a seating area with a sofa facing a fireplace.

"Not bad," Serena said.

"A lot better than a tent, eh?" Jason asked.

William tested the kitchen faucet. The pipes sputtered, and orange water poured out for a few seconds before running clear. "A *lot* better," he agreed. He explored deeper into the home.

A small bathroom and two bedrooms, each with a pair of twin beds, filled out the rear of the place.

"Who gets the beds?" Daniel asked.

William tossed his bag on one. "Mine."

"I got the other one," Daniel said.

Serena and Lien claimed the other room.

"Where do I sleep?" Jason asked as he walked in.

"Sofa city, sweetheart." William gave a cheesy grin and snapped his fingers.

"No you don't," Mr. Zeus called from the front of the cabin. "You get the floor. The sofa belongs to me."

Jason stalked off, grumbling under his breath.

"We'll take a more thorough tour of the environs tomorrow morning," Mr. Zeus said. He gave William a meaningful glance. "Let's settle in and have some dinner."

"As long as I don't have to cook," Jason said. "If I have to sleep on the floor, I should get out of having to cook."

"More like we should get out of having to eat your cooking," William replied.

Mr. Zeus ended up mixing some frozen corn and okra he'd brought along with fresh vegetables, sausage, chicken, rice, and spices into a jambalaya. Afterward, a stuffed Serena, Daniel, and Lien decided to call it an early night.

William was about to follow suit, but Mr. Zeus called him back. "We need to talk. There are further truths we need to discuss, but before we do, how are you feeling?"

"Fine. Same as always," William answered. "But didn't you say I'd feel different in a *saha'asra*?"

"You will," Mr. Zeus said. "You haven't actually entered a *saha'asra*, though." He gestured outside. "It's the meadow. That's the *saha'asra*. But even there, you'll only experience a shadow of what you would on Arylyn."

"Why's that?" William asked.

"You're wearing a *nomasra*, a device that can do many things. For us," he pointed to Jason, "it can hold enough *lorasra* to keep us alive in the Far Abroad. For you, the one I gave you, suppresses your *lorethasra* so it won't awaken when you walk into the meadow."

Irritation riled William. He was tired of all the secrets, the choices made on his behalf and without his consent. “What’s this magic thing I’m supposed to be wearing?” he asked.

Mr. Zeus pointed. “The pendant on your chain. It’s the *nomasra*.”

William fingered the locket, staring at it for a moment. “Any other secrets you want to tell me?” he asked Mr. Zeus, not bothering to hide the annoyance in his voice.

“You’ll learn what you need to when you need to,” Mr. Zeus said, which wasn’t much of an answer in William’s estimation. “As for the locket, it’s best that you never take it off until you’re absolutely sure you want to become a magus.”

“I thought I was sure,” William said with a scowl, “but if it means lying to everyone and hiding who I am, then maybe this isn’t for me.”

Jason sighed. “I thought we already went over that. We would have told you everything sooner, but the timing never worked out.”

William glared at the two of them. “I thought the pendant was a thoughtful gift. I loved it for that.” He knew his tone sounded petulant.

“Are you sure that’s the only reason you’re angry with us?” Mr. Zeus asked. “There isn’t someone else who stirs your passion? A beautiful, young woman perhaps?”

“Serena has nothing to do with this. It’s about what I said before: secrets, lies, and manipulation.”

“I understand why you’re upset,” Mr. Zeus said, “and I can only apologize again for what we’ve kept from you, for what you feel that we’ve tricked you into doing. If you decide other than what we hope, then so be it.” He paused. “But please don’t make your decision now while you're angry. Give yourself time to consider your choices. Go over them carefully, deliberately. There is no reason to decide today, or even tomorrow or any time during the Christmas holidays. And talk to Serena. Make sure you know where you stand with her."

Some of William's anger ebbed away. "Yes, sir."

The next morning dawned cloudy and gloomy, a typical Appalachian winter's day. A wicked wind gusted, and the remnants of an early snowfall littered the ground. The smell of wood smoke rose from some of the other cabins.

"Who's ready for a hike?" Mr. Zeus asked after breakfast.

Jason, Daniel, and Lien quickly agreed, but Serena said she wanted to read. William glanced her way, wondering if she wanted to be alone, but she winked at him.

He got the hint but hesitated. *Did he really want what she so strongly said she did? Maybe not, but he did need to talk to her about where they stood.* "I think I'll stay behind and read, too," he finally said, glancing at Mr. Zeus and offering him a barely discernable nod.

None of the others noticed.

Jason rolled his eyes. "Right. You're going to read."

"Is that what they call it," Lien muttered.

"*Fellowship* for the umpteenth time, right?" Daniel guessed. "By the way, did you ever learn to speak Elvish?"

"*Pedin edhellen*," William answered.

Daniel rolled his eyes. "Dork."

"I'm waiting," Mr. Zeus shouted from the front porch.

Jason, Lien, and Daniel shuffled out. After they left, William went to his backpack and drew forth his battered copy of *Fellowship of the Ring.*

Serena rose from her seat on the sofa and approached him. "Were you really planning on reading?"

His heart beat faster. "Serena, look . . ."

She silenced him with a kiss. Her fingers laced behind his head. Her lips were soft and warm. The scent of the apple she'd had for breakfast lay on her breath, and the kiss lingered.

Based on his limited experience, William figured it was a good kiss, but nevertheless, it left him disappointed. He found little passion or desire in it. Again rang that warning signal, that lack of trust, and he pulled away, unable to meet her eyes.

"You like me as a friend but not as anything more," Serena said. Her voice was frank and held no hint of anger.

William's head snapped up to meet her matter-of-fact gaze. "I don't know what's wrong with me. I should feel more. But, yeah."

Serena shook her head. "It's fine. Don't worry about it."

"But the kiss—"

"The kiss was nice," she said, "but you aren't the only one who's been wondering why you don't feel more than you do. The kiss . . . was a test. I guess for me just as much for you."

"You, too?"

"Yeah. Me, too," she replied. "Look. I like you. You're smart. You're nice. You smell good. But ever since I met you I've been trying to figure out why I don't think of you as anything more than a friend. I've wanted to, but I don't."

Burgeoning relief swept through William. "Then you're not mad?"

Serena chuckled. "No. Are you?"

"No." He smiled in relief. "Then we're good."

"We're good." Serena stepped away from him. "I think the others had the right idea, though. Why don't we go for a walk and clear our heads."

"Yeah. I'd like that."

"Any place you want to go?"

"Let's go where our feet take us," William suggested.

They laced up their hiking boots and stepped outside. On an impulse, William grabbed the keys to the Scout. "Wouldn't want anyone stealing our ride," he joked.

"Lead the way," Serena said as they stepped off the porch.

The wind had died down, but the weather remained cold, and William slapped on his gloves.

"Wimp," Serena said.

William shrugged. He didn't like the cold.

They headed down a well-marked dirt path leading into the woods from directly behind their cabin.

"This way," William said.

The trail they followed rose into the nearby hills before slowly descending into a narrow valley. It paralleled the course of a tumbling stream that emptied into a small pond. There they came upon a red fox. William couldn't tell who was more surprised, Serena or the fox.

"Shit!" Serena exclaimed as she came to a lurching halt.

The red-furred fox took one startled glance at Serena before darting off into the underbrush.

Serena clung close to William. “You think there are any other animals out here?” she asked, sounding worried.

“Nothing that can hurt us,” William replied. “No wolves or anything. Maybe some coyotes, but the bears should be hibernating.”

Nonetheless, he picked up a stout stick and swung it experimentally a few times before giving a grunt of satisfaction. *Better safe than sorry.*

Serena found one as well and they pressed on, following the meandering trail with staffs in hand. They bypassed a fork that seemed to lead deeper into the woods, and took the one that ascended out of the valley. Serena cast occasional nervous glances at the surrounding forest, but they came across no more wildlife.

“I could use a drink,” Serena said as they crested a final rise and reached the end of the trail.

They stood on the far side of the meadow from their cabin, and Serena took William’s hand, tugging him forward. She led him toward the meadow, the shortest course back to their lodge.

William hesitated. The meadow contained the *saha’asra*, and it would change him if he set foot in it. Then again, he had the locket to keep him safe, and he mentally shrugged before following after Serena.

The field lay barren, its wildflowers wilted with bent, brown stems. A solitary oak soared up and out from the center of the meadow and stood silent sentinel. The tree’s bare, brown branches rattled in a stiff wind beneath a gloomy sky.

William stepped into the meadow . . .

The field came to life as the clouds seemed to part and warm, golden sunlight poured down, flavored with a taste of dandelions in summer. Birdsong carried the promise of a day as sweet as lemonade, and green, vibrant leaves filled out the oak. Butterflies flitted about with neon-bright colors, and the sweet fragrance of honeysuckle in bloom suffused the air. All of the sensations were an imperfect echo of a singing light that called from faraway, but was as near as William's truest desire.

The meadow. This was the touch of a *saha'asra.*

William spun around in a full circle with his arms held out, and laughed, a deep, belly-laugh that rose from his heart and his soul. He hadn't laughed so truly, so purely, so fully in his entire life.

"What is it?" Serena asked.

William laughed again. There was nothing he could say or do to explain what he felt. He took Serena into his arms. She squealed when he spun her about in a circle.

Serena likely thought him mad, but he didn't care. When he looked at her, a silver halo surrounded her and her raven hair winged about, floating as if buoyed by water. The ringing of bells seemed to jingle from her lovely lips when she laughed.

How could he have not desired a woman so beautiful?

"William Wilde," she said, sounding breathless when he put her down, "what has gotten into you?"

He silenced her with a kiss. A spell had captured him. He wanted to stay in this perfect place forever. He wanted to drown in this moment, to make time stand still.

A bellow rose from the nearby forest. Deep-throated and powerful, the roar captured the tenor of a bell tolling doom.

Serena broke from William and her head swiveled to the woods. Her face held utmost horror. "Lord save us," she whispered.

"Run!" Mr. Zeus came tumbling out of the trees near where William and Serena had just exited. On his heels sprinted Daniel, Jason, and Lien, all clearly terrified. They tumbled onto the far side of the meadow, beyond the oak. "Run!" Mr. Zeus repeated. He appeared to throw something into the air. A golden nimbus extended along the perimeter of the meadow. "It won't hold him for long."

William stared about in confusion and fear. "What the hell's going on?"

"I have it," Mr. Zeus said. A doorway opening onto a bridge that seemed to disappear into infinity split the air before him. It swirled with all the colors of a rainbow. "Tether to it," he instructed Jason, Daniel, and Lien. "I'll bring William and Serena."

Another bellow came from the woods, this time much closer. From the edge of the forest, trees swayed. Something big lumbered swiftly through the brush.

William didn't wait to see what would emerge. Mr. Zeus and his rainbow bridge, or whatever it was, were too far away. The cabin was closer. William grabbed Serena's hand and raced toward the lodge.

They'd only taken three steps, running just past the edge of the meadow, when Serena pulled him to a halt. "The cabin won't stop whatever that is," she shouted.

"No! Come back! This way!" Mr. Zeus called. "Hurry!"

Something crashed out of the trees. William caught an impression of massive size, seven feet tall or more. Gigantic with misshapen features.

"I have you now, boy," the thing growled, staring hungrily at

William. "I'll feast upon you like I feasted upon your family."

William's heart skipped. Inchoate questions rambled through his mind.

"Hurry!" Mr. Zeus urged again.

Daniel and Lien leapt upon the rainbow bridge and disappeared with a stretching, snapping image.

William glanced back at the creature. It barreled toward him. *No more time for questions.* William and Serena raced toward Mr. Zeus.

The creature, the monster, whatever it was, rumbled toward them, charging faster than anything that size should have been capable, faster than any person could. It smashed into the golden nimbus. The impact sounded like a window shattering. The beast flew backward, careening through the air before smashing into a tree and thudding to the ground. It quickly regained its feet.

The golden nimbus had been thick as honey, but now it appeared pale and washed away.

The creature laughed. "Your pitiful shield will not avail you." It charged again.

William and Serena were yards away from Mr. Zeus when the creature smashed once more into the golden nimbus. This time the barrier tore apart like a spider web and dissipated into the winter air.

"Down!" Mr. Zeus cried.

William and Serena ducked.

A crackle of lightning sizzled across the distance from Mr. Zeus' hands, lashing the monster.

It screamed, a sound like tortured metal, but once more came horrid laughter. "Little *asrasin.* Your lightning feeds us. It doesn't rend our being. For my kind, only blood washes away blood.

The lightning faded. In its place came a gale. The creature nimbly side-stepped Mr. Zeus' attack.

William placed himself in front of Serena. The creature loomed only a few yards away.

It sneered at them. "You've yet to ignite your *lorethasra.*" It sounded disappointed. "No matter. These other *asrasins* will do nicely in your place." It lunged, moving too fast to dodge, and grabbed William by the throat.

When its hand contacted William's chain, the creature screamed, as if from deep pain.

William cried out, too. His skin beneath the necklace burned as if on fire. Wetness seeped down his shirt. *Blood.*

The beast snarled. A hard shove sent William tumbling through the air. His chain snapped, and he lost all sense of direction, until he crashed into Mr. Zeus.

William rolled off the old man and leapt up with a groan. His locket lay at his feet, and unthinking, he stuffed it into his pants pocket.

Jason raced toward the creature. From his hands burst a blaze of white-hot fire. William felt the heat all the way to where he stood. It would have set the creature alight, but no matter how quickly Jason cast his fire, the creature moved quicker. It evaded his attack and circled closer.

"There's no time to tether you," Mr. Zeus said, his voice slurring. "I'll hold him off." He stumbled to his feet, almost falling over again.

William wasn't listening. Serena stood there, past the oak. Her face was set, as if she intended on attacking the creature herself. William ran to her side, unsure what he could do.

"Grandfather! Go!" Jason shouted.

Serena cried out and fell away from the monster. A line of blood trickled down her arm.

William shot a quick look back. The rainbow bridge flickered.

"You have to," Jason continued. "The necrosed can't cross the bridge."

"No!"

"You must. It can't get to Arylyn."

William glanced at Mr. Zeus whose face clouded with indecision before firming into an expression of frustrated fury and sorrow. "You stay alive!" Mr. Zeus shouted to Jason. His voice throbbed with pain and passion. "No matter the cost, I will bring you home."

William reached Serena's side. The creature continued to dodge Jason's fire. William heard a high-pitched whine. Mr. Zeus and the rainbow bridge were gone.

"I'll split your bones and drink your marrow," the creature roared.

Jason's fire caught it full on its torso. It howled in anguish, stumbled, and fell flat, but managed to rise and dart away, too fast for Jason's fire to set it alight again, though it ran more slowly than before.

Jason shot another blaze at the monster. It dodged once, twice, three times. The fourth time, the flames blasted it head on.

The creature screamed, and this time it retreated.

"What the hell is that thing?" Serena sounded hysterical.

A gale from Jason's hands caught the creature flush and hurled it through the air. "Fire and wind won't hold it forever," Jason said. "We have to make a run for it."

"What about that bridge-thing Mr. Zeus made?" William asked.

"It'll take too long," Jason said.

"The Scout. I've got the keys," William shouted. "Follow me!" He led them in a flat-out sprint, keys out and ready.

Jason's fire roared like an open blast furnace, but William didn't dare look back. An instant later, the creature's scream rang out again.

Good!

"I'll kill you all," the monster cried out.

William unlocked the Scout, and all three of them tumbled into the vehicle. He gunned the engine and threw it into reverse.

"Go! Go! Go!" Jason shouted.

Through the windshield, William saw the creature. It had risen up and shambled toward them, gathering speed with every step.

William slammed the Scout into first gear. He hit the gas and spun the steering wheel. Tires squealed, and with a stutter the vehicle began to move.

Hurry up!

"It's coming!" Serena screamed.

William glanced in the rearview mirror. The creature filled it, gaining steadily. William cursed and pressed the gas pedal to the floor. He plowed through the gears as fast as he could.

A thump hit the Scout, and it shuddered and shook. The creature had slammed into the right rear-quarter panel, threatening to tip it over. The Scout tilted for a moment before banging back onto all four wheels. Miraculously, it remained pointed in the right direction.

The creature roared.

"He's still there!" Jason shouted.

William glanced in the rearview mirror again. The Scout was finally getting up to speed. The creature couldn't keep up. It dwindled in the distance, shaking an impotent fist at them before loping into the woods.

William breathed out a shuddering sigh of relief before punching the ceiling in triumph. "We did it!"

Serena and Jason shared in his joy. They laughed, delirious at their survival.

When their euphoria died down, Serena turned to face Jason. "You better tell me what's going on," she demanded. "What was that thing?"

William kept his eyes forward, concentrating on the road, but he listened to what Jason had to say.

"I don't know," Jason muttered. "I'm just glad we—"

The long, gravel driveway took a right hand turn just before it intersected the old, country road. A warning siren went off in William's mind.

"You know *exactly* what that thing was," Serena snapped. "Don't pretend you don't."

William noticed a disturbance in the trees. Something big was pushing through the forest. Something coming on fast, and headed toward the Scout. It would intersect them when they reached the right-hand turn.

Fear clambered at William's heart and his mouth went dry. "Hold on!" he shouted.

Serena faced forward and must have seen the disturbance moving toward them. "Oh no," she whispered.

William never let off the gas. The creature raced out of the woods to their right. It burst from the foliage, angling closer. Parallel to them. Massive and terrifying.

Time slowed.

The monster grinned.

William kept the pedal down. They hit the turn. The Scout wheel hopped. Tires squealed. The creature loomed closer and reached out. Closer.

CHAPTER 15: REVELATIONS

The Scout slipped, right wheels lifting. William's heart seized. They managed the turn, barely. Then all four tires were on the ground. The vehicle roared out onto the old country road, and they quickly outstripped the creature.

It bellowed and roared in frustrated fury. This time when William glanced in the rearview mirror, the creature simply stood staring after them.

"It'll be back," Jason muttered.

"Talk," Serena demanded of him.

Out of the corner of his eye William noticed that, for once, Jason was the focus of her intense gaze. The observation didn't bring him any relief. When she learned the truth, especially his part in it, she'd be pissed.

"What was that thing?" Serena asked.

William wanted to hear this as well. He glanced through the rearview mirror at Jason, who sat ashen-faced and quiet.

"It's called a necrosed," Jason said. "It's a creature of magic, dead and alive at the same time, and they kill. That's all they do.

There is no talking to them. No reasoning with them. No begging for mercy. We run if we ever see one."

"Exactly who is *we*?" Serena asked. "You and Mr. Zeus? How did you do that thing with the fire? And that bridge-thing Mr. Zeus created? Who *are* you?"

"They're magi," William answered. He glanced at Jason, surprised that he could talk about magic.

"I lifted Mr. Zeus' collar. You can tell Serena all you want about us," Jason said.

"You know about this?" Serena accused William. Now *he* was the focus of her intensity, and as he'd figured, she was angry at him.

"I only learned a few weeks ago over Thanksgiving," William said, defensively. "I wasn't allowed to tell anyone. Mr. Zeus did something to me so I couldn't."

"What do you mean, he did something?" Serena demanded. She sounded more furious than scared.

William kept his eyes on the road. "He cast a spell on me," he explained, mentally wincing at how stupid it sounded when put like that.

Serena scoffed. "A spell?"

William chanced a glance in her direction. She glared at him, and he quickly returned his attention to the road. "That's what happened. I couldn't tell anyone what I knew. I couldn't even write it down."

"Or maybe you just lied to me."

William's irritation, fired up by his recent fear, stirred. "If you don't want to believe me, that's your problem."

"My problem is being lied to."

"And mine is that you can't seem to understand simple English," William snapped back.

A tense silence fell over the Scout.

"You're saying Jason and Mr. Zeus are magi," Serena said, eventually breaking the quiet.

"So are Lien, Daniel, and their parents," William said.

"Right. Can't forget that," Serena jeered. "I guess that makes all of you wizards or something."

"We're magi," Jason corrected. "The plural of magus."

Serena gave him a hard stare.

"Wizards are something else," Jason said. "So are witches. We're different from them."

"Fine. You're magi," Serena said. "And this monster that attacked us, this necrosed, is like a magical Terminator."

"Pretty much," Jason agreed.

William glanced again at Serena again. She didn't seem quite as angry. He took it as a good sign.

"It seemed to know me," he said, speaking softly. "It talked about my parents. It talked about killing them."

Serena's angry expression softened. "I'm sure it was just saying that to make you—"

"It killed your family," Jason broke in. "It wouldn't have said it if it wasn't true."

"I thought you said no one knew anything about these things," Serena said.

"We know some," Jason said.

"Then why do you think it was telling the truth about my family?" William asked.

"When we first saw you in the hospital after the accident there was a smell on you, like spoiled meat. Mr. Zeus and I didn't think much about it. We thought it must have been the air in the hospital or something to do with the accident. But it was the necrosed. They're animated corpses. Rotting flesh. Some of its stink lingered on you."

"A zombie Terminator," Serena muttered.

"You think that thing really killed my family?" William asked. Even as he spoke the words, uncertainty gave way to surety. He recalled his dreams of the accident, the brutal figure watching in silence from a nearby embankment, menace and cruelty pouring off it like a miasma. His lipless mouth, gorilla arms, and massive size. It had been the necrosed.

William's anger flared to fury and his fingers tightened on the steering wheel. He had trouble concentrating. His family was dead because of that abomination. "Why did it kill them?" he asked through clenched teeth.

"Who knows?" Jason replied. "The necrosed use the flesh of others to maintain themselves, but to thrive they require the *lorethasra* of an *asrasin*. Maybe it was on the hunt and was attracted to you because of your potential as an *asrasin*." He shrugged. "I don't know why it didn't kill you, though. Maybe it was hoping you'd come into your power and it could kill you then."

Son of a bitch! "That thing dies," William vowed. "I don't care what it takes."

"How long has it been watching William?" Serena asked. Her prior outrage at being deceived seemed to have dissipated.

"Since it left him alive," Jason answered, "probably since last winter, after it killed his parents and his brother."

William shot a glare at Jason. "You knew nothing about it?"

"Believe me, if any of us had known a necrosed was stalking you, all of us, including me, Mr. Zeus, and the Karllsons, would have immediately evacuated to Arylyn."

William grunted acknowledgment. "What else do you know about these necrosed? What are their weaknesses?"

"They don't have any. Only a holder—think of them as monster hunters—can kill one, but they all died out a long time ago," Jason said. "Once a necrosed has a target, it won't stop until it kills it. Almost everyone who has fought one ends up dead. The only way to survive it is to escape to my home."

"Your house in Cincinnati?" Serena asked, sounding confused.

"No. The place I come from. Arylyn. It's an island. It's where Mr. Zeus, Daniel, and Lien went on that rainbow bridge."

"They're okay?" William asked.

"Better than we are."

"Where is this island?" Serena asked.

"I can't tell you," Jason replied. "I'm not allowed."

The Scout grew quiet again, and for the first time, William noticed a niggling sensation in the back of his mind. He'd been too scared before to pay it any attention, but now that the immediate danger was past he could feel it more clearly, like a bug crawling on his skin.

He feared what it meant and wiped sweaty palms on his pants. "What does it mean if I can feel him?"

"Feel who?" Jason asked.

"It. Him. Whatever. I can feel him. I can feel the necrosed. I even know his name."

Jason leaned forward and eyed him in uncertainty. "You sure about this?"

William nodded. “He’s a male. I can even tell where he’s going. I can almost feel his emotions.”

Jason sat back with brows furrowed as he stared out the window. “I don’t know what that means,” he finally said. “I don’t know much about the necrosed. No one does. I’ve never heard of someone feeling anything from one of them.” William caught a worried look from Jason. “You really know his name?”

William nodded. “Kohl Obsidian. And he’s coming after me.”

The winter breeze carried the cheery scent of smoke from a fireplace, along with a wetness that tasted of a pending snowfall. Another gust of wind blew, and William shivered. The breeze bit hard, and he hoped whoever was enjoying the fireplace was warmer than he was. His numbed fingers, stiff as frozen sausages, could barely work the gas pump as he fed fuel into the bottomless maw of the Scout’s tank.

They’d had to stop in a small village in Ohio, a place named Rio Grande. Rolling hills and farms gave it a picturesque beauty, but it was most famous for being the home of the Bob Evans Farm. The billboards lining the road said so but William didn’t care, not about Rio Grande’s history or the village’s beauty. He might have once—he did love Bob Evans—but not now. Not with a zombie Terminator out to kill him.

“Can you still tell where the necrosed is?” Jason asked.

An old pickup interrupted William’s answer as it rumbled to life and sputtered away in a cloud of gray smoke. Other than the

Scout, the gas station now stood empty and only occasional traffic traveled the nearby state highway.

"He's behind us," William replied. "I can't tell much more than that. I don't know if he's even moved off that *saha'asra*."

Jason muttered under his breath before glancing at the gas station. "What's taking Serena so long?"

They stared through the windows of the gas station, but she was nowhere to be seen. The only people visible inside were a skinny, teenage girl standing behind the counter chatting with a husky boy.

"I think she's calling her dad on the pay phone inside," William said. "She also wanted to clean off the cut on her arm."

"She's using the gas station bathroom?" Jason asked in obvious shock. "Why didn't you warn her?"

"I did warn her."

"You should have warned her harder."

William shrugged. He didn't really want to talk about Serena right now. He needed to talk about the attack from a few hours ago. "What are we going to do?"

"Survive," Jason answered. "If we can."

"That's not much of a plan."

"I know, but it's all I've got," Jason said. He paused a moment before speaking again a beat later. "Serena will have to come with us."

"Why?" Until now, William had planned on just dropping Serena off at home and figuring out the rest afterward.

"Because Kohl cut her. It means she's been marked," Jason said. "The necrosed won't stop until she's dead, too."

"Have you told her?" William asked, already dreading how that conversation would go.

"No. I was hoping you'd do the honors."

William grimaced. "I'll take care of it," he said with a sigh.

"Listen, there's more you need to know. Remember I told you about the *saha'asra* in Cincinnati? It's in Winton Woods, but it's not connected by an anchor line to Arylyn."

"That rainbow bridge?"

"Yeah," Jason said. "That's how we travel from one *saha'asra* to another. But the one in Cincinnati doesn't have an anchor line to Arylyn."

"Does it have any anchor lines at all?" William asked.

"One. It leads to a *saha'asra* in Thailand. That one leads to Arylyn."

"Then why can't we use that one?" William asked, hope burgeoning. "Or why can't we just go back to the park in West Virginia and leave from there?"

"The necrosed bled on the *saha'asra* in West Virginia. I saw it," Jason answered. "The blood is like a signal to others of its kind. It's a sign of weakness. Any necrosed that comes across Kohl will eat him, if he can. Some might be on their way to the meadow right now, hoping we or Kohl will be stupid enough to return there."

"I hope they get him," William muttered.

"So do I, but I doubt they will," Jason replied. "You have to understand, the necrosed have a way of traveling that we don't understand. You say Kohl is hours behind us, but if he wanted to he could cover that same distance in seconds."

"What about the *saha'asra* to Thailand? Why can't we use that one?"

Jason shook his head. "Because the anchor line going from

Cincinnati to the Thailand *saha'asra* is only large enough to transport small items like the *nomasras* Mr. Zeus and I use to stay in the Far Abroad," he said. "It's not big enough for a person to cross."

"*Nomasras. Lorasras. Lorethasras,*" William scowled in disgust. "Why did your people have to make everything sound the same?" He knew the question was petty even as he asked it.

"They're your people now, too," Jason said.

"Don't remind me."

"You wish you weren't one of us?" Jason asked.

"If I wasn't, then Kohl Obsidian wouldn't have attacked my family. They'd still be alive," William said with a bitter snarl.

"Maybe," Jason said, "but there's more you need to learn about us."

The Scout's tank was finally full, and William screwed on the cap. "Like what?"

"Arylyn isn't the only *saha'asra* where our kind can survive," Jason began. "There was a war once, a long time ago, so long that no records of it exist. But the generals had names, Shet and Shokan."

"Sounds like some kind of ancient gods."

Jason nodded. "Yeah. A lot of ancient gods were probably our ancestors. They had powers and skills that we can only dream of. And they warred. Their battles reshaped entire continents, left lands barren and ruined. It's not surprising that people would think they were gods. Those *asrasins*—"

"Another word with '*asra*'," William interrupted.

"I know. It's stupid, but anyway, '*asrasin*' is the general name for people like us—"

"People like you. I'm not an *asrasin* yet."

"Fine. You're not one of us. But you will be," Jason said. "Anyway, the war I was talking about almost destroyed my kind. The *saha'asras* were drained. Only two survived that could sustain us. Arylyn, which you know about, was founded by the magi—the followers of Shokan—while Sinskrill was founded by a rival branch of *asrasins*—the *mahavans*—those who followed Shet.

"Where's Sinskrill?" William asked.

"I don't know," Jason replied. "Only someone from Sinskrill could tell you. They know nothing about Arylyn's location either. The war goes on."

William rubbed the bridge of his nose. He could feel a headache coming on. "You're telling me I just signed up for some ancient war no one else knows about?"

Jason had the grace to blush. "Pretty much."

William sighed. "Great. You got any other good news?"

"That's about it. I really don't know all that much. I was born out here, just like you."

"You never did tell me how you ended up in Arylyn."

"Yeah, well, I was born in New Orleans, just a normal person. But my mom and I were canoeing out in the bayou and we came across a *saha'asra*. I got sick right afterward, and Mom didn't know what was wrong with me. None of the doctors did either, but she'd been told stories about *saha'asras*, and a few days later Mr. Zeus showed up."

"How'd your mom know? I thought no one was allowed to talk about it."

"We can't, but Mom's grandmother, my great-grandmother, Grandma Layla, was born on Arylyn. Mr. Zeus and his wife, Mrs.

Edith, were her parents, but since Grandma Layla didn't have any *lorethasra*, she had to leave the island. If she stayed, she would have died, but Mr. Zeus and Mrs. Edith loved her. They wanted her to remember something of Arylyn, so they kept her there until she was about ten. It was the longest she could stay before Arylyn's *lorasra* killed her."

"There was no other way? Like one of those *nomasra* things?"

"Maybe. But she'd have been the only person on the island without *lorethasra*," Jason said. "Would you have wanted that? To be the only one unable to do magic on an island full of magi?"

William smirked. "I'm pretty much the only one of my kind as it is. There aren't a whole lot of people with Indian and Irish ancestry are there?"

Jason shook his head. "This is different. We don't have black, white, Chinese, or any kind of races on Arylyn. Everyone there has some kind of mixed up ancestry. But if Grandma Layla had stayed there, she would have watched all her friends master magic while she was left unable to do anything. Personally, I think it would have been awful."

William tried to imagine the kind of life Jason had described, to look like everyone else but be different in a way guaranteed to evoke pity. He would have hated it.

"Your Grandma Layla left the island before she realized that she was different, but she remembered Arylyn because Mr. Zeus didn't take that away from her?" William asked.

"He let her remember," Jason said. "He and Mrs. Edith came with Grandma Layla to the Far Abroad and raised her here. But then Mrs. Edith got sick. I'm not sure what happened, but she ended up dying in Mississippi." He shrugged. "Mr. Zeus doesn't talk about it. Anyway, right after she died, Mr. Zeus returned to Arylyn, because by then Grandma Layla had married."

"Did he ever visit?"

"When he could, but it's not easy," Jason said. "He doesn't like it out here. None of us do. But back to my mom and how she knew about Arylyn. Since Grandma Layla had her memories of her parents and of Arylyn, she was able to pass her history on to her son and later to her granddaughter, my mother, and then to me."

"How old were you when Mr. Zeus found you?"

"Nine," Jason said. "He pretty much raised me."

"Do you ever get to see your mom and dad now?"

"No," Jason said. His face became harsh and closed off.

William knew not to press for details. "Does Mr. Zeus find a lot of people like us?"

Jason's expression cleared. "You don't know?"

William shook his head.

"That's his job on Arylyn. He finds and trains those like us, the ones who come to Arylyn from the Far Abroad."

William nodded, but something continued to puzzle him about Jason's story. *The timing couldn't be right.* "When did you say Grandma Layla was born?"

"Eighteen eighty-one. She had my grandmother in nineteen-nineteen. My mom was born in nineteen forty-three."

William's brow furrowed. *That didn't make sense.* "Then when was Mr. Zeus born?"

"Eighteen fifty-two," Jason said.

William's mouth gaped.

"We magi live long. Age and illness don't touch us like they do everyone else."

CHAPTER 16: TEMPORARY RESPITE

Tension had William's shoulders tight and him leaning forward the entire drive back to Cincinnati. When they finally arrived and pulled into the driveway, he fell back into his seat and exhaled in relief. *Home.* It felt good to be back, even if for only a few minutes.

The neighborhood lay quiet with the streetlights turned on, but their illumination wasn't needed. Strings of Christmas lights and decorations lit up most of the houses, and the entire setting seemed perfectly ordinary and safe.

"C'mon," Jason said. "Let's get this done." He trudged past William. "We've got to pack up everything we need, including our swords, and get going as soon as possible."

"I'll be up in a bit," William said, waiting while Serena got out of the vehicle.

"I'll meet you at Winton Woods, like we talked about," Serena said, her voice calm and steady. So far, she'd handled everything a lot better than William had expected. Serena leaned her back against the Scout and closed her eyes. Her face was filled with fear. “I can feel him,” she whispered. “He’s there, in the back of mind, like an itch I can’t scratch.”

“I know. I’m trying to ignore it.” William hesitated. “Do you know what you’re going to tell your dad?”

She opened her eyes. “I’ll figure it out. I called him from that gas station and told him we were coming home early for a party at Winton Woods we’d all forgotten about.”

William eyed her, askance. “That’s a pretty weak excuse.”

Serena gave him a flat glare. “Next time you’ve been chased by some monster, found out magic was real, and that all your friends have been lying to you for months, let me know how you take it.”

“I already apologized for that.”

“No, you didn’t. You never once said you were sorry for any of what’s happened.”

“Then I’m sorry,” William said. Even though none of this was his fault—Kohl Obsidian could be blamed for that—guilt gnawed at him. He’d never wanted Serena to get caught up in any of this awfulness. “And I’m sorry you’re stuck having to come with us.”

He’d told her the truth about the necrosed and what it meant to be scratched by one back in Rio Grande, right before they’d left the gas station. She hadn’t been happy.

“Forget it.” Serena pushed off the Scout.

“I really am sorry,” William tried again. “If there was a way to make this go away, I would.”

Serena’s face softened briefly. “I know,” she said. “But right now I’m not in the mood for criticism, and I hate lying to my dad.”

“You can’t tell him the truth,” William warned.

“I know,” Serena said, “because Jason *collared* me, just like what Mr. Zeus did to you." She shook her head. "Anyway, this may be the last time I get to see him. In case . . . You know."

"I know."

In case they died or reached Arylyn, since once there, none of them could ever leave.

William imagined it wouldn't be so bad for himself. He would become a magus. But for Serena it would be awful. She'd hate being the only non-magus on the island, as Grandma Layla would have been.

Then again, maybe none of this would come to pass. Maybe they'd find a way to kill Kohl. Jason thought Mr. Zeus or someone else on Arylyn might figure out a way to do so, which was why they were going to Winton Woods first. Mr. Zeus had left a stash of *nomasra*s and weapons there. Maybe one of them would work on the necrosed.

"Get your stuff together," Serena said, breaking into William's thoughts. "I'll see you soon."

"Yeah. See you."

He climbed the steps to the front door. Before entering, he glanced around again at his quiet neighborhood. Christmas lights twinkled everywhere, somehow tacky and comforting at the same time. Leafless trees, young like the subdivision, stood like sentinels in their front yards. A cloudless sky revealed the stars, and many houses had lights on in every room.

Warm and peaceful. He wondered if he'd ever find such warmth and peace in his own life. After all, they'd started running from the necrosed early this morning, and it seemed like they'd always be running.

The thought left him melancholy.

"It would help if you answered the phone, sir," Serena said as she stepped through the front door.

Isha glanced her way, surprise on his face. He'd dimmed all the lights except for a single one he kept focused on the book he had been reading. "You're home early."

"And you'd know the reason why if you'd answered the phone."

"I must have been out when you called." Isha said. He set his book aside.

"I've been marked by a necrosed," Serena said.

The blood drained from Isha's face. "What happened?"

For the first time since Serena had known him, Isha looked fearful. Terrified even.

For my safety? Why? I'm just his bishan.

"What happened?" Isha asked again.

Serena explained succinctly, as she'd been taught.

"The creature touched William?" Isha asked.

"He grabbed a chain from around William's neck. It was likely a *nomasra*. But in doing so the necrosed was hurt," Serena said. "I heard the creature cry out in true pain. Something about the *nomasra* injured it."

"Did it bleed on you?" Isha asked, his gaze more raptor-intense than ever.

"No. It only cut me," Serena answered. "That's probably why I can sense it. But it might have bled on William."

"Think," Isha said. "This is very important. If William has the blood of this creature within him, he may eventually become a necrosed."

Serena startled. "Are you sure?"

"Who can be sure of anything when it comes to such creatures?" Isha said. "But it's possible, maybe even likely."

"But only an *asrasin* can become a necrosed," Serena argued. "That's one of the few truths we know about the necrosed."

"William was in a *saha'asra*," Isha said.

"But his *lorethasra* had not come to life. I'm not sure how it was done, but I think his *nomasra* prevented it."

"But the chain, this supposed *nomasra*, was it torn from him?"

"I don't know," Serena said with a frown.

"Then William's *lorethasra* may, indeed, have come to life. It may be growing even as we speak."

Serena's brow furrowed in uncertainty. "If it is, and he also has the corrupted blood of the necrosed within him, does that mean he's destined to become one of those creatures?"

"Possibly," Isha said. "But if his developing *lorethasra* is able to overcome the corruption of the necrosed, he might become more powerful than any *asrasin* born in centuries." Isha's face hardened. Whatever earlier softness might have once been there vanished. "William must be preserved at all costs. We need him."

"And me?" Serena asked, wearing a sardonic smile. "Must I be preserved as well?"

Isha didn't answer at first. Instead, sorrow appeared to flicker across his face. Serena would have dismissed such a possibility out of hand if not for his earlier, obvious fear when she'd told him she'd been marked by a necrosed.

"Ours is a harsh life," Isha said. "We're taught that those

closest to us are faithless, that they'll disappoint us, betray us, and ultimately fail us. We're taught to keep our emotional attachments to a minimum, to let no one into our hearts." He sighed. "I failed in this. You are in my heart, Serena, and if given a choice, I would preserve you over William Wilde."

Serena's mouth gaped. She could use what Isha had just told her against him for all time. He'd all but voluntarily bent his knee to her, and all she had to do was accept his submission. But did she want Isha as a servant, or as her teacher? She'd come to trust him, a vulnerability she would never admit to him or anyone else.

"I think the shock of learning about the necrosed must have addled your mind," Serena replied. "Be careful no one learns of it."

"You would tell them?"

"No. I won't betray you." The words were honest.

"But now it is *your* words that betray *you*," Isha said with a smile.

Serena mentally cursed.

"It seems we both have failed to keep our hearts chained in iron boxes," he said. "Strangely enough, this brings me peace rather than fear."

In a day full of shocks, what she and Isha had just admitted was perhaps the greatest.

"What do I do?" Serena asked.

"You go with William Wilde," Isha said. "You stay with him. Support him if he manages to overcome the corruption in his blood, and kill him if he does not. We cannot allow him to transform into a necrosed."

Serena stiffened. She didn't like the idea of killing William even while she recognized the possible need to do so. She also knew how Isha would respond to her next words, and she didn't like that, either. "Jason plans on taking William to Arylyn through a *saha'asra* in Arizona. They spoke of it on our way back."

"You'll stop Jason as well, or see William dead. Arylyn cannot have someone with his potential."

Isha's statement wasn't a request but a command.

Further unhappiness filled Serena's heart, but she bowed and kept any weakness or defiance from showing. "Yes, sir."

"Take your sword," Isha ordered. "Keep it with you. Protect yourself. You know the rest."

Serena nodded. Preserve William at all costs, even if the price was her own life.

However, her mind flitted elsewhere. She might have to kill a young man she liked and admired, as well as his friend, another young man she liked and admired. An awful situation all around, and truthfully, Serena didn't know if she could actually take either of their lives.

In that moment, a large part of Serena wished she'd never met William Wilde, or at least wished she didn't like him. Then she wouldn't care what he'd think if he learned the truth about her. She wouldn't care that he'd end up hating her. *It'd be so much simpler to not care.*

"Remember to conceal your true nature," Isha advised, interrupting her thoughts. "Right now William and Jason think you're a normal girl. Keep it that way. They'll expect you to be angry over what has happened. Make sure they see it."

"I *am* angry."

"Then you'll have no trouble maintaining a sense of outrage. Be angry with William for a time before you forgive him."

"Yes, sir," Serena said.

"When do you leave?"

"Tonight. We're meeting at Winton Woods."

"Why there?" Isha asked with a frown.

"It's supposed to contain a *saha'asra*, one I wasn't aware of until tonight. Mr. Zeus is said to have secreted a number of *nomasras* and weapons within it or nearby."

"So be it," Isha said with a brisk nod. "Stay as safe as you can. Stay alive, if possible."

"My father would rather have victory than the life of any of his children," Serena said.

"How are we going to pay for all this?" William asked, gesturing to their overflowing grocery cart.

Jason eyed him in seeming disbelief. "Magic, remember?" Suddenly he held a fistful of twenties.

"Handy trick," William said. "Wish you'd used it more often when we went to the arcade."

On the way to check-out they passed the medication aisle, and William held up a hand. "Hold on a sec. I need some cough syrup or something. I think I'm getting a cold."

"Okay," Jason said, sounding distracted. A moment later his focus snapped to William. "Wait. What do you mean, you think you're getting a cold? Since when?"

"Just now. Or maybe on the way back from West Virginia. Why? It's just a tickle in my throat," William said.

"When the necrosed grabbed hold of you, did it do anything other than throw you?"

"Well, yeah. The necklace got hot, like it was on fire." William pulled down his shirt to show a set of raised, red marks around his neck and a scabbed-over cut. "It snapped, and the next thing I knew I was flying through the air."

"What about your *nomasra*, the pendant?" Jason demanded. "Did you lose it?"

"No, I found it. After I rolled off Mr. Zeus, it was just a few feet away."

"But it was off your person?"

"Yeah, but just a few seconds," William said. His impatience grew at the cryptic nature of Jason's questions. "Why is this so important?"

"It's important," Jason said, "because without that particular *nomasra*, your *lorethasra* has come to life. It only takes an instant." He snapped his fingers. "You're one of us now."

"Yeah, but that was the plan all along anyway, right?" William said.

"Yes, but now you need another type of *nomasra*, one that contains enough *lorasra* to keep you alive," Jason said. "This cold you have is going to feel like pneumonia in a few days. After that, it becomes worse and you die."

William paled. "You never mentioned that."

"That's because we never thought you'd be in this situation."

"Do you have one of those other *nomasras*?"

"Only mine," Jason said. His voice and face seemed filled with regret and sorrow.

"What about back at the house?"

"Mr. Zeus had the other one."

William's heart sank. "What do we do?"

"What do you think?" Jason asked. He grinned widely.

William silently cursed. He'd been played. "You've got another one, don't you?"

"You should see your face." Jason laughed.

"Ass-hat. Do you actually have an extra one or not?"

"Of course, I do." Jason continued to laugh.

"Dickhead."

Jason kept grinning and passed him another pendant. "Here's your *nomasra*. Put it on the chain, and don't lose it. Keep the other one on you, too."

The drive from the grocery store to Winton Woods only took a few minutes, and William made the final turnoff for the location where Serena should have been waiting alone for them. Instead, in this quiet, middle of nowhere portion of the park, music blared, car headlights blazed, and people they recognized from school—their classmates—stood around drinking what looked like beer. Rather than a secluded spot to pick Serena up, it looked like they'd chosen a place where someone had decided to have a party.

"Shit," Jason muttered. "What the hell is going on?"

"There's Jake Ridley," William said, pointing out his longtime nemesis. "I see Sonya Bowyer and Steve Aldo too. Looks like a party."

Jason grimaced. "Great."

"It doesn't matter. There's Serena." William gestured. "Let's find Mr. Zeus' stash and get gone."

"Where's the necrosed?"

"Still in West Virginia," William said, pulling the Scout into an empty parking spot.

"You made it," Serena said when they exited the vehicle. She hefted a large bag.

William took it from her, and noticed the hilt of a sword and what felt like a bow and quiver of arrows. He shot her a questioning glance before deciding it wasn't important. She could explain it later.

"Is that a sword?" Sonya Bowyer asked Serena, sounding both scornful and curious. "Can I see it?"

"Yeah, but not now," Serena said.

Jason entered the darkened woods with a flashlight in hand. "Come on," he called. "Let's get this done."

"What? Are you like She-Ra or something?" Jake asked Serena. His question elicited a laugh from the others.

"Something like that," she answered, never slowing as she followed Jason into the woods.

"Hey! Where are you guys going?" Steve Aldo shouted.

"We dropped something in the woods," William replied.

"You're going to get lost if you go in there this late at night," Steve advised. "Better hold off 'til morning."

"It can't wait," William said. "We have to find it now."

He missed whatever response Steve might have given when he stepped into the dark woods. Only a few muffled shouts and peals of high-pitched laughter penetrated the trees, and soon even those sounds faded away. Jason and Serena were yards farther down the trail, and William hustled to catch up with them.

"Where's this stuff that we're supposed to get?" Serena asked.

"Down a little ways. Not far," Jason said.

They pressed deeper into the forest, and Jason led them off the path they had been following. A wind moaned, setting bare branches clacking as they pushed through the underbrush, moving slowly and carefully. Even with their flashlights they could trip on unseen limbs or stumble over loose stones.

The woods contained a dark, eerie, quiet, and William didn't like it. Something felt off about Winton Woods tonight, something menacing. He shivered.

"There," Jason said, sounding satisfied. He stood next to a stream. "Look for three rocks leaning against each other. That's where Mr. Zeus left his emergency supplies."

Serena and Jason bent low, searching for the rocks. William was about to join them when he felt a strange tingling in the back of his mind. He couldn't shake it, and it took him a moment to understand what he sensed. He gasped.

"Oh no!" Serena whispered at the same time.

"Found it," Jason said. He cast aside the rock formation, and buried a few inches under it lay a long, narrow satchel. From within it, he drew out a knife and a few gems.

"Kohl's here," William said.

Jason shoved everything back into the satchel as terror flashed across his face. "Where?"

"Close. In the woods. Nearby."

"We have to go!" Serena said.

"Follow me." Jason stood and darted back toward the path.

A ragged whisper came to William. "Run, little *asrasins*. Run fast."

William glanced back. A hulking shape hunkered on the far side of the stream. From it came a hideous laugh, low-throated and cackling.

William's mouth went dry, and he raced away, following after the others. His heart thudded. Adrenaline surged and fear coursed through his veins, urging him to run faster. Branches cracked and snapped as he raced by.

Where was Kohl? He'd only been yards away, on the other side of the stream.

A rock cracked against a tree, inches from where William's head had been.

"Next time, I'll pulp your brains," Kohl promised, and again came that horrible laugh.

William ducked low and kept on running.

A crackling of broken branches and a chuckle that made William's blood run cold arose behind them. "Faster, little *asrasins*. Make it interesting for me, and I promise to kill you quickly."

"He's toying with us," Serena panted.

"Just run," Jason ordered.

"Your *lorethasra*. Succulent as blood."

The beams of their flashlights bobbed as they pumped their arms. William panted with effort and terror. The smell of moldy leaves mixed with a rank stench of decay came to him.

Kohl.

They hit the path back to the Scout and picked up speed.

"Where is he?" Jason demanded.

"Still there. Still coming," William answered.

Another rock smashed into a tree, this time next to Jason's head.

A thud fell directly behind them and vibrated the ground. William chanced a glance back. Kohl stood on the path. Even shrouded in dark, William sensed the monster smiling.

"I see you," the necrosed taunted. He charged, his wide shoulders shoving trees aside. Branches broke. The ground shook with his heavy steps. Kohl raced toward them. He chewed up the distance.

"He's on us!" William shouted.

"Go! I can see the edge of the clearing," Jason said. He slowed, and William passed him by.

"What are you doing?" William exclaimed.

"Slowing him down. Just keep going."

A banshee wail rose. William peered back. A wall of fire had sprung from Jason's hands.

The necrosed never had a chance to evade. He lit up like a bonfire and roared in pain. "Then a slow, painful death shall be your future. I promise to make it so!"

The necrosed had paused. The fire engulfing him slowly died. Embers littered the ground at his feet, casting a glow about him. Kohl waved his hands and the forest went dark.

The monster howled, "Go on, then. Your fear will make the feast all the sweeter."

"We're almost out," Serena shouted.

"Don't slow down," Jason ordered.

"We have to warn Jake and his friends," William said. "We can't just leave them on their own."

As they burst from the woods, Jake Ridley ran towards them. "What the hell is going on in there?" His face wore a look of anger and worry.

"Something bad is coming! You need to get out of here!" William said.

"What the hell are you talking about, Wilde? What was that scream?" Jake persisted.

William gritted his teeth. *Why couldn't Jake just do what he was told?*

Jason arrived. "Why are you still here? Kohl disappeared, but you can bet your ass he'll be on us if we stand around like a bunch of numbnuts."

"Who's coming?" Sonya Bowyer asked, starting to look spooked.

A noise from farther away than expected spun William around. *There.* A hundred yards away or so, a shadowed figure pushed out of the woods. Kohl. His gait was jerky, but swift, and in seconds, he'd moved to stand beneath a distant streetlight, effectively blocking the only exit from the park.

"He's here," William whispered, his eyes wide with fear.

"Who's here? That guy?" Jake asked. "That's what's got you girls so scared?

"That's not some guy. We all have to go. *Now*," William said.

"It's probably just Officer Wilson," Jake scoffed. "He's nothing. He'll give us a speech about littering and underage drinking, but so what. He's just a rent-a-slob."

"I don't know," Steve said, sounding doubtful. "That dude doesn't look like Officer Wilson."

The horrible laugh echoed again, clicking and clacking.

"That doesn't sound like Officer Wilson, either," Steve said. He backed away. "I've got a bad feeling about this."

"We're too late," Serena said, stepping up and handing

William and Jason their swords. She drew a *jian*, a Chinese longsword. "He's blocked our exit. We have to fight our way past."

"What are you guys doing with those swords?" Jake asked. Worry finally tinged his voice.

CHAPTER 17: FLEE

William didn't answer Jake's question. He waited, sword ready, with Serena and Jason on either side of him, trying to control his terror. All the while, the necrosed stalked toward them, deliberate and unhurried.

"Guess we know how fast a necrosed can move," Jason muttered.

"I don't understand," William said. "He was hours behind us when we left the grocery store, even when we first got here. Then he's right in front of us. If he could move this fast all along, why didn't he do it before? Or just kill us in the woods?"

"I told you, he's toying with us," Serena answered.

"What's that smell?" Sonya asked. "It smells like rotten meat. Ugh." She covered her nose and mouth.

"It's coming from that big, ugly guy," Steve said. "I think we should take William's advice and go." He edged further toward his car.

"Yeah. Maybe we should," Jake said. But he and his friends stood unmoving, apparently wanting to see what would happen next.

"I'll kill you now, boy," Kohl Obsidian growled in his grating voice. "I'll kill you and your friends and these others. I'll eat their flesh while they're still wriggling."

The necrosed stopped beneath a streetlamp. He stood a hundred feet away, but even from this distance William could make out the monster's hideous features. Earlier, in West Virginia, he hadn't paid much attention to Kohl's face, but as in his dream, he discerned a horror of melted flesh and misshapen features. The monster's arms hung low and apelike, past his knees, and claws long as a bear's tipped his fingers.

"Oh, my God!" Sonya said.

Serena unpacked her bow and nocked an arrow. "Lead him to my right," she ordered Jason.

A stream of fire roared off Jason's hands, straight at the necrosed.

Jake and his friends scrambled into motion, shouting and screaming as they raced for their cars.

The creature moved. Kohl's earlier jerky motion smoothed out. He spun to his right, evading Jason's fire and ducked beneath Serena's arrow.

The necrosed howled before calling out again. "You die tonight. All of you!"

William noticed that Jake and the others had finally reached their vehicles. They frantically scrambled into them. Engines roared to life.

"Again!" Serena ordered. "My left this time."

Another stream of fire burst from Jason's hands.

William watched helplessly.

An arrow bloomed from Kohl's shoulder, and the necrosed hissed in fury.

"You and Serena get in the truck," Jason called to William. "It's you he wants. Run him down with the Scout. I'll be right behind you. We'll try to get away in all the confusion."

William shot a disbelieving glance at Jason.

"Go. It'll work," Jason urged.

William and Serena tossed their swords and Mr. Zeus' satchel in the back seat and hopped into the Scout.

"Go!" Serena urged.

William keyed the engine to life.

Jake and his friends peeled out, and William followed.

The necrosed swung his arms lazily, as if he was warming up before a game. "You will not escape me this time. I—"

His words cut off. The necrosed danced about. The earth trembled beneath him. Cracks appeared in the pavement.

William didn't know what Jason had done, but it gave him time to get the Scout rumbling up to speed.

Kohl stepped into the road and threw his arms wide. His bulk blocked further passage. Jake's Corvette screeched to a halt.

Kohl laughed, but it became a scream of pain as Jason lit him up again. A whirlwind howled, and the necrosed tumbled through the air, flying over treetops. His echoing cry grew distant.

Jake gunned his Corvette and roared away.

William waited on Jason, who jumped into the Scout an instant later.

"That's not going to stop him for long," Jason said.

William got the vehicle rolling. The taillights of Jake's Corvette were far ahead. William followed, swinging the Scout through fast, tight, wheel-screaming turns.

He touched the area of his mind that could sense Kohl. Right now, the necrosed was ramming his way through the trees, seeking to cut them off before they left the confines of the park.

William floored the pedal.

The necrosed took a straight line through the forest.

"Where is he?" Jason asked.

"In the trees," Serena said. "He's heading right for us."

Jason swore.

William gave his entire attention to the narrow, winding road leading them out of Winton Woods.

"There's the exit!" Serena cried.

A hard left at a stop sign.

William slowed only enough to take the turn without rolling the Scout. A stoplight glowed red at the intersection leading into and out of the park. Cars zipped through it.

Kohl closed in from the right. Yards away.

Too close.

William kept the pedal down. He ran the red light and swung left at the intersection. The Scout swayed and nearly tipped. Tires squealed as other cars swerved to either side of them or braked hard. Drivers laid into their horns.

William didn't let off the gas.

William's fists remained clenched and his shoulders tight as they drove further and further from Winton Woods. Every shadowed movement along the road, every darkened alley they passed, every place of hiding had him jumpy. Kohl might be hiding in any of them, ready to leap out and ambush them.

Jason and Serena also remained tense during the drive along Cincinnati's streets. The red lights, the endless minutes waiting for the green . . . What if Kohl caught them while they idled? In any other setting, such concerns would have struck him as ridiculous, but earlier that night, Kohl had covered hundreds of miles in a meager few seconds.

Only when they hit the highway, with the Scout motoring along at over sixty, did William finally relax. With each passing mile he sensed the necrosed falling farther and farther behind.

The interstate cut through downtown Cincinnati, but the brightly lit city, with many buildings and offices decorated with cheerful Christmas lights, did nothing to lift William's spirits.

"Where is he now?" Jason asked. "Still at Winton Woods?"

"He hasn't moved," Serena answered.

"I say we drive non-stop to Arizona," Jason said. "We only stop for food and bathroom breaks. Two people awake, one person asleep."

"Maybe," William said, "but even if we did, Kohl just covered five hours of driving in five seconds. Until we figure out how, we're screwed."

"I think I know the answer to that," Jason said. "Kohl must be able to travel along the anchor lines, no matter how disconnected or how small. For us, the *saha'asra* in Winton Woods is too small to transport anything other than small objects, but Kohl's magic must allow him to use a *saha'asra*, no matter how narrow its anchor line. That has to be the answer. It's the only thing that makes sense."

"Then we have to make sure to avoid any *saha'asras* on our way to Arizona," William said.

"Monsters, magic, and hidden islands," Serena said, with a headshake of disgust.

"I'm sorry you're stuck in all this," William said.

"Being sorry doesn't really matter now, does it?" Serena said.

William's grip on the steering wheel tightened, and an artery throbbed at his temple. While he sympathized with Serena—she'd never see her father again—she wasn't the only one who had lost someone she loved because of the necrosed. "I'm stuck with this, too," he reminded her. "I never asked for magic, or some unstoppable killing machine chasing us, and I sure didn't ask to be the reason for my family's murder."

"Forget it," Serena said.

"We shouldn't be arguing," Jason said. "We've got to figure out our next step."

"I'd be happy to," William said, "but I'm tired of having my apologies thrown back in my face, especially over something I didn't do."

"And I'm unhappy that I might die because of something *I* didn't do," Serena snapped at him.

"Well then maybe you should—"

"Stop it!" Jason shouted. "That's enough."

Other than the engine, the Scout fell quiet, but William sensed that Serena still seethed. Well so did he. His head throbbed in time to his pulse, and his shoulders remained tense.

Jason broke the quiet. "I didn't know you knew how to use a sword and a bow," he said to Serena.

"Did you think only boys should learn martial arts?" Serena asked.

"That's not what I said," Jason replied in an even tone.

"There's a lot you should have said to me, though, isn't there?" Serena demanded.

William rolled his eyes. *Get over it already.* No, they hadn't told her everything. So what? Mr. Zeus and Jason hadn't told him everything, either. Besides, who told everyone every last thing about themselves? Everyone had their secrets.

"If the necrosed can travel so easily from one *saha'asra* to another," he asked, "what's kept them from going to Arylyn?"

"Because Arylyn's anchor lines are all gated. You have to know the right tune to open them."

"Like a song?" William asked.

"Sort of," Jason said. "When you've been trained as a magus, you'll know what I mean."

"Do you know where all the other magic places are located?" Serena asked.

"When I was going through Mr. Zeus' stuff back home, I found a map," Jason answered. "It's got all the ones we know of listed."

"Then we need to avoid all of them," Serena said, echoing William's earlier advice.

"Can we use a *saha'asra* that takes us to the one in Arizona?" William asked.

"There's always a few minutes of disorientation whenever we travel along an anchor line," Jason explained. "We could be resting up for the next part of our journey when the necrosed shows up."

"Can we fly to Arizona?" Serena asked.

"Fly where? I know the *saha'asra* is in Arizona, but that's a big state," Jason said.

"Hold on. I thought you said you had a map of the

saha'asras," Serena said.

"I do, but for some of them, all that's indicated is a rough approximation," Jason said. "All I know about the one in Arizona is that it's by a lake."

Serena gave him a wide-eyed stare of disbelief. "That's it? That's all you got?" She shook her head. "This just gets better and better."

William did his best to ignore Serena's pessimism. "Then what do you think we should do?" he asked Jason.

"I think we should stay away from all the *saha'asras*, like you and Serena said, but we should also make sure we're always around a lot of people," Jason said. "The necrosed don't like crowds."

"Kohl didn't seem to mind much when Jake and the others were around," Serena said.

"That's because it was dark and secluded," Jason replied. "We need to make sure that we're never caught alone in the middle of nowhere like that. We need to stay in public as much as possible."

"Then we drive to this place in Arizona, and we stay with large groups of people as much as we can," William said. "And once we're at this *saha'asra*, how long will it take to open up the anchor line to Arylyn?"

"Just a few seconds." Jason said. "And during the drive out there, I can hopefully figure out which lake the *saha'asra* in Arizona is located next to."

They drove through the night, and even Jason ended up taking the wheel. He climbed into the driver's seat in Louisville, Kentucky.

As they traveled west on I-64 and the night set in, the traffic grew lighter. Other than a few lonely, long-distance truckers, they had the interstate to themselves. They passed the time in quiet reflection. There wasn't much to see, as the surrounding fields and farms of Indiana were still and dark.

None of them wanted to talk much, anyway.

William took over driving duties in a tiny town called Lynnville, Indiana, and drove for a few hours more. With the sun yet to rise and his eyes heavy-lidded and tired, he saw a sign that made him straighten from his slouch. They approached Wayne City, Illinois, and while they needed to stop for gas, it was a promotion on a billboard that had caught his attention. The advertisement offered an answer to a pressing problem, and William took the exit.

Several miles later, Serena woke up. "Where are we?" she mumbled as she uncurled herself from the back seat. She and Jason had traded positions in the middle of the night.

He sat in the passenger seat, dozing with his head resting against the door.

"Illinois," William responded.

"Why'd you leave the highway?" She muffled a yawn.

"I saw a billboard," William said. "It said there's a campground a few miles up the road, near a town called Wayne City. We might have found what we were looking for."

"What was it?" Serena asked.

"We should be there soon," William said, not wanting to raise a hope that might turn out to be a whole lot of nothing. "Just wait."

Jason stirred. "What's going on?" he asked, yawning mightily.

"William saw something that might help us," Serena said.

Jason rubbed at his eyes and yawned again. "Where are we?"

William answered. "And don't ask what I saw. We'll know if I'm right in a few minutes."

The fallow farms and fields passed by beneath the light of a crescent moon and the stars. The Scout chugged along, and several minutes later, William breathed a sigh of relief. A red-and-white striped tent became visible. A big-top.

"A circus," Jason asked, sounding confused. "Why'd you bring us here?"

William didn't answer. Instead, he took the turnoff to the campground.

A large sign at the entrance, similar to the one on the highway, proclaimed the presence of *Wizard Bill's Wandering Wonders* and the dates when it would be in town. Small print at the bottom of the display indicated the names of the owners, Bill and Nancy Londoner.

This early, the circus rides remained closed and unmoving, and the big-top entrance closed up. No one appeared yet awake, but despite the emptiness, a quiet, watchful vigor stirred the grounds, a sense of hidden glories and wonders.

"What are we doing here?" Serena asked.

"We need to hide from Kohl Obsidian," William explained, "and we need to stay out in public."

Serena groaned. "You want us to join the circus?"

"Hear me out," William entreated. "The circus travels. If this one is heading west, we can join them and we'll be heading roughly the same direction that we want to go anyway. Best of all, there's always lots of people around. There's the circus folk, and the crowds coming to see them. They might even have a bunch of animals."

"Necrosed don't like animals," Jason said. "They mess with their senses."

"This circus has them," Serena said, pointing out a number of animal trailers and stacks of hay.

"They've even got bears," William said. He pointed to a hauler.

"Momma Bridget's Balancing Bears," Serena read before turning to Jason with a wondering smile. "Is it just me or is this starting to actually make sense?"

"It's not just you," he replied, smiling in return. "Kohl will *never* come close to us as long as we're with the circus."

"As soon as the circus folk wake up, we should find out what it takes to join them," William said.

"But can we afford to sit here and wait that long?" Serena asked. "Until they wake up, I mean. What if they're all hungover? Kohl won't wait for them to sober up."

"Kohl's back in Cincinnati," William said. "I can feel him. He's miles behind us."

Jason fumbled about through his things before finally hauling out a book. He flipped through the pages and seemed to study it with rapt focus. He grinned in relief after a moment. "No nearby *saha'asras*."

"Then it looks like we're running away to join the circus," William said with an answering grin.

Jason groaned. "I can't believe you said that."

"We still have to convince these people to let us join them," Serena said.

"We'll figure it out. *Asra* and all that." Jason wiggled his fingers.

"*Asra?*" Serena asked.

"Magic. I'll explain later," Jason said.

"I'd appreciate it," Serena said, smiling at him again.

She seemed to be smiling at Jason a lot all of a sudden, and William had to stifle a tide of conflicted emotions, jealousy amongst them. He had no romantic claims on her, so what was with the feelings?

CHAPTER 18: THE CIRCUS

Soon after their arrival, the circus began to rouse. People stepped out of their trailers and moved about to start various tasks. Horses were led out of their stalls, washed down, and let loose in a nearby field.

From a large hauler echoed a series of deep-throated whoofs.

"Guess you were right about the bears," Jason said to William.

"What?" Serena asked, sitting up in the back seat. She had fallen asleep again while they waited for the circus to stir.

"I was right about the bears," William said. "Guess you could call me Nostradamus."

"More like Nostradumbass," Jason said.

Serena rolled her eyes. "Is it too early to check on the owners?"

"The sun's barely risen," Jason noted.

"But all these other people are already up and at it," Serena said.

"If we want to join the circus, it probably isn't a good idea to piss off the owners by waking them," Jason said. "I say we give it a little more time."

Serena muttered something inaudible and lay down on the back seat again.

While they waited, William studied the circus. From a distance, the tents and trailers had a certain allure to them, but up close, they seemed rundown and shabby. Rust marred some of the equipment, and the red stripes on the tent were faded.

Minutes later, William sat up straight. "It's time," he said. "Look." He gestured to a trailer that proclaimed itself *Bill and Nancy's Place*. Someone had just exited. "Bill and Nancy. Those are the owners. Someone just left their trailer. They're up."

"Let's go," Serena said, sliding out of the backseat.

They walked up to the trailer, and their breath misted in the winter air.

"Where's Kohl?" Jason asked.

"Same as before. Way back there," William said. He rapped on the trailer door.

"Hold on," someone grumbled from inside. "This better be important, or I'll feed your balls to the bears." A short, pot-bellied man with a red face and a handlebar mustache threw open the door. "What do you want?"

"Excuse us, sir, but—" William began.

The door slammed shut in their faces. William shared a look of confusion with Serena and Jason before knocking again.

"What do you want?" the red-faced man growled. "And if you call me 'sir' again, you'll get my boot up your backside. Hurry up."

"Are you Bill Londoner?" William asked.

"Who's asking?" the red-faced man demanded followed by an epic belch.

William mentally rolled his eyes. *The red-faced toad was hungover.* "We're but three lost folk who would like to become circus performers," William said, mangling a quote from *The Princess Bride.*

"Who's at the door?" a nasally voice asked. A tall, thin woman with an impressive bouffant hairdo pressed past the red-faced man.

Both of them appeared to be in their fifties or early sixties. They wore matching pink-striped pajamas, although the man's stretched unsuccessfully in an attempt to cover his bulging belly.

"Who are you?" she demanded. "If you're a mite slow, I wouldn't be calling Bill 'sir', either. We're circus folk. We aren't sirs or ma'ams."

William was about to repeat his line about being lost folk, but Jason spoke first. "We were hoping to join your circus."

"Not interested," the man said.

"Stop being such a grumpy, old troll," the woman scolded before turning back to William and his friends. "I'm Nancy Londoner. Call me Mrs. Nancy." She eyed them up and down. "So you want to join our circus, eh? What can you do?"

"I'm a magus," Jason said.

"I don't know what a magus is, but we already have a magician," Bill said.

"What about sword-fighters?" William asked.

"You any good?" Bill asked.

"We're the best." William infused his voice with enthusiasm.

"I don't care. I mean, is your act any good?" Bill asked. "Are you as good as the ninjas in the movies?"

William and Jason shared a glance.

Bill smiled sardonically. “Thought so.”

“We are good,” Jason said. “But we can also cook and clean, do anything you need.”

“We could use the help,” Mrs. Nancy said. “We’ve been short-handed ever since Randy and Todd left last week.”

“Arrested, you mean,” Bill scoffed. “Worthless idiots. Starting a bar fight.” He shook his head. “What about you?” he asked Serena. “Can you do anything more than cook and clean?”

“I’m an acrobat,” Serena replied, her voice smooth and confident.

“We’ve got acrobats.”

“Not like me.”

“Sure of yourself, aren’t you, girl?” Bill said. “Well, you better not be wasting my time or I’m going to have Sam the Strongman twist the lot of you into pretzels.”

“Be quiet, Bill,” Mrs. Nancy admonished. “Stop trying to scare them. We can use the help. You know it. And we’re thin on acts since Mysterio the Magnificent quit.”

“Maybe, but I’d rather be thin on acts than waste the audience’s time,” Bill said.

Mrs. Nancy rolled her eyes. “At least find out what they can do before passing on them.”

“I need a drink,” Bill grumbled. “You handle this.”

“You always need a drink,” Mrs. Nancy shouted at his retreating back before returning her attention to William and his friends. “There are three kinds of folk who want to join the circus. The first love performing. That’s admirable. The second think our kind of life is glamorous. That’s stupid. And the third are running from something, which is sad. What kind are you?”

"Does it have to just be one kind?" Serena asked. "What if we like to perform, but also have private reasons for wanting to join?"

Mrs. Nancy broke out into a warm smile. "And the fourth kind—Did I mention there's a fourth kind?—are smart enough to know that no one is just one type of anything. Head over to the cookhouse. They should have breakfast ready by now. Find Jimmy and tell him Mrs. Nancy said to feed you."

William perked up.

"When Bill's ready, we'll come see what you can do," Mrs. Nancy said. "And he wasn't kidding. You better not be wasting his time."

"Where did Mrs. Nancy say the cookhouse was?" William asked.

"Just follow your nose," Serena said. "We'll find it." She inhaled deeply and captured the lovely scent of sizzling bacon. "This way."

She trailed the delicious scents of cooking food and led them to an area walled off by a number of haulers and campers, and apparently closed to the public. From within came the unmistakable aromas of sizzling bacon and sausage.

"I'm starving," William announced.

"Same here," Serena said.

She hummed *"Gloria"* as she pushed past the rough gate shielding the cookhouse and paused inside the entrance. Several awnings leaned off the campers, and from a large smoker came the smell and sound of sizzling bacon and sausages. A picnic table groaned beneath a pile of food, and an open fire pit provided heat. A small group of people milled about, some with the graceful movements of athletes, and others who moved like ordinary folk. They all turned when Serena, William, and Jason entered the cookhouse, unwelcoming expressions on their faces.

"Public ain't allowed here," said an old, beefy, bald man who stood behind the picnic table. He spoke with a deep Southern drawl and wore a stained apron that might have been white at one time and a scowl every bit as unwelcoming as the others'.

"Mrs. Nancy sent us," Serena answered. "She said to find Jimmy and ask him for breakfast."

"I'm Jimmy," the bald man said, his expression still unfriendly. "Who's you? And what business you got with the Londoners?"

"We want to join the circus," William said.

"You ever been in one before, boy?" Jimmy asked.

"No," William answered.

Serena suppressed a sigh. William was honest to a fault, a habit he'd have to break when her father got hold of him.

Jimmy scoffed, and amused chuckles broke out from the others seated or standing around the cookhouse.

"Mrs. Nancy says that Bill will be by later in the morning, when he's ready, and see what we can do," Serena said.

"You mean when he's over his hangover," someone muttered.

"Or when he's sober," someone else said.

Jimmy glared about before turning back to Serena, William, and Jason. "Don't mind these nattering nabobs and gossip-mongers. They don't know nothin'," he said. "Here, grab a plate and some food. And it's *Mr.* Bill to you, missy. Mrs. Nancy is the only one who gets to call him Bill.

"Thank you," Serena said when Jimmy handed her a plate. She smiled at him, pleased when his scowl softened. Isha had taught her to use every advantage, and a smile offered by a pretty girl to a man, no matter his age, always worked wonders.

"Mr. Bill ain't at his best in the morning," Jimmy said, "but he'll have you sorted out soon enough." He gave them a stern expression. "And you best not be wasting his time."

They each gathered some food, and William took an appreciative whiff of his hearty meal of bacon, eggs, sausage, and fried potatoes, and Jason did the same. The two of them dug in and wore expressions of concentration as they gobbled their food as quickly as possible.

Serena wanted to follow suit, but she ate her breakfast slowly and daintily. After all, she did have an image to maintain.

However, while she ate, she caught William glancing around and appearing worried. She could guess what had him concerned. "Kohl's miles behind us," she reminded him. "Besides, Jason said that a necrosed won't show up during the day with all these people and animals nearby."

"I know," William said. "But I hope that by being here we aren't putting these people at risk."

"It'll be fine," Serena said and without thinking, she reached out and squeezed William's hand.

William offered a smile. "I'm glad you're not mad at me anymore."

Serena withdrew her hand. For a moment she'd forgotten she was supposed to be angry at William for his lies and for putting her in danger. "Who says I'm not," she said in a frosty tone.

William's smile fell, and a worm of guilt curdled her stomach.

"You ever going to tell us about that sword and your bow and arrows?" Jason asked around a mouthful of food.

Serena had worked out her explanation before she'd left to join them at Winton Woods. "My dad spent a lot of time in China," she said. "He taught me what he learned there."

"And you never mentioned it before because . . . ?" Jason persisted.

Serena shrugged. "I knew you and William practiced the longsword, but I didn't want to poke my nose into what the two of you were doing."

"Why not?" William asked.

"Because then you'd have wanted to spar against me," Serena said. "Besides, your practice always seemed like it was something private, just the two of you. I didn't want to butt in."

"Well, there's no butting in now," Jason replied. "You have to show us what you've got."

"We'll see," Serena said.

"You have to," Jason persisted.

"I said we'll see," Serena said, this time with more steel in her voice.

"Sword. Bow and arrow," William mused. "What else can you do?"

Serena grinned slyly. "My dad taught me kung fu."

Mr. Bill came stomping into the cookhouse an hour later. “You’re still here.”

“Mrs. Nancy told us to wait for you,” Serena said. “We can show you what we can do now.”

Mr. Bill held up a finger. “Not yet. First I need some coffee and some food.” He glanced around. “Jimmy!”

Jimmy stepped out of a camper. “You know me, boss. I kept it warm in the oven.” The beefy, old cook brought out a cup of black coffee and a plate piled high with crispy bacon, fried eggs, and flapjacks. “All the way you like ‘em.”

“Thanks, Jimmy,” Mr. Bill said with a nod.

“You need anything else, boss, you let me know,” Jimmy said before waddling off toward a large tub full of dirty dishes.

William thought Jimmy was walking weird, and Mr. Bill noticed, too.

“You okay, Jimmy? You’re walking funny,” Mr. Bill said.

“I feel like my butt crack’s eating my britches is all,” Jimmy answered with a dejected frown. “Can’t pick it out ‘cause my hands is all wet. If I do, it’ll look like I soiled myself.”

William had a sudden case of coughing to suppress his laughter, and so did Serena and Jason. They studiously avoided meeting one another’s eyes.

“Go dry your hands off, fix your britches problem, wash your hands, and then clean off the rest of the dishes,” Mr. Bill said.

Jimmy nodded vigorously, a relieved expression on his face. “Sure thing, boss. That’s a good idea.”

He waddled out of view, and Mr. Bill briefly shook his head. “Poor man’s thicker than a bank vault,” he said before taking a sip of coffee. He sighed in appreciation. “That’s the stuff.”

William had tried the coffee too, but it wasn't for him. The stuff was thick enough to tar a driveway.

But it must have been just what the doctor ordered for Mr. Bill. After that first sip he dug into his breakfast. He ate steadily and without stopping, relentlessly plowing through his food but never gulping. He finally finished and sat back with a satisfied pat of his belly and a jovial smile. "Now, my young lads and lady, tell me your names."

Introductions were made, and Mr. Bill greeted them all with a handshake. "I believe you wanted to show me what you can do. Let us make haste to the parking lot, where the three of you will have plenty of space to offer up your performances."

William shared a glance with the others. Earlier in the morning, Mr. Bill had been as irritable as a thorn-pawed bear. Now he was as friendly as a cat with a nose full of catnip.

"Don't dawdle," Mr. Bill said, exiting the cookhouse. "We haven't all day."

"Best not keep the bossman waiting," Jimmy advised with a shooing gesture.

William shrugged at Jason. "Weird."

"Definitely weird," Jason agreed.

"Hurry up, you two," Serena said as she departed the cookhouse.

William and Jason jogged to catch up with her.

"Why don't we start with the boys," Mr. Bill said when they reached the parking lot. "Show me what you can do with your swords."

"Yes, sir," William said.

Mr. Bill scowled.

"I mean, yes, Mr. Bill," he immediately amended.

He and Jason drew out the training blades they'd retrieved from the Scout while they'd been waiting. The edges were dull, but a strike from one of them could still hurt like hell. For the winter talent show at St. Francis, they had planned to do a demonstration with their longswords, so they already had a routine worked out.

Halfway into their performance, Mr. Bill waved them off and called them to stop. "Boys, you've got promise, but there's no spark. Can't you mix in some jumps and flips, like in a ninja movie?"

"I guess so," Jason said. He sounded as doubtful as William felt.

"Is that *'I guess so'*, or *'I guess no'*?" Mr. Bill asked with narrowed eyes.

"We can do it," William answered. "We can add in backflips and stuff."

"Well, work on it. If you get it shiny enough, I'll give you a shot," Mr. Bill said. "For now, though, I can't use you in the show, but like Mrs. Nancy said we need some help with the crew. If you're willing to clean, fetch, and do whatever the foreman tells you, you're hired."

William and Jason shared a smile of relief. "We'll do it," Jason said.

"Good. Now let's see what the girl's got."

"We need to go to our truck," Serena said.

She led them to the Scout, and once there, she shucked off her coat, shoes, and socks, and from a backpack removed two long, sheer scarves, one green and the other one yellow. Longer than a sari, they both seemed to go on forever. Serena weighted one end of each scarf with a large washer, twirled the heavy ends, and flung them over an overhanging streetlamp.

"Tie them to the Scout's bumper," she said to William, handing him the weighted ends. "Make sure they don't come undone."

After William did as she'd told him, Serena gripped the scarves and climbed them.

William had never seen her bare-limbed before, and he stared in appreciation as the muscles in her arms and shoulders rippled as she ascended.

When she reached the same height as the overhanging streetlamp, Serena stretched her arms out and hung suspended in the form of a crucifix, held aloft by only the sheer fabric. Serena rotated, a graceful inversion until she swung upside down. Again she rotated. Again. And a final time, all the while her muscles flexed and moved beneath her smooth, brown skin. She now had the scarves looped around her arms and hung right-side up again. Serena opened her hands and released the fabric.

William gasped. He wasn't the only one.

Serena remained suspended by the portion of the scarves that she'd wrapped around her arms. She grasped the fabric again and did the splits. In that position, Serena wrapped her feet in a tight binding of the sheer material and again let go of the scarves.

William instinctively reached out to catch her.

"Sweet Father," Mr. Bill mumbled. "We've got to find her the right costume, and the right story."

Once again, the material held Serena up, but this time by the fabric around her feet. She rotated upside down and spun in mid-air. Then, with a gentle flick of her wrists, the scarves coiled around her arms. With a snap of her legs, the material unwrapped from her ankles. Rotating to right-side up, she resumed the form of a crucifix. A moment later, she unwrapped the scarves from her arms and climbed to the level of the lamppost. Up above them, she scissored her legs and rotated her arms. Most of the scarves' lengths were now wrapped around her body.

"What's she doing?" William asked.

"I have no idea," Jason said.

Serena let go of the scarves, and they unspooled from around her.

This time William did dart forward, arms held up, prepared to catch her before she smashed into the ground.

Several yards before she would have smacked the concrete of the parking lot, Serena snapped to a halt. She gracefully descended the last few feet to the ground, alighting in William's arms. He set her down, and she grinned as she stared him in the eyes, her hands resting on his shoulders and his on her waist.

He managed to smile back through his conflicted emotions, desire warring with the inexplicable caution he couldn't seem to shake.

"Fantastic!" Mr. Bill clapped loudly. "You'll be the prize. I can see it now. William and Serena are circling one another on the ground, like you're young lovers dancing. You're about to kiss, but then Jason shows up. William doesn't know how to fight. All you've got is a stick."

"But I thought you wanted us to do ninja moves," William said.

Mr. Bill waved his words aside. "Later. For now, you've got a plain outfit. Jason's is much fancier. He's an evil, master swordsman while you're a nobody. Jason drives you off. Then Serena does her performance." Mr. Bill punched the air for emphasis, and he grew increasingly animated. "Serena is dancing in the scarves. She's in the air doing her routine, rotating in the air. The crowd's gasping, sure she'll die.

"Then William shows up again, but this time you're in a fancy outfit, too. You're a master swordsman now. You and Jason fight, but the two of you have to sell it. You're fighting for Serena. She's the center of your performance. In the end, William is victorious. You wait for Serena under her scarves, catching her just before she hits the ground." His eyes lit with enthusiasm. "It's perfect!"

"Does that mean we're hired on as circus performers, also?" Jason asked.

"Artists. We don't say circus performers," Mr. Bill said. "Right now you're crew, but you'll eventually be artists. We'll see how it works out. Go see Mrs. Nancy. She has all the paperwork about wages and stuff. After that, ask her to send you on to Jane, our seamstress."

Mr. Bill stared at the still-hanging scarves, wearing a broad grin. "The crowds will love it."

CHAPTER 19: A TRAVELING CIRCUS

When William, Jason, and Serena returned to Mr. Bill's camper, Mrs. Nancy greeted them at the door with a warm smile. "Did Bill like your performances?"

"He liked Serena's," Jason said. "Me and William, not so much. He's got a lot of changes he wants us to make."

"I'm sure you and William will be fine," Serena said, offering Jason a warm smile.

William once again suppressed a surge of jealousy. *What was going on between those two?*

"Then you'll be crew for a while," Mrs. Nancy said. "That's better than what my own children did. Neither of them wanted the circus life."

"Why?" Jason stated.

"You'd have to ask them." Mrs. Nancy shrugged. "They seem happy enough with their lives, but it's a world away from what Bill and I have built. A tax attorney and a dentist." She barked laughter. "Can you imagine two professions less like the circus?"

"Their loss," Jason said with a grin.

"Did Bill tell you to meet with Jane?" Mrs. Nancy asked.

"The seamstress? Yes, he did, ma'am," William said.

"You keep saying 'sir' and 'ma'am," Mrs. Nancy said, her head tilted in puzzlement. "Why?"

"It's how I was raised," William answered. "It's considered polite."

"I suppose so," she said. "Just remember what I told you about calling Mr. Bill 'sir'."

"I remember."

"Good. Right." Mrs. Nancy became all business. "I have some forms for you to sign." She fetched a binder full of papers and had the three of them sign some liability waivers and non-disclosure agreements.

Afterward, she directed them to Jane, the seamstress who travelled with the circus. She was a slender, owl-eyed woman of an indeterminate age. She could have passed for anywhere between sixty and eighty. Her white hair and seamed face indicated great age, but her eyes, despite being hidden behind Coke bottle-thick lenses, were young and curious.

Jane smiled when they entered her trailer. "Bill stopped by earlier. He told me to expect you." She clapped her hands. "Now. Let's get started."

Her camper was crowded with bolts of cloth, pieces of fabric, and spools of thread with the center of the room dominated by an old Singer sewing machine. Jane shifted items aside, muttering all the while. "It has to be eye-catching."

While she searched, William asked, "I thought circuses only traveled in the summer."

Jane glanced up from her search. "We do, but in his august genius, Bill Londoner wanted to try a winter tour, with no competition from other circuses."

"It hasn't worked out so well?" William guessed.

"It's worked out fine," Jane corrected. "But I think I speak on behalf of most everyone when I say we'd rather be home for the holidays instead of touring."

"How much longer is the tour?" Serena asked.

"Not long. We're only running from Thanksgiving to New Year's. Then it's home."

"Where's home?" Jason asked.

"Salt Lake City, Utah."

"That's your last stop?" Serena pressed.

"No. That's Las Vegas, Nevada."

"Just two more weeks and it's all over," William mused.

Jane peered at him over the rim of her thick glasses. "You picked a strange time to join us," she said. "After Las Vegas, you'll have to find some other work until the spring tour." She gave a grunt of satisfaction. "Found it." She hefted a bolt of shiny, yellow fabric and held it up to Serena's chest. "You'll look wonderful in this. It contrasts so nicely with your dark hair." She eyed Serena up and down. "And we'll make it form fitting, of course. You have a lovely body, dear. Perfect bosom. Not flat-chested like so many acrobats."

Serena reddened. "Thank you," she said.

Jane continued as though she hadn't heard or seen Serena's embarrassment. "Yes. The yellow fabric, and dark piping to match your eyes. We'll also have some flowered patterns to act as a highlight. I think I have some leftover material. It should work perfectly. Now let's measure you." She pulled out a tailor's tape and had Serena turn this way and that, stand still, walk, hold her arms out to the side, all sorts of postures.

Jane wrote down the measurements, and when the seamstress felt satisfied, she turned her attention to William and Jason. "Now for you two," she announced. "We'll have to make sure to highlight your packages. Make them pop," she said, tapping her teeth. "The women love that. Some men, too."

William and Jason reddened while Serena chuckled.

Jane had them turning, standing, arms out . . . all the things she'd had Serena do, and after she finished she stepped back with a satisfied smile. "I'll have the costumes ready in three days."

The circus packed up and left Wayne, Illinois the next day. Early in the morning after the final performances, everyone, even the artists, helped break down the tents, stalls, and rides. They packed everything, including the vehicles, onto a train to carry it to their next stop. The long day of labor didn't finish until late afternoon, and by then, most everyone was ready to have an early supper and go to sleep.

Of course the senior performers, such as Sam the Strongman, Mistress Purdy the Mistress of Cats, and Dr. Devious the Enchanter from the Farthest East and his assistant, the Fabulous Winona, dozed in the best spots. William, Serena, and Jason had to accept a set of blankets rolled out on the floor of the combine car.

Jason snored lightly in his nest, but William wasn't ready to rest. His mind and emotions roiled, and he sat in the open frame of the side door, staring outside. The train rattled along the tracks with the wheels striking a regular rhythm, and the winter-fallow cornfields lay beneath a fresh dusting of snow. His breath misted in the air, and the blaze of lights from a small town briefly brightened the night before the darkness took hold once again. The landscape seemed to unspool before him like a slow, hypnotic film.

"You're not freezing out here?" Serena asked, sitting down next to him.

William glanced at her. She was wrapped up in a thick coat and a scarf—a normal scarf, not one of the long, silky ones she used in her act. "I can close the door if it's too cold for you," he said, rising to his feet.

Serena shook her head. "Leave it open."

Her voice was as cool as the night, and William figured she was still upset with him. The truth was, he was also upset with her. He didn't see why she was taking out her frustrations on him, and right now, he didn't want to be around her. "I was about ready for bed," William lied. "The door's yours. Good night."

"Don't go."

William looked her way. She stared out the open door. "You sure?" he asked.

"I'm sure." Serena held up a hand. "Stay."

William ignored her hand and sat down.

"I'm sorry for how I've treated you," Serena said. "I shouldn't blame you for what happened, but you have to understand—"

"Your life's been torn apart," William said. "I get it."

"Maybe you do, but it doesn't make it right that I took it out on you."

"What about Jason?"

"What about him?"

William glanced back at his friend. Jason lay buried beneath a mound of blankets. He appeared comfortable. "You blamed me for what happened, but not him or Mr. Zeus." His jealousy stirred, and with it the anger that never seemed to entirely dissipate.

"Jason's safe. He's simple, easy, you know? Around him, I don't have to worry about . . ." Serena paused.

"Worry about what?"

She shrugged. "It's nothing. Maybe I blamed you more for getting me in this mess because I care about you more. You kept this secret from me, and it felt more of a betrayal coming from you than it did from Jason."

"I would have told you if I could have," William said.

"That's the only reason why you didn't say anything?" Serena asked.

William nodded. "It's the only reason."

"And you've apologized enough for it." Serena wore a guilty expression. "I should have forgiven you a long time ago." She took his hand and gave it a squeeze. "Just don't keep anything like that from me ever again."

William offered a hesitant smile. "Are we still mad at each other?"

"Only if you want to be," Serena said with a faint smile of her own.

"I'd rather not," William said. A wash of relief ebbed through him. "I'll tell you the truth next time."

"You'd better." Serena playfully punched his thigh. "I know how to use a sword, remember?"

"I only have your word on that," William said. "For all I know, you might not know the pointy end from the hilt."

A challenging glint lit Serena's eyes. The last of the tension between them dissipated like a phantasm. "Think so, huh? Then maybe you should try me."

William unaccountably got the sense that she'd wipe the floor with him. "My mom taught me not to fight with girls."

"Because she knew you'd lose." She gave him another playful punch to the thigh, and William captured her hand before she could do it again. Her punches stung.

Serena wore a wistful expression. "Can you feel him?" she asked.

William didn't have to ask to whom she referred. "Yes," he said. "But not as much. He's way back there, probably still in Cincinnati. Waiting."

"Maybe Jason's right and animals really do mess with his senses. Maybe we'll be safe here."

"I hope so," William said. "But you know we'll eventually have to deal with him."

"I don't want to talk about it right now," Serena said with a shiver.

"Are you cold?"

"Is that why you think I shivered?" Serena gave him an arch gaze. "Or is that your subtle way of asking if you can put your arm around me?"

It hadn't been, but William went with it. "I plead the fifth."

"Even though you only think of me as a friend?" Serena asked.

William had no ready answer. Until recently, he'd thought friendship was all he felt toward Serena, but with everything that had happened in the past twenty-four hours, he wasn't so sure any more.

"No answer?" Serena pressed, staring at him with her oddly intense gaze.

"I don't know," William answered.

"Honesty," Serena said. "At last." She immediately ducked her head, appearing contrite. "I'm sorry. I said I forgave you, and I did."

Their conversation quieted, and they stared in silence at the world beyond the train.

"You're really just going to let me stay cold?" Serena asked at last.

William returned her arch gaze. "Is that your subtle way of asking me to put my arm around you?"

Serena chuckled. "Well played."

William drew her close, and she rested her head on his shoulder.

"I like this," Serena said. "It's much nicer than being mad at you."

William squeezed her shoulder in silent agreement. It was nice, but not enough to overcome his odd disquiet.

"You know, you're a very unusual person," Serena said.

"How so?"

"You like *Lord of the Rings, Star Wars,* so many things that aren't of this world, and yet here you are, part of a world of magic, and you act like you hate it."

"Yeah, I guess I do hate it in a lot of ways," William said. "My family died, and . . ." He trailed off.

"Yeah, I see what you mean."

A horse whinnied, and William glanced into the interior of the railcar before returning his attention to the world outside. The scenery passed, dark and quiet except for the train chugging along. The moonlight reflected off snowy fields.

Serena closed her eyes and spoke.

Fleet-footed, I race across stubbled ground,
Aglow with warm magic and the pale moon.
Unseen lines anchor my hope, and a sound
Of welcome breathes life into my cold heart.

"What was that?" William asked, moved by the words even though he didn't understand them.

"It's an old poem."

"It's beautiful."

"I'm glad you like it," Serena said, "but it's not really all that old." She smiled. "I wrote it."

"You?"

"Me. You're the only person I've ever told it to." Serena gazed up at William. "Don't tell anyone."

"I won't," William said, touched by her gesture. "But you should know something about me."

"What's that?"

"My brother Landon used to call me a bladder-mouth."

"You mean a blabbermouth?"

"No. A bladder-mouth. He said I leaked secrets." William grinned, waiting for her response.

Serena made a moue of disgust. "Gross. Now I'll never get that image out of my head."

"Then my work here is done," William said with a chuckle.

"Really? That's what you think your work is?" Serena's eyes

twinkled. "Disgust the person who was mad at you a little while ago?"

"It did make you smile, though, didn't it?"

"I didn't smile."

"Your eyes did. They don't lie."

A fleeting flash of sorrow passed across her face, so quickly that William doubted he saw it.

"Where are we?" Jason asked, yawning mightily.

The sun had risen hours earlier, and the clamor of grunting bears, growling tigers, and cursing crew filled the air. The train cars that had hauled the animals stood open, and the stench of soiled bedding lingered despite the water hoses washing them down.

A blustery wind blew, chilling Serena. "Newton, Kansas, our next stop," she answered. "Get up. We're supposed to help unload the train and set up at some campground."

"Where's William?" Jason asked, sitting up and stretching.

"He rolled the Scout off the flatbed and went ahead with Mr. Bill and some of the advance team."

"I'm surprised he's not hungover," Jason said. "Mr. Bill, I mean."

"I knew who you meant," Serena replied. She tried to imagine William drunk, and came up with an image of him giggling like a girl. She hid a smile at the thought.

"What are we supposed to do?" Jason asked.

"Clean out the cars where the animals were housed. We've got to haul out all the shit—"

"Language," Jason chided her.

"It won't be the last time I curse, given the amount of *shit* we have to clean out," Serena said.

Jason grimaced. "I wish I'd gone with William."

"Then you should have gotten up earlier."

"Speaking of William, why didn't you go with him? The two of you still arguing?"

"No. He and I made up last night while you were asleep." Serena felt grateful that she didn't have to keep pretending to be angry at William. Maybe it was because she thought of William as a friend, and friends didn't lie to each other. Which was ironic, because Serena lied about everything. Her true nature and motivations, her interest in William, even her supposed feelings for him. In all ways, Serena was a liar, so why had that lie, pretending anger toward William, bothered her so much?

She didn't know the answer, but whatever the explanation she recognized it as another chink in her armor, another point of vulnerability. She was also vain enough to wonder why her ploy with William, her intention for him to desire her hadn't worked.

"Good," Jason said. "He didn't deserve you yelling at him."

"Careful," Serena warned. "You aren't entirely blameless in this."

"How's any of this my fault?" Jason asked. "I didn't create the necrosed, and I didn't ask one of them to show up and try to kill us."

"You lied to me."

Jason waved off her words. "So what? If the necrosed hadn't

shown up, you'd have never learned who we are. You'd have been happy in your ignorance, and not knowing the truth would never have hurt you."

"You think so? You think not knowing the truth about you, Lien, Daniel, their parents, and Mr. Zeus didn't hurt?"

Jason eyed her for a moment. "Well, when you say it like that," he muttered sourly.

Serena laughed. "I'm going to remind you of that one of these days. Now let's get this done. Those cars aren't going to clean themselves."

"You sure about that? I am a very powerful magus, you know." Jason wiggled his fingers.

"Then what's stopping you?"

"Maybe I don't want to."

"Or maybe you can't. Weren't you telling William that you have some sort of thingy that helps you use your magic?"

"Yes, I have a *nomasra*, a device that stores *lorasra*. It's how I stay alive in the Far Abroad."

"Then it's finite, isn't it? Meaning you can't risk wasting it to wash down the cars."

Jason frowned at her for a moment before muttering something that sounded like a curse.

"Well?"

Jason sighed. "Even on Arylyn, I couldn't waste *lorasra* like that."

Interesting. Her people had very little knowledge about the magi, their abilities and limitations. Yet Jason had just divulged up information that might prove useful later on.

But how best to use it?

"You sure do know how to take the fun out of something," Jason said.

Serena blinked. She had to replay Jason's words in her mind as her attention snapped back to the here and now. "I'm sure I do," she said. "Now grab a shovel and a rake and let's go."

Half an hour into the work, Jason cast down his rake in disgust. "How do animals produce so much . . ." He seemed to fumble about for the right word.

"You can say it," Serena said with a smile.

"Shit. How do animals produce so much shit?"

"Didn't you take Biology like the rest of us last semester?" Serena asked. "I'm pretty sure we covered that topic early on."

"Very funny."

"Don't feel bad," Serena said. "We're almost done with this car. Just two more to go."

Jason groaned. "How did we end up with this work, anyway?"

"We were voluntold."

Jason frowned. "What's voluntold mean?"

"It's a portmanteau."

"A portmanwho?"

"A portmanteau. A word that combines the sounds and meanings of two other ones. Like brunch: breakfast and lunch. Voluntold: volunteered and told what to do."

Jason grinned. "I like that. I should voluntold William next time we have to clean Mr. Zeus' workshop." His grin fell away a moment later.

"Kohl's still back there," Serena said.

CHAPTER 20: CHRISTMAS FORTUNE

William backflipped over Jason's lunge and countered with a thrust. He parried, and angled a horizontal slash that made Jason slide aside to avoid it. Another exchange of blows ended with both of them doing front-flips in parallel.

He and Jason practiced in a small corner of the big top. Other performers also went over their routines in different areas of the tent.

"Break!" Mr. Bill called out. "Fantastic! The crowd will love all that jumping around, and the jabbing makes it come off as so much more dangerous than when you just slap swords at each other."

William, tired and drenched in sweat, smiled in relief at Mr. Bill's enthusiastic response.

When he and Jason had first been told what was expected in their act, they had commiserated with each other with head shakes and eyerolls. All that jumping around would be ridiculous, but they also knew that if that's what Mr. Bill wanted, then that's what he would get. They'd worked hard to make it so, and with the fruits of their labor now seen as successful, they shared a grin of triumph.

"William's flips could use some work," Luc Dubrovic observed, a balding, middle-aged man of medium height who had the bulldog build of a gymnast. He headed the famous Dubrovic family of tumblers from Croatia, but his real name was Stanley Wilson, and there was no Dubrovic family of tumblers from Croatia. The artists in *Wizard Bill's Wandering Wonders* were all American gymnasts who were unrelated to one another and had been thrown together by Mr. Bill's manic madness.

But family or not, William thought them amazing tumblers. Yesterday, their second day in Newton, Kansas, Mr. Bill had asked Luc to help spice up William and Jason's routine, and the gymnast had added a bunch of backflips and handsprings, so many that William doubted he'd be able to do them all. Of course, Jason had no such concerns—he was a born athlete, but William wasn't so blessed. Somehow, though, he'd muddled through, mastering all the rolls, flips, tumbles, and jumps that Luc had built into their act.

"It needs to be tighter," Luc advised William. "You need to keep your knees and feet together. Otherwise, your legs will eventually throw you off balance and down you'll go."

"Fine. Fine. Work on the flips," Mr. Bill said, waving aside Luc's criticisms. "But otherwise, it looks great! I can't believe how quickly the two of you picked things up. At this rate, you'll be able to perform by our last night here." His red face brimmed with excitement and a faraway gleam lit his eyes.

"You can't be serious. There's no way they'll be—" Luc began.

Mr. Bill had already wandered off. "Where's Serena?" he shouted. "She needs to get in more practice, too."

Luc sighed before turning back to William and Jason. "Take a break," he said. "Be back here in five."

"Yes, sir," William said. "I mean. We will, Luc," he hastily corrected.

He and Jason trudged off toward an unoccupied corner of the big top. Along the way they called out greetings to Sam the Strongman and Dr. Devious. Both artists were getting in some last-minute practice before their first performance later that day.

"I could use some coffee," Jason said.

"Didn't you just have some at breakfast?"

"Yeah, but I'm still sleepy. I had some weird dreams that kept me up."

"Hi, boys," Elaina Sinith, the fortune teller, called out as she approached them. Elaina likely wasn't much older than them, but William couldn't tell for sure. Not with her always having her hair bound up inside a turban, wearing creepy ghost-like face paint, and dressing in over-sized clothing that wouldn't have appeared out of place on a bag-lady. Still, Elaina possessed an exotic quality, something that hinted at a beauty hidden beneath her ugly clothing and makeup.

William wasn't sure why, but he found himself following Elaina's movements whenever she was around, unable to understand what drew his attention to her.

"What are you two doing?" she asked.

"Luc and Mr. Bill have us practicing our new routine," Jason answered.

"I saw some of it," Elaina replied. "It looked great. The two of you sure have come a long way since . . . What's it been? Less than a week?"

"I guess hard work pays off," William said with a grin. "But Luc thinks my handsprings are sloppy."

Elaina rolled her eyes. "Luc thinks Nadia Comaneci's handsprings are sloppy."

William and Jason laughed.

"But you have to tell me your secret," Elaina said. "Yesterday only Jason could do the tumbles." Her eyes twinkled as she stared at William. "How'd you get so good so fast? It wasn't magic, was it? I heard Jason says he's a magus, whatever that is. Are you one, too?"

William's face got hot while Jason chuckled nervously.

Elaina threw her head back and laughed. "You should see your faces," she said. "I was just kidding. I know you aren't real magicians."

"In some small towns, they still believe in witches," Jason told her. "The people there don't react well to them."

Some of Elaina's humor left her. "No, they don't." She nodded to William and Jason. "I have to work out some kinks in my act." She sashayed on her way, elegant and graceful, and even in her baggy clothes, she was a view to behold.

"I could watch that all day," Jason muttered.

"Amen, brother."

Jason eyed him in surprise. "I thought you only had eyes for Serena."

William tried not to fidget. He wanted to like Serena, but something in him simply wouldn't easily bend in that direction. "Maybe I do, but it doesn't mean I'm blind."

"I think even a blind man would appreciate Elaina," Jason agreed.

William laughed, but even to him, his humor sounded half-hearted.

"What is it?" Jason asked, apparently picking up on his uncertainty.

"Kohl," William quickly said, which wasn't a complete lie. "All this running. Being afraid. I'm just tired of it." His ever-present anger simmered. "After what he did to my family, I don't want to just escape from him. I want to kill him."

Jason gave his shoulder an understanding squeeze. "I know. And maybe someday we'll find a way to do that. But right now our best bet is to get to Arylyn."

"Run, you mean," William said bitterly.

"Run," Jason agreed. "Kohl's still chasing us, and we can't stop him."

"He's still back in Cincinnati."

"A small blessing," Jason said, "but at this point, I'll take any blessings we can get."

"I still don't like sitting in one place like this."

"We ship out after tomorrow night's performance," Jason reminded him.

"Can't come soon enough," William said. "I'll be relieved when we get to Arizona. I'll be relieved *if* we get to Arizona."

"We'll get there," Jason assured him. "Then you'll see Arylyn, and all of this will be worth it."

William shrugged. "I hope so, but maybe I'm more of a pessimist than you."

"More like a pest-imist."

Serena took in William's pallor and reached for one of his hands and gave it a supportive squeeze. Tonight was their first performance, and his nervousness was obvious in everything from his posture, the woeful expression on his face, and the way his eyes flitted about like he was having a seizure.

"It'll be fine," Serena assured him, no longer surprised by the compassion she felt for William. No matter how many times she sought to expunge her emotional frailties, they continued to rear up, refusing to be cast aside. Witness the supportive squeeze she'd just given William. Serena hated her weaknesses. Detested them for how they'd invaded and hollowed out her hard core, and she couldn't seem to do anything to rid herself of them. Worse, she wasn't always sure she wanted to.

"You're not nervous?" William asked.

"Maybe a little," Serena said. A moment later. "Maybe a lot, but we'll be all right."

"I hope so." William sounded as if he was offering up a prayer, and afterward, the small trailer in which they waited fell quiet.

Serena ran her hands down her outfit, smoothing it out. A large keyhole opened in the front, exposing an ample amount of her breasts, and the back plunged low. Panels of purple silk extended from her waist to her ankles, and while they mostly covered her legs, with every step she took the fabric swirled about, exposing flashes of her calves and thighs. The outfit left very little to the imagination. In fact, when Serena had first seen it she had pretended to pitch a fit, figuring a tantrum was in order for what she was being asked to wear. Of course, she *had* eventually agreed to don the outfit, but only after letting everyone know exactly how unhappy she was.

It was all so silly, though: the provisional morality of those in the Far Abroad. The minimal clothing didn't embarrass Serena—she'd worn less in the past and would do so again if circumstances required it.

She caught William staring at her. "What?"

"I wish Jane hadn't given you such a skimpy outfit," William said with a frown.

"So do I," Serena said, although truthfully, she didn't care. "But you look nice. Real nice."

And William did look nice in his bright-blue, velvet pants with beads and gold piping running up the sides, and the vest that left most of his chest bare. He filled it out nicely.

William blushed, and Serena smiled at him in genuine fondness. He was sweet and innocent, and she liked that about him. She liked a lot of things about William and his friends. She liked smiling without faking it, who she was—

She cut off that line of thought with a mental scowl.

There again with the weakness, sneaking up on her when she least expected it. Even her attempts at continual diligence couldn't keep it away.

Serena closed her eyes and tried to recall Isha's teachings.

We have no friends in this world. We simply have temporary allies whose needs occasionally align with our own.

And based on those teachings, William was nothing more than her target, someone to be bent to the needs of her people, or failing that, someone she'd have to kill.

She frowned when she considered killing William. Could she actually do that? When she didn't even like hurting him? Three months ago, the answer might have been an easy and obvious 'yes'. But now?

"What's wrong?" William asked. His face filled with concern.

"I'm fine."

He quirked a half-smile. "Is it because of having to prance around in that outfit with all those people watching?"

"I hadn't really thought about it until you mentioned it just now," Serena said. "Thank you for that."

"I'm sure no one will notice the clothes," William said, grinning now. "They'll be too busy staring at other things."

Serena smiled, and unconsciously reached for an unruly lock of his hair, intending to tuck it back into place. *He was so . . .*

Serena hid a scowl. *Idiot*. She attempted what she hoped was a challenging smile. "And I'm sure no one will be staring at your manly chest."

William glanced down and blushed. "Oh, no." He went back to fidgeting, and the trailer fell silent again.

After a moment, Serena eyed him askance. "Can I ask you a question?" She waited until he looked her way. "How did you and Jason get so good with your sword routine so fast?"

William frowned, appearing troubled. "I don't know. It just happened."

"Is it because of your magic?"

"*Lorethasra?*"

"Yes. That. Was it your *lorethasra?*" Serena made sure to stumble over the word that was supposed to be unfamiliar.

"I don't know. I'm just stronger and faster than I used to be. Maybe it's all the training I've been doing."

"Then you should count your blessings," Serena said. She kept her face composed, although alarms went off in her head. William's newfound physicality might be due to the blood of the necrosed. The disease might be growing in him. She smoothed her outfit again and reached for something to distract her from her worried thoughts. "What do you think Mr. Zeus would think of *The Highlander*?"

Serena wanted to smack her head. *What an inane question!*

William pondered it, though, as if it deserved serious consideration and stroked his chin in thought. "He wouldn't like it," he finally said.

"Why?"

"It would remind him too much of his own life."

"What do you mean?" Serena asked, genuinely curious.

William slapped his forehead. "That's right. We never told you about Mr. Zeus. He was born before the Civil War. He lived to see his brothers and sisters, his nieces and nephews, his own daughter and granddaughter all get old and pass away. He wouldn't like watching a movie portray something he's actually lived through."

Serena stilled. *The Civil War? Impossible. William had to be mistaken. He couldn't mean that Jason's grandfather was over one hundred and twenty years old and yet looked to be in his sixties.* "Mr. Zeus was born before the Civil War?" she asked quietly.

William laughed. "It's hard to believe, right? I didn't believe it either, but Jason swears it's true."

Serena grew numb. "Is Mr. Zeus' longevity exceptional?"

"Jason says most of our kind live to be over two hundred, some to over two hundred and fifty."

"Two hundred fifty?" Serena whispered in shock. She had no idea the *asrasins* of Arylyn lived so long. No one did. They lived half again as long as what her own people thought possible.

The door to their trailer opened, interrupting whatever Serena might have said.

"You're up in five," a runner told them before dashing away.

William watched as Fire Lord Ignis reached the finale of his performance. The stocky artist, graceful despite his bulk, swallowed a flaming sword and blew fire out of his mouth as he spun about in a circle, lighting up a ring of torches. The crowd cheered enthusiastically.

Despite the busy season of Christmas shopping, the folk of Newton, Kansas had still come out *en masse* and on multiple occasions for the circus. Mr. Bill had been thrilled.

"We're up next," Serena whispered. She gave William an encouraging smile. "Don't be nervous."

"I'm not nervous," he said. Earlier, in the trailer, his stomach had been aflutter with butterflies, but now he felt steady enough to play *Operation* while driving. "We'll kick ass."

A surprised expression passed across Serena's face.

Before she could respond, the ringmaster had introduced them to the audience. "Now, Ladies and Gentlemen, for the first time ever, I give you *The Lovers*!"

William paused when he stepped out of the shadows into the bright lights of the center ring. The smell of popcorn and gray smoke from when Master Aero had been shot from his canon permeated the air, and he could barely make out the crowd. They appeared distant, faraway and silent, as they watched Serena glide across the center ring. Given how she looked in her outfit, he thought it understandable. She reached her scarves and struck a pose.

The lights had followed her as she made her way across the center ring, and William stood in darkness again, just outside the lights.

Music began, melodic and slow. “Rhapsody on a Theme of Paganini” by Rachmaninoff. All the music had been chosen by Mrs. Nancy.

Serena high-stepped around her scarves, each movement controlled and graceful as she swayed in time to the rhythm of the music. She twirled about the scarves, into them, hiding away from the crowd before poking her head out a moment later.

Beautiful.

Serena pirouetted around the ring, oblivious to anything but the dance, until she saw William standing in the darkness. She feigned startlement, and her hands went to her mouth in an exaggerated expression of surprise. The big-top’s spotlight angled on him so the audience could see him as well. Serena crooked a finger and urged him out.

William took a deep breath and stepped forward. Before leaving the trailer, he’d donned a shepherd’s robe over his fancier clothes, and held a shepherd’s crook. He pointed it at Serena, and she mimed a laugh before darting away from him. Now began the chase. William followed Serena, dancing after her, chasing her lode star around the center ring. They picked up speed, and the music changed to “Rite of Spring” by Stravinsky.

The movement paused when Serena, enshrouded amongst her scarves, allowed herself to be caught. William held her in his arms, and bent low as if to kiss her.

The music changed, becoming dark and sullen. “Totentanz” by Liszt. Jason entered the ring, dressed in black with silver piping. William placed himself protectively in front of Serena, and Jason sneered at him. William held his shepherd’s crook at the ready, and Jason drew his sword. Serena climbed her scarves to safety.

William made wild swings with his crook, which Jason easily batted aside. William grew more desperate, and Jason laughed at his feeble attempts. The crowd groaned when their short battle ended with William driven off the stage.

He left the spotlight of the center ring, standing again in darkness as he watched Serena’s performance.

The music changed again. Dark choir music now, with occasional light tones hinting at hope.

Serena had the scarves wrapped about her arms. She held the crucifix pose, and the audience gasped when she let go of the scarves. She looped them about her ankles and did the splits. She held the pose before suddenly plunging downward, snapping to halt when she hung upside-down. The crowd gasped again before breaking into enthusiastic applause.

No matter how many times William had seen Serena’s routine, it always left him mesmerized, if not terrified.

“Get your robe off,” Mr. Bill hissed.

William started, and hurriedly undid the shepherd’s robe. Beneath it gleamed the blue costume that matched Jason’s black outfit. “Where’s my sword?”

"Here." Mr. Bill handed him the sheathed weapon.

William belted it on before returning to watch Serena. She had the crowd spellbound. They held silent, raptly following her every movement. But she was nearing the end of her performance. William would have to go back out in a few seconds.

Serena came to a halt high above the center ring, and the music changed again, this time to the theme from *Conan the Barbarian.* William had no idea why Mrs. Nancy had chosen that music for the final battle between himself and Jason, but by Crom, he would make this a performance to remember.

William stepped back into the light and faced Jason. Once more, he beheld his friend's sneer of derision. William's adrenaline began pumping, and for some reason his anger flickered to life. He quickly squashed it.

William struck a heroic pose, one mirrored by Jason. As one, they drew their swords and attacked. The clang of steel striking steel reverberated throughout the big-top. The sound served as an accompaniment to the music while William and Jason ranged across the center ring with handsprings and somersaults. The crowd whistled approval, while Serena, wound in her scarves, watched from above.

With one final pass, William drove Jason off the stage. The audience cheered wildly.

Once again the music changed, this time upbeat, happy, and modern, "I Melt With You" by Modern English. Serena tumbled down her scarves, unwinding all the way to the ground and alighting in William's arms. The lights faded to a single spotlight that focused upon them. The crowd grew silent. William held Serena in that famous pose between Rhett Butler and Scarlett O'Hara. The spotlight slowly faded.

But Serena changed the final scene. Her eyes were filled with something William couldn't describe. Longing, or sadness maybe. She cupped a hand to the back of his neck and pulled him close, kissing him. Surprise held him frozen while the spotlight faded to black.

Serena was nowhere to be found after their performance, or even later that evening when William and Jason helped break the circus down. They loaded everything onto the train to be shipped out to their final destination, Las Vegas, New Mexico.

The long night's work ended up bleeding into the next morning, and it wasn't until shortly after sunrise that the train pulled out of Newton. Afterward, while everyone tucked in for some sleep, William and Jason stayed awake, too keyed up to rest. They sat before a small opening in the combine's car, wrapped in thick blankets and watching the unchanging prairie pass by. America's heartland with its stubbled harvested fields appeared as a vast, unending wasteland this time of year, and the thin winter sun, often hidden behind a scudding blanket of gray clouds, did nothing to resolve the bleakness. Someone had the radio on and "Mama" by Genesis was playing, the perfect song for the setting.

"I hate winter," Jason said with fervor.

William merely grunted agreement.

"What I'd give to be home right now."

"Cincinnati or Arylyn?" William asked.

"Either, but if I had to choose, it'd be Arylyn."

"What's it like?" William asked. "You never told me."

"We wanted it to be a surprise."

"What if . . ." William trailed off.

"What if you never have a chance to see it?"

William nodded. He hadn't wanted to give voice to his worries. It felt as if doing so might make the fears come true. At least that's what his Mom always used to say. Some of her superstitions must have rubbed off on him.

"I can't describe Arylyn. You have to see it for yourself." Jason surprised William by reaching out to cup his temples. "This is what I saw the first time I set foot on the island."

The world blurred, and William no longer saw the barren, winter prairie outside. Instead, he stood on Arylyn.

William breathed deep and clean, citrus-tinged floral scents filled his lungs. Then he saw *Arylyn and his jaw dropped.*

Cupped within the protective embrace of a series of bluffs lay a turquoise bay. A pencil-thin golden beach framed the border between violet-veined, ruddy cliffs and water. The cliffs, five of them, soared four hundred feet or more into the air and were sculpted into staggered terraces. It reminded William of pictures he'd seen in National Geographic *of Bali's rice fields, except Arylyn's were more majestic and far more beautiful.*

Upon the terraces were perched an eclectic blend of homes in styles from around the world. They varied from English cottages to some that appeared vaguely Asian. Flowering bushes, palm trees, and fruit trees—mango, orange, apple, and pear—decorated front yards, while tall, wooden fences draped with red jasmine and honeysuckle, divided the lots.

Innumerable staircases and slender, white bridges, each with intricate carvings of dragons and unicorns and other fantastic animals, linked the various terraces and cliffs. The spans shimmered fragile as glass, and some were even translucent. A river split the cliffs and cascaded down as a misty waterfall as permanent rainbows stretched from sea to sky, dappling rooftops with colored shadows as rich as those of stained glass.

The image slowly faded from William's mind.

"Arylyn," Jason said, with a deep-seated note of loss.

"Arylyn," William managed to whisper past a throat dry with awe.

Arylyn, an island more beautiful than anything he could have ever imagined, as perfect as a place could be. Waking up every morning to see a village and island like that would be a miracle.

A sudden restless need filled William. He didn't want to be on this train anymore. He didn't want the life he was leading. It felt so bland and washed-out after the vibrancy of Jason's true home. It felt like the rest of the world existed beneath a pale, frigid light, and only Arylyn held a golden, summer sun.

"You want to go there, don't you?" Jason asked.

"Yeah" William said, his single word answer unable to encompass the depth of his desire. "Why did you ever leave?"

Jason gave him a wry grin. "Arylyn is gorgeous, but so is the rest of the world. There's always more of it to see and experience."

"I guess," William said, in a voice full of doubt. "Do you think I'll ever get to see it?"

"Yes."

"How? Have you figured out where the *saha'asra* in Arizona is?"

"It's only a matter of time," Jason said, sounding confident.

"Mr. Zeus will tell me."

William frowned in confusion. "What?"

"He's been sending me directions."

William's confusion deepened. "How?"

"Dreams. Magic, remember? He can send impressions and images in my dreams. They fade out pretty fast, so I have to make sure to remember whatever he sends."

"If he can send you a dream, why can't he just tell you?" William asked.

"Magi have a lot of skills," Jason said, "but telepathy isn't one of them. The best we can do is share impressions and images when someone else's mind is totally at rest."

"What's he told you?" William asked.

"The *saha'asra* is next to a lake, along the north shore," Jason answered.

William eyed him askance. "Not to rain on your parade, but Arizona's pretty big, and it probably has a lot of lakes."

"I'll figure it out," Jason said with his normal confidence.

"Then we just have to get there before the necrosed catches up with us."

"Where is he, by the way?" Jason asked.

"Back there." William gestured vaguely in the direction he sensed Kohl. "Still in Cincinnati as far as I can tell."

"You sure?"

"Positive," William replied. "But you saw how fast he caught up with us in Cincinnati. Did Mr. Zeus tell you how to stop him?"

"No. But I'm sure he's working on it."

William hoped Mr. Zeus would figure it out before they got to the Arizona *saha'asra*. "Have you seen Serena?" he asked.

Jason shook his head. "I saw her get on the train, but other than that I haven't seen her since the performance."

"Me, neither," William said. "I think the kiss bothered her."

Jason smirked. "You mean the one that wasn't in the script?"

William blushed. "Yeah."

"Whose idea was it? Yours or hers?"

"Hers."

"Then you're lucky," Jason said, sounding wistful. "To be kissed by a girl like her."

William shrugged. He didn't want to discuss it anymore, and he sure didn't want to talk about his ambivalent, nonsensical feelings toward Serena.

"Well, I haven't seen her," Jason said, replying to William's earlier question. "She's probably busy with her own things."

"You're probably right," William agreed, although it felt like she was avoiding him.

"Of course, I'm right," Jason said. "By the way, Merry Christmas."

William startled before breaking into laughter. "I can't believe I forgot about it."

CHAPTER 21: A NIGHTMARE ENCOUNTER

The minuscule *saha'asra* in the winter-bare forest where Kohl had almost trapped the boy and his *asrasin* friends held barely enough *lorasra* to sustain a werewolf, much less a creature of a necrosed's stature. He'd been tempted to stay anyway, though. Perhaps those young ones the boy had been with, the non-*asrasins*, might return. Kohl could always supplement his decaying form with a plethora of new organs and extremities.

In the end he declined to remain. Too many folk walked the trails around it. Too many people with dogs, on leashes or unleashed. In either circumstance, they left Kohl, not fearful—he feared only one creature in any world—but uncomfortable, with an unsettled sensation in the middle of his back that penetrated to his pustulant heart. His stomach roiled, and he didn't like the feeling.

Therefore, Kohl returned to his home in the low-shouldered mountains farther to the east, a place far from any roads or trails. No one came here. Even the animals scurried past the entrance of his home, giving it a wide berth.

Once there, in a cavern deep in the heart of a rounded mountain, the *saha'asra* he'd made his own, Kohl prepared to wait. The boy sought safety. Only two such places existed where he might find such an illusion on this world, Arylyn and Sinskrill. But to make it to either of them, he needed a *saha'asra*, and the moment he entered one, Kohl would be ready.

The necrosed slept, resting after the exertion of chasing the boy. He gave himself over to his favorite fantasy, the one in which he devoured an endless line of *asrasins* and slew Sapient Dormant. But he couldn't fully enjoy the dream.

The boy.

His ongoing survival aggravated like an affront, one that stained Kohl's sleep. The boy should have been dead by now. His pure *lorethasra* should have been Kohl's, filling his corrupted being as the boy's flesh should have filled Kohl's stomach. Instead, the boy had escaped, not once, but twice. How? The unjustness of such a calamity filled Kohl with outrage.

Kohl sighed and shook off his unhelpful sleep. His dreams would have to wait. He cracked open his eyes as he considered the boy's situation.

A possibility came to him then, one he had pondered deeply.

The boy traveled south and west, steadily and smoothly, which meant he likely traveled by car, or possibly a train. But if he continued his current journey far enough, a *saha'asra* lay near his path.

Kohl unfurled his limbs and stood. He stared unseeing at the far cavern wall, his focus entirely on the boy. Would he truly offer Kohl such an easy hunt? Would he truly pass so close by that faraway *saha'asra*?

A smile came to Kohl's face. Yes. The boy's course never wavered. On he journeyed, unknowing and ignorant, toward that distant *saha'asra*. On he journeyed, to his doom.

"Wake up."

William shrugged off the annoying voice and rolled over.

The voice followed him. "Wake up!" it said, sounding urgent.

Hands shook William awake and he groaned, cracking open eyes still bleary with sleep. Jason crouched by his side, his face filled with worry. "What is it?" William asked.

"We've got a problem. A big one."

William rubbed his eyes and sat up, trying to get his brain and body in gear. "What?"

"I should have paid more attention." Jason said with a scowl as he pounded a fist into an open palm. "The train passes close to a *saha'asra*, no more than a half a mile."

It took William a moment to understand what Jason was saying. *Oh, God. Kohl.* "When?"

"Soon. A few minutes from now."

William immediately reached for his sense of the necrosed, searching the itch in the back of his mind. "We've got a little time. He's still east of us," he said. "Where's Serena?"

"Sleeping," Jason said.

"We need to wake her up and figure out what to do."

Serena slept nearby, and she roused more easily than William had. She sat up, fully awake, and glanced from one to the other, her gaze holding its usual intensity. "What happened?"

They told her, and she frowned, tilting her head as though in thought. "Kohl's still far behind us," she said, confirming William's senses, but he won't be for long. Not if we're passing that close to a *saha'asra*."

"We need to hide," Jason said. "Find a place to hole up and . . ." He trailed off when Serena shook her head.

"It won't work. He'll find us." She gestured to herself and William. "He feels us the same way we do him. He'll know *exactly* where we are."

"Then we find as large a group of people as we can," Jason suggested. "Necrosed don't like crowds."

This time it was William who shook his head. He didn't like that idea, either. "We can't. I don't want to put anyone else in danger. What if Kohl doesn't actually care about the presence of other people? It didn't help us back in Winton Woods."

"Besides, everyone is spread out in a whole bunch of cars," Serena added. "There isn't a crowd of people around to help us out, even if we were willing to put them at risk."

"Which we're not." William put a definitive end to that idea.

"Then what do we do?" Serena asked.

"Whatever it is, we better choose quick." Jason said. "We're coming up on the *saha'asra* any second."

William's brow furrowed and he pondered furiously. *Where was the safest place on the train?*

"What about one of the animal cars?" Serena suggested. "Maybe he won't come after us if we're hiding in one of them."

Hope dawned on Jason's face, clearing the lines of worry. "That might actually work."

William thought it a good idea too, but not good enough. He still frowned, heart pounding and mind racing as he tried to figure out what had him bothered. "We hide with the animals and hope Kohl doesn't come after us there," he said, hoping talking it out would expose the flaw he intuitively knew existed in Serena's plan. "But what about later? What happens when the train pulls into Las Vegas? Kohl will still be on the train with us. He'll attack any time he wants after that."

Jason's hope seemed to spill away. "Shit."

"We have to choose what we're going to do. Now," Serena said, her face growing tight with fear.

Jason's head shot up. "I got it," he said. "We let him find us."

"What?" Serena protested. "Are you crazy?"

"Hear me out," Jason said, holding up his hands. "We let him find us, but we retreat to the large animal car, the one with the elephants—"

"The bears are in there, too," William interrupted. He had a sense of what Jason was proposing.

"Right. It's the final car in the train. We lead Kohl to the elephants and bears, and we fight him there."

"Fight him?" Serena asked in disbelief. "Weren't you the one who said that no magus ever stood his ground when faced with a necrosed?"

Her incredulity echoed William's own thoughts. Jason's plan wasn't at all what he had in mind.

"I am, but what choice do we have?" Jason argued. "Besides, we don't have to kill Kohl. We can't do that anyway. We just have to toss him off the train."

William opened his mouth. "But—

"We're running out of time," Jason interrupted.

"Then we'll go with your plan," William said, "but we also have to keep Kohl from reboarding the train after we toss him off."

"There's a small river not far past the *saha'asra*," Jason said. "There's no way Kohl will follow us across the water."

"Why can't he just use the bridge?" William asked.

"He could, but I'll shield the entrance to it," Jason explained.

"What's that mean?" Serena asked.

"A shield is that golden screen Mr. Zeus formed in West Virginia. You remember? The thing that slowed Kohl down?"

"It didn't slow him down by much," William said. "He punched through it in two blows."

"Yeah, but I'm a lot better at shielding than Mr. Zeus is," Jason said. "His might be stronger, but I have better control of mine. I'll angle my shield so that when Kohl tries to ram through, it'll toss him into the water."

The itch in the back on William's mind heightened, and Serena's tense expression mirrored his. "He's here," they said as one.

"Oh, shit," Jason said.

"Run!" said William. "We can still make it to the animal car. It's only five cars behind us, the last one in the train."

"How?" Jason asked. "Not every car has front and rear entrances."

"The outside ladders. We'll climb to the top of the cars and jump the gaps," William said. "We don't have time to debate this!"

"Come on!" Serena said. Panic raced through her. With every wasted second, Kohl drew nearer. He couldn't be more than a minute away. She led them toward the rear of their car, where they stepped out into the pitch-black of late night. She leapt over to the next railcar.

“Hurry,” William urged.

“I’m hurrying,” Serena snapped.

She climbed the ladder to the top of the boxcar and shuffled forward. She had to move carefully, bending low against the icy wind as she strained to keep her balance and footing on the slick roof. She cursed under her breath. She could have traversed the roof of the car far more quickly if she’d been allowed to utilize all of her skills, but Isha had forbidden it. He had stated she could only tap into those other abilities if there were no other alternative.

Jason shoved past her, and the pressure from the wind suddenly eased. “I’ve got a shield around us,” he explained. “It’ll keep the wind from slowing us down, and keep us from falling off the train. Now, go!”

William tentatively reached out to both sides, but Serena didn’t need to. The shield Jason had created didn’t glow like Mr. Zeus’, but even with her eyes closed she knew what she’d find all around them: they stood in a closed tunnel that stretched along the length of the railcar with a roof to protect against the wind.

“Hurry up!” Jason called from the end of the railcar.

Serena set off at a sprint, with William following on her heels. Fear gave wings to her feet. She dashed along the roofs of the railcars, sprinting as hard as she could, leaping from one to the next.

“He’s close,” Serena said. The itching in the back of her mind had become a throb.

“Only one more car to go!” William shouted.

Jason had already reached it and clambered down the far ladder. From the gap between the two cars, he screamed for them to run.

A shudder shook the stock car upon which they stood. Serena glanced back, and her eyes widened.

Kohl. He must have leaped from the ground to the top of the train. He'd landed on braced knees before slowly rising to his feet and grinning. "Where do you delicious morsels think you're going?" he asked.

The animals in the car below, goats and sheep from the petting zoo, went crazy. They bleated, racing around inside the car in panic.

"Come on!" Jason urged.

His voice broke Serena's panic. She turned away from the necrosed and leapt across the void between the two stock cars. She tumbled down the ladder with William close behind. Behind them raced Kohl. Jason slammed the door shut just as the necrosed crossed the linkage between the final two cars of the train. He threw the bolt, locking it in the creature's face.

As one, Serena, William, and Jason stepped away from the door, deeper into the depths of the stock car. Dim, red-hooded lights provided barely enough illumination by which to see.

Serena glanced about, her thoughts fragmented by fear. Her heart pounded. Sweat beaded, and she had to swallow to work saliva into her mouth.

Several elephants and a few of Momma Bridget's bears rode in the car with them, and the animals were clearly agitated, likely sensing Kohl's presence. However, unlike the sheep and goats, they grew angry rather than afraid. The bears roared in fury while the elephants trumpeted.

From without, mocking laughter answered. "The animals are wise to fear me. And so are you, it seems. Here now ends the hunt for my tasty meals."

"What now?" William asked.

Serena gritted her teeth and forced her mind to work. With an angry snarl, she mastered her fear and threw open a side door. "We carry through with the plan." She hoped she sounded more courageous than she felt. Even during her Tempering, she'd never been so scared. "We knock him off the train and keep him off."

A moment later, a scrabbling noise, like some giant insect clattering along the sides of the stock car, reached them. Serena followed the sound with her eyes. She traced its path. An instant later, Kohl leaped through the open doorway.

Jason met him with a blast of air, but Kohl leaned into it and spun aside.

Another blast of air was . . . consumed, and Kohl Obsidian loomed before them. The creature chuckled. "Oh, my little treats. I shall savor each of you while I split your bones and suck dry your marrow."

"Do something!" William cried.

"I'm trying," Jason shouted back.

They pressed deeper into the car, away from Kohl. Serena's gaze darted about, desperate for a weapon. They should have brought their swords. Or purchased a pistol somewhere along the way.

The bears and elephants continued to thunder their fury, and an insane idea popped into Serena's mind.

"Look out," she hollered before freeing the bears.

With a roar, the animals surged out of their cages, charging straight for Kohl.

William and Jason flattened themselves to the sides of the railcar as the animals lumbered by.

Kohl backed away from the bears, an expression of concern on his face. The animals, a sow and a young male, reared, standing eye-to-eye and toe-to-toe with the necrosed. William and Jason peeled away from the walls and moved to join Serena.

Kohl flicked a punch at the sow, knocking her back. He raked the male across the chest, slashing him. A backhand slammed the young bear to the floor.

"He's going to kill them," William said.

"No, he won't," Jason vowed.

A blast of air from Jason hammered Kohl into the far side of the railcar before he could further injure the bears. Next came a roar of fire, blazing through the gap between the bears and catching Kohl full in the chest. Kohl slipped aside from the stream, but by then the bears had recovered.

Once again, the ursines faced off against the nightmarish creature, but they needed more help. Serena cast about, searching for something else that might aid the animals.

There! A pitchfork. Two of them. She reached for one.

William followed suit. "Ready?" he asked her.

Fear again thrummed through her veins, but she made herself nod and press forward.

The bears didn't go after Kohl as they had earlier. They still snarled and reared at him, but this time they were wise enough to stay out of his range.

William stepped between the bears and stabbed at Kohl. The male used the distraction to slap the necrosed across the face. The blow would have decapitated a human, but it merely stunned Kohl. Serena stabbed as well, but the necrosed reached out, swift as a snake, and grabbed her pitchfork, nearly pulling her into his embrace.

The sow struck Kohl's arm, and pustulant blood flowed from a series of slashes. The necrosed snarled and leaped upward to safety, hanging beetle-like from the ceiling as he glared at them. Serena was about to stab at him with her pitchfork, but an elephant, a cow, reached her trunk through the bars of her cage. She grabbed one of Kohl's legs and yanked.

For a moment, the necrosed's eyes widened comically before he slammed into the floor. The elephant didn't release his leg, however. She pulled the necrosed to her, battering him into the cage and stabbing at him with her tusks.

Kohl managed to free himself, but the bears lunged again. Despite her fear, Serena laughed at how they took turns slapping him until he ended up against the other elephant cage. The necrosed scrambled to his feet, but the bull within the enclosure snatched at him. The elephant repeatedly battered his face into the bars of the cage.

Again came the bears, slapping, clawing, and biting.

But as before, Kohl managed to free himself of his attackers, shrugging them off and escaping their claws, teeth, and trunks. He stood silhouetted before the side entrance, battered and wrecked.

"The animals can only hurt me," he said. "They cannot kill me. I'll slay them after I slay each and every—"

His words ended in a scream as Jason blasted him out the side entrance. Kohl tumbled end over end across a wheat field.

Serena leaned out of the train, staring back at the necrosed. The creature lay still for a moment before slowly rising to his feet. He swayed, almost stumbling before eventually regaining his balance. Impossibly, he set off after them again.

Serena cursed, simultaneously angry and fearful. What would it take to bring the creature down?

Her worries were short-lived. Kohl's pace proved far too slow to keep up with the train, and he stumbled to a stop.

Serena imagined she could feel his eyes boring into hers, promising death.

The bears whuffed, wrenching her attention to the interior of the railcar.

The ursines eyed them, and the young male reared up, growling.

"Uh-oh," William whispered.

"We're fine," Jason said with a grin.

A wave of his hands, and both bears dropped down to all fours. The animals whuffed again, more quietly this time and looking quite docile.

Serena's eyes widened, impressed with Jason's control.

Jason scratched the young male behind an ear, and another hand-wave helped heal the animal's injuries.

"*Asra*, remember?" Jason led both bears to their respective cages. "No worries."

CHAPTER 22: A WITCH'S PROPHECY

The next afternoon, Serena, William, and Jason remained huddled in the car hauling the elephants and bears, staying there until the train pulled into Las Vegas, New Mexico. There they helped unload the circus equipment and set it up in the campground outside the town. Evening had fallen by the time they finished.

"I know Kohl is probably back in Kansas or wherever," Jason said, "but we can't hide out with the animals forever." He shrugged. "But I also don't want to be alone right now."

Serena felt the same way. "I heard Jimmy was supposed to prepare a Christmas dinner for everyone today. We should go."

She led the way to the backyard. There they found a jumble of people mingling about, many of them stopping by to get food, drink, or both, and chat with their friends. The mouth-watering aromas of roasting meat and spices filled the air, along with the musky odor of spilled beer.

Some of the artists and crew were already well on their way to drunkenness. Sam the Strongman was laughing too loudly at something Lily Reed, one of the younger Dubrovics, had said, while the Fabulous Winona and one of the crew tossed back shots. Dr. Devious carried on a serious conversation with Elaina Sinith, who seemed quite bored with the good doctor. The entire area was a welter of light, laughter, and sound, as more people straggled in by the minute.

While Serena waited at the buffet table, she tried to soak in the sights of revelry, hoping they would ease her tension. Maybe seeing other people happy might unfurrow her worried brow or loosen her tense shoulders. She couldn't take much more. Her strength and courage were reaching their limits.

Last night's attack by Kohl merely previewed what would occur at the *saha'asra* in Arizona. There would be no running then. Worse, Serena's options had grown increasingly narrow. She would either have to see William die at the hands of the necrosed, or she would have to kill him herself. Those were her only choices with no obvious options in between. Not if she wanted to see Selene, safe.

"What would you like?" Jimmy asked, interrupting her thoughts. "I've got roast beef, turkey, honeyed ham, mashed potatoes, mac 'n' cheese, a green bean casserole, and five kinds of deserts."

"You cooked all this today?" Serena asked in amazement, taking in the tables loaded down beneath the weight of all the food.

"Did my best," Jimmy said with a proud grin. "But I can't take all the credit. I had some help."

"It smells amazing," Serena said.

"You're welcome to all you want," Jimmy said, puffing up. "And if you ask nice, you can even have some beer or liquor. Boss' orders. Ain't no cops around tonight."

"I'll take a rum and Coke, hold the rum," Serena said.

Jimmy laughed. "Anything for you, little lady."

"Hey, Jimmy," William said, surprising Serena as he appeared at her elbow. "You put on a good spread."

"And you 'uns put on a good show," Jimmy replied. "Had my doubts about y'all when you first signed with us. What's your poison?" he asked William. "Drink, I mean."

"Just a Coke."

"Two rum and Cokes, hold the rum," Jimmy said with a wink. "Now get y'selves some food, and I'll bring your drinks out to you."

Serena led William to the tables of food, and when they each had a plateful, she found them a corner where they could talk. Jimmy brought them their drinks and chuckled as he left. Serena heard him mutter under his breath about young love.

"By the way, I got you something for Christmas," William said. He held out a small box covered in pink wrapping paper.

Serena unwrapped the present, and within it found a small, silver anklet. She smiled. A thoughtful gift that left her more melancholy than before.

How would she find the strength to hurt William? To maintain all the lies she told him?

"You don't like it?" William asked.

"I love it," Serena said. "Thank you."

"Then what's wrong?" William asked.

"It's nothing," she said.

"It doesn't sound like nothing."

Serena sighed. Why couldn't William leave it alone? The present was a kind gesture, but it left her even more worried about the future, a future she didn't want to think about.

But William insisted on dragging her thoughts in that direction. Fine. If he wanted to talk about it, then she'd talk about it. "You want to know the truth?" she asked. "You're right. I'm not okay. In a few days, Jason will probably find that *saha'asra*, and then we're all going to die." Blunt truth. Let him chew on that for awhile.

"We're not going to die," William said, clearly trying to soothe her worries.

Serena's irritation flared at his condescension. "I'm not an idiot," she growled. "We barely survived last night."

"But we did survive. I talked to Jason about it. There's never been any record of a person marked by a necrosed surviving an encounter with one, and we've done it three times."

"Then none of this scares you?" Serena challenged.

"What, me worry?" William said with a silly grin.

Serena blinked, trying to place the words and the stupid smile. It took her a moment before she realized they belonged to the singularly mad Alfred E. Neuman, a character William evidently thought hilarious.

Serena didn't, and she rolled her eyes.

"I'm actually terrified," William said.

"That doesn't inspire much confidence."

"We'll get through it, though," William said, more seriously this time. "We have to. We'll just have to be clever about it."

Serena blinked. "Clever? You think we have to be clever?" Disbelief briefly overcame her unhappiness with herself. "Cleverness won't stop a necrosed. Nothing will. Last night should have taught you that."

"Last night we fought Kohl to a standstill. We can do it again," William said with an obstinate set to his jaw.

"Fighting to a standstill isn't the same as winning."

"In our case it is. We're not trying to kill Kohl," William reminded her. "We're just trying to get away from him. And if we fight him to a standstill again, we can escape to a place he can't follow. We win."

And then what would she do? It was a question to which Serena still lacked an answer.

"William! Jason! Wait up!" a voice shouted.

William glanced about from where he stood in the parking lot, and it took him a moment to recognize Elaina Sinith. With her dark hair hanging unbound from her turban and her face free of its usual creepy ghost-face makeup, she looked completely different. Her skin turned out to be a dusky brown, but more importantly, she was every bit as pretty as William had always suspected she might be. And instead of her bag-lady attire, she wore tight jeans and a form-hugging T-shirt, both of which looked several sizes too small for her. Or maybe she just filled them out really well.

After a few seconds of study, William decided it was definitely the latter: she filled her clothes out *very* nicely.

"You thinking what I'm thinking?" Jason asked in a strangled voice.

"Probably," William said.

"And what are the two of you thinking about?" Serena asked, surprising both of them with her unexpected arrival.

William paled, and hoped Serena didn't notice. "Err . . ."

"Cat got your tongue?" Serena asked with a knowing grin. "Let me guess. You're probably thinking that our fortuneteller over there fills out her clothes real well."

"Amen to that," Jason said.

"It's all right to look," Serena said to William. "Just don't stare. Girls don't like that."

William gaped.

"Now close your mouth, or people will think you're a cretin," Serena advised.

William reddened while Jason snickered.

"Say 'hi' to the fortuneteller for me and try not to drool all over her," Serena called over her shoulder as she left.

William stared after her, feeling as if a boulder had run him over.

"Hi," Elaina said as she drew up. "Where's Serena going?"

"No idea," Jason said.

"Oh." Elaina looked unhappy for a moment but brightened an instant later. "I just wanted to tell you guys how much I loved your performance the other night."

"You saw it?" William asked.

"Didn't I just say that?" Elaina asked with a smile to take the sting out of her words. "By the way, why don't you come by my tent and I'll read your fortune? On the house."

"We'd love to, but you know how busy Mr. Bill keeps us," Jason said.

"Plus, we wouldn't want to intrude," William added.

"No intrusion. Come by after your performance tonight. You won't be busy then, and neither will I."

"Maybe," Jason said. "We've got an early start in the morning."

Elaina frowned. "Why? You aren't staying with the circus?"

"Isn't Las Vegas the last stop?" Jason asked.

"It is, but after that we head home to Salt Lake City. You're not coming?"

"I've got relatives nearby that I want to visit first," William said with an inspired lie. "We'll catch up later."

Elaina made a moue of disappointment. "Too bad," she said, "but if you change your mind, you know where I am." She flashed them a wink and a smile before sashaying on her way.

William watched her hips sway hypnotically from side-to-side as she walked away.

"Lord have mercy," Jason whispered reverently.

Elaina turned a corner and was lost to view. "Did you see her wink at me?" William asked.

"She did not!"

"She did, too!"

"No way."

"I'm telling you, she winked."

Jason grimaced. "What for? I'm standing right here. If she should be winking at either of us, it should be me."

William gaped. "Think much of yourself, do you?"

"It's the truth."

"Not the way Elaina sees it," William said, offering a smug smile.

Jason grimaced and mumbled under his breath.

"What was that?"

"Nothing," Jason muttered, still scowling.

William sighed. "You know, you could be happy for me. It's not like a pretty girl does this to me every day." He reconsidered his words. "Or ever."

Jason's face partially cleared. "Yeah, I know. I'm being a dick. It's just . . ."

"What?"

"You already have Serena," Jason said, an uncharacteristic whine in his voice. "She doesn't see anyone but you, and now Elaina, too?"

William gaped again. Jason was jealous of him? Why? There were plenty of girls interested in Jason. "You can't be serious."

Jason sighed. "Forget it," he replied. "It'd just be nice if a pretty girl winked at me once in a while."

"That's what's got you bothered?" William shook his head in disgust. "You're a dummy. Maybe you should look around once in awhile. Then you'd see all the young Dubrovics and other artists staring after you like you're a glass of water and they're parched."

"Really?" Hope bloomed on Jason's face.

"You haven't noticed?" William smacked Jason upside the head. "Dumbass."

"Ow." Jason rubbed his head. "Guess I need to surface from worrying about stuff all the time."

"We're going to be fine. I have a feeling about it."

Jason blinked. "William Wilde, an optimist?" His features became mock severe. "Okay, who are you and what did you do to my friend?"

With the work before the night's performance done, the campground housing *Wizard Bill's Wandering Wonders* stood nearly empty, and everyone had a few hours to kill. Jason had gone to the backyard, presumably for food, his favorite pastime, but more likely to talk up Josephine Sandler, one of the Dubrovics, while Serena had to see Jane the seamstress about a tear in her outfit.

For the first time in what seemed like forever, William found himself alone and with nothing to do. As a result, he decided to take up Elaina's offer to have his fortune read. After she'd spoken to him and Jason, he couldn't get her invitation out of his mind. It sat hunkered in the back of his thoughts like a bothersome itch he couldn't scratch.

Still, he hesitated at Elaina's tent, almost afraid to ring the bell that would announce a customer's presence. *Did he really want to do this?*

"Come in, William," Elaina called from within the tent.

William sighed. *How had she known he was out here?* He shrugged aside the question, pulled open the curtain that served as a door, and entered her tent. Stepping inside felt like walking into a trap. He wondered if a fly felt the same way when it lighted upon a Venus flytrap? Knowing it was in danger, but unable to resist the carnivorous plant's allure?

Inside the tent, he discovered long drapes of purple, red, blue, and yellow hanging from all corners and adding color to what would have otherwise been a drab interior. Candles provided a soft, almost ethereal glow, and from a small statue of a wizard smoking a pipe came the scent of sandalwood incense.

Elaina, back in her fortuneteller getup, with her ghostly

whiteface makeup and sack-like clothing, stared as William stepped inside. She might have been intimidating or even scary, except that from a curtained off area in the tent came the unmistakable strain of the theme song to *Murder, She Wrote*.

Elaina must have noticed William's amusement because she flushed. "Sorry about that," she said, "but I've always loved Angela Lansbury. Ever since I saw *Bedknobs and Broomsticks*."

"And now you watch *Murder, She Wrote*?" William asked, still amused.

"I think the show's clever, and it's neat seeing her solve all those mysteries," Elaina replied.

"Don't you think it's weird, though?" William asked. "Everywhere she goes, someone gets murdered. She's like a walking plague. I mean, if I ever saw Angela Lansbury walking toward me, I'd run the other direction as fast as I could. And if I knew she was visiting a town, I'd get as far away from it as possible. Someone's bound to be murdered there."

Elaina threw her head back and laughed, a bright, musical sound at odds with her ghastly attire. "That's one way of looking at it," she said. "Now, what can I do for you?"

"I thought I'd let you read my fortune."

"You thought you'd let me? Isn't that generous of you?" Elaina teased.

"Sorry. That didn't come out right," William said, reddening.

Something about Elaina threw him off-balance, something he couldn't identify. She couldn't be much older than him, but she acted as if she had seen so much more of the world, done so much more than him. Whatever the reason, William found himself both fascinated and intimidated by her.

"It's fine," Elaina said. "Sit down, and we'll get started."

William sat in the indicated chair. "Now what?"

"Now put your hands in mine and we'll see what we see."

William did as instructed. "Where did you learn your fortune-telling skills?"

"I didn't learn them. I honed what was already there," Elaina explained. She had her head bent to study his hands. "I was born with my abilities. But as for where I honed my skills, that was in the village of Sand, the place where I grew up. It's far from here and remote, and the folk there are all witches." Elaina lifted her head and stared him in the eyes, her gaze challenging. "Which is what I am. Does that scare you?"

William shook his head, trying to shake off his nervousness. "How could I be scared when you're really just a sand-witch?" He grinned at his pun.

Elaina offered a sarcastic smile. "How original," she said. "Now be quiet so I can figure out the lines of your past."

While Elaina probed at his hands and studied them, William became aware of the heavy calluses on her palms. Apparently, she was a woman who worked hard. William wouldn't have thought a fortune-teller would have to do a lot of manual labor.

Elaina's head remained bent over William's hands, and she wore a frown. "You have suffered a terrible tragedy," she pronounced. "Recently. At such a young age."

"It was my—"

Elaina *tsked*. "Don't tell me. Don't you know how fortune telling works?" Her head remained bent. "You lost loved ones."

William shifted about, uncomfortable at her close guess.

"Family. Grandparents. No, parents," Elaina said. She glanced up again. "They died unexpectedly."

William nodded. “Last winter.”

“A car accident?”

William nodded again, not bothering to tell her the cause. She wouldn’t understand. No one normal would.

“There was another involved in that accident, was there not? Let me see.” Once again, she peered at William’s hands. “Who’s this?”

“It was my—”

Elaina *tsked* again. “Quiet.” She continued to study William’s hands, running her fingers along the creases and folds of his palms. “A sibling.” She glanced at William once more. “An older brother.”

“How did you know?” William shivered, creeped out by her ability to divine what had happened to him.

“You aren’t the only one with magic,” Elaina said with a mysterious smile.

“What?” William asked in shock.

“You and Jason. Your performance with the swords. It’s magical,” Elaina explained.

“Oh,” William said, hoping his face and voice seem as weak with relief as he felt.

Elaina laughed. “You look like I just took away a death sentence.”

“I’m just nervous,” William said, which was the truth, if not the entirety of it.

“Is it because you’re alone with me, and you wonder what Serena will think?” Elaina asked. “Or is it something else? Fear, maybe? Fear of the unknown, of true magic?”

“Pretty much all of that,” William replied.

Elaina nodded. "At least in this one instance you're honest."

What did that mean?

Elaina didn't explain. Instead, once again she peered at William's hands. A frown creased her face. "You said your brother died?"

"He died in the same accident as my parents."

"The accident that wasn't an accident," Elaina murmured.

Once again, William's hackles rose.

"What is hiding from my sight?" Elaina mused, sounding frustrated. "Something dark." Her head shot up. "Walking death came for you and your family last winter, and yet you live. So, too, does your brother." Elaina sounded utterly sure of herself.

William snatched his hands from her, his blood instantly at a furious boil. He tried not to shout at her. "I buried my brother. He's not alive, and it's a cruel joke you're playing on me, saying he is."

"Landon."

A chill crawled down William's spine. "How do you know his name?"

"Because a true witch can see that which is hidden even from the eyes of the magi." Elaina held his gaze the entire time. "That is what you are, is it not? You and Jason and Serena. You have true magic, and your brother does as well. And he lives. He is lost and searches for himself."

William stood up on shaky legs, wishing he'd never come here. His heart thudded, and he breathed as heavily as if he'd run a marathon.

Elaina's performance had been impressive but only a performance and nothing more. Most of it had to have been guesswork on her part, just like her heroine, Jessica Fletcher,

Angela Lansbury's character on *Murder, She Wrote*. Elaina was no witch.

Landon was dead. Of that, William was certain. The notion that his brother was out there alone, wandering and lost, didn't bear considering. It couldn't be true. William had buried Landon's ashes alongside their parents.

"Believe what you wish," Elaina spoke into the silence, "but I speak the truth. The living death walks—"

"Thank you for your time," William interrupted. He backed out of the tent, keeping his eyes on Elaina the entire way. Now he understood what it was about Elaina that bothered him so much. She stared at him like a predator.

It was hours after the final performances of *Wizard Bill's Wandering Wonders* in Las Vegas, late at night. Tomorrow the circus would pack up and head home to Salt Lake City. Meanwhile Serena, William, and Jason would leave for the *saha'asra*.

The enormity of what would happen afterward filled Serena with fear and doubt. Neither *"Gloria"* or the Colt automatic that she'd purchased in a local pawn shop assuaged those worries. The hours of her life might be measured in hours, and while she wanted to succeed at the task set to her by Isha and her father, even more she wanted to live. She wanted to see the New Year. She wanted to dance in the ocean. She wanted to climb the mountains of her island home. She wanted so much from life, so many things that she couldn't even name.

Serena had never before known such longings or such disquieting uncertainty, and it left her wanting the company of others tonight. So when Mrs. Nancy, Jane, and Josephine Sandler had invited her to a late-night raid on Jimmy's dessert pantry, she had gladly accepted.

Better than spending time worrying about William, or lying to him. Not tonight. Not now. She couldn't. Tomorrow Serena would lie as skillfully as always, but tonight she wanted peace.

Right now, they had the backyard to themselves, a blessed quiet.

"Mmm. That's good," Jane said after taking a bite of strawberry cheesecake. Her voice had grown husky and her expression became one of sheer bliss. Jane took another bite, and her eyes rolled up. "Better than sex."

Josephine Sandler, the pretty, young Dubrovic with whom Jason had been flirting the past few days, snickered. "Nothing's that good."

Jane's eyes snapped open and she pointed her fork at the younger woman. "Get to my age, missy, and then come talk to me." She took another slow, sensuous bite of her cheesecake.

"Or maybe you're just doing it wrong," countered Mrs. Nancy with an arch of her brows. "I'll take the small death over a slice of cheesecake any day of the week, and three times on Sundays."

"Three times on Sunday?" Jane snorted. "With Bill?"

"The Lord does tell us to be fruitful and multiply," Mrs. Nancy responded with a pious expression.

"What does the Lord tell you to do?" William asked as he walked in from the shadows. He'd apparently only heard the end of Jane's pronouncement. Jason walked alongside him.

Serena mentally groaned. *A single night of peace. Was that too much to ask?* She wanted to gnash her teeth in frustration. She didn't have it in her to deal with William and Jason right now.

"There you are, Nancy," Mr. Bill said, striding into the backyard.

Serena sighed. The peacefulness that had existed among the four women was officially over.

"Can't I have just a moment to myself?" Mrs. Nancy complained, echoing Serena's thoughts.

"Sure, you can. When we get back to Salt Lake. Then you can take a nice, long soak in a tub or whatever," Mr. Bill said. "Right now, I need your help. Elaina doesn't want to tour with us next season."

Mrs. Nancy did a double take. "Why not?"

"College."

"Not this again," Mrs. Nancy groaned. "Is she still up?"

Mr. Bill nodded. "Can you go talk some sense into her?"

"I'll be right there," Mrs. Nancy said. She offered hasty goodbyes to everyone in the backyard before departing with Mr. Bill.

"I think I'm done here, too," Josephine said, yawning mightily.

"I'll walk you back to your trailer," Jason said, hopping up with an overabundance of eagerness.

Jane glanced at Serena and William. "I think that's my cue. Make sure to see me tomorrow morning before you leave."

"We will," William told her.

Serena sighed. Here he was despite her best efforts to avoid him. She could have whined about the unfairness of it all, but what was the point? Instead, she set aside her disappointment and mustered her energy. "Looks like everyone left us," Serena said with a smile.

William shrugged. "I just came here for something to eat. I'm hungry." He sat down and drew Jane's half-eaten cheesecake and Josephine's untouched slice to him and focused on devouring the food.

Serena shook her head in amazement. *How did he eat so much?* She'd have been as big as a houseboat if she ate like William did.

"Are you a magus?" William asked casually.

His head remained bent as he focused on his food, so he missed Serena's wide-eyed expression of shock. She gazed at him in disbelief before quickly schooling her features to stillness. Once again, she leaned on her training and answered his question with one of her own. "Why would you think that?" she asked, hoping he didn't notice the quaver in her voice.

William looked up from his cheesecake slices. "Are you all right?"

"Just a tickle in my throat," Serena lied.

William shrugged. "Are you?"

"Am I what? A magus? Absolutely not," Serena answered, her voice now firm. "Why would you think I was?"

"Elaina Sinith," William said. His face had gone uncharacteristically flat.

Serena's hackles rose. William liked her. But that wasn't what made Serena nervous about the other young woman.

It was something else.

Serena knew the truth about Elaina Sinith. The fortuneteller was a being of magic, like William and Jason, except Elaina was a witch. While they weren't as powerful as *asrasins*, they were still dangerous.

"She read my fortune," William said. "She said that you're a magus, and that my brother is alive."

Serena exhaled in relief. The witch's pronouncement could be easily explained away. "Well, I'm not a magus, and your brother is dead." Serena tilted her head in consideration. "Not much of a fortuneteller, is she?"

"I didn't think so," he agreed, "but something keeps bothering me."

"What's that?"

"She knew Landon's name. I never told her that."

"Did Jason?"

"He says no."

"Lucky guess?" Serena asked, hoping to set aside William's concerns. He couldn't be allowed to think too deeply on what Elaina told him.

William snorted. "That's one helluva lucky guess. Landon isn't exactly a common name. And Elaina says that she's a witch, a real one from some place called Sand."

"A Sand witch." Serena snorted laughter.

"That's what I said." William grinned, but his smile quickly fell away.

"What is it?" Serena asked, her own smile fading.

"I wish she hadn't known Landon's name."

"What are you thinking then? That I might have it in me to become a magus like you and Jason? And that your brother is alive?"

William perked up. "I hadn't thought of it like that. You aren't a magus now, but maybe you can become one."

Serena breathed out a quiet sigh of gratitude, thankful that her distraction had paid off. William hadn't seen through her ruse, hadn't seen how she had guided his thoughts. She smiled and mimicked a faraway expression of longing. "How wonderful would that be? I wouldn't be the only bland, boring normal person on Arylyn."

"Yeah, and best of all, Landon would be alive," William enthused, his face also filled with longing.

CHAPTER 23: DREAM DETAILS

"William, you awake?" a voice asked.

William rolled over.

"William," the voice repeated.

He covered his ears with his pillow.

"I need to talk to you," the voice persisted.

"Leave me alone. I'm sleeping," William grumbled.

Someone clicked on the battery-powered lantern they used to light their small tent. "How about now? You still asleep?"

William poked his head out of the pillow, growling like a bear and knowing that he'd find Jason smirking down at him. "What?" he demanded.

"I was asleep and—"

"So was I," William grumbled. "Besides, I thought you'd be with Josephine after you walked her back to her trailer."

"I did, and she let me kiss her goodnight, but that was it." Jason looked crestfallen. "She didn't even let me inside so we could talk."

"Is that what they call it in Arylyn?"

"I swear that's all I wanted to do," Jason protested. "I just wanted to tell her how much I like her."

"What did you want to talk to me about?" William asked. He really wanted to go back to sleep.

"After I left Josephine, I went back to my tent and fell asleep. That's when I heard from Mr. Zeus," Jason said. "I know where the *saha'asra* is. It's on the north shore of Black Canyon Lake in Arizona."

"You've got the *saha'asra* dialed in?" William woke up more fully.

"It's in this small hollow next to where a dirt road leads right up to the lake. We won't even have to do any hiking, just drive right there."

Hope blossomed in William's chest.

"Best of all," Jason said, "some of the *saha'asra* extends into the water."

"Why's that good?"

"Because the necrosed don't like water. They hate it."

"Why?"

Jason shrugged. "How would I know? And more importantly, who cares? Maybe they melt in it and die or something."

"That'd be cool, right?" William said with a grin. "We kill the necrosed, and none of us have to go to Arylyn. We can all go home and finish high school."

"St. Francis," Jason said in fond remembrance. "It seems like a million miles away."

"A long time ago, in a high school far, far away."

Jason chuckled. "What would you have done after graduation?" he asked. "You can't stay with Serena, you know?

Your *lorethasra* is awake. You'll have to come to Arylyn, but the longer you wait, the harder the training will be."

"How much time do I have?"

"Plenty," Jason said. "But college is definitely out. Four years, or in your case, seven, Mr. Bluto Blutarsky, is way too long to be away from Arylyn."

"Fat, drunk, and stupid is no way to go through life, son," William quipped, quoting *Animal House.*

They laughed, but the seriousness of what might happen tomorrow quickly stole away their humor.

"We go up to the north shore of Black Canyon Lake and then this is all over," William mused.

"That's the plan."

William only hoped it would work as easily as it sounded in the safety of their tent.

"Is Serena your girlfriend?" Jason asked out of the blue.

The abrupt change of topic had William flustered. "None of your business," he said, trying to shrug aside the question.

"Have you kissed her?" Jason persisted. "I know you've kissed her at the end of our performances, but how about other times?"

"Twice." William recalled the times he'd kissed in West Virginia, and wished, as before, that he knew why he couldn't make up his mind about her.

"Once?" Jason asked, incredulous. "That's it?"

"There's this thing about a necrosed that wants to kill us," William replied dryly. "It kind of put a damper on the whole romance business."

"I guess," Jason said, and thankfully, he let the topic slide.

"You remember what Jake looked like when he saw Kohl Obsidian?" William asked.

Jason grinned. "If I hadn't been so terrified I'd have peed myself laughing."

"He sounded like that scream thing, you know?" William said. "The one they use in the movies whenever a man falls to his death."

"The Wilhelm scream?"

"Yeah. That's the one. That's what Jake sounded like." William mimicked the Wilhelm scream, and Jason laughed. "I wish we had a way to video tape things as they happen."

"Could you imagine Daniel and Lien's reaction if they'd seen it? They would have loved it."

"What an asshole that guy was," William said.

"Still hate him, huh?"

William shrugged. "He wasn't so bad at the end, but I guess some people will always stay enemies."

Serena started when Mr. Bill wandered into the nearly empty backyard. Not because he didn't typically get up that early in the morning, nor because he didn't appear to have his usual hangover, but because of the teary-eyed 'thank yous' and bear hugs that he delivered to each of them. She'd never expected him to have such a sentimental side.

"You have to promise to join us for the summer tour," Mr. Bill said, his eyes shiny.

"If we can, we will. Sir." Jason wore a crooked grin.

Mr. Bill shook a fist under Jason's nose in mock aggravation before he broke out into a grin. "Scamp."

"Thank you for all you did for us," William said in his mild North Carolina drawl. "We were just three dumb kids who thought they knew more than they really did. You didn't have to hire us on."

"No, I didn't, but you worked out."

Jimmy, in the backyard as always, snorted. "They did all right for young 'uns who didn't know the difference between a big-top and a rag-top."

"None of you are dumb. You all have good heads on your shoulders," Mr. Bill said to William before gesturing to Serena and Jason. "Lead them straight and true, and you'll do well by them."

Serena pursed her lips in surprise. How had she missed it? William *was* their leader. He was the one who generally made their final decisions. Even before this entire disaster with the necrosed, it had been the case.

"I'll do my best," William replied with a solemn nod.

"Sorry we can't stay long enough to help pack up," Serena said.

"No worries. I'm not paying you for today's work anyway," Bill said with a dismissive wave.

Mrs. Nancy hustled into the backyard. "Oh good! You're still here."

Her skinny frame appeared particularly skeletal in the tight-fitting, white jeans and T-shirt she wore, and despite the ungodly hour, she had still found time to apply her makeup and tease her hair into its typical bouffant.

"I've got some goodies for you," Mrs. Nancy said, reaching into a large sack. "Cookies. Right out of the oven."

Serena's nose tickled and her mouth watered. Chocolate chip cookies. Her favorite.

"I'm so glad you haven't left yet," another voice called out.

Disquiet traced Serena's spine.

Elaina Sinith.

"I've got some presents, too," the witch said.

William shifted about, visibly uncomfortable.

"For you, Jason, I have this." She pulled out a single glove with a theatrical flourish.

Jason held it in obvious confusion. "One glove? I don't get it."

"It's a right-hand glove, just as you are the strong right hand of your trio of adventurers," Elaina proclaimed.

Serena somehow managed to keep herself from rolling her eyes.

"To you, William, I give this fountain pen. I sense that where you journey, the sword will prove mightier than the pen. But having a good pen is never a bad thing."

Elaina wore a broad smile as she turned to Serena. "I haven't forgotten you," the witch said. "You are unforgettable. But a word in private, sister."

Serena felt the need to fidget, but she forced herself to remain still.

Elaina stepped closer and spoke softly. "I know who you really are, and I know they don't." She gave a barely perceptible motion of her head. "I'll keep your secret."

Serena gave her a bland smile of confusion. "What secret?"

"I'm not stupid," Elaina said. "Nor am I your enemy. In the

end, that honor belongs to yourself. If you don't let go of your falsehoods, they *will* trap you in sorrow." She shrugged. "But it's your life to live." She stepped back and once more donned a bright smile. "Now. Your gift. To you I give this pendant." She presented Serena with a silver locket in the shape of an *om*. "Though the mind lies, the heart is always true. Find your truth, and you'll find your joy."

For once, Serena's training held no suggestions on how to respond. She merely nodded her thanks for the witch's gift.

"And with that, it's time for us to hit the road," William declared.

"You all packed up?" Jimmy asked.

"The Scout's ready to rumble."

"Then may good luck and a fair wind allow you to safely reach your destination, and annoy those who deserve it," said Mr. Bill.

Serena stared out the window and watched as the barren reds and tans of the desert flowed by like a static image. The view went on and on, a never-ending expanse of eye-aching dreariness. Once the colors had been fascinating, but fascination had long since faded, and the colors had long since grown aggravating. All the reds, orange, and earth tones—in her mind's eye Serena imagined green forests, white-capped mountains, and an indigo blue ocean, soothing images from a not-so-soothing home.

Jason napped in the back while William drove them along a

monotonous highway heading south. They took a circuitous route to Black Canyon Lake that they hoped wouldn't allow Kohl Obsidian to so easily guess their final destination.

Serena doubted it would work, but it wouldn't hurt to try.

"You don't like the desert," William said to her, breaking the quiet within the Scout.

"Why do you say that?" Serena asked, turning to him.

"Because I don't like it either," William said. "And you sighed."

Serena quirked a wry smile, surprised at his insight. "I don't like it," she admitted. "I was imagining the sea. All the blues and greens. Something tranquil. Anything other than these stupid reds and oranges."

"Same here, except I was thinking of a forest, like when my family went camping in the Smokies."

"What's it like?" Serena asked.

"Pretty," William replied.

Serena waited for him to elaborate, but he didn't. His eyes faced forward, and he remained silent.

"And?" she prodded.

"I'm getting to it," William replied with a frown. A moment more of silence, and he began to talk. "It's pretty," he repeated. "A morning fog blankets the ground, and the world is so quiet. Dad and I would wake up early—Landon and Mom always slept in—and we'd talk. It was like we were the only people in the world."

"Sounds peaceful," Serena said, her wistful tone a true expression of her feelings.

In times past when William had spoken of his family, or when he and his friends had shared their stories and laughter, she had tried maintain her aloofness, to disregard what she considered a weakness. Now that same supposed weakness had become a longing, a desire for the comfort and safety of family and friends who truly loved her.

The time left to her in this life might span less than a day since tomorrow they would reach the *saha'asra*. Tomorrow her future would be decided, and she didn't want to face the end with regrets and unanswered questions.

"You okay?" William asked.

Serena forced a smile. "Not really," she said. "Tomorrow . . . It's scary to realize that tonight might be the last sunset I'll ever see."

"It is scary," William agreed softly. He reached for her hand and gave it a comforting squeeze.

Serena squeezed back. Doing so no longer filled her with guilt. If comforting another was a weakness, then so be it.

After all, look at William. He was exactly the kind of person every one of her people would have categorized as weak: kind, decent, and easily manipulated. And yet, he had survived three attacks by a necrosed, and he'd done so mostly because of his friendship with Jason.

How many of her people could have accomplished such a feat in a similar set of circumstances?

None.

Which meant that William wasn't weak, and neither was friendship or love.

It was a strange and startling insight.

"We'll make it through this if we stick together," William said. "That's what friends do."

Serena nodded before turning to stare out at the wasteland. Friendship: a terrible and heavy burden, and yet, how freeing and wonderful it must be.

CHAPTER 24: AIA

William huddled alone near the fire while Jason and Serena slept in their tents. On what might be his last night on Earth, William didn't want to be cooped up in some Days Inn or a Best Western. So they'd foregone a hotel, choosing instead to camp under the wide, open desert sky. William needed to see the stars and feel the world and the living night.

The desert cold had him rethinking his wishes, and he shivered, shifting closer to the fire.

He tried to keep his mind from dwelling on tomorrow, and tomorrow's turmoils and terrors, but it proved difficult as the night stretched on, cold, lonely, and troubled.

However, in the hour just before dawn—earliest morning or latest night—the sky began to pale but not yet pink, and a hush, serene and still, overtook the world; a magical moment that was fragmentary and fleeting.

When the sun fully rose, life's hectic cacophony would resume and the world's temporarily forgotten problems would stir once more, but for now, William embraced the peace.

The sun pinked the sky, and a cold breeze blustered. The wind stirred the coals, crackled the fire, and sent tumbleweeds scattering along the ground like errant balls of yarn. It blew harder, and William shivered as the peace ended. He pulled his coat tighter about him, but as the breeze died away, a faint, noise came to him: the cry of a baby.

William straightened and searched the darkness around him, seeking the source of the sound. Seconds passed, but the cry didn't repeat, and William relaxed, thinking it must have been his imagination.

The cry repeated, and William surged to his feet. He turned about in a circle, trying to localize the source. *What was a baby doing out here? Were there other campers nearby? And where was their fire?* The baby sounded close.

Help!

William startled at the word. The plea had rung out in his mind rather than his ears. He shook his head and tapped it a few times.

Help!

The plea cried out again in William's mind, but this time he also heard again the plaintive baby's wail. There *was* a baby out there.

William frowned and glanced at Jason's tent, wondering if he should wake him. Maybe he'd know what was going on.

He stood frozen with indecision before finally muttering at his stupidity. *Let Jason sleep. Magi didn't possess telepathy.* Jason had told him that once. It was a lost art. Whatever he thought he heard in his mind had to be a product of his overactive imagination.

But what about the baby he'd heard? He hadn't imagined that.

William stepped past the light of the fire and flicked on his flashlight. He washed the light in the direction of the occasionally crying baby. It sounded close, and again William wondered what the infant was doing out here in the winter desert. If it was outside, why didn't the parents have a fire going to keep their baby warm?

Please help me!

William stopped. A trickle of uncertainty made its way down his spine, and he frowned. *What was going on here?*

Is someone there?

The voice spoke in his head at the same time that he heard the baby's mewling cry. Both sounds seemed close, only a few yards away. William swept the beam of his flashlight in the area where he expected the other campers to be. The baby should be right there, directly in front of him. But other than cactus and scrub, the desert stood empty.

The trickle of uncertainty became a trickle of fear. William reached into the back of his mind, the part that always knew the location of Kohl Obsidian. He breathed out a sigh of relief when he felt the necrosed hundreds of miles away, back in Kansas somewhere.

A silence fell across the desert. A stillness stole all sound, and the world seemed to wait. A rustling arose next to a scrub brush. William's heart nearly stopped.

From the scratchy depths of the brown bush came a small form, a calico kitten with a black patch over her right eye.

She looked at William and mewed, the same mewling sound he'd mistaken for a baby's cry. The kitten padded up to him and sat down, her tail curled up before her front paws.

I'm cold.

William stared at the kitten in astonishment. *Who had said that? Surely not the kitten.*

Yes. Me. The kitten. I'm cold.

William stumbled back from the calico.

What the hell was going on here? The kitten was talking to him. In his mind! How?

Maybe he'd accidentally burned peyote as part of the kindling for the fire? Maybe the kitten was just a drug-induced hallucination? And if so, how long would the peyote keep mucking with his mind? All day? Just a few hours? Long enough to render him useless when they had to face the necrosed?

The Shining Man told me I'd find a friend here. Are you a friend?

William didn't know what to think. He stared at the kitten in confusion and fear.

"What are you doing out here?" Serena asked from behind William.

A yip escaped William's lips as he nearly leaped out of his skin. Serena stared at him in bemusement.

William aimed the flashlight at the kitten. "What do you see there?" he asked.

Serena shifted her gaze to where he indicated. She tilted her head in consideration. "A kitten. What's it doing here?" Her words were matter-of-fact, not rising into that high-pitched, baby-talk that most girls used when they saw a kitten or something similarly adorable.

Her words, though, eased some of William's fears. The kitten was real, which meant there was no peyote-induced hallucination going on. But if he wasn't hallucinating, then why was he imagining that the kitten was talking to him in his mind?

Because I am talking to you in your mind.

William started again.

"What's it doing out here?" Serena repeated. "Did someone dump it?"

"I don't know," William replied. "I came out here when I heard her crying."

"Her?"

"Calicos are almost always female," William explained. "And this calico is . . ." He shook his head, not wanting to explain the impossible.

"What's wrong?" Serena asked.

"I think she can talk to me in my mind." William bent down and scooped up the kitten, holding her inside the warmth of his coat. She snuggled against him.

My chin itches.

"You are a demanding little girl, aren't you?" William said. He ignored Serena's look of astonishment as he marched back to camp.

"A cat that talks. That's what you're saying?" Jason asked. He didn't bother to hide the disbelief in his voice.

Serena felt the same way. *A talking cat?* She wondered if William had taken a blow to the head or developed frostbite of the brain with the overnight cold, anything rational to account for his weird hallucination. And why did he have to have it on today of all days? Just hours before they faced a life-and-death struggle against Kohl Obsidian.

"She can talk," William insisted.

"Then why won't she talk to me?" Jason said. "I haven't heard a peep out of her."

The kitten took that moment to mew.

"That doesn't count," Jason protested.

"I don't know why she won't talk to you." William held the kitten protectively against his chest, seeming like he'd already bonded with the animal.

Serena scowled. She didn't like animals as pets. Dogs, cats, hamsters, roosters—all creatures should have a useful purpose; not be doted upon like babies. And animals most certainly didn't talk. Not anymore, anyway. Maybe they had thousands of years ago, when the *asrasins* had far greater power than they did today.

Jason turned to her. "What do you think?" he asked.

Serena shrugged. "It doesn't matter what I think," she said. "William says the thing can talk to him. Fine. It can talk."

Jason looked at her, dumbfounded. "I thought you had more sense than that," he accused.

"I've got plenty of sense," Serena snapped, already tired of the argument. "But what difference does it make? We've got more important things to discuss, like how we're going to survive Kohl Obsidian. We don't have any plan other than showing up at the *saha'asra*, splashing into the water, opening the anchor line to Arylyn, and hoping the necrosed doesn't kill us first."

"I'm open to suggestions," Jason said.

"I didn't mean to criticize," Serena said.

"I'm just saying if anyone else can open the anchor line *and* protect the two of you," Jason said, speaking more vehemently, "then by all means, let me know."

"Calm down," Serena said, trying to stifle her irritation. "I know you have a lot to do—"

"I've got everything to do," Jason snapped back. "The two of you can't do anything to help me. Not one bit."

"I'm sorry we're such anchors," William said, "but maybe if you and Mr. Zeus had told me the truth earlier, we wouldn't be in this mess."

"You think this is my fault?" Jason asked, his voice rising.

"I'm not saying that," William shot back. "But what's happening now isn't my fault, either! Nor is it Serena's."

"I never said it was!"

"No, but you sure are comfortable saying we're dead weight," William said.

"You're not dead weight." Jason sounded frustrated. "But the kitten is. Or did you plan on taking her with us to Arylyn? You know what's going to be waiting for us at that *saha'asra*."

"I know *exactly* what's waiting for us," William snarled. "He killed my family, remember? I can feel him. And yes, I plan on taking Aia to Arylyn."

Jason threw his hands in the air. "Unbelievable. Today of all days you have to go crazy. I need you sharp and focused. Not worried about some cat you found."

"Aia isn't—"

"You've even named her?" Jason interrupted, sounding disgusted.

"No, I didn't," William said. "She told me."

"What?" Jason said. "That's the stupidest . . ."

Serena closed her eyes and imagined "Gloria". Lately it was the only thing that kept her sane and hopeful. William and Jason continued shouting at each other, and Serena wanted to stuff her ears with cotton so she wouldn't have to listen.

**They need a smack to their noses,* a small voice said.

Serena froze. "Who said that?"

I said that.

Serena opened her eyes and stared at the cat. *It couldn't be.*

Of course, it can be, the voice said, sounding oddly mature and amused. **And I'm not a cat. I'm a kitten.**

Serena's thoughts clamored in a mad dash. Chief among them was the simple hope that that both she and William were somehow sharing the same strange hallucinations. *Anything but a talking cat.*

"What did you say?" Serena asked, praying that the voice wouldn't reply.

I said that I'm a kitten, the voice replied.

"She's talking to me," Serena whispered, staring at the kitten in fascinated horror.

William and Jason didn't hear her, and they continued to argue.

I told you I could talk. The little animal blinked at her and yawned.

Serena gaped. All of Isha's training was of no use when faced with such an impossibility. She had no idea what to do. "She's talking to me," Serena repeated.

"What?" William asked.

"I said, she's talking to me," Serena said for the third time.

"Not you, too," Jason said, his disgust evident.

Serena shot him a glare. "Believe me. I'd much rather she *not* be able to talk to me, but she can."

"If she can talk to you, then ask her to do something," Jason said. "Prove she can talk."

Absolutely not. I'm not your pet, to do tricks on command. The kitten, Aia, sounded offended and imperious.

Jason's face stiffened, and he held himself unnaturally still. "Who said that?" he asked in a strangled voice.

I said that. I've been shouting and shouting at you, but you wouldn't listen.

"God save us," Jason whispered fervently. "The kitten's talking. A talking kitten." He sounded as stunned as Serena felt.

I'm a kitten now, but once I was much more. At least, the Shining Man said I was. I don't remember any of it, but he says I was grand. The voice sounded wistful.

Serena had no idea what Aia meant by the Shining Man, and she didn't care. Not yet, anyway. One impossibility at a time.

The Shining Man says that one day I'll become again what I once was, but first, I have to do something here. What's a dead thing that isn't dead? Aia asked. **I'm supposed to help kill it.**

Serena closed her eyes and sighed. She was already tired of this near-constant state of surprise. Aia was obviously talking about Kohl Obsidian. How had the kitten known?

How do we kill something already dead? Aia asked, sounding perplexed. **And can someone else scratch my chin? William's not very good at it.**

The rest of the drive to the *saha'asra* passed in relative silence, at least among William, Jason, and Serena. Other than

John Cougar Mellencamp—who'd always be John Cougar as far as William was concerned—singing *Scarecrow*, the Scout held a brooding quiet. None of them wanted to talk. Serena and Jason stared out the window, both apparently lost in their thoughts, while William kept his eyes on the road. Like the other two, his mind was elsewhere, mostly filled with worry.

The sky is so gray here, Aia said. William glanced her way. The kitten perched on the dashboard, and she wouldn't stop talking. She chattered non-stop. **The clouds are so ugly, and it's so cold. What's wrong with the sun? Is it too puny to make things warm?**

"There's nothing wrong with the sun," Serena said with a sigh of impatience. "It's the middle of winter. Rain or snow are on the way. It's supposed to be cold."

The kitten flicked her tail. **I don't like cold.**

"What were you doing out in the desert, anyway?" Jason asked.

Aia didn't answer at first. Instead, she licked a paw, appearing uncertain.

William wanted to roll his eyes at the notion. An uncertain kitten based on how she licked her paw? This day might be his doom, but it was already more ridiculous than any he could ever recall, and that included Kohl Obsidian tracking him down in West Virginia.

"How did you end up in the desert?" Jason repeated.

I don't know, Aia replied. She sounded meek and unhappy. **I opened my eyes and the Shining Man was there. That's the first thing I remember. He told me to trust him and to wait for someone who needs me.**

"Who's the Shining Man?" Serena asked, for the first time taking an interest in the kitten. William got the sense she didn't like Aia.

He's the Shining Man. He's my friend, and he loves me, Aia said, stirring to life and smiling, a slow blink of her eyes. **We've had many grand adventures. I wish I could remember them better.** She finished with a sigh.

"Loves you how?" Serena asked. "Like a pet?"

Aia laughed, a tinkling sound, as her eyes squinted and her head lifted up. **I'm no one's pet.**

"But you're doing what the Shining Man told you to do," Serena said.

Aia stared at Serena and her ears tilted back. **I'm doing what the Shining Man* asked *me to do. He didn't* order *me to do anything,** she said. **I think you know the difference between the two.**

Serena reddened at Aia's words, but William wasn't sure why.

I'm sorry, Aia said. She jumped down from the dashboard and scrambled onto Serena's lap. **I didn't mean to make you unhappy.** She nosed forward, pressing her face into Serena's hand. **You can run your hand along my fur now.**

"I can, can I?" Serena asked. She wore a small, surprised smile as she petted Aia, and the little kitten began purring like an engine before deciding to curl up into a small, furry ball. Serena tickled her chin.

That's good, much better than William, Aia said. She closed her eyes and appeared to fall asleep.

William glanced at Jason in the rear view mirror. "And you've never heard of a talking cat?"

Kitten, Aia corrected in a drowsy tone.

"No. Animals don't talk. They never have. No talking cats, kittens, dogs, or anything."

"Then how's she talking?" William asked.

"I have no idea," Jason said with a shrug. "Maybe Mr. Zeus can tell us."

"She's cute," Serena said, still wearing a smile of pleasure.

"Who? The kitten?" William asked. "I thought you didn't like her."

Serena glanced up at him. "It's hard not to like someone so precious and cute. You just want to keep them safe."

"Well all cuteness aside, we still have to come up with a way to get to the *saha'asra* and past Kohl Obsidian," Jason said. "We won't have lions and tigers and bears, oh my, to help us this time."

"He's fast and he's strong," William said, "but you also said he doesn't like water."

"He doesn't like *moving* water," Jason amended.

"Can you form a shield like Mr. Zeus made back in West Virginia?" Serena asked. "That golden thing?"

"I can, but you saw how little it slowed him down back there."

"But that's all we need," Serena said. "We just need to slow him down."

"What if you make a fake shield? Can you do that?" William asked.

"Sure, but how would that help?"

"If he runs into a fake shield, he'll stumble through it. It might surprise him."

"I can light him up with fire or fling him into the next county if that happens," Jason said, leaning forward in his excitement.

"That should give me enough time to form the anchor line to Arylyn, and we can escape."

"If you put the real shield inside the fake one, he'll have to punch through it. You'll have even more time then."

Jason broke out in laughter. "We've been thinking about this all wrong. We've been wondering how to beat the necrosed when all we have to do is distract him long enough to get away."

William chewed his lower lip in frustration. "I still wish there was more Serena and I could do."

"Don't worry about it," Jason said, sounding confident.

"You sure?" William asked.

"I'm sure," Jason said. "And forget what I said earlier. I don't think Serena's dead weight. You on the other hand . . ." He grinned.

William smiled, accepting the apology.

"Is there any way to actually kill a necrosed?" Serena asked. "I know we sort of talked about this, but you've always said there wasn't."

"There is a way, but it's almost impossible," Jason said. "A few nights ago, Mr. Zeus sent me another dream. He said the only way to kill a necrosed is to take his head."

William shared a glance with Serena. "You mean like what the immortals did in *The Highlander*?"

"Yes and no," Jason said. "Even removed, the head can continue to command the body, tell it where to go and what to do. You have to take the head, burn it, and scatter the ashes where the necrosed can never find it."

"What do you mean 'where the necrosed can never find it'?" Serena asked.

“All the body needs is a small piece of the head, either flesh or ash, and it can regenerate the rest,” Jason replied.

“How long does this headless thing wander around?” William asked, fascinated and horrified at the same time.

“It’s only been done once, and it took over a year for the body to finally die.”

“Jesus,” William said. “Then it’s a good thing we don’t have to kill Kohl.”

But if you did, you’ll have help, Aia said, still sounding drowsy. **What a long day. Rukh better not be wrong about this.**

“Who’s Rukh?” William asked.

The Shining Man.

CHAPTER 25: FINAL CONFRONTATION

Kohl Obsidian stood as immovable as a rusted out hulk, arms stretched out as he kept his focus on the boy. From far away he might have appeared an over-sized scarecrow in the winter-bare field, with the wind flapping his frayed garments. But from closer on, his thick frame revealed that this was no mere scarecrow. And in that darkening field, with the sun setting and shadows swaying and Kohl's hooded eyes moving as restlessly as his thoughts, his malice would have been unmistakable.

That malice focused upon a boy following a winding, wavering path.

Kohl frowned, a narrowing of eyes beneath his beetled brow.

In general, the boy's path took him west, obviously to a *saha'asra*. Of that, Kohl felt certain. From it, the boy and those other *asrasins* would seek to flee to Arylyn or Sinskrill. But which *saha'asra* would they choose? Three of them lay along the path the boy journeyed.

The sound of grinding gears breaking loose rumbled from Kohl's throat as he growled in impatience. Like the farmer who left his fields fallow in hopes of a more bountiful harvest in the future, Kohl had allowed the boy to live. He had delayed his gratification, but the delay had lasted too long, and Kohl's patience had reached its end. He needed that promised harvest.

Kohl's ruminations were ruined a moment later when he sensed a necrosed enter the *saha'asra* far to the east, the one where Kohl had first confronted the boy, where he had almost feasted upon a plethora of *asrasins*. His plans had first gone awry there, when he'd touched what he now recognized must have been a *nomasra*, one that nulled *asra*. The pendant hanging from a chain around the boy's neck had injured Kohl, and he'd bled upon the *saha'asra*, drawing his brethren like vermin to a rotting carcass.

They clustered there, and today's arrival marked the fifth of his kind, all of them seeking his death. Kohl imagined they stood as still as he did, stiff as stone and with arms held out, searching the wind for the blood of their injured brother. At least that's what Kohl would have done had their roles been reversed.

They wouldn't find him, though. Kohl was a finer hunter than any necrosed in any world. In his past life Kohl had been a holder, a warrior bred by *asrasins* to confront evil, and one of the few beings capable of killing a necrosed. Other than Sapient Dormant, none of his brothers could claim such a lineage. Yes, Kohl could easily remain hidden from those five necrosed searching him out.

Strangely, the memories of his past life as a holder had vanished from his mind. When and how those recollections had fled, he didn't know. But the skills remained.

Kohl's frown deepened for a moment as he examined the mystery. No answer came, and he eventually disregarded those concerns. Ancient, useless history.

A moment later, Kohl broke into a pleased smile. The boy still traveled west, but had changed direction to a course that took him north as well.

Kohl knew where the boy was heading. He would get there first.

William flipped on the fog lights and drove slowly along the twisting, narrow road that would eventually deposit them at Black Canyon Lake. "October" by U2 played on his mix tape, a perfect accompaniment for the gloomy, cold, miserable day with its misty rain and fog. William shook his head in disbelief. Rain and fog in a desert. The one day they needed to be able to see, and visibility was down to a few hundred yards.

Unbelievable.

His disgust was interrupted when the Scout slipped, threatening to get stuck in the muddy track of the dirt road. William goosed the gas, and the Scout lurched forward. *Thank goodness for four-wheel drive.*

He frowned when the itching in the back of his mind, his sense of the necrosed, grew more intense. Kohl was on the move. He wasn't in Kansas anymore. William shut off the radio.

From her perch on the dashboard, Aia hissed.

"What's wrong?" Jason asked.

Serena's face paled. *She knew.*

William didn't answer. Instead, he brought the Scout to a halt. The gloom had grown threatening. "He's here."

Aia's pupils widened, and she growled, a surprisingly deep-throated sound for such a small animal. She stared straight ahead, as if she could peer through the mist and see the necrosed.

"What do we do?" Serena asked, sounding a lot calmer than William felt. "Should we turn back?"

"I'd *love* to turn back," William replied, "but we can't. Not now. Not after we've come so far."

We attack, Aia said with a furious lash of her tail. **This creature is an abomination, one that should have never been fashioned.**

William did a double-take. *How did something so small manage to convey such ferocity?*

"Can you tell where he is?" Jason asked.

William flicked on the high beams, hoping to see farther along the road. The desert had plenty of low-lying hills, hollows, and blinds where Kohl could hide, and with the fog blanketing the ground, they might not see him until they were right on top of him. William continued to stare ahead, not that he could truly see much beyond the beam of the headlights. Instead, he focused upon the itching in his mind, using it to pinpoint the location of the necrosed.

"He's near the *saha'asra*," William said. "He's hiding behind a small rise."

"You can feel the *saha'asra*?" Jason asked in surprise.

William nodded. "Can't you?"

"Yeah, but—"

"Focus," Serena chided. "You can figure out what William can or can't do later. The necrosed is still waiting for us."

We'll have help killing him, Aia said. **We only have to hold on long enough for him to arrive.**

William's brows furrowed as he stared at the kitten. He had no idea what she was talking about, and he shared a glance with the others. They also shrugged in confusion.

"Is the necrosed between us and the *saha'asra*?" Jason asked.

William shook his head.

"Then I say we drive like hell, surprise the necrosed before he can stop us, get into the shallows of the lake, and go through with our original plan. Maybe the water will hold Kohl back."

It wasn't the best of ideas—it was actually pretty dumb—but no one had anything better to offer.

"I guess that's what we're doing," Serena said with a distinct lack of enthusiasm.

Her sentiment mirrored William's own uneasiness, and he grimaced. He waited, but no one had anything more to say. *Shit. They were really going to do this.* "Strap in," William advised. "The road's about to get bumpy."

Kohl traversed the anchor line from the cornfield to the lake in the desert and paused. The boy continued toward the *saha'asra* where he thought he could escape. He was mistaken. Only a few miles remained between the youth and his final fate.

Kohl secreted himself in a hollow next to the small dirt road upon which the boy traveled, the perfect vantage point from which to launch his ambush.

The necrosed smiled as he anticipated the feast to come. After he had fed, he would return to the *saha'asra* where he had bled, where his brethren had congregated. There he would kill them and feast again. Then would come Sapient Dormant. Kohl shivered in excitement.

An instant later his excitement ebbed, and a frown creased his brows. *Why had the boy come to a halt?* Kohl scowled. *What was that foolish creature doing? Did he not realize the* saha'asra *was right in front of him? This way lay salvation. The boy needed to keep coming.*

Kohl tried to remain patient as the youth dithered.

At last! The boy inched his vehicle forward once more, and Kohl licked his lips in urgent need.

"Closer," he whispered in his sandpaper-abrasive voice. His excitement built . . . only to falter again.

The boy no longer inched his vehicle forward. He raced it along the muddy track, picking up speed, going faster and faster. If he wasn't careful, he could crash and kill himself and the others. That couldn't be allowed. The boy and his friends had to be alive in order for Kohl to harvest their *lorethasra*. They were no good to him dead.

Kohl stood, and raced to the point where the road angled toward the lake. There he would put an end to the boy's mad plan, whatever it was.

"Here he comes!" William warned. "From the right."

"Punch it!" Jason urged.

"I'm going as fast as I can," William shouted back.

The Scout's engine rumbled, and the tires made slurping sounds as they cut across the mud.

Kohl raced toward them, still cloaked in the thick fog and drizzle. He moved faster than anything his size should have been able to. He bore down on them like a vision of doom, and his hideous face broke into a grin. A sight to give nightmares to hardened convicts.

Aia rose up on her hind legs, front paws on the sill of the side window. A growl emanated from her throat, displaying either foolishness, fearlessness, or a bit of both. **It dies.**

Serena, though, had too much good sense for such foolhardiness. She just wanted to live. She didn't care how. Her mind spun. Panic loomed, and she concentrated on the soothing exercises Isha had taught her. She deepened her breathing, focusing inward, trying to calm her mind's feverish visions.

It helped . . . a little. At least until she realized what was about to occur. Then her mouth grew dry, and her heart pounded. "He's going to cut us off!" Serena cried.

"Buckle up!" William warned.

Serena already had her seat belt fastened, and she grabbed Aia. She held the kitten close and cursed her luck. *Why had she been assigned to William Wilde? And why had he been so unfortunate as to attract the attention of a necrosed? Why couldn't she have been assigned to some budding* asrasin *in Siberia? Those frozen wastelands contained brutal winters, man-eating polar bears, and corrupt comrades willing to sell out a person for a bottle of vodka, but all of those were preferable to a necrosed.*

"If you're going to do something, do it now!" Jason shouted.

Through the windshield, Serena saw Kohl Obsidian. He stood directly athwart their path.

"We're going to ram him," William said. "Brace yourselves!"

The Scout swung left, wheels almost tipping into space and a long fall, before skidding to the right and hammering Kohl Obsidian. Serena heard a dull thud. The impact threw her about, and the necrosed roared. Her vision momentarily filled with stars when her head hit the side window. Aia yowled, and her sharp, little claws dug through Serena's pants and shirt.

The Scout spun. The world twirled. Torn metal screeched.

The grill had been ripped off.

Kohl Obsidian held it. For an instant he stood illuminated by their fog-lamps and headlights. Though he'd been thrown to the ground by the impact with the Scout, he'd already regained his footing. He loomed impossibly massive and threatening. He glared a promise of death.

Serena had no time to think about Kohl. The Scout still spun, and he disappeared from view. The lake took shape before them. William straightened out their rotation and aimed the Scout at the water, still several hundred yards away.

The Scout slammed to a halt, throwing Serena forward. Pain from the whiplash shot up her neck and head. Again, Aia dug in with her nails.

Serena shot a look back. Kohl had grabbed hold of the tailgate.

"You will die," Kohl promised. His voice rattled like mangled metal.

The Scout unexpectedly lurched forward, rolling free, straight toward the water. The tailgate had been ripped off its hinges. Kohl swung it like a club at the Scout. The impact sent their vehicle skidding.

I hate this! Aia cried.

Jason cursed floridly as he was slammed about. His seatbelt had come unfastened. “Drive better!” he shouted.

“If you want to take the wheel, be my guest,” William yelled as he brought the Scout back under control.

“How much farther?” Jason demanded.

Serena noted that he’d managed to buckle himself back in his seat.

“Close. A hundred yards,” William answered.

Somehow, they once more faced the lake, with Kohl behind them. Serena twisted about in her seat until she faced backward. Kohl sped after them. He couldn’t be evaded this time.

Serena murmured a prayer and breathed deep. She imagined her fears leaving her, and her clenched jaw relaxed. The tightness in her chest eased as the fear faded to the back of her mind. Once more, she could think clearly.

And she knew what was required.

Serena pulled out the Colt 1911 pistol she’d picked up in Las Vegas and stared down the barrel at the necrosed. He kept pace with them, holding aloft the broken tailgate, like a monstrous caveman holding his club.

Serena braced herself. The handgun she’d chosen had a powerful kick. She took a steadying breath. Aiming proved difficult with the Scout shifting and shimmying around so much, but there came an instant when Kohl held still in her sights.

She exhaled and squeezed off a round.

Serena slammed back, and her ears rang. The pistol sounded like a bomb going off in the confines of the Scout. Even braced, the recoil was brutal. Serena had almost dislocated a shoulder trying to keep the pistol from smashing her in the face.

Aia yowled. **Warn me next time you hurl thunder!**

"What the hell?" William shouted, clutching the side of his head.

Serena ignored her aching ears and aimed again, ready to ride the recoil this time. She fired another shot. Another. Her shots came more smoothly, and she managed to hit Kohl in the torso. She smiled when the necrosed roared.

"Almost there," William said, sounding far calmer than Serena would have expected.

Serena set herself for another shot. It would have struck, but a wave of Kohl's hand blocked her bullet.

Jason took advantage of the creature's distraction and let loose with a blast of fire and wind. The necrosed slowed to veer and dodge Jason's assault.

Serena loaded another clip into her Colt and readied herself. They drew closer to the lake. She could sense it. William's focus was entirely on his driving. Jason continued to hurl fire.

Kohl threw the tailgate at the Scout. The blow lifted the back wheels off the ground.

Serena grunted when the Scout slammed down.

Black lightning ripped from the necrosed's hands, and the right rear tire blew.

William wore a rictus of desperation as he sawed at the wheel. "We're going to hit!" he shouted as the Scout refused to turn. The nose of the truck aimed straight at a small embankment on their right.

Serena didn't pay the oncoming crash any attention. She returned to Kohl Obsidian. Once again, she calmly squeezed off a number of rounds, and again, a wave of the necrosed's hand swept aside her bullets.

The Scout rolled partway up the embankment before William could correct their path. The vehicle slipped and swerved in the mud. The fog and the rain . . . A plunge down a shallow incline, and there lay the lake.

The world went crazy. Up became down. Kohl had grabbed the rear bumper, lifted the vehicle, and hurled it forward.

Jason slammed into the roof while William cried out in pain. Serena braced herself, and Aia dug with sharp claws.

The vehicle landed in the water upside down, in the shallows where the lake was only a few inches deep. It came to a halt a few yards from shore.

William groaned. It felt like a mule had kicked him in the head. *Where was he?* Memory returned. *Kohl. The saha'asra.* With a surge of fear, he struggled to free himself of his seatbelt. Cold water filled the roof of the Scout for a level of a few inches. William fought to make his panicked mind and his stiff hands work. He couldn't seem to form a coherent thought, and the seatbelt wouldn't release.

The necrosed stood by the shore, illuminated through the fog and mist by the Scout's headlights. He seemed reticent to enter the water, but his hesitation likely wouldn't last much longer.

Hurry. Somehow, Aia had survived the tumult of the Scout being flipped end-over-end without an injury. **There's a battle to be fought, and that dead thing won't stay on the shore for much longer.**

William didn't need her urging. He grunted, mashing the seatbelt release, but it wouldn't come loose.

Serena appeared, startling him as she crouched down by his side, still within the Scout. She held a Bowie knife. "Hold still," she said, her voice calm and with no hint of fear. "When I cut through the seatbelt, you're going to fall," she explained. "Brace yourself or your head will smash into the roof. Ready?"

William gripped the steering wheel and nodded.

With a single slice of her Bowie, he dropped free. He caught himself before he dropped on his head, and scrambled upright.

Let's go, Aia growled.

"Climb out of the Scout on my side," Serena ordered. "I've already got my door open. It's the one farthest from the necrosed."

William clambered out and immediately slipped. He grabbed the door handle and managed to stay upright. His thoughts remained scrambled, and he had no idea how Serena was keeping it together because right now, he was almost overwhelmed with panic.

Don't forget Jason, Aia called out.

William spun about. Jason remained trapped in the back, working frantically to open one of the doors.

"Just blast it open," Serena said. "Use your fire or wind. Hurry up."

The fear momentarily left Jason's eyes, replaced by chagrin. With a gesture, the passenger side door slammed open and he scrambled out of the Scout. He, too, slipped and stumbled, and William steadied him.

"Thanks," Jason said. "What now?"

They stood behind the bulk of the vehicle, a slender bulwark between them and Kohl.

The anchor line, Aia advised. She sat on the upside-down Scout, her gaze focused on Kohl Obsidian. **A wise warrior retreats when necessary, fighting only when no other option remains.**

"Anchor line. Right," Jason said. "I need some time."

"You'll have it," Serena promised.

William's mind finally caught up with what had just occurred. All their blades were in the back of the Scout with the rest of their belongings. He hustled to the rear of the vehicle, reaching through the ripped-apart tailgate to grab their weapons. *Thank God they'd tied them down.* He tossed Jason and Serena their swords before unsheathing his own.

He immediately felt better.

Aia eyed him in approval. **Much better to fight as the lion than to die as the mouse.**

"Hurry up, Jason," Serena said. "I think he knows what you're doing."

"I'm going as fast as I can," Jason snapped.

"Well, go faster."

The blood drained from William's face when the necrosed took a hesitant step into the water. "He's coming into the water."

Kohl stepped gingerly, a mincing, fearful gait. The water bubbled with every step he took, becoming black like tar. He grimaced in pain. "The water won't stop me, boy. You're mine," he promised. "I'll feed upon you, and with your *lorethasra*, I'll heal. There's no escape for you this time. No tricks or animals to save—"

Serena interrupted him with a shot in the chest. The necrosed tumbled backward. She shot him again. Another shot. Kohl barely managed to keep himself from falling.

"I'm sorry. You were saying?" Serena asked with a smirk.

Aia sniggered. Even William chuckled.

Kohl rose to his full height. Serena again aimed and fired the Colt, but an imperious gesture from the necrosed scattered or halted the bullets. "No more games," Kohl said. He continued his methodical advance.

"What's taking so long?" William demanded of Jason. He tightened his grip on the sword.

"It keeps slipping away." Jason said in obvious frustration. "I don't know what's wrong. It shouldn't be so hard—" He paused and shot a horrified gaze upon the necrosed. "He's doing it! He's blocking me."

Kohl chuckled, a grim, woodchipper sound. "Foolish little *asrasin*. You cannot escape me."

"I can't lock onto the anchor line so long as he's doing whatever he's doing."

"Then we distract him so he can't keep blocking you," William said. His words sounded far braver than he felt. Right now, he wanted to run away from here, flee as far as possible from the horror of Kohl Obsidian. Instead, he moved in front of the Scout, and Serena stepped up next to him.

The necrosed laughed at their show of defiance. "Good. You come to me then, and hasten your doom. I will—"

Aia growled. **Shut up, you walking bag of pus.**

Kohl paused, clearly startled. "Who said that?

The one who has called your doom.

"Is that the kitten?" Kohl asked. "How?"

Aia lashed her tail. **Come closer, and I'll whisper the answer in your ears.**

William glanced back and forth between the two of them. The situation would have been hilarious if it wasn't terrifying.

The necrosed shook off his confusion. "No matter. I'll tear her apart, too and all her secrets will be mine."

"Then come and claim her," Serena challenged.

William took heart from her words, and his spine stiffened. The necrosed halted. Once again, his head tilted to the side as though in thought. Then, with a burst too fast to evade, he was on them.

William got his sword up in time to block a hammer- blow. He expected the blade to bite into Kohl's flesh. Instead, it hit with a hollow clang, like he'd struck an aluminum baseball bat. *What was that thing made of?* William fell back from the rebound of the blow, slipping again in the slick footing.

Serena ducked a swipe. Her return cut sliced Kohl across the stomach. But he showed no evidence that it hurt him.

William briefly wondered if there was any way they could more deeply wound the creature, but he had no time to ponder. He slipped another blow, twisting aside before snapping off a front kick. It caught Kohl in the solar plexus, and the necrosed's breath whooshed out. He stooped over, gasping.

Serena aimed a strike at his neck, but Kohl dodged her blow.

The necrosed stumbled away. William leapt toward him, launching a flying knee. His blow crunched into the creature's face.

Kohl grunted in pain and fell back. He shook his head as if clearing cobwebs and grinned. "Well done, boy. It seems I perfected you more than I intended. But you are no holder."

"Damn it! I almost had it," Jason screamed in anger.

Aia, ferocious and furious though her words had been, had wisely stayed out of the fight. **Not much longer,** she said. **He's coming.**

Who's coming? William wondered.

"Enough. I weary of toying with you," Kohl intoned. "This battle ends now."

The headlights from the Scout lit the gloom, and shadows twisted and twirled. Kohl stepped forward, and the fog and mist snaked about his bulking form. No longer did he act as if the water hurt him, though it still bubbled and blackened with every step he took.

William strode forward to meet him.

"Your little toy sword cannot harm me," Kohl said.

William didn't listen. He aimed a strike at the necrosed's chest.

Viper fast, the creature dodged. He swayed away from Serena, too. Before any of them could stop him, he reached an unprepared Jason. The necrosed hurled him through the air. Jason splashed into the water, tumbled out of control before finally sliding to a halt five feet onto shore.

William pressed forward. He struck at the creature's unprotected back, but impossibly, Kohl slid away before gliding inside William's guard. The creature grinned, and William reversed his sword. He struck with his hilt, but Kohl leaned aside. The necrosed raised his fist, ready to smash William to a pulp.

William had no chance to block or evade. *This was it. He was going to die.*

The necrosed howled in pain.

William stumbled away.

Aia had clawed the necrosed's face and darted back to the Scout before the creature could touch her.

Scratches marred Kohl's hideous face, and he glared at Aia. "You will die."

Only if you can catch me.

"Oh, I'll catch you," Kohl promised. "And I'll eat you slowly."

Serena attacked, but the necrosed shifted. He shoved aside her sword and grabbed her by her shirt. As with Jason, he flung her through the air. She would have crashed to the ground, but Jason had regained his feet. With a gesture, Serena's flight halted, and she dropped down next to him.

William swallowed. He stood alone before Kohl.

"Now it's only you and me, boy," the necrosed said with a mocking smile. "No one can help you now."

A flicker of William's ever-present anger flared to life, extinguishing any remaining fear. He smiled at Kohl, readying his sword. He gestured. "Come on, ugly. You're boring me."

"Your anger won't save you," Kohl taunted. "I know it well. I gave it to you last winter."

He's here.

William didn't know who Aia meant, but a rainbow bridge opened on the far side of the Scout. His heart lifted. *Mr. Zeus!*

But the person who stepped across the bridge wasn't Mr. Zeus. He wasn't anyone William had ever expected to see again.

"Landon?"

William's brother stood before him, leaner, bearded, and with unkempt clothes and hair, but otherwise, the same except for the vacant expression on his face.

Time ground to a halt. Even the raindrops hung suspended in the air.

“Landon?” William asked again.

His brother continued to stare at him, unseeing, focused on something else. Expressions flitted across his face like a silent argument. The timeless moment passed, and Landon shook his head. “Didn’t expect to see me again, did you?”

It took William a second to realize Landon wasn’t talking to him. His brother spoke to Kohl.

“I was sloppy when I tried to kill you before,” Kohl said. “I won’t make that mistake twice.”

“Pilot Vent,” Landon said. “You remember him, don’t you? He remembers you.”

Kohl edged back, unexpected fear flashing across his face. “Pilot Vent is dead.”

“Yes, he is,” Landon agreed, “but not before he helped create me. *You* helped create me. You were kind enough to bring Pilot back to life, and I wish to thank you for your gift.”

Landon leaped into the air. He cleared the Scout with ease and landed in front of the necrosed. A whip-swift punch hurled the creature toward shore.

“We must fight,” Pilot Vent commanded from within the vaults of Landon’s mind. *“It is why we are here, why that strange cat called us to this place. It is what is meant to be a holder: to fight evil and defeat it wherever it is found.”*

Landon tried to ignore Pilot, but it would have been easier to disregard a scream directed into his ears.

"My name is Landon Wilde."

"And I am Pilot Vent," the voice stated.

"Landon?"

Landon's attention shifted to the boy, the one who seemed so familiar. *Who was he?*

Landon's memories, his sense of self was fragmented and unreliable. He remembered little of his past life. Family, friends, happy occurrences—all were gone. He only knew for certain that a year ago Kohl Obsidian, a necrosed, had smeared his blood upon Landon's forehead, blessing him with an unholy baptism.

That marking, even now visible as a black streak that lingered like a tattoo, had done something else, something unexpected. Rather than simply set the necrosed's ruinous *lorethasra* into Landon's bones and essence, the blood had brought with it the remnants of Pilot Vent, the holder who had been transformed into Kohl Obsidian.

He, too, had a mind riddled with lacunae of memories and knowledge, but Pilot remembered enough. He had been the one who had thrown off Kohl's poisoned *lorethasra*, allowing both of them to survive.

"You know what we must do," Pilot said. *"Apart we are but a shadow of a man, but together, perhaps we can make something of this tragedy."*

They'd spent the past year as two lost souls housed in one body, each one fighting for control. Two souls for whom the past year had been an unending nightmare of muttered arguments, homelessness, and confusion as they both prayed for salvation.

"Only together, as one being, can we hope to destroy a creature as foul as Kohl Obsidian. Only then can we revenge ourselves upon the author of our shared misery."

"Landon," the boy called again. The boy who appeared so familiar, whose features sparked memories of home and family. The boy who had to be saved no matter the cost.

"Yes," Landon agreed to Pilot's request. The two of them had battled for domination in this one body for long enough.

"Our name?" Pilot asked.

"Landon Vent."

"A good name."

They dropped their defenses against one another and merged into a single being.

Landon Vent took his first breath before striding into battle—his birthplace, a powerful omen. Though his memories were worthless scraps, his purpose was certain. Clarity filled his mind.

He smiled as he stared at Kohl Obsidian, mocking him before surging to attack. The shallow water didn't slow him down, nor did the mist and fog cloud his vision. His footing was firm, and he could see as clearly as if the sun shone brightly.

He cried out vengeance as he dealt the necrosed a blow that sent the creature staggering.

William watched spellbound, stunned by what he was seeing.

Landon was alive! But how? He had died in the car accident, his body burned to ashes. William had never thought to question that fact. There had never been a reason to think otherwise.

But here he was, battling Kohl Obsidian.

Landon.

And yet he wasn't Landon. Not entirely.

Amazement lay like a stone in his mouth as William watched Landon launch himself against Kohl Obsidian. A punch, a kick. Each blow connected. The necrosed rocked on his heels, stumbling backward. Blood, foul as bile, trickled from the corner of the creature's mouth, and Kohl glared rage. The necrosed returned fire, and Landon took a blow that knocked him on his butt.

William threw off his shock and yelled to Jason. "Get the anchor line open!"

Jason, who had also been watching the battle, startled a moment before nodding. He seemed to focus inward, but a moment later he wore an anguished expression. "I can't," he said. "He's still blocking me."

"Then we kill him," Serena said. She stepped toward Kohl and Landon, who fought in the shallows, a few yards from shore. Her sword gleamed in the murky light of the Scout's headlights.

William closed his eyes. "Lord, keep me safe." He marched toward the battle.

Jason had recovered his sword and stood ready as well.

William charged from the right, while Serena advanced from the left. Jason attacked from the center.

Kohl shot a glance at the three of them and snarled. He front-flipped over Jason and landed on solid ground. "Come on," he snarled. "I'll tear you apart."

Landon took up Kohl's challenge. William only saw it now, but Landon's fingers ended in weird, glowing, silver claws. They were as long as a grizzly's, and his toes bore similar claws. From his mouth, large, sabertooth canines protruded past his chin.

Kohl retreated before Landon's slashes and kicks, blocking some and evading others. Shallow, furrowed cuts like windrows leaked blood from the necrosed's abdomen. Landon's claws were sharp if they could penetrate Kohl's steel-like hide.

"What do we do?" Jason asked.

"Can you distract Kohl?" Serena asked. "It only has to be for an instant. Just long enough for whoever that thing is that's fighting him—"

"Landon," William interrupted. "My brother's fighting him."

Serena did a double-take. "That's your dead brother?"

Landon grunted. He'd taken a gut punch, but it didn't slow him. He stayed in the pocket.

"Don't ask me how," William replied with a shake of his head. "But Serena's right. We need to distract Kohl." He turned to Jason. "Can you do it?"

Jason didn't answer. Instead, his face furrowed in concentration before white-hot lightning arced from his fingers. It blazed toward Kohl Obsidian . . . and was consumed when it struck the creature's body.

"Thank you," Kohl sneered. The cuts on his abdomen healed. "Foolish *asrasin. Lorethasra* lightning is food for my kind. Now, I will—agh!"

Landon had sliced open a new series of wounds across Kohl's chest.

"We need more like that," Serena said.

From Jason's hands came a gout of fire. Again, it struck the necrosed and was extinguished. This time the cuts on the creature's chest healed.

"Why isn't it hurting him this time?" William growled in frustration.

"He wasn't sourcing his *lorethasra* the other times. Now he is," Jason explained. "I can't do anything against him."

"You don't have to," Serena said. "We just have to distract him. Use wind or something."

Jason nodded and directed a gust of wind toward Kohl and Landon. Both combatants stumbled, but Kohl recovered first.

William took the diversion to enter the fray. All fear had ended. Only anger and an immovable certainty that he wouldn't let his brother fight this monster by himself.

Jason followed on his heels. Serena, too. They swept toward Kohl. Jason swung high with a sword strike. Serena angled low. The necrosed blocked and evaded both. William went low. His thrust struck the necrosed's thigh but bounced off. William twisted around for a snap front-kick. Kohl stepped away giving William room for another thrust, this one aimed at the necrosed's head. He missed.

But Jason didn't. For a wonder, his blade penetrated Kohl's armored skin, a score along the creature's bicep. The necrosed snarled. His backhand sent Jason tumbling to the ground, unconscious.

The return swing would have taken William's head off, but Landon sprang in. He blocked the blow. Kohl shot off a sidekick. It clipped Serena, and sent her reeling. She hit the ground with a groan and didn't get up. A shove from Landon saved William again, and he stumbled away from the fight.

Don't hold back, Aia urged William. Wet and bedraggled, she'd swum to shore and leaped purposefully toward the fight.

"Aia, no!" William shouted. His heart plummeted in fear for the brave but foolish kitten.

Aia never slowed. She leapt on Kohl's ankle.

"Now it is only me and the two of—" Again Kohl yelled in pain.

Aia's small teeth shouldn't have been able to penetrate wet paper, much less Kohl's tough hide, and yet they had.

Lightning flashed. In the afterimage stood a massive version of Aia, a giant, deadly predator who could stare Kohl in the eyes. *Death made flesh*, William thought. When she snarled, even the trees quavered.

Kohl did as well. He fell back, fear lighting his face.

The afterimage faded, leaving Aia as a kitten once more. The necrosed kicked at her, but she sprang to William's side.

Kohl stepped toward them. Landon put himself in the way. He checked Kohl's kick, and his own rocked the necrosed's head back.

Kohl grinned and wiped a spittle of blood. "Is that all you can do? I'd hoped for a real fight."

The necrosed blurred, shifting like a desert mirage until two versions of the creature were revealed. One seemed as solid as the mountains, the other a wispy phantasm. William could see through the ghostly version, and he didn't know what it meant.

"Now we'll see what you're made of, *holder*," Kohl snarled.

The solid version of the necrosed surged toward Landon. It kicked and punched, each blow faster than the one before. Meanwhile, the spirit held back, but from its fingers came sheets of black lightning.

Landon cried out as the energy coursed over him.

William stood frozen with indecision, wanting to help but not knowing how.

You have more strength than you know, Aia said. **Reach for it. Don't think. React. Trust yourself, and the answer will come to you.**

Trust yourself? What kind of stupid advice was that? William thought. *It sounded like something Master Yoda would say . . . or a fortune cookie.*

Landon cried out again. This time jagged crystals had scored his face, chest, and arms.

Both Kohls grinned.

William charged into the fray and took on the spirit version.

The ghost smiled mockingly and gestured William on.

Marble-sized stones lifted off the rocky terrain and rocketed toward William. He couldn't dodge, so he attacked. He lunged and stabbed the ghostly Kohl. Though wispy and insubstantial in appearance, it, too, had skin tough as armor.

But William's sword penetrated, opening a shallow gash that bled black light. The ghostly Kohl grimaced, and the volley of stones lost flight and fell to the ground.

William realized with a start that his sword glowed a dim silver-blue. It whined as it cut the air. He twirled it, and the sword left streaks of blue light in its wake. William took a stance against the ghostly Kohl, confidence flickering to life.

"You think you can stop me?" the ghostly Kohl asked. "Better men and *asrasins* than you have sought to do so."

"Shut up and fight."

The ghostly Kohl snarled. From his arms extruded a pair of swords, one long and the other short. Gangrenous and bile-colored like the necrosed's blood, they oozed corruption. The ghostly Kohl came at him.

William evaded a thrust from the short blade and blocked the long sword. William sensed more stones coming. He rolled beneath them, and kept rolling. The ghostly Kohl chased him, stabbing down over and over.

William swept his sword at the ghostly Kohl's ankles and regained his feet.

Black lightning arced at him. It buzzed the air, and instinctively, he blocked it with his sword. With a snapping crash, the lightning dissipated. William's blade blazed brighter, lit like burning magnesium, painful to look at.

He briefly gazed at it sidelong in amazement before returning his attention to the battle.

Icy spears hurtled toward him. William dodged some, but most he melted with a circular sweep of his sword. "Is that the best you got?" he mocked.

"I've got much more, boy," Kohl answered. "You'll learn all about it." The ghostly necrosed held his swords at the ready and advanced. "I'll make you eat those words while I eat your heart."

"Bring it."

Ghostly Kohl swept forward. He hammered with an overhand swing and thrust.

William sidestepped the swing, parried the thrust, and stepped back. *En garde,* Kohl came on. His longsword snaked forward. William swept it aside. Kohl followed up with the short sword, a disemboweling thrust. William blocked and jumped into the ghostly necrosed's guard, too close for swords.

A hard knee to Kohl's gut elicited a grunt. The necrosed disengaged.

It gave William the time and distance to reset himself. He offered Kohl a smirk.

Kohl glared. No words spoken, the necrosed attacked with fury.

William parried and slipped aside other blows, but Kohl always pushed him back. William circled to keep the longsword at a distance, disengaging when possible, and always searching for an opening. He found none. Kohl kept on him, constantly pressing forward, each sword swing coming harder and faster.

William's counters became sloppy. He struggled to maintain his guard.

The drizzly rain, clouds, and fog hid the sun, but the Scout's headlights gave the area near the shore an ethereal quality. They could have been fighting in the mists of fairie. The world held quiet except for feet shifting across wet sand, grunts of exertion, and the ringing of steel.

William moved his head off the center line and Kohl's short sword swept inches past his head. One-handed, he parried a swing at his chest. He flicked a punch at Kohl's hand holding the short sword, deflecting it.

William panted. He couldn't keep on like this. He could barely keep up with the necrosed's blistering pace.

Another sword slashed into view, defending William. Serena. He swung high, she thrust low. Kohl's longsword blocked William's angled overhand. His short sword blocked Serena's thrust as well. She slid along the parry, and her sword sliced the ghostly creature across his thigh.

Kohl grimaced in pain and shuffled back, out of position. The necrosed glanced from one of them to the other, trying to keep both in view. The cut on his thigh bled bilious light and slowed him. He limped, and an expression of panic passed across his face.

Again, William went high while Serena lunged low. Kohl parried Serena's sword. He would have parried William's, but small, calico Aia bit into ghostly Kohl's left ankle. The necrosed hissed, distracted. William shifted the angle of his attack. Kohl desperately moved to defend and partially deflected William's blow.

But not far enough.

William's sword gouged a line from eye to jaw. Kohl roared. Serena slipped behind him, and struck him across the backs of his calves. The necrosed fell to one knee. William's next thrust stabbed through the monster's thick skull. It punctured through hardened skin and thick bone. Kohl screamed.

Serena spun on one foot, her sword extended. It arced around, cutting off the necrosed's scream along with his head. The ghostly Kohl blinked out, and a cry of anguish rose from the flesh one.

Landon. William spun about, searching for his brother.

Landon's glowing claws dripped ichor. Jason stood with him, his sword nicked and dented, but bearing a line of Kohl's blood along its edge.

The necrosed gaped at the four of them. Multiple injuries leaked blood, none of them life threatening, but there were so many. Kohl had been savaged.

How was he still standing?

William and Serena advanced to Landon's side.

Black lightning stabbed forth from Kohl's fingers, but William's blade blocked it, protecting his brother.

"You die tonight," William said.

"Your pet holder cannot kill me," Kohl wheezed around his obvious pain. "His claws can cut but they can't kill. He is no true holder. He cannot do what is needed. He is pathetic. You're all pathetic. You'll break your swords on my flesh, and when you tire I'll rise up and slay you." Defiance shone in Kohl's eyes.

"Then we'll take your head and burn it and your body," Jason vowed.

Kohl laughed. "That tale was seeded by Sapient himself. Only a holder can kill my kind, and your supposed holder is too weak."

"I am weak," Landon agreed. "I know that. But William isn't. You touched him with your *lorethasra*, changing him to make him stronger of body. And we both have your blood. Except for a holder, the only way to kill a necrosed is with its own blood and *lorethasra*." Landon smiled grimly. "We have both."

True fear flashed across the necrosed's face. "You can't do this. I—"

His words were swept into a wrenching scream when Landon's clawed hands closed on Kohl's head. They dug into the necrosed's skull, holding him still as the creature kept screaming.

"Put your hands on mine and kill him," Landon shouted to William. "You'll know how."

William placed his hands on his brother's. At once, he knew what to do, as instinctively as he had during his battle with the ghostly Kohl. He reached for something within him, his *lorethasra*. Set it to white hot fire and poured lightning into Kohl.

The necrosed's screams rose in pitch. His body glowed. White light bled from his eyes, ears, mouth, and wounds. With a sizzle, his body blazed briefly before flashing to ashes.

CHAPTER 26: AFTERMATH

Silence descended upon the group, disturbed only by the misty rain that continued to fall.

Serena couldn't believe they'd destroyed Kohl Obsidian. *They'd overcome a necrosed!*

A wave of relief washed over her and her knees buckled. She knelt in the water, amazed and overwhelmed as she tried not to weep. She'd survived. They all had, and events no longer required that she had to kill William or Jason.

She was drawn out of her grateful reverie a moment later.

"Landon?" William spoke to his brother. The two approached one another.

The claws and teeth were gone, and while Landon was taller and swarthier, anyone could tell they were brothers. They had the same dark hair, complexion, and the same confused, hopeful expression.

"I should know you, shouldn't I?" Landon asked.

William reached for Landon, as if he wanted to hug him, but upon hearing his brother's confusing words, he pulled back.

"We're brothers," William said, softly, his voice filled with love and longing. "You don't remember?"

Landon's mouth opened and closed soundlessly. "I don't know," he eventually said. "It's all so mixed up. I remember some things, but not what's important."

"I don't understand," William said, disappointment rising in his eyes.

"Neither do I," Landon said. "Not entirely. All I know is that I have scattered memories of two men. One was Landon Wilde, the other was Pilot Vent, a holder. They . . . fused into one, creating me."

Serena frowned. *What did that mean*? She glanced at Jason, but he looked equally perplexed.

"I don't understand," William repeated.

Landon told them a story of stolen memories, of warriors called holders, and someone named Pilot Vent, who had once been just such a warrior. He spoke of how he'd spent the past year lost and alone, tortured as two men sought dominion over one body. Those two men—Landon and Pilot—had come to an understanding before engaging Kohl Obsidian, and now where there had been two, there was only one, a newly created holder named Landon Vent.

"I remember helping someone cook turkey and watching football," Landon said, "but it's all meaningless stuff like that, scattered images and pieces of who I once was, as both Landon and Pilot."

"Then maybe the rest of it will come back," William said. He seemed to be forcing a note of certainty into his voice, but to Serena's ears his optimism sounded flat.

Landon grinned, and Serena was taken aback by how eerily similar his smile was to William's. "I remember something else," he said. "I remember how we never let you eat green bean casserole, or anything with beans or onions."

William laughed. "That was you, not me! You always tried to blame me for it, though."

Landon's smile fell away. "I don't remember the rest."

"It doesn't matter," William said, pulling his brother into an embrace. "I love you, Landon. I always will."

Landon broke off the hug. "Who's everyone else?"

"I'm Serena Paradiso," Serena said, stepping forward.

"Jason Jacobs. Do you remember me?" Jason asked, offering a handshake.

"We know each other?"

"We're friends through William," Jason answered. "Neighbors. It's good to see you again."

Serena blinked back tears, pitying Landon. William's brother was powerful, that much was obvious, but what could he really do with all that power if he didn't know himself? Worse, he'd lost everything that gave meaning to his life. All his memories of his family and friends had been stolen. Love that couldn't be recalled was a curse rather than a blessing.

I'm Aia, the calico kitten said, strutting forward with her tail raised despite being wet as a dunked sponge. **I think we're supposed to have found one another.**

"You were the one who called me?" Landon asked. "You and that other one."

Aia nodded, a flick of her ears. **The Shining Man.**

"I don't remember much, but are talking cats common?" Landon asked the others.

Serena laughed. "Not that I ever heard." She wanted to bite her tongue an instant later. Jason was supposed to be the expert on magic and magical creatures, not her. Thankfully, no one seemed to notice her slip.

"Good," Landon said with a chuckle of his own. "I'd hate to think I forgot something so memorable."

"Why do you think you were supposed to find Landon?" William asked Aia.

An exclamation of triumph from Jason interrupted her. "Got it," he said. A line split the air before him. It rotated and opened out on a tall doorway filled with swirling colors. Shimmers like heat waves distorted the air, and a bell tolled as a rainbow bridge took the places of the colors. It extended into infinity.

An anchor line. They had always reminded Serena of a portal leading to a different world.

"An anchor line," Landon mused. He shrugged at everyone's surprise at his words. "I did say I remember some things. Where does this one go?"

"Arylyn," Jason answered.

Mr. Zeus appeared in the distortion of the anchor line. A second later, he crossed the threshold of the rainbow bridge and stepped into their *saha'asra*.

"You're alive!" he exclaimed, pulling Jason into a hug. The old man's eyes shone with tears when he stepped back. "I feared I'd never see you again, my boy. I kept trying to open an anchor line from Arylyn to this place, but I couldn't. Something kept blocking my efforts."

"Kohl Obsidian," Jason said.

"Who?"

"The necrosed," William explained.

Mr. Zeus started. "William! Serena!" He rushed to them and hugged them as well.

Serena smiled at the old man's obvious joy and relief. Her heart lifted when Jason's grandfather embraced her. For once she didn't feel guilty at the happiness she felt in seeing or hugging him.

I'm Aia. The calico moved forward to sit before Mr. Zeus with her tail before her front paws. **What's your name?**

Mr. Zeus glanced about. "Did anyone else here that?"

"It's Aia," Serena explained, grinning in anticipation of how Mr. Zeus would take the information. "The cute little kitten sitting in front of you."

"The kitten?"

Yes. The kitten, Aia replied.

"A talking cat," Mr. Zeus muttered in disbelief.

A talking kitten, Aia corrected.

Mr. Zeus pinched the bridge of his nose. "This can't be happening," he muttered. His gaze wandered over their party. And snapped back around as further shock filled his face. "Landon?"

"I should know him too, shouldn't I?" Landon asked William with a frustrated sigh.

"How is he still alive? I saw the car and the burned bodies. The ashes," Mr. Zeus told William, his voice rising in agitation as his eyes darted about. "What is going on?"

"Landon came back to life," Jason began. "I mean, he was never dead, and he came here and helped us kill Kohl Obsidian. The necrosed."

"Killed a necrosed? How?" Mr. Zeus said, his mouth gaping

in astonishment. A moment later he shook his head. "Never mind. If Kohl is dead, we have to get out of here. The other necroseds will sense his demise. They could be on their way any minute. Let's go."

"Arylyn?" William asked, sounding hopeful.

Mr. Zeus shook his head. "No. Somewhere else." He eyed Landon in uncertainty. "I can't take him there, not without knowing who or what he really is."

"Why can't we go home?" Serena asked. The girl she portrayed, someone with little knowledge of magic, would be expected to raise the issue.

"Can we discuss it later?" Mr. Zeus asked. He turned to Jason. "Uncouple the anchor line to Arylyn. We're going to Mexico."

Moments later, they stood on the shore of an ocean. A warm sun beat down on a narrow, black, sand beach they had all to themselves. A thick jungle rose north and south, all the way to the water's edge, and nearby a dirt track led off into the wilds.

Serena smiled. It'd been too long since she'd seen the ocean, even if this one shimmered aqua instead of the indigo she knew from home.

"There," Mr. Zeus said. The Scout landed softly on the beach with a groan of stressed metal. Mr. Zeus had floated it through the air, even the torn off tailgate, through the anchor line to this *saha'asra* before setting the vehicle down.

Despite herself, Serena found herself impressed by his power and control. Few of Sinskrill's mahavans could have done the same. It seemed Isha's description of the magi of Arylyn and their skill had not been an exaggeration.

"Now," Mr. Zeus said, as the anchor line extinguished, "tell me what happened."

Serena slipped into the background and listened as William and Jason explained everything they had been through during the past week. She needed to know what the others had truly thought during the time they had been on the run. Their information might prove important once they hopefully chose to return to Cincinnati.

The conversation lasted for hours, as Mr. Zeus asked detailed follow-up questions. "How did you know to call Landon?" he asked Aia.

The Shining Man told me to, Aia answered.

"Who's the Shining Man?"

I only know his name, but I don't know him, Aia said, ears flicking in what Serena read as irritation. **But I knew it once.**

"Did you lose your memories, too?" Landon asked, his expression sympathetic.

I did, but I'll get them back. The Shining Man said that in time, I'd remember myself.

Mr. Zeus shook his head, in apparent disbelief. "I think I've heard enough," he said.

"Can we go to Arylyn now?" Jason asked.

"Not yet. Not all of us," Mr. Zeus said. He faced Landon with a tight-lipped smile of regret. "I'm sorry, but you're too much of a mystery. Until we know more about who and what you are, you can't come with us."

"I don't want to go to Arylyn either," Serena said. "I want to go to home and see my dad. I want to go back to the way things were." Her words hid a deeper fear. William could never be allowed to set foot on Arylyn, the one inviolate rule Isha had given her. Her heart skipped a beat over what she might have to do, and her hand drifted to the Colt she still had tucked in the small of her back. *Please don't let him choose Arylyn.*

"William?" Mr. Zeus asked.

"If Landon can't go, then I don't want to, either," William said.

"I'm not going to Cincinnati, though," Landon said.

William darted him a stricken look.

"I'm sorry, but I don't know Cincinnati any more. I don't remember it," Landon said. "And there's something else."

"What?" William asked.

Landon gestured to the jungle. "There's something in there calling me. I didn't feel it until we came here, but I need to learn what it means."

"You can't wait until later?" William asked.

Landon shook his head. "I can't. I have to know. I think it has something to do with being a holder. We fight evil. It's what Pilot always said holders do. And there's something in the trees that's evil or has to do with being a holder. Or both."

"Maybe if you came home, you'd remember more," William urged.

"I have to do this first," Landon said. "That thing in the jungle is calling me. It's too loud to ignore."

Mr. Zeus turned to William. "If Landon isn't going to Cincinnati, are you sure you want to go back to Cincinnati?"

William glanced at Serena, brow furrowed as he seemed to

study her, and she gave him a wide-eyed, vulnerable expression, one full of hope and a subtle promise.

He must have seen what she hoped he would. His face cleared. "Arylyn can wait," William said. "Right now, I just want to go home, take a shower, and sleep in my bed. I want to go back to St. Francis and walk for graduation. I've had enough of adventure and seeing new places."

"So be it," Mr. Zeus said. "I'll stay with you in the Far Abroad. I imagine Jason will as well. Same with the Karllsons, but I give no promises on how long we can stay in the Far Abroad. You may not be able to finish out the school year."

I'll go with Landon, Aia said. **I think I'm supposed to stay with him until he doesn't need me anymore.**

"You sure?" Serena asked, surprised at how much she had grown to like the little calico.

I'm sure, Aia said. **But you can rub my chin one last time if you like.**

Serena bent down and brushed Aia's forehead before scratching the kitten's chin. "Keep safe," she whispered.

I will, Aia said. **May you always be brave.**

William and Jason knelt to say their goodbyes to the fearless kitten as well.

"I could use a vehicle," Landon said.

"You can have the Scout," Mr. Zeus said. "It's a wreck right now, but you should be able to fix it up."

"I could also use some money." Landon smiled wryly.

"Don't ask for much, do you?" Mr. Zeus said with a wry smile of his own. He conjured cash from the air, a large stash of pesos. "Anything else?"

"That's enough."

"Will I see you again?" William asked Landon, and his voice quavered.

Serena's eyes welled. Once more, she felt no guilt for feeling sympathy for William.

"Someday," Landon said. "Maybe when I know who I am and what I'm supposed to do. Then I'll come home."

By the last day of the Christmas holidays, three days after William, Jason, and Serena had arrived home, everything had returned to normal. As Mr. Zeus had expected, Daniel and Lien had also come back, and tomorrow would be the first day of school. They would drive in together, go to their classes as they always had, and do all the prosaic things teenagers did, acting as if nothing had changed, as if the events of the past week hadn't occurred.

In truth, for the rest of the world nothing *had* changed. The Earth still rotated on its axis. TV continued as always. Even now, Mr. Zeus sat in the living room watching a rerun of *Cheers*, and as in every other episode, everyone on the show called out "Norm!" whenever Norm entered the bar. Music and movies were the same, too. Bruce Hornsby played on the radio, while the dollar theater advertised for a second run of *Big Trouble in Little China*.

Meanwhile, William sat on his bed, listening to music, with a book propped open on his lap, while Serena sat in a chair reading *Blood Meridian*, a book William had never heard of.

Nothing had changed, and yet, everything had.

The world held a surreal quality. Landon was alive, monsters were real, and kittens could be ferocious warriors. So much had happened over the past week. Too much.

"What do you think Jake and his friends will say tomorrow?" William asked, shaking off his reverie. "You know, after what happened in Winton Woods?"

Serena glanced up from her book. "I think he's going to have a lot of questions. Same with his friends."

"Do you think they told anyone?"

Serena shrugged. "Does it matter? Who's going to believe them?"

Once again, Serena's pragmatic nature rose to the surface. Sometimes it could be annoying.

"What's wrong?" Serena asked, apparently picking up on his mood.

William couldn't explain his sudden irritation. "I don't know," he said. "I just feel . . ."

"Restless?" Serena guessed.

"Maybe," William said. "I know after what happened to us I should just be grateful to be alive. I am, but . . ." He shrugged in frustration. "It doesn't feel like it's enough. You know?"

"No, I don't know," Serena said. "You're home. You're safe. Your friends are with you. What more do you want?"

"I don't know," William said. He stood and paced, frustrated at his inability to explain what had him bothered.

Serena's eyes widened in disbelief. "Don't tell me you want another adventure. Because if that's what it is, then count me out."

"Not another adventure," William quickly agreed. "But magic is real. I knew it before, but now I *really* know it."

Serena set aside her book. "I sometimes wish I didn't know it," she said quietly. "Sometimes I wish everything was back to the way it was before all this. I wish you and everyone else, my friends, were just normal people. That's all I'd ever need."

"But I'm not normal," William said. "My sword glowed like a lightsaber when I fought that ghost version of Kohl. Mr. Zeus had never heard of something like that."

"What? The sword, or the ghost part?"

"Both," William replied.

Serena snorted derision. "That's because Mr. Zeus never fought a necrosed. No one has. Or if they have, they didn't live to tell the tale."

"Your point?"

"My point," Serena said, "is that in this new life of yours, this magical one, there may be mysteries that others can't solve for you. You may be the only one who can. Maybe what's got you so unhappy is that you don't like the idea of an uncertain future."

William paused as he considered Serena's words. *Could it really be that simple?* As he thought about it, though, he realized there was something else, something he had yet to figure out. "That's not all of it," he said. "There's more. Maybe it's also losing Landon so soon after finding out he's still alive. Or learning that evil really exists, or—"

"Or maybe you simply need to make some decisions, and you aren't sure how I'll take it," Serena said, her expression solemn. "You're a magus. I'm just a girl. That means something, and it's nothing good. Not for me, anyway."

William blinked, surprised by her insight.

Serena was right. Once again, she'd seen to the heart of a

problem. Months of wondering why he only considered her a friend, with a warning bell ringing every time he thought of her as something more, but now, no bells went off, and there was also no time to figure out what might have been. "I have to go to Arylyn," he said.

"When do you plan on leaving?"

"Right after I graduate high school," William said.

"Why not go now?" Serena asked.

William smiled. "Because my parents would rise up from the dead and kill me if I don't get my high school diploma."

"Rise up from the dead?" Serena asked with a smirk.

"Landon did."

Serena's smile faded. "Yes, he did."

"Plus, there's also what Elaina told me," William said.

"The pretty witch?" Serena asked with a knowing smile.

"Yeah, but I meant what she told me when she read my future. She said I'd find my brother, and I did. She also said you have magic. I'm thinking that if she was right about Landon, maybe she's also right about you. Maybe you have *lorethasra* that hasn't yet come to life."

"If I had magic, shouldn't it have awoken in those *saha'asras*?" Serena asked. "Isn't that how Mr. Zeus said a potential magus is born?"

"Didn't you just get done telling me that he doesn't know everything?"

"I think he knows enough."

"Then—"

"Listen," Serena interrupted, "I know what you're hoping for, and I'd like it, too. I'd love to have magic, but it isn't in the cards.

And according to what you just said, we have until graduation together, and then you're going to Arylyn. I can't follow you there."

"Then we'll have to make the best of the time we have."

Serena smiled. "I have no doubt we will."

THE END

ABOUT THE AUTHOR

Davis Ashura resides in North Carolina and shares a house with his wonderful wife who somehow overlooked Davis' eccentricities and married him anyway. As proper recompense for her sacrifice, Davis unwittingly turned his wonderful wife into a nerd-girl. To her sad and utter humiliation, she knows *exactly* what is meant by 'Kronos'. Living with them are their two rambunctious boys, both of whom have at various times helped turn Davis' once lustrous, raven-black hair prematurely white. And of course, there are the obligatory strange, strays cats (all authors have cats—it's required by the union). They are fluffy and black with terribly bad breath. When not working—nay laboring—in the creation of his grand works of fiction, Davis practices medicine, but only when the insurance companies tell him he can.

He is the author of the semi-award winning epic fantasy trilogy, *The Castes and the OutCastes*, as well as the YA fantasy, *The Chronicles of William Wilde.*

Visit him at www.DavisAshura.com
and be appalled by the banality of a writer's life.